Evening Standard Best Bc

Observer Best Début Nov

"Engrossing and moving." Fay Wel~~~~ ~~~~ ~~~~ Johnson,
Mail on Sunday Novel Competition

"Tender and subtle, it explores difficult issues in deceptively
easy prose. Across the decades, Ashdown tiptoes carefully
through explosive family secrets. This is a wonderful debut –
intelligent, understated and sensitive." *Observer*

"An intelligent, beautifully observed coming-of-age story,
packed with vivid characters and inch-perfect dialogue.
Isabel Ashdown's storytelling skills are formidable;
her human insights highly perceptive." *Mail on Sunday*

"An immaculately written novel with plenty of dark family
secrets and gentle wit within. Recommended for book groups."
Waterstone's Books Quarterly

"A brilliant début." *Sainsbury's Magazine*

"This stirring coming-of-age novel evokes the strictures of
the '50s and the tacky flamboyance of the '80s brilliantly.
Narrated through 13-year-old Jake's eyes, it's a heartbreaking
redemptive tale of family secrets that will take you on
an emotional rollercoaster. Arm yourselves with a box of
Kleenex as you'll be weeping into your pillow by the end."
Glamour

"Carefully observed, unexpected and mesmerisingly beautiful."
Easy Living

"It's an in~~~~ ~~~~ ~~~~ "
Boyd

"In Jake, Ashdown has created a beautifully realised character, totally believable as a 20th-century boy but imbued with qualities which should resonate with any reader and will surely stand the test of time. The prose is succinct and smooth, the dialogue crisp and convincing. An intriguing, atmospheric read with a healthy dollop of realism." *Argus*

"Isabel Ashdown's first novel is a disturbing, thought-provoking tale of family dysfunction, spanning the second half of the 20th century, that guarantees laughter at the uncomfortable familiarity of it all."
Juliet Nicolson, *Evening Standard*

"I love it. It's a book that's very fast and really rewarding for the reader. There's a wrenching end to the first chapter that switches the mood and absolutely hooked me for the rest of the book." David Vann

"Ashdown's début novel is accomplished, accessible and absorbing." *NewBooks Magazine*

"The beauty of Ashdown's writing is that readers are able to connect to the real characters presented and understand that life isn't always all that easy. Her character representations, no matter what sex or age, are flawless. It's hard to know who to recommend this to without encouraging everyone to go out and buy it. Ashdown is one to watch in British literature." *The Bookbag*

"It's very subtle, and subtlety is the key to this. The tragedy is happening behind the words and behind what people are saying, and you could be forgiven for wanting to read it again to catch all the nuances. It reminded me of Iain Banks. If you enjoyed *The Crow Road*, you'll get lots out of this book."
Joel Morris, *Simon Mayo Show*, BBC Radio 5 Live

Glasshopper

ISABEL ASHDOWN

Myriad Editions

First published in 2009 by
Myriad Editions
59 Lansdowne Place
Brighton BN3 1FL

www.MyriadEditions.com

5 7 9 10 8 6 4

A CIP catalogue record for this book is available from the
British Library.

ISBN: 978-0-9549309-7-4

Printed on FSC-accredited paper by
Cox & Wyman Limited, Reading, UK.

For Colin, with love

glasshopper / ˈglɑːshɒpəːr / *noun*: **1** a person or thing that shifts position or character without warning. **2** a fleeting, translucent object. **3** a person who balances precariously between sobriety and intoxication.

Prologue

There, framed against the steep backdrop of rock and sky, I see them, my two boys, bare-chested and brown as berries. The kestrel hovers between them, a wing tip on either shoulder. My foot is pressed hard against the floor of the car, and the speed is exhilarating. I forge towards them, a great pike, coursing through this ocean of blue sky. Jake sees me, cocking his head to one side, trying to work it out with his strange eyes.

"Does he see you too?" I ask the girl, turning to look into her deep face. "Does he see you?"

She shrugs, unconcerned, and as I tumble towards them, spitting grit and dust off the narrow mountain path, I smile at Jake, sending my heart out to him, longing for him to understand. The kestrel drops from view and the two boys part, making way for me to pass. Jake nods, a slight tip of his head, and when the car tyres leave the road, I'm really flying.

Memories flood through me, amorphous as March starlings, an ever moving cloud of voices, deafening in their clarity and number . . .

Part One

Jake, November 1984

I love November. I love the frosty grass that pokes up between the paving slabs, and the smoke that puffs out of your nostrils like dragon's breath. I love the ready-made ice rink that freezes underneath the broken guttering in the school playground. And I love the salt 'n' vinegar heat inside a noisy pub, when everyone outside is walking about under hats and gloves with dripping red noses.

This one Saturday afternoon, Dad and me are down the Royal Oak, getting ready to watch the match. Dad tells Eric the Landlord that I'm fourteen, so I can come into the bar so long as I only have Coke. Not that I'd want what they all drink.

Dad shouts over, "Fancy a bag of nuts, Jakey?" and I give him the thumbs up from the corner seat we've bagged. It's great today because it's just me and Dad. Andy's on some boring Scout trip, and he won't be back till teatime. And Matthew, well he just sort of disappeared a few weeks back. One morning I got out of bed, and went into Matt's

5

room to wake him up with this fart I'd got brewing. It kills him every time. Anyway, this one morning, I go into his room, and he's not there. His bed was empty. So were his drawers. He'd taken all his clothes and records, so I knew he wasn't planning on coming back anytime soon. Even his aftershave had gone. When I went in to tell Mum, she said, "He'll be back when he's hungry," and she rolled over and went back to sleep. But he didn't come back. Dad says he's old enough to leave home if he wants to, now he's seventeen. But I know that Dad wishes he knew where Matt was. The thing is, he couldn't stand being around Mum any more, and Dad's still in his bed-sit, so he couldn't have him there. It's not ideal, Dad says, but what can you do? The worst thing is, Matthew had only just got on to this Youth Training thing which was going to teach him bricklaying. He was gonna make a fortune, he said. I wish he'd phone or something. I could ask him if they've got YTS at his new place.

"There you go, Jake lad." Dad puts the drinks down on the round table, and settles into his seat. "We should get a good view from here, son. Here, 'ave you seen the new TV Eric's got up on the bar? It's the business – teletext, eighteen-inch screen, remote control – the works. Reckon I should save for one of them, don't you, lad? Trinitron."

It's a really nice telly.

"So, what's new, Jakey? How's it going at school? You still in the footie team?"

That's one of the things I like about Dad. All his questions are dead easy, and we never run out of things to say.

"Yeah, it's all cool. Because we're in the second year,

6

we're doing Classical Studies, and it's brilliant. We're learning about Odysseus. He has quests, and he has to kill monsters and cross oceans just to get back home. There's a cyclops and sea monsters and loads of others. It's brilliant – you'd love it, Dad. I think it's my best lesson now. Miss Terry's giving us Greek names as she gets to know us. Simon Tomms is Poseidon, Emma Sullivan is Artemis. She's still thinking about mine."

"Your mum got me to read the *Odyssey* when we were courting. And the *Iliad*." He takes a sip of his beer and smacks his lips loudly. "You'd like *Jason and the Argonauts*, son. Now, that's a good film. There's this one bit, when the Argonauts run into seven skeletons and they rise up from the earth, wielding swords and marching like soldiers of the dead. I tell you, that was one of the greatest achievements of twentieth-century filmmaking, Jake. And it was bloody creepy too. That's a film to stand the test of time." He takes another swig from his beer, wiping the froth from his top lip with the back of his hand as he looks around the pub.

"And Mrs Jenkins chose my bonfire night picture for the corridor display this week. She said that it's 'highly original'." I do her high-pitched voice to make Dad laugh. "It'll be stuck up in the corridor, so everyone will get to see it when they come for parents' evening."

"Parents' evening," Dad says, dabbing his finger in the dew around his glass. "Is your mum going?"

"She says yes. I mean she signed the slip saying she would. And I gave it back to Mr Thomas."

"When is it, son?"

"Sometime at the end of the month," I answer. I know what he's getting at.

7

"Well, if there are any problems, you give me a ring. Here's 10p for the phone box, in case you need to phone from school. Stick it in your pocket. You can get me at the workshop. Alright, son?"

I smile at him, sucking up my Coke through two straws. It feels different drinking Coke out of two straws instead of one. If I had to choose, I think I'd go for one straw. It's less gassy. I wonder what Odysseus would choose, one or two. Mind you, Coke wasn't even invented back then.

"Dad, I don't s'pose you know what Mum's done with our library cards, do you? It's just they won't let me take out—"

"Stu!" My dad shouts across the crowded pub. Stu's this new mate of Dad's, and he's come to watch the match too. Sometimes, when he comes to the pub, he brings his son with him, Malcolm. Malcolm's the same age as me, and he's mostly OK, but sometimes a bit of an idiot. Once I saw him trip up this little kid in the pub garden, on purpose, just for a laugh. Then this other time we saw some woman struggling with a pram in the paper shop, and he helped her lift it over the step. Dad reckons Malcolm's a bit of an oddball. I think Malcolm's OK.

"Alright, Bill mate!" Stu bundles over with their drinks, grinning at Dad, unwrapping his scarf and hat. "Glad to see you could make it. This should be a good 'un, eh? Room for two more? Budge up, Jakey boy."

Dad's pleased to see Stu. "Just in time for kick-off, mate. Good timing."

Malcolm's cheeks look all shiny and red with the cold. Like apples. We nod at each other, and then Eric whacks up the volume, and shouts, "Alright lads!" and everyone turns to the TV as the players run on the pitch and take position. Stu lights up a cigarette and squashes further into the seat so I have to budge up to get out of his smoke.

"Should be a good match," he says knowingly, leaning on to his knees like an excited kid.

Dad agrees and helps himself to one of Stu's fags. "Just the one," he says to me with a nudge.

As it turns out, the match is a really boring one, and by half time it's still nil-nil. In between, Dad and Stu give us each 30p and let us go off to get some sweets from the newsagents. We leave them in the pub getting another round in.

On the way back from the shops, Malcolm's been telling me about the BMX he reckons he's getting for his birthday next week. They're dead expensive, and I ask him how his dad can afford it. He squats down next to a drain in the road and drops his lolly stick through the gaps, before carrying on along the path.

"It's cos him and my mum are divorced. Cos I live with Mum and Phil. So Dad always tries really hard to get me a better present than them. Then they say stuff like, who does he think he is, flash git, and then they get me something great too. It's brilliant. Win-win."

Sometimes I don't get Malcolm, but he's got a point. It does sound quite good.

"Is Phil loaded then?" I ask.

"Nah. But they get the money from somewhere. That's what counts."

Malcolm looks like a spoilt kid. He's too big, and too chubby, and his black hair is a bit square. But he talks like he thinks he's cool. He shoves his hands in his pockets and pulls out a liquorice shoelace, shovelling it all in at once.

"What about your lot?" he asks, an end of shoelace poking out the corner of his mouth. "Do you get good stuff off them? I mean, they've split up, haven't they?"

We reach the phone box on the corner of Park Road.

"You ever played Mrs McSporran, Malc?" I ask him, heaving open the chipped red door, releasing the stench of old piss and cigarette burns. Malcolm's frowning at me like I'm a right prat. "Come on," I urge him, as he stands outside the glass, chewing. Half-heartedly he comes inside, which is a bit of a squeeze with his chubby belly.

"It'll be a laugh," I say. "Watch the master at work."

I dial 100. "Reverse call please," I tell the operator. I give her a made up number and name – "Yes, Albert" – and we wait for the connection. Malcolm keeps looking around, to see if anyone's coming. He looks really nervous.

"Hulllooo!" I shout when the operator puts me through. "Hulllooo? Is that wee Ethel McSporran?"

Malcolm's eyes are like saucers, and his mouth has dropped open like a cartoon.

"Ach, Ethel! D'ye need any haggis, Ethel?" I hoot, as the woman on the other end tries to explain that I've got the wrong number.

"Ooh Ethel, pipe down will ye, wee lassie! Ye dinne wan' iny haggis? Hoo aboot some bagpipes?"

Malcolm has tears welling up in his eyes.

"Eh? Oor hoo aboot a kilt?" This one is so high-pitched that I crack up too, and just manage a final "tatty-bye" before hanging up.

Malc is thumping his fists on the glass, choking on his Hubba Bubba. "You're nuts, mate—" he splutters, still chuckling, his shiny cheeks redder than ever.

I offer him the receiver, "Wanna go?" but he shakes his head, laughing, pushing out of the phone box backwards. As we carry on back towards the Royal Oak, we see an old dear sat at the bus stop on the other side of the road. She looks quite sweet, with a big shopping bag on the floor by her little brown shoes, and she seems to be smiling at everything. I notice the bag's made of a kind of plastic tartan material. Malc sees it too, because he snorts and shoves me.

She's a little way off, and I come to a stop facing her over the road, hands on my hips, legs wide. In my deepest Scottish bellow I shout over to her, "Hulllooo deary! D'ye wanna haggis?"

The little old lady tips her head to one side, like she's trying to hear better.

Malc tugs at my sleeve, and screeches in a rubbish accent, "Oor perhaps a hairy sporran!" and we tear off down the street before she has a chance to get a good look at us.

An old man with a poofy little sausage dog angrily waves his newspaper at us as we run past. "Bloody hooligans!" he shouts, like a character from Benny Hill. I smirk at him, running backwards so he can see I'm not scared of him. His dog cocks his leg and pisses against the litter bin, and the steam rises like smoke as it trickles down the pavement and off the kerb.

When we get a safe distance away we stop, hands on our knees, catching our breath between sobbing laughter. A gob-stopper slips out of my mouth on to the toe of my plimsoll, before rolling along the pavement and coming to a stop by Malcolm's foot. We look up at each other, and now we're almost screaming, holding our bellies and gasping like we've got asthma.

"Was she Scottish then?" Malcolm asks as we get a grip of ourselves, "—the woman on the phone?"

I shake my head.

"Then what's with all the Scotch stuff?"

"Dunno, it's just kind of funny," I answer. "Shit! I forgot the oatcakes! You should always ask if they want any oatcakes!"

As we get closer to the pub, we run out of things to say for a bit.

"Malc, do you do Classics at your school?"

Malcolm wrinkles up his nose, and snorts, "Yeah. Why?" like he can't believe I just asked it.

"Oh, nothing really. Wanna jaw-breaker?" I say, offering him the bag, and then we turn the corner, across the road from the pub, and Malcolm nudges me, grinning.

"Fuckin' 'ell mate – look at the state of that!"

And there's this woman, swaying around outside the door of the pub, arguing with Eric the Landlord. She looks like she's just crawled off a park bench, wearing a summer dress and slippers. She must be freezing. Eric is shaking his head, sorry love, no chance; trying to get rid of her. There's a match on, they don't need this kind of bother.

Malcolm's laughing; he doesn't know it's my mum. I try to act normal, pull a face, rummage in my sweet bag.

"Yeah, fuckin' 'ell," I reply. My head's throbbing. "Malc, mate – I need a waz. You go on in – tell Dad I'll be there in a minute." And I pretend to head off towards the pub's outside loo.

Malcolm nods, stuffing in more sweets, looking the

12

drunk woman up and down as he passes her in the doorway. Eric the Landlord spots me, shakes his head as if to say, don't worry about it, Jakey. For a moment, I'm stuck to the spot. I just stand and stare at the back of her head. She's like a gorgon, and I've turned to stone.

Quietly, I walk over and slip my hand into hers, and lead her away from the pub.

"I'll make you a nice cuppa, Mum. I think we've got some logs out the back. It's cold enough to make a fire, I reckon."

Mum shuffles along, shivering silently beside me, till we reach the house. We get inside and she wraps her arms around me and sobs against my shoulder.

"You know I love you, Jakey. Never, ever forget that, darling. I love you."

On top of Devil's Dyke the sky is bright and clear. I stand at a little distance, watching Mummy shake out a fresh white tablecloth, as the wind tries to whip it away from her fingers. She sets it down on top of the picnic blanket and reaches for her wicker basket, but the wind snatches at the cloth again. Rachel sits on the grass beside me, sulky and bored. She says she's too old for birthday tea parties.

Mummy narrows her eyes against the sunlight. "You're only twelve, for heaven's sake, Rachel! Come and help me hold down this blasted cloth."

Daddy strides back up the hill, after a walkabout. His usually neat hair lifts and sways in the wind, and I like the jaunty way he marches towards us in his tweed suit. He sees me watching and raises his hand.

Rachel's cheering up now she's been given a job. She lays out the jam tarts she made this morning, placing them on the plate, one by one in the right pattern. Mummy always lets Rachel in the kitchen to make things. "You'll make a mess," is what she tells me. Rachel's good at it, naturally, so I suppose that's the real truth.

"Shall we give her a little present now?" Daddy asks Mummy as he reaches us, out of breath. He stands with his hands on his hips, his stomach thrust forward. Lately his waistcoats seem to be getting tighter around his tummy. Whenever Mummy mentions it he pats his stomach with both hands and calls it Good Living.

"As you like," says Mummy, not taking her eyes off the lunchtime preparations. She unpacks a stoppered bottle of home-made lemonade and four china cups.

Daddy squats down and rummages through the wicker basket. "Are you sure you packed everything?" he calls over his shoulder.

"Well, if you put it out where I asked you to, I will have packed it." Mummy reviews the picnic spread seriously. She reaches into her handbag, then briskly fixes a headscarf over her head to keep the wind from ruining her hairdo. She wears no makeup except for lipstick, which is a perfectly applied slick of tomato red. From a distance she has no features, except for her lips. I can't remember if I've ever seen her without her lips.

"Aha!" says Daddy, and he turns to hand me a long flat parcel, wrapped in brown paper and ribbon. "Sorry the wrapping's not too good. That's down to me, I'm afraid. Happy birthday, ten year old!"

He always chooses us something himself, usually something fun that Mummy wouldn't have thought of. I kneel on the edge of the blanket and start to untie the ribbon, with Rachel and Mummy looking over my shoulder. Daddy hunches down in front of me, studying my face expectantly. As I turn back the brown paper, a flash of bright red and yellow is revealed, bound up in white string.

"A kite?" I ask.

"Yes! A paper kite. It's supposed to be the latest design; extra thin paper – but also extra strong. Shall we try it out?"

"Yes!"

Mummy shakes her head and gets back to the picnic display. I've always wanted a kite.

Once we get it into the air, the breeze sucks the paper diamond way up high, and the spool of white cord tugs reassuringly in my hands.

Daddy shouts instructions to me, as he shields his eyes from the sun with his hand. "Reel it in! Let her out! That's it . . . good girl!"

We run and loop and whoop with the kite, until Mummy calls us back to the blanket for lunch. I can feel the cool heat in my cheeks, and Daddy beams at me, flushed and breathless, pleased with his gift.

"I love it!" I tell him as we flop down to eat. "I love it!"

Mummy passes around china plates and we each pick out sandwiches and cakes. She's a good cook. No one's better. And she remembered to do egg for me, which is my favourite. She leans back to produce another parcel from the basket. As usual, it's book-shaped. *Little Women* by Louisa May Alcott. I kiss Mummy on the cheek and thank her.

"Not as good as a kite, I suppose," she says, casting Daddy a wounded look.

"It's super, Mummy, really. I love them both."

Mummy clicks her tongue and gives me a dry smile.

16

Rachel passes me her gift, a needlepoint bookmark to go with my book. It says "Mary Murray, Happy Birthday 1957", and it's decorated with hearts and flowers. It's beautiful, with not a stitch out of place. I hug her and she hugs me back.

After we've eaten, Daddy, Rachel and I take turns flying the kite. The day was just made for kite flying. Mummy is busy clearing the plates.

"Come and have a go, Penny!" Daddy shouts to her.

She shakes her head and carries on packing away lunch.

"Leave that!" he tries again. "Come and have a go! It's great fun!"

Mummy turns her back to us, pretending not to hear, and Daddy returns to concentrate on the kite flying.

I run to her, and tug at her blouse. "You'll love it, Mummy. Have a go!"

When she pulls her sleeve from my fingers, I can see that she's crying.

"I love the book, Mummy. Really! I can't wait to read it! Mummy?"

She nudges me off, turning away again. "It's not the blasted book," she says, and I take a step back, embarrassed. "I'm fine, Mary. You go and fly your kite. Go on – they're waiting for you."

I kiss her, and she nods, not meeting my eyes. There's nothing to be done when she's like this, so I run back to Daddy and take the spool from his hands.

"Carefully does it!" he shouts after me. "Keep her steady. And she's away!"

The kite dances and weaves on the currents, bobbing every now and then as if trying to escape, before pulling

17

itself back up on high. Rachel and I giggle and shriek each time the kite drops from the sky, threatening to break free of the breeze. Daddy looks on, clapping as we recover the kite from its downward spirals. He looks like a little boy. Mummy sits at the top of the hill, her knees drawn in to her chin, the white tablecloth fluttering beneath her. When I squint she blurs away, so that she's just a rock on a hillside. I squint for ages, but the rock never moves, just sits there, a grey mound buffeted by a bright white light. For a brief moment, the flapping cloth looks like a young girl kneeling beside Mummy, whispering in her ear. It looks like me. When I bring Mummy back into focus, you might think that she's staring back at me. But I know she's not.

"I think we should go and see Mummy now," I tell the others, and we wind up the string and start up the hill.

As Daddy lugs the basket back towards the parked car, Mummy puts her arm around my shoulder and kisses my hair.

"Happy birthday, Mary," she whispers.

I smile up at her. "I really do like the book," I say. "Lydia has it, and she's always telling me that I have to read it. Now I can."

"Well, that's just grand," Mummy says, happy again.

When we reach the car, she turns to look back the way we came. She grabs both my hands and spins me until we're dizzy.

"What a view!" she shouts into the breeze. The Downs spread out behind us, bathed in light. "What a magnificent view!"

Jake, November 1984

It's Wednesday afternoon when Matt phones. I've only been home from school ten minutes, and I'm so surprised when I hear his voice that I drop the sick sponge and it splatters up the kitchen cupboards.

"Jakey!" he says, and he sounds really far away, and really happy to hear me. "What you doin', Jakey boy?"

I'm gob-smacked, it's been weeks since he left. All at once I think of his empty bed, and what it'll be like when he comes back home, and what Dad'll say when I tell him. I don't even mind going back to sharing with Andy just to have Matthew back home again. Even though he's out chasing girls most of the time, it's just good to have him about.

"Matt! I'm just mopping up Mum's sick," I tell him, clicking the kitchen door shut behind me. "I found it on the kitchen floor when I got up this morning, and it was still there when I got home, so I thought I'd better clear it up before Andy sticks his clod-hoppers in it and treads it through the house. You know what a messy bugger he is. But anyway, Andy must've gone back to Ronny's house or something cos he's not here and I didn't see him on the way home . . ."

"Alright, alright, boy! Slow down!" Matt's laughing at me down the phone, and I think I must have been gabbling. "So, guess where I am?" he asks me. "You'll never guess in a million years!"

I pause, realising that he must be far away if he's asking that. I feel my eyes well up and the drip from the tap seems to just hang there, not dripping quickly like normal, but hanging there, getting fatter and fatter. There's a massive pile of dirty pots on the side that wants washing. I suppose I should do them next, before Andy gets home wanting something to eat. The empty space down the phone line is waiting for me to answer. The fat drip plops on to an eggy plate in the sink.

Matthew shouts his answer, still laughing: "Germany! I'm in bloody Germany! *Guten Abend!* What d'ya think of that, Jakey?"

I can't talk, and suddenly all I can smell is the sick and the sick sponge and then Mum's shouting from her bedroom, *"Who's that?"* and I find that I don't want to talk to Matthew after all.

"That's great, Matt," I tell him, and for some reason all I can think to do is to put the receiver back in its cradle on the wall.

"Wrong number, Mum!" I shout, and I get on with the sick scrubbing.

When Andy gets home I make us some Marmite on toast, and we go up and watch the Lions Club fireworks from the top window. We talk about what it would be like if we could have our own fireworks one year, when we've both got jobs. Roman Candles; Snowstorms; Zodiac Fountains; the lot.

Mary, April 1961

The house is full of clients and family friends. On the other side of the door, I can hear Mummy welcoming them in, taking their coats, calling to Daddy. I sit on the toilet seat, staring at the door handle as someone tries it from the outside, pauses and walks away. A little patch of long awaited blood nestles in the cotton of my white knickers. I look at it, and wonder what Rachel does when she has hers. I know she has them, but when she's tried to talk to me about it I've told her she's making me squeamish. Now it's here, it's not what I thought it would be. It's so small, so insignificant. I wish I'd listened now, so I'd know what to do. I need to get fresh underwear, but Mummy's designated our bedroom as cloakroom. I roll up a wad of toilet roll and carefully balance it in my knickers, before flushing and washing my hands. I stand over the lavatory to make sure that everything's gone down, that there's no trace left behind.

"Mary!" Mummy calls when she spots me in the

hallway. She's wearing a pretty white blouse with ruffles down the front, and a neat little pencil skirt. Her hair is rolled up into a loose bun, with escaped ringlets tumbling around her neck. "Come and say hello to Mrs Stokes. Mr Stokes works with Daddy – you remember?"

I nod, and smile at Mrs Stokes. Mrs Stokes isn't as pretty as Mummy, and she looks serious and sensible. She's what Rachel would call "frigid-looking". Mrs Stokes smiles back at me, briskly, then carries on talking to Mummy. I run upstairs to see if I can find Rachel.

There's no one in our bedroom, so I quickly find a clean pair of knickers in my drawer, and ball them up into my cardigan pocket. I poke my head in all the other rooms, but Rachel's not there. The sounds of jovial cheer and adult conversation ripple across the floorboards and up the stairs. The hallway chandelier twinkles and sways with the noises of the party. If I go down now, Mummy will give me a plate to offer around, and I'll smile and smile until my face muscles ache. My knuckles are white against the smooth oak of the banister. Below me, Rachel hurries by, back towards the kitchen with an empty nibbles tray.

I dash down the stairs after her, and divert her into the lavatory.

"I've started," I whisper, pushing the door closed behind us.

"Started what?" asks Rachel with a frown.

"You know!" I say, impatiently. "You know!"

"Oh! Your periods!" she says, too loudly. "About time too. I was starting to wonder when they'd arrive. Does Mummy know?"

I shake my head. "It just happened. I don't want to tell her. She'd probably tell the next person she speaks to, then the whole houseful will know that I started my periods at the party. Oh my God."

Rachel nods. "Right, you wait here. I'll go and get the stuff and we'll sort you out." She kisses me and runs off, leaving me biting my fingernails and holding my breath until she comes back.

After everything's in place, Rachel stands back admiringly, as if I'm a masterpiece of her own making. "I think this calls for a celebration," she says, wickedly.

I follow Rachel through to the kitchen. The table is laden with plates of tasty treats for the guests, and bottle after bottle of wine.

"Mmmm," says Rachel, with wide eyes on me. "Hungry?"

I giggle, and we both grab a plate.

"Good girls!" Daddy bellows, making us jump as he leans across the table to pick up a bottle of red wine. Rachel and I both watch as he removes the foil and unscrews the cork. "You doing another waitress round then? Chop chop!" He leaves the kitchen with his bottle.

Quickly, we load up our plates, grab a bottle of white wine and a corkscrew and dash out of the back door before we can be seen. We head down the side of the house and out into the blinding sunshine of Hove seafront. The gulls screech and squawk overhead, adding to the sense of urgency and deceit, and we hurry along like double agents on a secret mission. With one last look over our shoulders, we cross the road and trot down the steps to the pebbles below, where we scrunch into a windless hollow tucked up against the breakwater.

Rachel expertly opens the wine. "Damn it! No glasses. It's straight from the bottle, I'm afraid."

She hands it to me, and I drink it back, coughing at the sharp flavour. Rachel laughs, and swigs it back herself.

"So, what's it like? Having a period every month?" Even though I'm practically fourteen, I still don't know much about this stuff. All the other girls at school have started already, so I never asked them, because then they'd know I hadn't yet.

"It's a complete bore, to be honest," Rachel says, leaning back knowingly. "But it's the burden of women. If you don't have periods, you can't have children. Mind you, I'm not even sure I want them, so the bloody periods might be a complete waste of time. Tania says if you don't want children, you can get your womb removed and then you wouldn't get periods. She says she's seriously thinking about it. But then Tania is full of funny ideas that she never follows through." She hitches her skirt up high, to stretch her legs out for tanning. I do the same, noticing how white my legs look against hers. The warmth of the sun is heavenly.

"But isn't it meant to hurt when you get your period? I didn't feel a thing when it happened."

"It will. It can hurt like hell sometimes. The cramps. In your back and tummy. That's usually how you know it's coming – like a warning sign. And you can get moody – PMT. Really moody, or kind of sad feeling. We'll have to tell Mummy, though, so she can get you your own sanitary stuff."

I'd rather keep it to myself, not tell her at all. The sea line is hazy and slow, and the backs of my knees are full of butterflies. "Are we drunk?" I ask Rachel, as I take another swig from the bottle.

"Will be," she says, taking the bottle from my hand.

"Is that why Mummy gets like that? PMT?"

"No. Mummy's is different. Hers isn't a monthly thing, is it? It comes and goes. Maybe some people are just like that. Up then down. Don't know how Daddy tolerates it, to be honest. She's a cow sometimes. It's best when she just goes and lies down in a dark room, keeps out of everyone's way. Have you got a bra yet?"

I shake my head.

"Oh my God! You must get one – they might be small now, but if you don't get a bra soon, they'll be round your knees by the time you're twenty-one. I'm not kidding! I'll talk to Mummy for you."

I throw my arms round Rachel's neck and pull her close. The deep, clean smell of her hair reminds me of being tiny, of snuggling up together like puppies. "I love you, Rachel," I tell her, and I gaze into her dark, kind eyes.

Rachel thrusts the bottle high in the salty bright air. "To womanhood!" she shouts into the wind. "To breasts and fannies and periods!"

We shriek in disgust and roll about on the pebbles, knocking our vol-au-vents off Mummy's best china plates.

Jake, December 1984

I had this really weird dream last night. It went like this. It starts off with me walking. I'm on my way to school, and then I look at my digital watch, but it's dark so I have to press the light button to see the time. Then I realise that I'm really late for school, and that it's near night time, so I start to run as fast as I can, and as I run my books start to fall out of my bag behind me. It's like they're in slow motion, and I turn and see them landing, one by one, in this massive puddle of dirty water, and one of them flaps open and I see all the words floating off the page and trickling away down a drain in the road. And then Malcolm cycles past on his shiny new bike, going, "Jake, what are you getting for Christmas?" I can see he's got these little wings sprouting out of the back of his trainers. And I say, "A puppy," and he snorts at me like it's a really sad thing to want. So I keep on running, but then I'm running towards home instead of school, and I get to the house, and see Andy in the top window, and he's banging on the glass from the inside, shouting, but I can't hear what he's saying. So I stick the key in the lock, and turn it, but it just won't open, the door's jammed solid. My heart's really pounding by now, with all the running, and I step back to look up at Andy, to tell him to let me in, but he's gone. So I try to shout "Andy!" but nothing comes out.

When I woke up, my stomach muscles were all bunched up like I'd really been trying to shout, but I know I hadn't because everyone else in the house was still asleep. Anyway, it was a shit dream, and I kept thinking about it all today at school. I wonder if Malcolm did get that BMX bike for his birthday. Probably, spoilt git.

I've got a job! It's brilliant; Andy and me went into Horrocks' newsagent on the way home from school, and I asked about the paper round.

Mr Horrocks said, "Have you got a bike, lad?" and I said yes, and he said, "Can you get here at six a.m. to pick up the papers?" and I said yes. He rubbed his stubbly chin between his finger and thumb like he was thinking hard. Then he said, "You got a hat and gloves, lad?" and I nodded yes. He looked serious, like he'd changed his mind halfway through, but then he told me, "You can start on Monday." And he patted me on the back and that was that. Didn't even ask my age!

When we get down the road a bit, Andy pulls out a fistful of Flying Saucers and shares them.

"I could only get a few," he says, his eyes squinting against the sherbet, "cos he was right by us this time. D'you get anything, Jake?"

I finger the Twix that I'd slipped up my sleeve as Mr Horrocks was telling me about the job. I don't think I've ever talked to Mr Horrocks before today, even though he's run the shop for as long as I can remember. There's something calm about him, in his eyes under those bushy white eyebrows. He must be really old, but he's got all his hair, only bright white. And he gave me the job just like that. I can't wait to start, and I'm going to get my bike out as soon as we get back, to check the tyres and WD40 the rusty bits. I didn't even ask how much I'd get paid.

"You can have it, Andy," I say, handing him the Twix from my pocket. He's chuffed to bits, and scoffs it before we get home.

My clock says 8.29 and it sounds like someone's banging the front door down. After a pause, the doorbell rings. "Saturday," I say out loud, pushing my eyes awake with the heels of my hands. I'm sure I can hear Dad shouting up at the window as I swing my legs out of bed, but we're not meant to go to his until eleven. And even then, we usually have to bang down his door, and get him out of bed. Anyhow, I don't like the sound of it, and I leg it down the stairs in my pyjamas, sticking my head in Mum's room on the way past. She's fast asleep. I wonder how she can sleep through that. When I get to the door, Dad pushes straight in, waving a letter around, looking really pissed off.

"Where's your mum, Jake?" he asks, looking about the room, checking out the mess. "Out for the count, no doubt. Jake?"

I start to straighten up the cushions on the sofa, feeling the goose pimples pop up through my skin. Dad's standing in the doorway with his hands on his hips, still holding on to that bit of paper. I look at him, seeing the icy air puff out of his mouth into the cold room, and I say, "It's bloody freezing, Dad."

"Watch your bloody language," he says and he clips me round the back of the head. "Come on, son. Get a jumper on and I'll make you a cuppa. Andy still in bed?"

"Yep," I tell him, and I run upstairs to put on a woolly. Upstairs, I check in on Andy, and then Mum again, and I'm glad to see them both asleep. I know there's trouble brewing, but if I'm lucky I might get a bit of time with Dad before the shit hits the fan. When I get back downstairs, Dad's cleared the fold-up table in the living room and the kettle's starting to boil in the kitchen. He's got his back to me, washing up a couple of mugs for the tea. The white letter is folded up in the middle of the living room table. I guess it must have been delivered in the first post for him to come over here all agitated like this. I straighten up the rag-rug by the fireplace while Dad finishes making the tea, and then he comes in with the two mugs and sits at the table.

"Sit down, son," he says, nodding at the empty seat. Shit, I'm thinking, what've I done now? Maybe it's not me, maybe it's Andy. I've tried to keep an eye on him but I can't be around all the time. At least next year he'll be moving up to my school. Dad looks scruffy, puffy-eyed. What could be so urgent that he'd come rushing round here in just a T-shirt and jeans on a freezing Saturday morning? He looks like he hasn't shaved, and one of the things I know he always does on a Saturday morning is shave. It's part of his Saturday ritual, like putting a bet on the horses, and having a couple of pints in the Royal Oak, and having me and Andy for the afternoon. And a Mars Bar, he usually gets us all a Mars Bar on a Saturday.

"How was parents' evening, Jake?" he asks me, as his fingers fiddle with the scruffy corner of the letter. There's a smudgy blue colour to its edges, where he's had it in the back of his new blue jeans. "Jakey? Are you with me, son? I asked you how parents' evening went?"

It was just another of those things I thought he didn't need to know. Sometimes staying quiet does avoid a whole load of hassle. I try to take a sip out of my tea, but it's too hot.

"I'm sorry, Dad," I say, and I don't want to look at him, because I know he's disappointed. He doesn't say anything, and I say, "I'm sorry, Dad," again, and then my stupid face starts blubbing, and my nose is bubbling snot, and I just can't stop, and I'm crying like a stupid baby. Blub blub blub, like a stupid baby. I should be able to handle this. It's just a stupid parents' evening.

"Jakey, lad – come on, son," Dad says and he comes round the table, pulling me in to him like I'm little again, and all I want to do is stay there.

"I couldn't get her out of bed, Dad!" I'm nearly shouting. I've got to keep my voice down. "I tried, and tried, but then it was gone five thirty, and it was too late to call you, so I thought, if we just don't go, maybe they won't even notice, so we just didn't go. I'm sorry, Dad. I'll give you your 10p back – it's still in my pocket upstairs." I swipe at my soggy face, and bury it in my tea, which is nearly drinkable now. Dad pushes the hair off my face, and I'm embarrassed about him seeing me cry. The folded letter sits in the middle of the table. I nod at it. "So what does it say then? The letter."

Dad sits back in his own chair. "Nothing much, son. They just want to see me. They were a bit worried that your mum didn't turn up, and they know we're not together any more. That's all, Jake, nothing for you to worry about." He looks at me long and hard. "Jakey – we've just got to get on with it, son. None of us wants the school busybodies poking about, do we? Let's just do our best, eh? Phone me next time. That's all."

The stair creaks and Dad goes, "Andy, mate! How's my little man then?"

Andy shuffles down the stairs, pyjamas twisted and his hair standing up on one side. He rubs his eyes as Dad ruffles his yawning head, and I go off to wash my face. The last thing Andy needs is to see that I've been crying.

"Jake!" Dad calls up to me. "You might as well get yourself dressed now – we'll head straight off if it's alright with you. There's no need to wait around for your mum to wake up – we'll leave her a note."

That's two more hours with Dad than normal. Bonus! I catch my skinny reflection in the mirror as my face breaks into a smile, and even the rotten feeling inside starts to shrink.

"Dad?" I yell down the stairs. I love you, Dad.

"What?" he yells back.

"I like your new jeans," I tell him.

There's a pause, before he answers, "Alright, Jakey. Don't wake your mum up, for God's sake."

I can't stop grinning now, and I pull on my own blue jeans and plimsolls, before skidding down the stairs, two steps at a time, still wearing my pyjama top under my jumper. On the way out I quickly fill the kettle, and put a tea bag and a clean spoon in a mug on the side, next to Dad's note. Andy and I grab our parkas and we ease the front door shut behind us.

As we all head off down the street together, Dad's got us either side of him, hands in his pockets, trying not to shiver.

"Thought you could help me choose a little tree for the flat?" he says. "Cheer the place up a bit. Only three weeks to go, you know. Wa-hay, boys!" Then he does his usual Noddy Holder impression. "*It's Christmas!* So, have you been good little boys for Santa then? Eh? Eh?" and he's scruffing our hair, and poking our ribs, and it's a laugh being with Dad.

When we get home from Dad's at 6.30, the kitchen bin is on the doorstep, scrubbed clean and drying upside down. Mum is up. We open the front door and hear the TV on in the living room. I look at Andy, putting my finger to my lips to shush him, and creep into the kitchen to check it out. It's spotless. I give Andy the thumbs up and we take our coats off and go through.

"Hello, my lovely boys!" Mum smiles, throwing her arms out to beckon us to the sofa. She's wearing her nice purple tunic and her black hair is brushed shiny and long.

"Did you have a good time with your dad? I've bought a Battenberg for tea – and *Doctor Who*'s on in ten minutes. Come here, you handsome princes!"

And she grabs us in this sort of huggy neck-lock, one under each arm like she hasn't seen us in a week. She smells clean and warm. Andy's face is level with mine, and I give him a cross-eyed spanner face. Andy laughs and I know he had a good day today.

Mary, March 1963

Rachel's so tall and lean, she might almost look like a man. Except she doesn't; she looks long and elegant and effortless, as if her limbs are made of mercury, the way they swing and gesture at her side. Every movement is fluid, and her dark curls tumble around her brown shoulders, picked up by the sea breeze to swirl about her face.

"Do you know about our brother?" she asks me casually, as she bends to pick up a nugget of polished green glass. "Look," she says, inspecting it against the light.

The damp wind is howling around my ears, and I wish I'd brought a jacket down from the house. I frown at her.

"Mummy had a baby boy, and it died. That's probably why she gets how she does." Rachel says this like it's everyday news, nothing to make a fuss about. She brushes her sandy hands over her tight red slacks.

"When?" I ask, not really believing her.

"After you, I think. I heard Mummy crying to Daddy

34

about it the other day. So I snooped around in their things when they were out one afternoon, and I found the medical papers."

"What would they say if they caught you? Rachel! Are you sure? About the baby?"

"Yes. It was there in black and white. Male, date of birth, weight, name, time of death. Urghh. It gives me the shivers to think about it."

"So what was his name?"

"Oh, I can't remember. What's it matter anyway?"

"He was our brother, Rachel! Of course it matters. Sometimes I think you haven't got a heart."

"Well, I seem to recall it was William, now I think harder."

"William. How sad. Poor Mummy. Can you even imagine the pain of losing a little baby like that?"

"As I say, it explains a lot. Mind you, poor Daddy too, but you don't see him moping about feeling sorry for himself."

"Rachel! This is so horrible! How can you talk like that?"

Rachel strokes her fingers down my arm, and smiles warmly. "You know I don't mean it. I'm just sick of everything revolving around her all the time."

Her eyes are full of water, and I wish I could see into her thoughts. She strides ahead over the pebbles.

"Is there a grave?" I call out to her.

She turns and walks backwards, leaning into the wind. "I don't know. They don't know I know, so I can't exactly ask about it. Maybe."

When we reach the next groyne, we sit at the water's edge, cross-legged, and skim pebbles out to sea. The sky is a murky grey, and a salty mist lies between the horizon and the clouds, obscuring the distant piers of Brighton. I think about that little baby boy, pale and dead.

"I've got a bit of a dilemma," says Rachel, still skimming stones.

I study the side of her face. She's always so full of news, whereas nothing ever happens to me. She knows everything first, and everything happens to her before me. She's the robber of new things.

She sighs deeply. "So, the dilemma's name is Darren. He's a dreamy dish, like Paul Newman, bright blue eyes and sun-kissed hair. When he's near me, I'm a wreck. My heart beats like a drum. But he's not our type at all, and Mummy would have a fit if she met him. And Daddy would load up that shotgun he's always going on about. But I can't stay away from him. He does the gardens up at the college, and I wag off to meet him when it's double typing, because I've already got a speed of a hundred and twenty words a minute. When he kisses me, I'd do just about anything." Her face is misty and flushed. She turns to look at me. "In fact, I have done just about anything with him."

She grins, and I gawp at her. "You mean, you've done it? You've actually done it? With a gardener? Oh my God, Rachel. Oh my God. You're right about the shotgun. Daddy must never know."

Rachel looks very pleased with her story. "That's not all. He's asked me to marry him."

"But Rachel, you're just eighteen!"

"God, Mary, I'm not actually going to marry him. He's a gardener, for Christ's sake. He might be a Greek god, but he's no provider. Mummy would never recover, and I'll not be the one to finally send her over the edge, thank you very much. I've just got to work out how to let him down gently. And I'm not quite ready to finish it yet. Mary, if you could see him! This is lust, pure and simple. Sometimes I just stare out of the window as Mrs Fanshaw drones on about salutations and punctuation, and I'll spot him in the distance, pushing a wheelbarrow, or bending to pull out a weed in the borders, and I swear my thighs start to tingle, just like they do when he runs his rough fingers under my skirt."

"Rachel! You did not let him do that! You're lying. Or you're a hussy!"

She leans back and inspects her bust, tugging the hem of her blouse down, tight over her slim figure. "I guess I must be a hussy, then," she says, and she smiles at the sea with satisfaction. "I'll think of something," she ponders. "Secretarial school finishes in a few months, so I'll make the most of it until then. Come July, it'll be au revoir Darren the Gardener."

Rachel closes her eyes, and stretches her long arms behind her head. She's a lithe sea serpent. She could just slither across the wet pebbles and slip down beneath the waves. She's the most beautiful thing I've ever seen.

"Your time will come, Mary," she says. "When you've felt the undeniable power of physical passion, you'll understand."

Miss Terry is drawing one of her chalk pictures on the blackboard.

"So, does anybody know who these figures are supposed to be?"

The picture shows a great round sun, with two winged men flying towards it. I know that it's Icarus and Daedalus, but I don't want to be the one to answer again. Miss Terry's arm is raised as she points to the board, and the light from the window blazes through the white material of her shirt. I'm sure I can see the outline of her bra from here.

"Jake?" She's looking at me. Standing right beside my desk, at the front of the classroom.

"Miss?" I feel my cheeks glowing hot.

"You must know, Jake?" She's smiling at me now, her fingertips resting on the corner of my desk.

"Icarus and Daedalus, Miss."

"That's right, Jake, good. And what's the story of

Icarus and Daedalus?"

My palms are sweating. "Um, well, King Minos was angry when the Minotaur got killed. And Daedalus was the inventor, who invented the maze. So King Minos blamed him. He locked Daedalus and his son Icarus in a high tower." I pause, looking up at her, hoping I can stop now.

"Very good, Jake. That's right. So, how could they escape? Anyone hear what Jake just said about Daedalus' job? What was his job?" She looks about the classroom with wide eyes. They're green eyes, like mine. I can see them from here. I can see the pupils of her eyes from here.

"Inventor," a few muffled voices call out.

"That's right! Daedalus was an inventor. The tower was filthy with the bodies and feathers of dead birds that had used the tower as their home. So, Daedalus created two pairs of enormous wings, using the feathers and bones of these dead birds, bound together with candle wax. Icarus and Daedalus strapped the wings to their shoulders and launched themselves from the window of the tower." Miss Terry weaves in and out of our desks, like a bird gliding through the sky, her arms held wide. "'Stay away from the sun!' cried Daedalus. 'For the heat of the sun will melt the wax, and you will fall!' But Icarus was having a fine time, and wouldn't listen to his old dad. He did his own thing, looping and whooping through the sky. And guess what? He flew too close to the sun. The wax of his wings was turned to liquid in an instant and as Daedalus landed safely on an island nearby, he saw his son, Icarus, plummeting into the Aegean sea far below, leaving nothing but a few feathers floating and bobbing in the sunlight."

She comes to a stop, back at my desk, her wings now hanging limp by her side, her head bent forward to signal that her story has come to an end. A few of the cocky boys at the back of the class clap and shout, "Bravo!" Miss Terry is smiling now, doing a little bow to the class, her face pink and shining.

"And the moral of the story is?" she asks us all, expectantly.

"Listen to your dad?" someone calls out from behind me.

"Yes, that. But, more to the point, it's about respecting the wisdom of your elders. If Icarus had respected his dad's advice, and known his own limitations, he may have made it to the island in one piece too. OK – that's it for today – thanks everyone!"

The class bundle out just as the bell rings in the hallway.

"Didn't see you at parents' evening, Jake," Miss Terry calls after me as I leave, behind everyone else.

"No, Miss. Flu. Mum had flu. Really bad, actually. We nearly had to get the doctor out, but then she got better suddenly, so we didn't have to in the end. So – yep, that's it. Actually, we thought it was pneumonia at one point, but it wasn't."

"OK, Jake." She's cleaning the blackboard, and the hem of her blouse top lifts up and down as she stretches and sweeps. I can see a little stripe of creamy skin each time she lifts her arm. "Well, tell your parents I'll look forward to seeing them at the next one."

I wait for her to look over her shoulder at me but she doesn't.

The corridor is deserted as I leave her classroom.

There's only Maths left today, but my brain is full of arrows and ships and Miss Terry. I slip out of the back exit, across the playground and through the gap in the hedge. I dump my school bag, and lie down on the cold grass, where I'm close enough to the school to hear all the comings and goings at the end of the day. I hear the rumble of the caretaker's wheelbarrow. The screams and shouts of the first years on the netball court. The car engines of teachers who've finished for the day. No one will notice me gone.

I've been doing my paper round for two weeks now, six days a week with Sundays off. Every week, I stash my savings in my Secret Literature Hideaway Book. It's a money box in the shape of a normal book, and you put it on the bookshelf with all your ordinary books, so thieves wouldn't have a clue. Matthew gave it to me for my last birthday, said he got it off the market. I'm saving for a new dynamo set for my bike, and I want one of those bike horns that make an electronic sound. If I don't get them for Christmas, that is. At the end of my round every Saturday I return my paper bag to Mr Horrocks' shop and he hands me a small brown envelope and a chocolate bar of his choice. He half smiles and winks, passing it to me secretively like it's a message from the FBI or something. One week it was a Texan bar, the next a KitKat. It doesn't really matter, I like them all. Andy is desperate to get a job here too, but he's only ten and Mr Horrocks wouldn't have him yet.

A few days before we break up for Christmas, I turn up at the shop and hang my paper bag on the hook at the back of the till where Mr Horrocks keeps them. It's 8.30, and I guess I must be the fastest paper boy because my bag is always first back on the rack.

"Good lad," Mr Horrocks says as I'm doing it, and as usual he heads towards the counter to get my money envelope. But before he opens the till we hear Mrs Horrocks from out the back, upstairs, and she sounds really old and weak.

"*Ted? Are you there, Ted?*"

Mr Horrocks pauses, his hand wavering over the till.

"*Ted?*" she calls again, this time sounding worried, sounding like a little child. Mr Horrocks' forehead wrinkles up.

"Can you hang on a minute, Jake? Keep an eye on the shop – I'll just be a couple of minutes." And he's gone through the beaded curtains, to the upstairs I've never seen, to the wife I've never met.

The shop is small and dark, with every shelf packed with things to buy. It's a newsagent, but it sells loads of other bits and pieces – custard powder, toilet rolls, Basildon Bond envelopes, Bic biros, sheets of wrapping paper on a stand, shaving brushes. It's a bit of everything. The shelves are dusty in places, I guess in the spots where stuff doesn't sell much. The cigarettes and lighters are on a shelf behind the till, and penny sweets in plastic tubs run all around the front of the counter. I'd love to know what's out the back. I bet there's a loo, and a phone, and maybe towering boxes of biscuits and things that he brings out to fill up the shop.

A few minutes go by, and Mr Horrocks still hasn't come back down. Luckily no one's been in the shop; I wouldn't know what to do if they did. I wander over to the beaded doorway that leads through to the back, and stand there casually, straining to hear what's going on upstairs. It sounds like someone's crying, and I can make out the odd word from Mr Horrocks. *"It's fine, love. Don't get upset, Marcie."* I can't think what's going on up there, and I start to wonder why I've never seen his wife before. All these years, and it's always been him behind the counter or stacking the shelves in his navy blue apron. I stay where I am, scanning the shop, thinking about Christmas coming, wondering how Mum will be this year without Dad. There's a stumbling, bumping noise from the room above, and it goes quiet for a moment. Then I hear Mr Horrocks' voice again. *"There you go, love. You sit there and watch a bit of telly. I'll be back to make you a cuppa."* And I hear his footsteps moving across the floor towards the stairs I can't see. I grab a pack of twenty Benson & Hedges and stick them up my sleeve, before moving round to the front of the till, to stand with my hands politely behind my back. I can hear him shuffling through the back room, towards the beaded curtain and the front of shop where I'm waiting. I can feel a bead of sweat in the dimple above my lips. I drop my arms down by my sides and stand awkwardly waiting for him to appear.

"Sorry about that, son," he says, and he pops open the till, pulls out my wage packet and hands it to me directly. No FBI secret stuff today.

"Thanks, Mr Horrocks," I say, feeling a bit embarrassed. He looks at me in his particular way, when he seems to be thinking about something else altogether. Then he leans over the counter to reach for a box of Dairy Milk, and passes it to me before I start to leave the shop. Brilliant, I think, that'll save me a bit of cash.

"You're doing a good job, Jake lad," Mr Horrocks

says, not smiling. "You've not been late yet. Keep it that way, lad. Work hard, show us all what you're made of."

He puts his hand on my shoulder as he's saying this, his glassy blue eyes glittering in his crinkly face. I wish I had a grandfather, like all my mates have. He'd have a dog, and a fishing rod, and he would've fought in the war and have tales to tell. He might even have a scar to show for it.

"Can I give them to my mum?" I ask him, holding up the Dairy Milk.

"That's why you're a good lad, Jake," he says, and he turns his back on me as he starts to empty a new box of crisps into the racking.

I push the chocolates up my jumper and cycle towards home, swallowing a lump of anger, my face burning against the cold morning air. I pass some of the other paper boys on their way back to Horrocks' with their empty sacks. I wonder if they'll all get a box of Dairy Milk like me. Probably. When I get halfway back, I stop at the footbridge that runs over the stream behind the school. There's no one about and I dump my bike in the nettles and scoot down under the walkway, to the spot where the big lads used to keep a stash of porno mags. The mags went long ago, but the ground is littered with freshly dumped cans, cigarette butts and sweet papers. I plonk myself down on the hump of the bank that rolls down to the stream. It's a filthy stream; doesn't belong here. It should be somewhere else, out in the countryside where it can run clean, without being bunged up with beer cans and johnnies. I rip open the Dairy Milk and stare at the pictures on the menu. *Toffee Delight. Hazelnut Whirl.* They're the best. Andy and me always fight over them. Not that we get that many boxes of Dairy Milk, but at Christmas we'll always scrap over those ones. *Orange Cup.* Urggh. The morning is cold and damp, and the light under the bridge is grey. As I run my fingers across the chocolates I notice my knobbly knuckles look red with the cold and my nails are bitten down to the quick. What a state. After I've gorged all of the nuts and toffees I turn the box over, sprinkling the remaining chocolates across the muddy ground, before jumping up and grinding them in with my heels. I stamp and stamp and grind and grind until the chocolates are nearly invisible in the mush of mud, and then I drop to my bum again, and sob into my knees until I can't sob any more.

When I walk to Rachel's college, it's just to look, just to see what he's like.

I creep about the grounds, like a trespasser. The buildings are shut up, the students and teachers all gone home for the holidays. I left my hair down today, and brushed it a hundred times to make it shine. Mummy asked me why I was wearing my best dress when I left, and I told her I just felt like making more of an effort today because the sun was shining. She smiled, pleased.

As I turn the corner of the main building, the light reflects off the long greenhouse and I pause, pressed against the brick wall, my breath zipped up tight. That's where he'd be, if he were here. I feel the sting of the sun as it singes the tops of my bare shoulders.

When Rachel came home last night, she was in a black mood. I asked her if she'd finished with him, and she told me of course she had, and to bugger off and stop asking questions. She called me a pathetic child and slammed the door in my face. Through the dusty little panes of the greenhouse I can make out pots and leaves; tomato plants; bags of earth; steam. His wheelbarrow is parked neatly by the door. But he's not there; no sign of him at all. Perhaps when the students go home for the summer, so does he. Rachel says he has skin like hard silk.

"Can I help you?"

I spin and gasp, and I'm staring at him, and he's staring at me.

"Do I know you?" he asks, a quizzical frown dancing around his eyebrows. His eyes are sharp and sad. His shorts are too big for his slim frame, sitting low on his hips, exposing the deep grooves that run down below his tanned waistline. He has his shirt in his hand, and there's a film of sweat covering his sinewed torso.

I can't speak.

"Are you looking for someone?" he asks, looking concerned and annoyed at the same time.

"Are you Darren?"

He puts his hand in his pocket, pushing the waistline down lower. My heart is thumping and I think I should probably leave.

"Who's asking?" He leans in to the brick wall, smirking.

"I'm Mary," I say, flicking my long hair off my face.

He looks blank and shrugs.

"I'm Rachel's sister."

His hand comes out of his pocket and the cocky expression disappears. He turns to walk away, towards his greenhouse. "You should go home," he says.

I run after him and touch his arm lightly, and he spins around as if he's stung.

"What do you want?" he bristles.

He thinks I'm a child too. I put my hand on my hip, and flick my hair again. "I think she's mad, that's all."

Darren shakes his head and strides into the greenhouse. I follow him, and stand in the doorway as he starts potting up some seedlings, scooping up fistfuls of earth and pressing down with his wide thumbs. His shoulder muscles flex as he works, and his face is set in an angry glare. Rachel's right, he is like Paul Newman.

I pull up a stool and sit on it, crossing my legs. My shift dress rises up, and from where he works, I know if he turns and looks at me he'll see my knickers. The moist heat in the greenhouse smells green and clear.

"So, is that it, is it completely over then?" I ask.

Darren turns, runs his eyes over me, lingering on my legs. "Apparently so," he says.

"Well, I for one can't understand it. Can I help with the potting?"

He shrugs, and I stand beside him so the hairs on our arms are touching.

"What can I do?" I look up at his face and he looks at mine. Tiny beads of sweat cling to his brow.

"Go get a few pots from under the bench down the back."

I walk to the back of the greenhouse, aware of his eyes on me. I bend to my knees and reach under the bench for the pots. "These ones?" I call out, holding some little black ones up over my shoulder. I know he's still watching me, trying to see up my skirt.

I drop the pots on the surface in front of him and wait for him to look at me. He doesn't. "You know, Rachel can be a bit of a cow sometimes. And she'll only marry someone who can look after her properly, so she says."

Darren's hands are suddenly on my hips, strong and hard, pushing me into the workbench as he presses his mouth down on mine, parting my lips with his forceful tongue. His teeth catch my lips and I taste blood. I kiss back, smelling the earth and perspiration rising from his naked chest. In one movement, his hand is up my skirt, stripping my knickers and forcing his finger inside me. I yelp at the brief stab of pain, and see his hands in my mind, tanned and dirty. His mouth silences me. One hand holds my hip bone, as the other pushes at my leg, making a space. He shoves, angrily grunting and pushing, and he's inside me and the pain is searing. I press my eyes shut and see the winter tide on Hove seafront. The wave pulls up high, like a monstrous thing, so high that you think it will never come down, and then it does, viciously thudding against the shoreline, tossing the pebbles asunder, grabbing at the debris on the beach, before it roars back and upwards again. A little girl in a blue shift dress runs along the water's edge, trailing a red ribbon from her hand. I squint hard at a gull as it sweeps high above the wave, bombing beneath the water as the foam hits the shore.

Darren shudders, pauses, then yanks out of me, backing away to the workbench opposite, horror smudged across his face. I drop my head and see a thin stream of pale blood running down the inside of my legs, snaking away to nothing beyond my bare ankles. Darren sees it too. I hear a sob, and look up as he turns away and leans into the bench. My body throbs mechanically, but my heartbeat has slowed to a dull tremor. When I take a breath, it surprises me, aloud, like a cry. Darren starts and turns back to me.

"There's a toilet in the building opposite." He hands me my sandals, his eyes averted. "Sorry," he whispers towards the bench.

As I leave the toilet block, I look back and see Darren through the door of the greenhouse. He's sitting on the stool, bent over his knees with his hands to his forehead.

Jake, Christmas 1984

When we get home from school on the last day of term, Mum announces that we're going to spend Christmas on the Isle of Wight, with her sister Rachel. The bags are packed already, and within half an hour we're in the back of a tatty cab, on the way to the ferries at Portsmouth Harbour. None of us talk. Mum sits in the middle, smiling as if in a daydream, staring at the road ahead; Andy sits on the other side of her, turning his thumb, first one way, then the other, frowning and quiet. The taxi driver in front smokes all the way there, with his window wound down an inch, so that the second-hand smoke streams past his headrest and into my face. I try coughing from time to time, but he doesn't get the hint. Every now and then his eyes check us out in the back. But even he doesn't break the silence. The grey sky is turning black as we approach the terminal, which is lit up with fairy lights that twinkle in the December drizzle. When the taxi pulls up by the ticket desk, Andy and me start to unload the boot as Mum pays the driver with a few crumpled pound notes. Andy shoots me a worried look as we dump the bags on the grimy pavement a few feet from a mangy-looking Alsatian dog and his trampy owner.

"What about Dad?" Andy whispers, his eyes flicking to Mum as she climbs out of the car, clutching her patchwork shoulder bag.

I scowl; shake my head at him before Mum can see. Andy doesn't say another word until we're in the café on board the ferry, drinking hot chocolate and watching the lights of Portsmouth drop away, as we sail towards the smaller lights of Fishbourne Harbour on the Isle of Wight. I wonder if it will snow this year. I wonder what we'll get. Mum hasn't packed a lot, so maybe she'll be doing her shopping there. She still has that quiet, calm look on her face and it's making me uneasy. She's getting my nerves on edge, just by looking like that. And Andy's right. What about Dad? I bet she hasn't thought about him in all this. It's like kidnap, I think, but worse because she's our mum, and she kind of tricked us into coming before we could even talk to Dad or give him presents or work out when we would see him over Christmas. I want to scream at her, shake her until she snaps out of this zombie act. And who's bloody Aunt Rachel anyway? If she was all that great, we'd have met her before, wouldn't we? That's the trouble with Mum; she's always changing her tune.

"How come she lives on the Isle of Wight?" I ask her.

"Who?" Mum asks, looking up from her coffee, surprised.

I tut, and look out the window. All I can see is my reflection in the glass, unless I press my face up close and shield the sides of my eyes with my hands. The wind is blowing a polystyrene cup about on the deck, whooping it up like a bird, plopping it down like a stone.

"Oh! Yes – of course. Aunt Rachel," Mum blurts out. "I'm not sure, darling. We'll ask her. You'll like her, and the kids are lovely."

"So you've met them, then?"

"No. No, not yet."

"Then how do you know they're lovely? They could be right little gits for all you know."

Mum's hand goes to her necklace, twisting it nervously, her thumb squeezing the silver cross, making her nail turn white and angry. She's trying not to look at me, because I'm ruining it.

"Well Rachel says they're lovely – in her letter." She looks up at me now, with pleading eyes.

"What did you tell her about us, then?"

"Well, I told her that you're thirteen, that you're a great little artist, and a brilliant runner. I told her that Andy is a bit of a maths wizard, might end up being the brains of the family! And that he's nearly eleven, and about to go up to the High School next year, with you. I told her that you're neat and tidy, and Andy's messy. You've got green eyes and Andy's got brown."

She looks up at me, and I can see she wants me to be pleased with all this rubbish she's told Aunt Rachel.

"Yeah, Mum. But what about the other stuff? Who's my best friend, for example? What's my favourite TV programme? What do I want for Christmas? Even, what do I have for breakfast in the morning?"

She stares at me. And Andy stares at Mum, looking worried, as her eyes well up again. It's always me. I just can't keep my mouth shut for five minutes. I rip open a tiny packet of sugar cubes and stuff them in my mouth as I storm away. I can't stand to be near them.

I take a walk around the open deck to cool off, feeling good about the icy spray on my hot face. The glass windows run all around the inside decks, letting me spy on the other passengers as I stroll around hidden in darkness. There are laughing groups of men at the bar, drinking pints and smoking; and a bored-looking barmaid wiping down the slops and sloshes their clumsy drinking makes. Every time she runs the bar towel along to dry up the puddles, another splash sloops up and over and on to the dry surface. After a couple of times, she realises the men are winding her up, and she laughs and leaves them to it. It's all friendly enough.

In the lounge seats in the next room along, lots of kids and mums are huddled around tables, colouring in pictures with crayons and eating biscuits. There's the odd dad here and there, reading a paper, leaving the children to the mums. One little kid sees me as I go by and presses his grubby hand against the window, smiling like he knows me. He's only about two or three. I wave back at him, and press my hand against the glass on the other side.

The mist off the sea is getting heavier all the time, and I'm really wet now, with no coat on. As I head back towards the café, I spot Mum and Andy through the salty grease of the window, bunched together into the corner sofa seat, her arm loosely hugging him into her, him looking warm and happy. They're both smiling, and Mum's unwrapping sugar lumps and passing them to him to eat. Mum looks more awake now, pretty even from this distance. I stand a while watching them like that, them on one side of the glass, me on the other.

Aunt Rachel is there to meet us when we step off the ferry at the other end. She's tall and slim, in a long dark brown duffel coat and green wellies, with wiry, greying hair piled up in a loose bun. Although she's scruffy, and even a bit older than Mum, she has a face like a film star, all cheek bones and bright eyes. She stands under a lamp post in the dark mist, lit up.

"Rachel," Mum calls out, as we struggle down the walkway with our luggage.

Aunt Rachel sees us, raises her two gloved hands, and rushes over with a smile. She and Mum hug each other for ages.

"Oh my!" She stands back, looking us over. "Mary, you said they were handsome – but I had no idea!" She doesn't kiss us, but holds out her hand to shake. "A pleasure, boys – and long overdue."

Mum looks proud, and tearful.

"No Matthew, then?" asks Aunt Rachel. Mum throws me a look, like a warning. I look at my shoes, bend down, pretending to tighten up my laces.

"He's gone . . ." tries Andy, but Mum cuts him off quick.

"He's gone travelling," she lies. She doesn't know where he is. "Itchy feet – you know he's seventeen now, Rachel!"

Rachel's nose wrinkles, just for a moment, and her eyes dance over each of us. "Of course he has! I'm sure you must have told me already," she laughs, brushing her hand down Mum's arm. "We can't keep them babies for ever, can we? Come on then, the wagon's over here." And she grabs a bag, slings it over her shoulder and strides towards a mud-spattered old Volvo parked on double yellow lines.

"Sorry about the dog hairs," she apologises as she clears a tangle of rope and a gardening spade off the back seat to make room for us. "Ellie goes everywhere with me normally – the kids are looking after her at home – waiting for you to arrive!"

The moon is high now, and I'm starving. I'm not sure I want to meet these cousins, let alone spend Christmas with them. But Aunt Rachel is alright, so maybe they will be too. Andy nudges me, and pulls a face, holding his nose and blowing his cheeks out like balloons.

"Doggy-doo-doo," he whispers, and even though I shove him off me, we both snigger. It really does stink of dogs in here.

The journey takes no time, and within half an hour we pull into a long muddy drive and head towards a huge house, in the middle of miles of lawn and fields. There are cows in the fields to one side, and white chickens peck freely in the gravel around the steps up to the front door. The moon lights up the driveway, showing the bright white of the house and its sparkling windows. The dog, Ellie, comes bounding down the driveway towards us, a big hairy old thing, a grey and white ball of fluff. When she reaches the car, she turns and trots alongside us, her tongue lolling out as she tries to see in our windows through her shaggy fringe. Andy holds his nose again, looking at me with rolling eyeballs, pointing at the dog and chuckling. I squeeze his knee so he shrieks.

"Those chickens shouldn't be out in the drive. Someone's left a door open," Aunt Rachel grumbles, as she pulls up alongside the house. She bundles out of the driving seat as she pulls up the handbrake, calling, "George! George? Chickens!"

Mum gets out too, and Andy turns to me, wide-eyed. "Bloody 'ell, Jake. It's a bloody mansion!"

I clip him round the head, "Watch your bloody language," and we laugh, scrabbling out of the car to catch up with Mum.

Two children appear in the doorway, a boy and a girl. The boy, George, is lean-faced and small, like me. Across one eyebrow he has an angry scar that's left a bald stripe through it, and his mousy hair hangs down the sides of his face, resting in small curls on his shoulders. George and I share the same birthday, Mum told us on the way here; same day, same year. Born hours apart. We're practically twins, she said. He looks really pissed off to see us.

"I'll do the chickens," he mumbles, and he slopes off towards the darkness of the sheds.

I hear Mum's sharp intake of breath as she watches George disappear down the side of the house. She puts her arm round my shoulder, bringing her hand up to brush my hair to one side. I shrug her off. I hate it when she does that.

"This is Katy," says Aunt Rachel, and to Andy's embarrassment, the girl skips down the steps to grab his hand. Katy is just ten, a bit younger than Andy, and it's obvious she's over the moon to have some big cousins come and stay. Her long dark plaits look as if they were done days ago as they're all fuzzy and untidy like she's slept in them over and over. She's got freckles right across her face and a dimple on one side. She's like one of those *Little House on the Prairie* girls, right down to the

57

oversized rag doll dress and boots. Andy's trying to play it cool like me, but I can see he's desperate to get inside the house and poke about. The dog has flopped down in the middle of the drive, looking exhausted from the short burst of excitement.

"Ellie!" Katy calls to the dog, and we gather up our bags and trail inside the house to see where we're staying.

The house has five bedrooms, two living rooms, an office, a huge square kitchen, and an extra bit that Aunt Rachel calls the Boot Room, where the shoes and coats are all kept along with the washing machine and the dog's basket. In the Second World War, the house was used by British soldiers, and Aunt Rachel tells us that Andy and I will be sleeping in the officers' room on the second floor. Andy wants to know if anyone actually got killed here, but Aunt Rachel says that there wasn't any real fighting, that they just camped out here in case the Germans tried it on. All the rooms are tall and wide, and every one of them is a complete mess. There's junk everywhere, spilling out of boxes and tucked behind doors and sofas. In one room, the office, there are seven boxes along one wall, every one of them packed with newspapers going back years. Aunt Rachel says that Uncle Robert was a hoarder, and she can't bring herself to clear out his stuff just yet. It's only been six months since he died, and she says it still doesn't feel right to start interfering with his things.

The kitchen is gigantic, with a great big old-fashioned oven called a range, which throws out a toasty heat all day long. Strings of onion and garlic hang from the beams, and all the pots and pans are on show, hanging from hooks above. The weird thing is, you can see everything

– there are hardly any cupboards to hide stuff away in. Aunt Rachel says it's a working kitchen; that everything has to be where she can see it and use it. It's cluttered and loud looking, and I love it. It makes me want to cook. Aunt Rachel doesn't fuss over us, just tells us to go off and explore while she and Mum knock up some dinner. As I disappear up the hallway, I hear the sound of a cork popping from a bottle.

Andy ran off with Katy pretty much as soon as we arrived, and George hasn't come back from feeding the chickens. So I'm free to wander about the house as much as I want. Ellie's sticking with me, sniffing along by my side, or looking up at me for a stroke. They said she's an Old English Sheepdog – the proper name for a Dulux dog. She looks a bit daft, because Aunt Rachel insists on tying her fringe back with one of Katy's pink grips. But the best thing is, she's got one brown eye and one bright whitish blue eye, just like David Bowie. It makes her look a bit alien, and really cool. Her brown eye is exactly the same shade of brown as Dad's eyes. Exactly the same. I'm glad that she's decided to stay with me; it makes me feel less like a snoop when I check out all the rooms. I mean, she's got a right to wander about in her own house.

Mine and Andy's room is right up at the top of the house, and has a linking door to Mum's. Our single beds are made up with puffy, soft duvets and pillows. I could tell Mum liked them earlier, when she sat down on the bed and stroked them, gently squeezing the feathers under her fingers.

She said, "We'll get duvets for your beds soon, Jakey – much better than sheets and blankets."

I felt bad about the ferry then.

I decide to unpack my things now, get them into some sort of order, so I know where everything is when I need it. There's a chest of drawers in between the two single beds, and I give myself the top two, leaving the bottom two for Andy. I lay out my pants and socks in the top one, which is thin, and my trousers and tops in the second, deeper one. I already wrapped up the presents for Mum and Andy, when we were back home, so that they wouldn't know what they were if they found them. I take them out of my bag now, and carefully slide them behind my underwear. I wonder if I need to get something for Rachel and everyone now. I haven't got much money with me – most of it's back home, in my bike light fund. Mum might have got them something, I suppose. I refold my pyjamas and put them under my pillow, then lie down for a minute to see how it feels. Our beds are directly under a sloping window, built into the roof, so we can go to sleep looking at the stars. It feels good in this small room, and I close my eyes and imagine being alone here, completely alone with Miss Terry. She would be sitting on the edge of my bed, brushing the hair across my forehead with her long white fingers. She won't call me Jakey, it's too childish. Shall I read to you, Jake? Slide along, Jake, make room for me, she'd say, and we'd both move under the covers, bunched up real close where the bed's so small. Do you know about the Trojan War, Jake? she'll ask me. Tell me, I'll whisper in her ear.

Ellie's snuffling at the door; I must have shut her out when I came up here. I sit up, feeling red-faced and flustered, and stumble over to the door, readjusting myself as I go. I try not to feel irritated at Ellie, but I am. She looks up at me with sad eyes, so I haven't got any choice but to forgive her and give her a playful ruffle. I take a pee in the loo next door, and decide to inspect the rest of the house while it's still quiet.

The stairs down from the attic rooms are dark wood and narrow, twisting. Ellie scrabbles and lurches behind me, too big for such a small and slippery staircase. There are creepy old portraits all the way down the walls; probably ancestors. On the next floor are all the family's bedrooms, plus a big bathroom and playroom. I check out the playroom, and find floor to ceiling shelves straining under the weight of every board game you can imagine. Monopoly, Cluedo, Guess Who, Yahtzee, dominoes, jigsaws, Tumbling Chimps, Operation. There are posters on all the walls, and loads of little round grey spots where Blu-tack has pulled the paint away. One of the walls is painted black, and it's covered with pink and blue chalk drawings and writing. There's a big trunk underneath the window, full of bears and plastic dolls, some of which have had their hair cut close to the head, so they look like naked chemo patients. The carpet is filthy, and it seems they're allowed to eat and drink up here, judging by the crumbs on the floor and the purply-coloured stains on the carpet. There's a really old-looking rocking horse by the wall, and an electronic keyboard plugged in and ready to play. There's even a full-size drum kit set up in the far corner.

"Whadda you want?" growls George, in a near whisper, right up close to my ear.

He scares the life out of me and I spin round, making this unexpected squeaky noise. I must look really stupid and scared, because he snorts a laugh at me, then picks up his drum sticks and sits at the seat, cocky. I think I'm meant to be impressed. Ellie flops down on the floor next to George, laying her head on her paws with a huff.

"Go on," I say, "give us a demonstration then."

George sneers at me, scratching behind his ear with his drum stick.

"So, what're you into then?" he asks, like he's asking me for a fight. "Music? What're you into?"

I look at him blankly. "Dunno, loads of stuff. Yeah, I've got quite broad tastes really," I answer, thinking I sound knowledgeable enough.

"Like?" he pushes on. He's really scoffing now, like I'm some pansy who's into Abba or something. I try to stop my eyes from checking out the band posters stuck up around his drum kit.

"Like all sorts. What about you, then? Who're you into?"

He snorts again, shaking his head, then starts drumming, first slowly, staring me out with each beat. The more he stares at me, the more I want to laugh in his stupid face. I wonder which one of us was born first, which of us is older than the other by a few hours. Me, let it be me. His drumming starts to build up, faster and harder, and it's really quite good, and as it builds, he starts shaking his head rhythmically, his floppy hair moving back and forth across his eyes that he won't tear away from me. I can't keep this staring up much longer; my eyes are starting to water. He looks like a madman, some weird, mad animal. And then, I don't know why, but I start to dance in this crazy, jazzy way – still stuck to his eyes – jigging about like an elf, mooning my face up to his, wheeling my arms by my sides, lifting my knees like a string puppet. And I never lose eye contact.

He's drumming and drumming, and I'm leaping and yelping, ta-ta-ta-boom-ta-ta-ta-boom-ta-ta-ta-boom, and I'm laughing like a loon, and he's swinging his girlish hair, starey-starey, and then he's throwing down his drum sticks into a clatter of cymbals, screaming, "Alright, you fucking Joey Deacon nut-nut! You win!"

He's sitting there with his cymbals spinning like plates, hands on his hips, shaking his floppy-hair-head and grinning at me. Then he steps out from behind his drum kit and offers me his hand. I grin back at him and shake his hand, feeling sweaty and bold.

"Food," says George, when the bongs ring out downstairs. It's the first time I've ever been in a house so big that you need to sound a gong to tell your kids to come down for tea.

"You'll soon see," he adds, carefully sliding *Blue Monday* back into its 12-inch sleeve, checking the disc for dust as it slips into place, "she's completely mad. Not only since Dad – just mad, naturally."

"No way," I say, "I think she seems really cool. Really together." I pause, feeling his silence. "I mean, is she really, though? A bit mad?"

He shrugs, gets to his feet, and rests his hand on the doorknob. "Nah, she's alright. Just a bit annoying at times."

We head down the stairs, to hear Aunt Rachel yelling, "*Boys!*" and banging the gong again. Down in the kitchen the heat and smell of the cooking is like a magic hunger potion, and my stomach growls painfully. It's nearly nine o'clock, and I've only had a hot chocolate since lunch. We all help to carry the food from the kitchen into the dining room, where Katy and Andy are laying out the knives and forks. It's noisy with chatter and clatter, and they've got a fire going in here as well as the front room, so it smells smoky and alive. Ellie's wagging about, begging as we put the bowls out on the table.

"Leave it! Ellie! Leave it!" yells Katy, who tells us that she's in charge of dog training. Ellie is only two, but it's hard to believe, as she already looks like such an old lady with all that grey fluff around her. Ellie doesn't seem to take much notice of Katy, and just carries on weaving in and out around the table and chairs until we all sit down.

"OK, do we do grace?" asks Aunt Rachel when she comes in, flinging her apron over the back of her seat. The chairs are all the same, high-backed and carved in dark wood, to go with the huge table. The table looks really ancient, like an old knights' table, with deep scratches and ring marks all over the surface.

"Oh – George! Candles, let's do candles, shall we? Yes, let's do candles!"

George pulls a lighter out of his jeans, and leans in to light the four red candles in the middle of the table. He shoves it back into his jeans pocket with his thumb, like he's done it a million times before. He clocks me watching him and smirks.

"So, do we?" Rachel asks Mum. "Do grace?"

Mum laughs, shakes her head. "Not since home, Rachel. You?"

"No bloody chance! OK, well, for old times' sake then: For what we are about to receive, may your stomachs be truly grateful. Amen. Tuck in, everyone!"

She's done jacket potatoes, and there are bowls of chilli, and baked beans, and grated cheese, and salad, and sausages and beefburgers. Katy walks around the table pouring Ribena into our huge wine glasses, while Aunt Rachel pours real wine into hers and Mum's. When all our glasses are full, Aunt Rachel raises her glass.

"To family, absent and near. To new friendships – and old ones. To all of us in this old wreck of a house. Bottoms up!"

"Bottoms up!" we all cheer, and we plough into the food like a swarm of locusts. There's no best behaviour to worry about, everyone just talks across the table at each other, and leans over to get what they need without having to say excuse me or thank you every time. It's not how I'd have thought people in houses like this would be. Mum and Rachel are chatting away, finishing sentences for each other, patting one another as they laugh. Mum gets out her cigarettes, and George leaps up to offer her a light. He doesn't just give her the lighter, he actually lights it for her. She bats her eyelashes at him and smiles, brushing his sleeve with her fingers. He looks chuffed to bits with himself as he slumps back down in his chair, twirling the lighter between his fingers and thumb.

"Mary and I used to be quite a pair, didn't we, Mary?" Aunt Rachel says, as she plonks a big cherry cheesecake down on the table. "Real party animals. And that was in the days when people really knew how to party!"

"Oh God, Rachel, don't be daft!" cries Mum, flicking at Rachel's wrist, as she prepares to cut into the pudding. Mum grinds her cigarette into the ashtray, then goes to the fireplace to empty it into the flames.

"Oh, come on, Mary, we were gorgeous! D'you remember those minidresses we made – matching – and they barely covered our frilly knickers! And couldn't we dance too? The Twist, the Monster Mash. We did them all."

George has his head in his hands. I can't imagine Mum partying like that, young and lively, and without kids.

"Cheesecake, George?" Aunt Rachel says, passing a plate over to him, winking at me. "Come on, George, eat up and I'll tell you more about my partying days. I'll show you my dance moves if you like."

George looks up at me like a condemned man, and says, "See?"

I laugh, scooping up my last mouthful of cheesecake, all sweet and biscuity. I didn't know if I'd like it, but it's not even slightly cheesy. Aunt Rachel whips away my plate and serves up another huge portion, sliding it across to me without a word or a look.

As dinner comes to an end, I can't help staring at the photograph of Uncle Robert, hanging on the wall behind Aunt Rachel, opposite George and me. His smiling eyes look right out of the picture and follow you about the room wherever you are. It's kind of like having his ghost in the room. I scan George's face and I can see that he's not at all like Uncle Robert; just like I'm not like my dad. It's weird how it works. Even though George's face keeps trying to be grumpy, it's still a nice face. I'm good at faces.

"What're you looking at?" asks George, sounding annoyed again.

"Nothing," I reply, and I run my finger over my licked clean plate.

After dinner, George disappears to his bedroom to be on his own, and the rest of us move into the living room where Aunt Rachel has built up the log fire. There's a real Christmas tree in the corner by the huge window, covered in hundreds of tiny handmade baubles of glass and glitter. They're nothing like the metallic plastic ones we've got on our small tree at home, and there's no sparkly tinsel, but instead, strings of little iced biscuits that Aunt Rachel and Katy made together this afternoon when they knew we were coming. Ellie is lying on the grubby rug in front of the fireplace, her hairy chest rising and falling as she snores, and Aunt Rachel is opening a box of chocolates to celebrate our arrival. Mum and Aunt Rachel sprawl out on the big old leather sofas, and the rest of us sit on cushions on the floor. The After Eights go round and round, and me and Andy can't get enough of them. Better than Dairy Milk. Andy's stopped frowning altogether, and he and Katy seem to have hit it off. She's foot wrestling him under the coffee table, and they both giggle as one tries to out-wriggle the other. I ask Aunt Rachel if she's got any photos of Uncle Robert, and she fetches an album and a box of loose pictures. She looks quite young in the firelight, and she flicks through the album with lively eyes. Mum uncorks the red wine and tops up both their glasses.

"What did Uncle Robert do?" I ask Aunt Rachel. Mum glares at me, like I'm asking a terrible question.

"It's alright, Mary. He was a partner in a law firm for many years. George and Katy were at boarding school in the country, and I was doing bits and pieces of charity work. But then Robert was rushed into hospital with a massive heart attack. Three years ago. Probably too many business lunches and too much stress."

She's flicking through the photos as she speaks. "So,

we upped sticks, moved here, and your uncle became a writer, while I looked after the animals and children. A little piece of the good life, a lot of people would call it."

I look at a grainy photograph of Aunt Rachel and Uncle Robert sitting outside a café on holiday in Tunisia, holding their posh cocktail drinks up to the camera, both smiling behind big sunglasses. They look happy, rich. Her skin is brown, and her hair is dark and loose. She's like a Bond girl.

"God!" she screams. "Look at me there! What a cracker. Didn't know it at the time, of course. You never know what you've got until it's gone." She takes a swig from her glass of wine, pushing back her wiry, wild hair, and moves on to another photo.

I wonder what Uncle Robert was like; I'm really impressed at the idea of having a writer for an uncle. I ask Aunt Rachel if I could see some of his books.

"Oh, he never actually got anywhere with it, darling," she says sadly, "but it was his dream. He really meant to do it, you know. Maybe he would have got on with it if he'd known he wouldn't be around so long. Live for the moment, darling, because we're dead a long time." Aunt Rachel gathers up the photos and places them carefully back in the box. "God only knows what he did in his office all day long – because there was no sign of a novel that I could see. Perhaps we'll find it when we're least expecting it."

Mum reaches across the table and places her hand on Aunt Rachel's.

"You should have told me, Rachel." Mum has tears in her eyes. I hope it's not the drink.

"And you should have told me, Mary," Aunt Rachel

replies, and gathering up the box of pictures, she stands, kisses Mum on the forehead and leaves the room.

For a while, we sit there in easy silence; me, Mum, Andy and Katy, all of us staring lazily past Ellie into the crackling fireplace. Full of good food, and at home with these new people, for a short moment it feels like this living room is our whole world.

"Bedtime," says Mum, as she re-corks the bottle. And leaving her glass of wine half full, she takes us up to our beds on the second floor and we all settle in for our first night in Manningly Farm.

Mary, December 1965

As we turn into our gate we see Mummy rise and look out of the window. It's ten past ten, and we're late.

"Great," says Rachel. "She's probably been having a seizure during the last ten minutes. Probably imagines we've got caught up in some Mods and Rockers skirmish on Brighton seafront."

"Or worse still, run off with them," I add.

Mummy opens the door, her face surprisingly animated. She looks over her shoulder and calls out, "See? I'm so glad we persuaded you to stay, Robert."

Rachel glares at me as I stifle the giggles behind my gloves. We go through into the living room, where Daddy sits with Robert, drinking whisky. Robert stands and immediately holds out his hand to Rachel.

"Rachel. Mary. Lovely to see you both." He's nervous as hell, and Rachel's expression shows that she's pleased to see him. "I was just passing, and, well, your parents very kindly asked me in for a drink." He smiles at Mummy and Daddy, who look delighted to have him here. "Don't know where the evening's gone! I'd best get out of your hair, Mrs Murray. Good grief, is that the time?"

Responding to a meaningful look from Mummy, Daddy insists that Robert stay for another drink, and instructs us to take our coats off and join them for a glass of wine. In the hallway I nudge Rachel as we hang our coats, giving her a pout and a sexy wiggle.

"Bugger off," she hisses, before smoothing down her miniskirt, plumping up her hair and walking elegantly into the living room.

Rachel is directed to sit next to Robert, with me on the sofa beside Mummy. Daddy stands with his back to the fireplace. The fire's simmering behind the guard, reflecting pretty flickers of light in the Christmas baubles that cover the tree.

"Rachel, did I tell you that Robert's coming on board at Murray-Stokes?" Daddy sounds almost rehearsed.

"No," she says, smiling at Robert coyly. "That's wonderful news."

"Well his old man says he's got a good brain in that head of his, and we've been looking for a bright young thing to bring up through the ranks. Starts next week, isn't that right, Robert?"

Robert puts his empty glass on the side table. "That's right, Mr Murray. And I must say, I can't wait to get stuck in. I think I'm going to be very happy there." He turns to Rachel and gives her such a wonderful, open smile that I want to kiss him on the cheek and ruffle his hair.

Daddy looks severely at Robert. "I think we can stretch to Derek, now we're to be working together, Robert."

Robert nods. "Derek it is."

For a moment, there's an uncomfortable silence. Mummy breaks it. "Rachel's twenty now, aren't you, darling?"

Rachel's eyes open wide at the floor in embarrassment.

"Yes," I say. "This birthday, she had twenty candles on her cake, didn't you, Rachey?"

Mummy tuts. "Robert, how old are you now?"

He blushes. "Twenty-four."

"How lovely," says Mummy.

"Anyone for a top-up?" asks Daddy, and Rachel and I offer our glasses. Daddy gives us both a censorious look, but fills our glasses anyway. "So, where've you been tonight, girls?" he asks.

I was hoping that someone would ask. "Cochran's. It was party night – oh, the band was amazing! The singer was just like Adam Faith. The girls were going crazy! Rachel and I danced and danced all night. We had to fight off the chaps too, didn't we, Rach? In fact, fake-Adam Faith was definitely giving you the glad eye from where I was standing. If we'd stayed on a bit longer, I'm sure he would've been down to ask you for a dance." The silence returns to the room, and it's suddenly really funny. I take another big swig of wine, just to hide my face. Rachel looks mortified. No one says anything, and when I look up at Robert's polite face and Mummy's anxious one, I have to excuse myself before I upset someone by howling with laughter.

In the downstairs lavatory, my vision spins as I look at my clammy reflection in the mirror. I flop on to the toilet seat and let my head drop on to my knees, as the floor slides from side to side beneath my feet. I can hear Mummy in the hallway, telling Robert that she'll let Rachel see him to the door as she's got some clearing up to do in the kitchen. Daddy says he'll give her a hand. They whisper together as they pass my door on the way to the kitchen.

After a few minutes, I poke my head out of the door, where I can spy down the hallway to where Rachel stands primly on the doorstep, saying goodnight to Robert. He kisses her on the cheek, and she gives a shy little wave as he goes down the path. I watch and wait for her to close the front door, then rush out to grab her by the wrist.

"Upstairs. Now!" I whisper and despite her annoyed expression, she rushes up ahead of me to our bedroom.

"Well?" I ask. "Did he ask you out?"

"Of course," she says, aloof.

"And?"

"We're going out for dinner next week, if you must know. No thanks to you, you child."

I stand and stare at her as she strips off her clothes and wriggles into a shapeless winceyette nightie. "God, Rachel," I say, slurring a little. "You're amazing. The dancing whore of Babylon one moment. The Virgin bloody Mary the next."

Rachel tries not to smile, but she can't help it. "Bugger off, Mary. Just because I know how to handle my drink doesn't mean you have to get bitchy."

"I'm not getting bitchy. After your performance with Robert tonight, even I believed your virginity was still intact. I'm just very, very impressed. That's all."

Rachel smiles contentedly, gazing at the ceiling as I clamber into bed. We lie in silence as we listen to the sounds of Mummy and Daddy settling into their own bedroom.

"But he is rather sweet, isn't he?" Rachel asks as she tugs the light pull that dangles between our beds.

"He's lovely," I say.

"So bugger off, and go to sleep then," she whispers, the smile still in her voice.

"Love you, Rach," I murmur, already half asleep.

"Love you too," she says. Her hand reaches out to mine in the darkness, to squeeze the soft pads of my fingers before I slip away.

Jake, Christmas 1984

On Christmas Eve, I overhear Mum on the phone in Uncle Robert's study. She's talking in an angry murmur, like she's sneaked off to make the call and doesn't want to get caught.

"Because I knew what you'd be like if I told you, that's why!" she whispers. "You're a bloody arse, always wanting it your own way! You're like a spoilt child."

There's a pause as she listens to the other end.

"You're being an arse right now! No – no – that's not the point, Bill, you know that's not the point!"

I knew it could only be Dad. Mum never talks to anyone else in the way she talks to him. I'm pressed up against the door frame now, and I can see her through the crack, sitting behind Uncle Robert's huge desk, leaning forward with the phone to one ear, a hand over her eyes. Her hair hangs around her face like a black curtain.

"You patronising little shit, Bill! It's Christmas – of course I've had a drink. You bloody hypocrite. I don't suppose you've been down the Royal Oak every night since you downed tools on Friday? But that's alright, isn't it? I don't suppose that's the same at all, is it, Bill? I tell you what – if Women's Lib thinks its job's done, it's bloody well wrong, Bill, with chauvinist pigs like you roaming the streets. You shit."

Mum looks pale and tired. She's listening to Dad talking, shaking her head every now and then, swiping away the tears. After a pause, she sniffs, shakes her hair back and straightens herself in the chair. Her face is changing, her eyebrows arched, her mouth fixed. She pokes her finger into the crystal glass of gin and tonic in front of her, making the ice cubes bob around. She wipes her wet finger on her lap.

"They're not here, Bill. They've gone out with Rachel for the afternoon, so I'll have to get them to call you when they're back. – No, I'm not having you ringing here all hours, we'll phone you."

Her eyes are cold and icy, all the softness and tears gone. There's nothing of her to love when she's like this.

"Well, you'll have to be happy with it, Bill, because that's the way it is. The boys will call in the next few days. – Of course I know it's Christmas Day tomorrow, Bill. Credit me with that much intelligence. I said we'd call."

And she hangs up.

I slip away like a thief, down the hallway and up to my attic room in the roof.

Christmas Day is great. Mum's pleased with the fags – six packs – and she says the Charlie perfume is really lovely. She's gonna save it for special. And for Andy I got a bunch of *2000AD* mags and a pile of sweets. He said, "Skill!" and punched the air in this really annoying way he's picked up from his mate Ronny, and I had to resist the urge to thump him. He's had his head stuck in a comic ever since. George's presents were really expensive by the look of it – a *Smash Hits* annual, loads of albums and a pile of cash to spend in the sales. Katy got the standard girl stuff – Care Bears, girls' annuals, hair bobbles and that kind of thing. She seems happy enough though. As usual, Mum got me and Andy the same as each other, and because she forgot to bring our stockings, we both had to hang up a stripy pillow case, which was different. There are new pyjamas, a Cadbury's selection box, socks and pants, a spud gun (plus spud), books – *Stig of the Dump* for Andy and *The Owl Service* for me – and of course, nuts and tangerines and whizzing balloons at the bottom. When she sees George's presents, she slips me and Andy a tenner each, "to spend in the sales", she says, and we hug, Andy on one side, me on the other. I wonder where Matt is, what he's doing on Christmas Day.

I get to speak to Dad twice. The first time we speak, Mum's there, so I'm careful what I say so's not to upset her and cause a fight or anything. It's 10 a.m. and we've just had a massive breakfast of bacon and eggs and Bucks fizz, which I loved. Dad answers the phone on the second ring.

"Happy Christmas, Dad!" It feels like weeks since I saw him.

"Jakey!" he shouts, and I can tell he's sitting up in bed, running his hand through his hair, half asleep. "Jakey, son – happy Christmas! How ya doin', boy? God, I've missed you two – you know that? It's not Christmas here without you."

"So, what're you doing today, Dad?" It's our first

Christmas not together.

"Oh, you know. Probably pop over to see Gran, and then I've got some friends who've invited me over for lunch. I might go there."

There's a voice in the background. Definitely a woman's voice. There's a rustling as Dad puts his hand over the receiver, I can tell, and then he's back.

"What about you, Jakey?" he asks, like it didn't just happen.

"Oh, you know, lunch with Aunt Rachel and everyone. They're really nice, Dad. Really nice. And the house is amazing. They've got a dog. Dad – who's there – I heard a voice?"

He doesn't answer straight away, and then I know to feel bad. I know it's a woman and that's it.

"No one, Jake," he finally says, "it was just the – I've got the TV on, that's all. Go on then, pass me to Andy!"

And that's it, he's gone. My stomach is bunched, and my heart is pounding. I think about the voice, and what Dad said. Yes, that's probably it. He must have had the telly on, and that's why I thought it was a voice. I hand the telephone over to Andy.

"You alright, Jakey?" asks Mum as I leave Uncle Robert's study. She cups my chin with her hand, looks in my eyes deeply to see what she can see.

"I'm fine, Mum. I just miss him, that's all."

"Who's with Dad, then?" she asks, too casually.

"No one," I reply. "It was the telly."

Later, I sneak back to the study, and call him by myself. It's about six thirty, and it sounds like I woke him again when he answers. I can hear Scarlett O'Hara in the background, so I guess he's been watching *Gone With*

The Wind like us. I listen hard for any other voices, but it's just him there. It must have been the TV earlier, like he said. Dad says he's been to Gran's and she said to say happy Christmas. Old bag. He ended up staying there for lunch after all. They had turkey and Christmas pudding, and Gran moaned about the price of everything. I'll bet she moaned about how selfish the rest of the family are, and how no one bothers with an old 'un like her, like she usually does. Dad says he tried to cheer her day up a bit, did the washing up and made cups of tea for everyone when they visited in the afternoon. He said I'd like my cousins; that we ought to get to know that side of the family too. After meeting Aunt Rachel's lot, I guess I'd like to. But I know we'd never hear the end of it from Mum.

I tell Dad that we had roast beef, and how it was so much tastier than boring old turkey. We didn't have a Christmas pudding, because no one here really likes it that much, so instead we had a huge, lovely trifle and a big chocolate yule log. He doesn't say much to that, but tells me he's got a present for us both, that he didn't get a chance to give it to Mum before we left. But we'll like it, he says, it'll be worth the wait. Then his doorbell goes, and he stops, and says, "That'll be Stu," and we say happy Christmas again and he's gone. I sneak back to the front room, and Mum's still asleep in front of the fire. Ellie's on the rug, and when she looks up at me I can see that she's wearing one of Katy's disgusting new Care Bear hair clips in her fringe. She huffs and plonks her head back down to sleep. I'd be pissed off too, if I was her.

The day after Boxing Day we all go on this massive six mile walk over Tennyson Down. It's cold and bright, and you can see all around the island, with the sea on both sides. It's getting towards tea time, and the sky is beginning to show pink. When we get to the highest point, there's a big stone cross, in memory of the poet, Tennyson. I've heard of him, but I couldn't tell you what he's written. At the cross, we all sit to catch our breath and eat beef sandwiches on the wooden benches that run around the monument. Aunt Rachel's also packed some orange juice and mince pies, and it feels just like the taste of Christmas Day all over again, but right here, high up on top of the world.

Mum and Andy are a bit behind us, and they make it up to the summit a few minutes later. Mum's eyes fix on me and George as she takes the last few paces. She brings her hand to her mouth and gasps.

"Look at them, Rachel!" she cries out, pointing to us. "It's uncanny – have you had a good look at them?"

I stare at Mum as George frowns at me for an explanation.

Rachel looks us over, and shrugs. "Well, they're cousins after all, Mary. It's not so surprising. Remember how everyone used to say that about you and cousin Anne?"

"I know, I know. I still can't believe they were born on the same day!"

Mum stands for a few moments, hands on hips, feet planted wide, looking at us from one to the other, smiling and shaking her head. George rubs his eyebrow scar and looks at his feet. I can tell he's smirking, trying to not let her see it. I pull an annoyed face at her, but she doesn't seem to register.

Mum's attention is suddenly caught by the view. "Oh my God, Rachel! What a place! What a view!" Her face is shining and bright, almost mad-looking with happiness. "How could you bear to live amidst such beauty?" She flings her arms wide, her head back, deeply breathing in the cold air, and blowing it out in great white billows. Her eyes sparkle wildly, as if she's just discovered the meaning of life.

Rachel laughs, and goes to hug Mum, like a mother to a daughter. But Mum grabs her hand and starts running down, down, down the hill that we've just climbed, pulling Aunt Rachel screaming and laughing behind her, her scarf trailing in the breeze. As they stop in the dip below us, I see a dark cloud rising above the sea. It moves and soars, leaving the sea behind it, and as it draws closer we see clearly the hundreds, even thousands of tiny birds that make it up. Mum and Rachel see it too, and I can make them out below, pointing and staring at the air display, way up above. Mum looks tiny in the huge dip of land. The flock cartwheels and loops, swooping high and bombing low, black as night against the deepening pink of the gigantic sky. It seems to throb like a heart.

"Starlings," says George, as we sit on the bench with our faces to the sky. He's taken the lid off a mince pie, scooping out the filling with his finger.

Below us, on the wide grassy plain of Tennyson Down, Mum has dropped to her knees, with her face in her hands. She hugs the ground as Aunt Rachel reaches down to her uncertainly.

"There'll be sparrowhawks around before you know it," says George, still looking at the sky, "picking them off, one by one. A starling cloud's like a moving banquet for a sparrowhawk. Or a peregrine."

"Got a fag?" I ask him, and we disappear around the

other side of the cross where Mum can't be seen.

"Didn't know you smoked," he says, lighting up.

"Oh, yeah," I lie, puffing away in the cold shadow of Tennyson's monument. I nod my head in the direction of our mums. "She doesn't like it much, but you know, if it's OK for her to do it, it's OK for me. Know what I mean?"

"Too right, J. Too right," he says, waving his fag in the air. "Solidarity, comrade."

Katy and Andy have already run further on, throwing sticks for Ellie. Darkness seems to be coming down fast now, the red behind us deeper and lower than before. I grind the stinking half-finished stub into the stone paving with my heel. My head feels light and a bit queasy. When I spy round the other side of the cross, I see them walking back up the hill towards us, Rachel's arm around Mum's shoulders, Mum nodding, blowing her nose into a hankie. Aunt Rachel spots me, puts up her gloved hand, turns it into a thumbs up.

"J! Over here!" shouts George from behind me. He's tearing down the hill on the other side, making wings from his jacket like me and Andy used to do when we were little kids. "Geronimo!" he yells, hurtling downhill. Andy and Katy are screaming away from him, with Ellie leaping about, in and out of their legs, joining in with her barks.

"Geronimo!" I answer, and we're flying like starlings, bombing, whooping, looping, free.

Mary, December 1966

The first time I see him, he's standing in the kitchen window of my student halls and I know he will be my one great love. I want to ask him his surname, to know if it suits me. Somehow, I recognise his steady brown eyes, his slow smile, his broad hands with their deep set nail-beds. He's replacing a broken pane of glass, and he's framed in the high window, looking down at me, a tape measure gripped in his tanned fist, a stub of pencil between his teeth. The rich, red sun throbs through the buildings beyond the window, casting him in dark relief.

"Oh!" is all I can say to him, as he looks down on me, barely moving.

"Milk and one sugar," he says, his slow grin emerging. And he turns back to the window and presses putty into the wooden frame edges.

I fill the kettle and place it on the hob to boil, casting careful glances at the side of his face. He works steadily, confidently.

"I'll leave your tea on the side," I say, loitering by the kitchen door.

"Thanks, darlin'," he calls over his shoulder. I leave the room quietly; wanting to flee, desperate to stay.

Here on Frith Street the Christmas lights are twinkling under a haze of December evening mist. If I squint, the passers-by blur in pretty flashes, like oil on canvas. Oils and a loose arm. I arrive at the corner, at 7.30 sharp, and quickly hide my London street map so Billy won't see it. After a few minutes, he strolls towards me, radiant in the lamplight. His arms hang casual in his pockets, his loose curls skimming the shoulders of his tan jacket, his eyes holding me steady. I can hardly bear the weight of my attraction to him.

"You came then," he teases. "Not so contrary after all."

I blink at him.

"You know – Mary, Mary."

I smile into the pavement. "Actually, I am," I respond, arching my eyebrows, suddenly bold.

And he likes it. He lights a cigarette, drapes his arm across my shoulder and leads me along Frith Street, past the bars and restaurants bubbling with activity.

Café Emm has a Latino spirit, with a lone acoustic guitar playing out from a darkened corner, and attentive young foreign students carrying plates in and out. The tables are placed intimately close to each other, each with a low candle lamp and a crisp red tablecloth. A fug of smoke hangs across the room, sexy and white.

We sit at the back of the restaurant, and Billy offers me a cigarette. I hesitate, and take one. His mouth smirks, just out of one corner. He strikes a match, grins again, sits back.

"So, what are you studying?" he asks me, as we wait to be served. Billy slouches back in his chair, one ankle resting on his knee, his arm over the back of the chair. It's the pose of a Grecian hero at rest.

"Fine art," I reply, fiddling with the corner of the menu card. "I wanted a more design-based course, but fine art was the only way my parents were going to let me come to St Martin's."

He frowns at me.

"They're old-fashioned. They'd have had me at secretarial school if I'd let them. Like my sister. So fine art it is."

Billy nods, listening carefully. "First time away from home then?"

"No. Well, yes, kind of. It's great, though. I love being able to do my own thing. Get in when I want, eat what I want, drink what I want. Actually, it's bloody marvellous!"

Billy laughs, and I frown at him.

"What?"

"It's you – I've never been out with anyone quite like you before."

"Like what?" I ask him, feeling annoyed.

"Posh! That's what it is. You talk like the Queen!"

"Bugger off, I'm not!" He's making fun of me. I stub my half finished cigarette into the glass ashtray, and flick my long hair over my shoulder, throwing him a withering look.

"See! You even say 'bugger' with a posh accent! Oh, that's brilliant!"

I hate him.

The waiter arrives to take our drinks order.

"What do you drink?" Billy asks, recovering his composure and pulling himself up in his seat. Every question seems loaded with booby traps.

"What wines do you have?" I ask the waiter.

He indicates to the list on the back of the menu. I can feel Billy growing uncomfortable.

I smile at him. "Perhaps you'd like to choose?"

He pauses, staring at the list. "What do you like?" he asks me without lifting his eyes.

"Well, that depends on what we're eating," I say, in clearly enunciated syllables. "Tell you what. You choose. Yes, you choose – what we eat, and then which wine to have with it. I know you'll make a good choice." I bat my mascara-heavy lashes at him, feeling wicked.

He rubs his chin, leans back in his seat, and looks at me under his dark eyebrows. The waiter shuffles awkwardly from foot to foot. The candlelight bounces off the moisture of Billy's eyes, and he looks like Lucifer himself, ready to devour me whole.

"Fuck it," he says, his rough accent bared full. "Let's drink beer. Let's drink cold beer and eat hot food, and then we'll drink Mescal. We'll polish it off with a strong coffee, and then we'll find something else to drink. You in, posh girl?"

He flashes a full smile at me, his teeth bared white like a wolf, and yes, I nearly cry out, I'm in! I'm in!

Billy's flat is an unconverted warehouse space in London Bridge. He gets it rent-free whilst he's working for some Egyptian businessman with properties to maintain. It's freezing, with bare brick walls and almost no furniture. Except for a huge iron bed, piled with blankets and sheets, that looks out over the street. There's a stack of books on an orange crate that doubles up as a bedside cabinet.

When I wake in the morning my breath billows out before me like the smoke of the night before. Three trapped starlings circle high above us, twittering and looping together, separated from the rest of their flock. There's a single broken pane, high, high up in the glass wall of windows, and I will them to make it out into the cold and open air, but they don't even attempt it. They're crowd creatures, starlings; they don't function alone. I feel pity for them; for ever in the need of others. Billy lies on his back, his lips slightly parted, one strong arm hooked over his head in sleep. I wonder, will I be missed? I can see my flatmates gossiping. It's unlike her, Gypsy will tell them all with a knowing glint in her eye, and later she'll take pleasure in grilling me for the gruesome details. But still, they'll all just pack their portfolios, slick on their eyeliner and take themselves to college to swoon over the art technician or dishy Professor Hibbert. The muffled banter and trade from nearby Borough Market floats in through the broken pane; scraping carts, banging metal, gruff male voices. And not a seagull to be heard. Mother would die.

Billy stirs, rolling on to his side to face me, his fingers absently scratching at the dark stubble that's grown in the night. As I was lying here beside him, in his bed; it grew as we slept. His eyelids roll back, like slow venetian blinds, a smile entering them as he focuses on me, eye to eye.

"Where do you come from, Mary-Mary?" His eyes droop and rise again. His hand brushes a shot of long dark hair from my face.

I hesitate, closing my eyes to him. "The south," I say, attempting vagueness in my answer. Here, I can be anybody. Nobody.

"No!" He coughs, the stale tequila suddenly in the room with us. "Whereabouts? I'm a Pompey lad – Portsmouth! Who'd of thought it?" He's up on one elbow, suddenly alert, excited by the connection.

I roll away to stare at the high ceiling. I don't want this kind of intimacy. Not this. I want the fuzz of squinted eyes in lamplight.

Billy places his wide thumb across my dry lips, his expression growing troubled as his boyish enthusiasm fades. "You don't have to tell me, Mary. I don't need to know anything. I'm not about to scare you off. We've got something here." He trails off, and pulls my body against his.

Jake, New Year 1985

We get back from Aunt Rachel's the day before New Year's Eve. Dad's straight round with our present – a Pompey season ticket.

"Result, eh?" he grins.

He was right, it was well worth the wait. I'm not even that into football, but it'll be great to go to a live match with Dad some weekends.

"Skill!" says Andy, dodging out of my way the moment he says it. And anyway, I'm that pleased about the ticket, I'm not really bothered about punching him.

"Mum, I'm going round Ronny's," Andy gabbles as he grabs his jacket. "To tell him about the season ticket. Man, he's gonna be green! Pompey!" He slams the front door shut as he goes.

Mum shudders at the sound of it, then starts unpacking stuff from the travel bags that we dumped on the sofa when we got back half an hour ago. Dad stands awkwardly by the door, looking like he's about to go, but not going.

"What you doing at New Year, then?" he finally asks.

Mum looks up, frowning. "New Year? Um. Don't know. Why?"

I can't make out Dad's face at all. He seems nervy, even shy. He hands her a folded up piece of pink card, covered in little stuck-on gold stars.

"Sandy didn't know what to do, Mary. Actually, I think she was really embarrassed. Well they're friends with us both, aren't they – those things don't change just because we're not – you know, together. Anyhow, I told her, don't you worry about it – invite us both and we'll sort it out. We're both grown-ups, aren't we, love?"

Mum's turning the invite over in her hand. Dad's got his hand on the door latch, looking like he wants to bolt out like Andy did a few minutes earlier. Mum passes it to me to read:

Remember the Good Old Days? Let's twist again!
New Year's Eve Party
At Sandy & Pete's
8 till we drop!
(PS kids welcome too)

"Great, see you there, then," says Mum, smiling kindly. "The kids'll love it, won't you, Jakey?"

Dad is scratching his neck, frowning. He's dead good looking; dark and bright all at once. He's not like a film star, more like one of the famous footballers you see on telly.

"No, that's not what I meant, Mary. I meant, we're both grown-ups – we can decide between us which of us will go, can't we? I mean, it would be a bit awkward if we're both there." His forehead is all knitted up around his heavy eyebrows, and he keeps pulling his bottom lip over his teeth and rubbing his chin.

"Then I'll go," says Mum, still smiling.

"But," starts Dad.

"But I'm fine about it if you want to go too, Bill. You're right, we've got to be grown-ups about this. And the kids will have a really good time. OK?"

Dad's flummoxed. "Alright, then. Good. So – I'll see you all there then."

I watch him as he walks down the road, looking cool in his leather jacket and jeans.

"I like your new jacket, Dad!" I shout after him before he disappears. He looks over his shoulder and gives me a small wave before he turns the corner at the end of the street.

So, we're all going to the party together.

Pete and Sandy's place is a few streets away from our house, so at 8.30 me, Mum and Andy set off to the party. I've been going on to Mum about being late for the past half hour, but she says it's rude to turn up dot on eight, and that we should arrive "fashionably late". Seems strange to me – why bother saying the party starts at eight if you don't want them to arrive till half past? We pass the Royal Oak on the way, and I try to get a look in the window to see if Dad's there, but it's packed inside and the windows are all steamed up.

"Alright, Stu!" I call over when I spot him going in. He gives me a little salute, as if he's doffing a cap, then disappears inside the pub.

"So that's Stu, is it?" says Mum. "Your dad says he

works with Pete down the haulage yard. Hasn't he got a boy your age?"

"Yeah. But Malcolm lives in Southsea with his mum. Stu had to get a smaller flat near here when they split up. Bit like Dad I s'pose. Actually, I 'aven't seen Malc for a while."

"Haven't, Jake. It's 'I haven't seen Malcolm for a while'. Well, it's nice that your dad's got a pal to have a drink with, I guess." As we walk on, she looks over her shoulder, back towards the pub. The doors are open, and the sounds of the party spill out into the cold street.

Andy's been getting on my nerves all afternoon, asking me what I'm going to wear, if I'm gonna dance, if I think I'll be able to stay awake till midnight. He's such a prat. Sometimes he's just a stupid little kid who doesn't understand anything. "You're so un-cool," I told him. "Super-geek." He stood in the doorway and stuck his hand up his jumper and made a fart noise under his armpit. I went for him, but he legged it out the back door before I could clout him.

"You got your dancing shoes on then, Jakey?" Mum asks. She looks really pretty tonight, with sparkly makeup and glittery earrings.

"Yeah, right," I reply, rolling my eyes at her.

She laughs. She's got a bag full of drink with her, for Sandy and Pete, and she's made a Coronation Chicken too. The bottles clink against the Pyrex dish with every footstep, and I've got this urge to grab the bag off her, rearrange the bottles inside so they don't make that noise. At home, the booze is kept in a high cupboard above the cooker in the kitchen. The cupboard has got one of those stiff doors that pops open when you pull it, with this really clear click-clack sound. Sometimes at night I can't get to sleep waiting for the click-clack to be over and done with. It goes click-clack-clink-clink. Then I can sleep.

"I think there'll be quite a few other kids there tonight. You'll have a good time – have the run of the house probably. While we're all dancing downstairs! It's been ages since we last saw Auntie Sandy, isn't it?" I haven't seen Mum look forward to something so much in a long time.

"I wonder what time Dad'll get there," I ask her.

"No idea. I expect he'll be having a drink in the Oak. He never was one to arrive at a party without a couple of pints inside him first." She looks serious now, and changes her tone when she sees me frowning back. "Not that there's anything wrong with that – it's a free country!"

When we get to Sandy's door, we can see lots of people milling about through the windows, and over the wide-open door is a handmade banner that says "1985! HAPPY NEW YEAR!" We go straight in without knocking, passing some kids on the staircase who I don't know. They stare at us. One of them is a girl, maybe a couple of years older than me, and the other is a lad about Andy's age. The boy's a bit of a Casual, dressed in burgundy and grey, with his thin hair slicked back, and the girl has heavy black makeup around her eyes, and strawy back-combed hair. They're each holding a can of Coke, and they look really bored. I feel embarrassed about my un-cool clothes, and think about my tenner for the sales.

"Mary!" screams Sandy, when we find her in the living room clutching a bowl of peanuts. "And your gorgeous boys! Come 'ere, you little heart breakers! Give us a kiss!"

Sandy – Auntie Sandy as she likes us to call her – plants a huge wet kiss on my cheek. She smells of powder and perfume and gin.

"Look at you! It must be a year since I saw you last! How old are you now?" She's saying these things about how grown up I look, but she's hunched down on her heels talking to me like I'm a toddler.

"Thirteen," I smile politely, my face burning.

"Thirteen! I would've said fifteen, easily!" she says, with a serious face that I don't believe, then she goes through the same routine with Andy.

Andy and me stand there like lemons until she's finished mauling us. Apart from the two on the stairs, there don't seem to be any other kids, and I'm starting to regret agreeing to come.

"Mary, love – it's been too long, sweetheart!" Sandy's hugging Mum again, whose carrier bags are clinking clumsily as she hugs Sandy back. "Know how long I've known your mum?" she asks us.

We shake our heads.

"What, sixteen years, Mary?" She looks at Mum.

"More like seventeen. I was just about to have Matthew when we moved here."

"He never is seventeen?" screeches Sandy. "And where is the handsome beast, then?"

"What, Matthew?" asks Mum, suddenly pale.

"He's travelling," I say.

Sandy turns to me with a big smile.

"In Germany, I think. Then on through Europe," I add for authenticity. "I think."

"Well, who'd of thought it?" says Sandy, looking as proud as if it had been her own son off discovering the world.

Mum puts her arm around my shoulder, the colour returning to her cheeks. I can't help but stare at Sandy as she beckons us to follow her towards the kitchen. She's nice enough, but a bit rough. She wears really tarty clothes for her age; I mean she must be at least forty. Tonight she's got on a short black leather skirt, with sheer black tights and stilettos, and a purple top with long flapping sleeves. Her perm's really fuzzy, and she smokes like a chimney. I remember her babysitting for us a bit when we were little, and she'd always stop sunbathing out in the back yard and play with us if we asked her to. One time, I was trying to make a Lego house, and one of the windows wouldn't stay in. It took ages, but Sandy took off all the top layers, then fixed the window in place and rebuilt the top. When she'd finished, she sat down and had a fag in front of *Emmerdale Farm*, and I had a custard cream and a glass of milk.

"Come on, boys," she says, after she's put the Coronation Chicken in the kitchen and ladled out a glass of punch for Mum. "I'll take you upstairs so you can meet the others."

The kids from earlier are gone when we head up the stairs behind Sandy. Her skirt is way too short and I can see right up between her legs. I don't want to look, but I can't help it, and I'm wondering if she's wearing any knickers under her see-through black tights. The backs of her calves are huge and muscly, even though her ankles are bony and thin. Mum waves from the bottom of the stairs, then turns to go through to the party.

Sandy smiles over her shoulder at me, before calling along the hall, "Shona! It's me, love! I've got a couple more here!"

Black-eyes girl opens one of the bedroom doors, and

looks at us coldly. Shona.

"Shona's my niece. Shona, this is Jake, and this is Andy. You look after them? Show them where everything is? And you know where we are if you need us, don't you, love?" She quickly fondles the back of my neck and then leaves us on the landing, face to face with scary-girl.

Shona nods her head for us to follow her, and she gives us the tour of the upstairs. Sandy and Pete's own kids have all left home now, so it seems really big for just the two of them.

Shona cocks a thumb at a closed door. "That's the bog." Then along the landing, another cocked thumb and a stern face. "Sandy and Pete's room. Off limits."

We turn the corner at the end of the corridor, to find another row of doors. She thumbs the first one. "Music room. That's where we are. Then there's the TV room. Bathroom. Snog Room." At this, she turns and looks at me for a reaction. "Do you know what the Snog Room is?" She's got her hands on her hips now, facing us. I reckon she could get a part in *Grange Hill*, talking all sarky and full of it.

"Well, I can guess, I suppose," I mumble.

"Well, you'd be right. There's quite a few of us here tonight, and if anyone wants a bit of privacy, that's where they can get it."

I try to avoid Shona's eyes.

"And nobody tells that lot downstairs," she adds with a touch of menace.

Andy's eyes are wide and unblinking. Black-eyes laughs and squeezes his cheeks between the palms of her fingerless-gloved hands. He looks like a scared guppy.

"Don't worry, baby-boy. You don't have to go into

the Snog Room unless you want to. It's not that kind of party."

She smirks, pleased with herself, and takes us into the music room, where a bunch of other kids are lying about on bean bags and cushions. There are piles of albums and a record player, and a tape cassette on the side. Loud music fills the room, and I recognise the track playing from George's collection at Manningly Farm.

Shona thumbs at us. "Jake. Andy." I wonder what she'd do if she lost her thumbs. The other kids all nod hello to us, and one smiles.

"The Cure?" I say, as I flop into a spare bean bag. Thank God for George and his excellent record collection.

"Yeah," says Shona, without looking at me.

"Cool," I say, and we spend the next hour going through music sleeves, comparing our favourite bands and tracks.

Shona keeps raising her voice, trying to get the attention of the older boys, but they're not interested. There's a small bunch of lads of about sixteen, who all seem to know each other, and keep themselves to themselves. Luke, the Casual, turns out to be Shona's younger brother. Despite his dodgy choice in clothes, Luke's alright, and he and Andy go off together to the TV room to see what's on. There are a few younger kids running about in the hallway, and now and again they pop their heads in the room, then run away looking scared. I remember that feeling when I was little, thinking how grown up the older kids seemed, spying on them at the same time as staying out of their way.

Shona leans backwards and sticks her hand behind the Flower Fairy curtains to drag out two cans of lager held together by their plastic loops.

"Want one?" She pulls the ring on hers and takes a swig, eyeing the older boys in the opposite corner. One of them glances at her, then takes a swig of his own can and carries on with his conversation.

Shona wriggles back in her bean bag, adjusting her baggy black skirt around her like a parachute. Her cardigan flops off to one side, showing a pale freckly shoulder and a white bra strap.

"I nicked them," she says. "The beers. I nicked them off my dad as soon as we got here. That's the good thing about being a Goth – baggy clothes. Loads of places to stash stuff. Beer, fags, gear. No one's any the wiser."

"Oh. Are you a Goth then?"

"Durr. Why else d'you think I'm dressed like this, straight-boy?" She's shaking her head, snuffling into her can. "S'pose you're gonna ask me if I've just been to a funeral next? You might as well. I hear it about eighteen times a day anyhow."

And I was worried about Andy embarrassing me.

"Act casual," Shona tells me when she sends me in search of more cans. I don't even want any more, but she obviously does.

The clock in the hall says quarter past ten, so it's nearly two hours till midnight. I wonder if Dad has got here yet. There are loads of people here now, although most of them I don't know, and most of them seem pretty drunk. I squeeze through the kitchen and spot Stu at the sink, cracking ice out on to the draining board. If Stu's here, Dad must be somewhere nearby.

"Stu!" I shout across the crush of people.

He looks over his shoulder, dropping the ice into a tumbler. Clink-clink.

"Jakey, mate! How's it going? Wondered if you were about, somewhere or other."

He pours a large slug of gin on to the ice, making it turn clear and liquid and gleaming.

"So what've you been up to then, Jakey?"

"Not much," I shrug, "listening to music, having a beer, you know." I don't know why I said that. "Malcolm here?"

"No – he's at his mum's tonight. He'll be over to mine in the morning. We'll be going over the rec for a kick about if you wanna come?" He reaches into the fridge and pulls out a big bottle of Schweppes tonic water. Mum always says it has to be Schweppes. The others are cheap tasting. A bit like fake Coke. Or fake ketchup. There are some things that you can't compromise on. Stu twists open the lid and the fizz escapes over the top like a fountain. He pours the tonic water into the glass, then sticks the bottle back in the fridge and pulls out a can of lager.

"Dad here yet?" I ask, but I've kind of worked out he's not.

"No, not yet, mate. He was getting another in at the Oak when I left. Shouldn't be long."

I'm still standing by Stu, leaning on the sink, watching him pull the ring on the lager. He catches my eye and grins, leans back into the fridge and pulls out two more.

"Stick 'em up your jumper and get up the stairs pronto," he says in a low growl, like a soldier to his comrade. He nudges me off, winks, and I leg it to the foot of the stairs.

As I get up a few steps, I can see Mum in the living

room. From my dark spy point, I stop and watch, as she stands at the fireplace, laughing and bright. She's got a couple of men standing to one side, Sandy to the other. Stu goes through with the drinks, and one of the men moves aside to make room for him. Mum takes the glass from Stu, raises it to the group and they all do the same, clink, cheers, drink, smile.

I wish Dad was here to see how pretty she looks.

Mary, February 1967

He's not their kind of person. I can feel our differences hovering above the dining table as we move to an awkward rhythm. Billy's wide, rough fingers are clumsy around the silver knives and spoons, and I'm sure that Mother has laid out courses of cutlery just to test his breeding. I see her watching his movements, checking to see which knife he chooses. As she studies his discomfort, the twilight catches his skin through the polished window panes, and the reflection from the silverware dances under his chin. He shines like a heavenly host, fixing me across the table with his brown gaze. Mummy can't take her eyes off him either.

"So, Billy. How long have you and Mary been courting?"

He smiles at me, as I cut across him, "Mum, don't interrogate him. He's only just got here!"

"It's a harmless enough question, Mary. And, darling, you know how I hate it when you call me that."

Billy looks at me, as if for permission to answer. I shake my head in resignation.

"It's been the best part of a year, hasn't it, Mary?" There's a phoney twang to his accent, which I despise instantly. He's picking up his h's.

"How nice," says Mummy, cutting into her smoked salmon. "I'm surprised Mary hasn't brought you back before. I mean, London's not that far is it, darling?" She looks to Daddy for an answer.

He agrees, and carries on eating.

"Sauce?" she asks, passing the Royal Doulton jug across the table to Billy.

He takes the jug, a closed-mouth smile on his face. A man of few words, she'd say, by way of insult. When he lifts his eyes to meet mine, I'm caught off-guard by the kaleidoscope of colour that radiates from him. I want to climb on my chair and cry out to them all, "This man is so good, can you not see it?"

Mummy looks along the length of the table, to where Daddy sits in the opposite head position. The four of us are posed like little figures in a neat Victorian doll's house.

"Well, it's certainly good to have you home, Mary. Isn't it, Charles?"

Daddy looks up, slightly baffled. "It's delicious, dear," he smiles. "Isn't it, Mary?"

Mummy glares at him. Billy tries to keep his expression neutral. And I'm dying inside, embarrassed by this odd couple who raised me. Mummy frowns at Daddy again, like a prod.

"Right," he says, as if suddenly awoken. "So, what do you do, young man?"

Billy straightens in his seat. "I'm a carpenter."

"Fine profession. Jesus was one," says Daddy. He's an atheist. "What d'you make? Cabinets? Churches?" He laughs at this, looking around the table for encouragement.

"Mostly doing up old buildings. I've been working in London Bridge for two years now, and the work just isn't drying up. It pays well too."

Mummy gives me a knowing look, which I ignore. I pull a large fish bone from the corner of my mouth and make sure she sees me place it on the edge of the plate.

"The owner is some Egyptian feller. Never seen him, but the money comes in, regular as clockwork, every week. And it's all rent-free."

"So, you have a flat in London? Lucky lad. Gold dust." Daddy is wiping his chin with a napkin as Mummy clears the starter plates away. "But of course, you should be investing that money of yours in your own property. That's where the real money is. But I don't need to tell you that, Billy. You're in the property game yourself, of sorts."

Billy nods silently, and rearranges his cutlery.

"And Mary. How's the painting going? Got anything worth hanging over the fireplace yet?"

"No. Not a jot. Everything I paint is rubbish. God only knows why they gave me a place at St Martin's." I pull a face at him, and he taps his nose and points his finger at me. "Perhaps I should have gone to secretarial college, like Rachel?" I add with pith.

Daddy slouches further into his seat. "Not at all, darling. Not for you. You'll be a great artist yet. Won't she, Penny?"

Mummy doesn't answer, but places another plate on the table in front of me. *Boeuf bourguignon*, with fresh vegetables. I smile up at her, but she doesn't see.

"My favourite," I say, as she sits at the table.

"I know, dear," she replies, passing the wine bottle down the table.

I top up our glasses and pass the bottle to Daddy.

"Cheers," he says as we raise our glasses.

The rest of the meal passes in reasonably good humour, and Daddy has opened another bottle by the time we get on to dessert. After a few drinks, Billy has loosened up, and Mummy has thawed out a little.

"It's a beautiful house, Mrs Murray. Who does your interior design?" He smiles charmingly.

Mummy flushes, taking another sip from her wine. "Interior designer! You're teasing me, young man! I do it all myself. Don't I, Charles? Charles?"

Daddy nods, distracted.

"Well, I love it," says Billy.

"Well, thank you!" says Mummy.

"Good," says Daddy. "Now that's settled, let's retire to the lounge for a brandy, shall we?"

Mummy gives the log fire a poke and puts on more wood. I feel the glow of the flames on my red wine cheeks, and I'm gripped by a nostalgic sense of being home. Daddy has taken the armchair opposite me, and he winks, indicating for Billy to sit on the sofa next to me. Mummy perches on the arm of Daddy's chair.

"Well, you're certainly a handsome couple. That's the truth." Daddy passes Billy a brandy glass. The liquid grips the inside of the glass like oil, and Billy follows Daddy in swilling it about in warming movements.

"I'd like one," I say.

Mummy raises her eyebrows at me.

"Just a small one," I add.

"Get her a glass then." He nudges Mummy with his elbow. She comes back with two, and joins us in the drink.

After a while, silence descends upon the room. It's time. My stomach lurches when Billy presses my foot with the toe of his shoe. He takes my hand. Mummy stiffens. Daddy continues to daydream into the fireplace.

"Mr Murray," Billy starts.

Mummy gives Daddy a little push.

"Mm?" he says.

"Mr Murray, we're here for a reason. I want to ask permission to marry your daughter."

Mummy gasps.

"Whatever for?" bellows Daddy, as if it's a joke. "You're too bloody young!"

"We love each other," I say. It comes out like a whine.

"Of course you do. You're young! She's still a bloody teenager, for Christ's sake!"

"I'm not a child!" I shout, sounding like one, and rising to my feet. Billy holds on to my fingers, and stands up beside me.

We look at each other with panicked eyes.

Billy turns back to them, now at his full stature, broad and tall. "Mr Murray, we'll do it anyway. We just want your blessing. I love your daughter."

Mummy brings her hand up to her mouth. "Oh, God!" she sobs. "You're pregnant!"

The tears come now. Not mine, but hers. I don't deny

it, but instead find my fingers cradling the tiny swell of my belly. My mother crumbles into my father's arms, and sobs hard into his shoulder. They are so complete, so utterly united, that there's no way in. There's just no space.

Daddy looks up at me with soft, bruised eyes. "You'd better go," he says, mildly, and he buries his face in her hair.

Jake, New Year 1985

Upstairs the Snog Room is in darkness, except for the light from the street lamps pouring through the curtainless windows. I see the shadow of Shona still at the door, and then the sound of the lock slotting shut. She walks towards me until I can see her clearly in the lamp light. She's not pretty – not even a bit. She would've chosen one of those other, older boys, if they'd been interested, but in the end she chose me. I hear the fizz of the ring pull from one of my nicked lagers, and Shona takes a swig and hands it to me. My hands are clammy. Hopefully, she'll just want to talk, maybe kiss a bit. Maybe she'll be my girlfriend.

"What d'you wanna do?" she asks, and already she's pulling off her tights.

"What are you doing?"

"Oh, come on, you dweeb," she slurs, hiccuping at the same time, and laughing. "Let's just mess about a bit. How far have you gone before?"

I just gape at her.

"OK. Nod if you've done them. Kissing?"

I nod.

"Tongues?"

"Yeah."

"Tits?"

Someone tries the handle from out in the hallway, and my heart jolts.

"Shouldn't we . . .?" I try saying.

"Oh, sod 'em. Fingering?" She smirks. "OK. Take that as a no then. Wanna?"

I can feel a vein throbbing in my forehead, and my legs are shaking. Shona unbuttons her cardigan, and hoiks up her white bra, revealing her small white breasts.

"Here," she says, settling on to the carpet and patting the floor in front of her. "No one's gonna see us. It'll be our secret. OK? Promise you won't tell anyone?"

I nod, and kneel on the floor in front of her. Her little tits are squished into a funny shape where the bra's pressing down on them.

"Lick them if you like," she says, staring me straight in the eye.

I do as she says, mechanically, like I'm licking an ice cream to stop it dripping down the sides of a cone. After a minute, she shoves my head off her with a huff, and stretches back putting one bare leg on either side of where I'm kneeling.

"Push up my skirt," she tells me. I do it. "Like my knickers?" she asks. They're black and lacy. I nod. "Take them off, then," she says.

For a few seconds, I just stare at the triangle of black fabric, afraid to move. She grabs my hand and pushes it down there. My feet start tingling where I've been kneeling back on them, and I have to change position before I can fumble about for the sides of her knickers and pull them off her. They snag and catch on her cold feet as I finally get them down. I look at her black eyes in the light, and she seems to be mocking me, daring me on.

"How old are you?" I ask her, trying to change the subject.

"Fifteen," she says.

"Me too," I say, and I settle back down cross-legged in front of her. She passes me the lager and I stare at the can, glad of the distraction. Kronenbourg. Kro – nen – bourg. Like burger. Like Cro-magnon.

"Cro-magnon. What's that mean?" I ask her. "I know I've heard it before."

She props herself back on her elbows, and flops her knees out, showing herself to me in the bright lamp light. My heart's going again. I look at my watch. Shona nudges me with her toe, and I glance up to catch a brief glimpse of her, down there. The hair is light brown and wispy, so different to her backcombed scare-hair.

"Touch it, then," she says. She swigs back another gulp of lager and wipes her lip on the back of her hand. "It won't bite."

I stroke the hair, like a pet, in downward movements. It's soft, but coarse all at once. A bit like a guinea pig or something.

"You got a boyfriend?" I ask.

"Carry on, you plank," she says, pushing herself up against my hand.

I gulp back another slug of lager. My head spins a little, and I carry on with the stroky movement like she wants me to. But then, with a huff, Shona sits up, grasps my hand and guides my finger inside her, right inside her, pushing against the resistance of skin, until it hits a wall of moisture, so unbearably soft and smooth that I start to think about how it would feel to climb on top of her, climb right in until there's nothing left of me at all. All gone. I freeze, uncertain what to do next, and then I realise that I'm just kneeling in front of her, motionless, like that little Dutch boy with his finger stuck in the dyke.

"Enough," she says, and she pushes me off.

We're back in the music room when Sandy shouts from the bottom of the stairs. "Kids! Come on down! It's five to midnight – we want you all down here!"

When she hears Sandy shouting up, Shona looks at me and tuts. "You can go if you want, but I'm staying here. It makes me wanna puke all that Auld Lang Syne stuff. I might have a smoke, actually."

Andy sticks his head round the door, beckoning me down, excited. All the other kids get to their feet and make their way out, trying to still look cool. I look back at Shona to make sure she hasn't changed her mind, but she won't meet my eye.

Downstairs it's all hectic, with husbands and wives milling around to find each other, and little kids shouting out for their mums and dads. Me and Andy are looking about for our own mum. I don't want to show it, but I do want to find her. For Andy's sake, really. The kitchen is empty now as everyone squashes into the living room in their little huddles. Mum was in the living room earlier but she's not there now. If I could spot Stu, I could ask him if he's seen her.

Andy's out in the garden, shouting, "Mum! Mum! It's

nearly time!"

I'm up the stairs, checking all the rooms, even Sandy and Pete's, and they're all empty. Even the music room where Shona was is empty now. I meet Andy in the hallway at the bottom of the stairs, and he shakes his head. We've looked everywhere.

We stand in the doorway of the living room as Sandy turns down the music, and motions for everyone to calm down.

"Together! FIVE! FOUR! THREE! TWO! ONE!" The room explodes with party poppers and cracker horns and streamers and everyone is kissing and hugging and jumping up and down and laughing.

Mary, February 1968

I haven't seen Rachel since I collected the rest of my things from home. On that last afternoon, Mummy had taken to her bed, and Daddy was out at a client meeting. The house pulsated with emptiness. My eight month belly pressed defiantly against Billy's Aran sweater; the only thing that would fit me. Rachel followed me around our room, silently passing me items to pack. I felt like the older sister, as she struggled for words. She'd hugged me, and then Billy, at Brighton station before we disappeared along the tracks towards Portsmouth.

Now, as I wait by the swings, I rock the pram to keep Matthew asleep. The morning sun is kind, thawing my icy breath. I spot Rachel at the other end of the park, a willowy figure turning on to the wide green in her red hat and gloves. She looks around, before marching purposefully towards the children's playground where I'm waiting. Halfway across the green she sees me, raising her two gloved hands, before breaking into a jog. I abandon the pram and run to meet her, swooped up in her familiar embrace.

"I've missed you!" she cries, brushing aside a stray tear.

I kiss her cheek and take her hand, not wanting to let go.

"Where is he then?" she asks, dragging me towards Matthew's pram. She leans in, cautiously, her hand rising to her mouth. "Oh! Oh, Mary. He's divine!"

Matthew's still sleeping, and his soft blond curls are coming through around his perfect ears.

"He's like Billy," I tell her. "Billy was blond. As a child."

We stand quietly for a moment, both gazing at the sleeping baby.

"So," Rachel says, patting her hands together in a muffled clap, "where can I buy you a hot chocolate around here?"

Edna's Café is along the harbour front, and Billy always says it's the best café in Southsea. Rachel orders two hot chocolates and two Chelsea buns.

"I only drink hot chocolate when I'm with you," I say, breathing in the sweet steamy aroma.

Rachel bites a large corner off her bun. "Mmm. I was starving."

I unwind my bun from the outside, popping it in my mouth piece by piece, working towards the doughy centre.

Rachel laughs. "God, you always ate them like that! No wonder your food always lasted longer than mine. Old gutsy here." She pats her stomach, and pours extra sugar into her mug, scattering grains across the table.

She's still thin as a bean. She smiles at me around bulging mouthfuls.

"How's Robert?" I ask. She'd never eat like that in front of him.

"He's fine. Anyway, what I want to hear about is Billy's family. What's it like living with them? I bet they love you! And that gorgeous baby."

I bring my mug to my mouth and meet her eyes over the rim.

"Oh, God! Are they awful? What's his mother like?" She stares at me expectantly.

"She's alright," I shrug. "They're not like our family, but it's not so bad. It's got to be hard having to adjust to a stranger moving in with a new baby. She's OK." I twirl my wedding band on my finger, watching the light catch its edges.

"I wish you'd asked me," Rachel says quietly. "I could have been your bridesmaid. Weren't you lonely, with just the two of you?"

I gather the spilt sugar into a neat pile beside my plate. "It was fine. Nice, even. No fuss. No guests to worry about. No speeches. We had a picnic on a Thames riverboat after the ceremony. It was romantic."

Rachel runs her forefinger through my sugar pile with a cheeky smirk.

"I've written to Daddy a few times," I say, "but he's not replied once."

Rachel stares into her mug of chocolate.

"I love Billy so much, Rach. If only Mummy could see that, maybe she'd come round?"

Rachel looks out of the window, dotting patterns in the steam with her finger. "She won't even talk about you,

Mary. It's her old convent schooling, probably. And Billy *is* a lovely man. You're lucky to have found him, Mary. Forget Mum for now. She'll relent, and then she'll regret this. So. When are you moving into your own place? I can visit you every month then. I could even babysit. Billy wouldn't mind, would he?"

"No, he likes you. We'd both love it."

Matthew stirs in his blankets.

"He's three months old now," I tell her. "Want to hold him?"

Rachel takes him from me, and cradles him tenderly. He gazes up at her, his brown eyes searching hers. He smiles, and gurgles, stretching out his chubby legs and fists in delight.

"Oh, Mary," says Rachel.

After Rachel has gone, I wander around the town, enjoying the sun on my skin. The seagulls are restless today, screeching and squawking overhead. Matthew smiles at me from time to time, before sleeping again. The fresh air's good for him. When I arrive home, the net curtains twitch as I turn my key in the lock.

Jean is icy. "I take it you had your dinner out?" she says, busying away into the back kitchen where her lunch plate sits besides the sink.

"Oh, I hope you didn't cook for me, Mum," I say, unwrapping Matthew from his blankets.

"Hmmph," she replies.

"Did you cook?" I ask.

She doesn't answer. There are no pots and pans out, just the bread board and knife on the side.

"Or did you have a sandwich?"

No answer.

"I hope it was just a sandwich, because then there's no harm done, is there?"

Jean shoots me an indignant expression, before running a sinkful of foamy suds. "Well. I'll just wash up, shall I?" she says briskly, and she turns her back on me.

I push the pram into the back courtyard, and take Matthew upstairs to our bedroom at the back of the house. It's about three o'clock, so Billy will be home in just over two hours. Plumping up the pillows, I settle on the bed to feed Matthew. I can't do it downstairs because Jean finds it distasteful. He's a good baby. He feeds from each breast, before dropping off, gently snoring. His soft, clear cheeks contrast against the dark rose of my nipple. I wonder how it would be to sleep so soundly, with no distractions or anxieties to trespass on one's peace. I don't remember a time like that. Even my memories of childhood appear now as a backwards extension of adulthood. I lift Matthew's gently snoring weight on to the bed beside me and pick up my book, *Wide Sargasso Sea*. Within minutes my eyes droop and I sleep, dreaming of Rachel and me running along Hove seafront, trailing our hair ribbons in the breeze.

When Billy comes in, he wakes me and Matthew, who starts crying. Billy drops his wallet and keys on to the window sill.

"Billy!" I say, startled. I swing my legs off the bed to greet him.

His hair is beyond his shoulders, and still retains a golden hint of summer in its curling ends.

"How was work?"

Matthew cries harder, now thrashing the bed with his hands and feet, his face perfectly crimson.

"Fine," says Billy. "I've just seen Mum. What's up?" His face is steely.

"Nothing's up," I answer, attempting a kiss.

He eases me back. "She says you're being a madam."

"I went out for a walk!" I shout, picking up Matthew to comfort him. "She had a go at me for not coming home for lunch. Sorry, I mean *dinner*. Which was a sandwich, by the way."

Billy glares at me. "I can't talk to you when you're like this. I'm going for a pint."

Matthew has stopped crying now, and nestles into my neck, red-faced and breathy. I sit on the edge of the bed, and nod to Billy to sit beside me.

"Billy. How long do we have to stay here? Jean can't stand the sight of me. And we need our own space." I look at Matthew in my arms. "He'll need his own room soon. It's not the same with a baby in the room at night time."

Billy sits beside me and takes my hand. We face the window, which looks out over the grey courtyard and on to row after row of terraced housing. The nights are drawing in now, and the sky is growing grey.

"Six months," he says. "Give it six months and we'll have enough to get started in our own place. I don't get paid London rates now, but we'll get there, darling."

I rest my head on his shoulder and his strong arm eases round to pull me in.

"We're a family, Mary. You, me and Matthew." He strokes Matthew's cheek where it rests on my chest. "But that includes Mum for the next few months. We can't do this without her."

I nod, kissing the top of my baby's soft head. "I know."

Billy gently caresses my neck, supporting the weight of my tired head in his one wide hand. He kisses me full on the mouth; a deep, muscular embrace. My heart thrills, just as it did when we first met. Matthew squawks between us.

Billy picks up his wallet and stands in the doorway. "I'll be back before we eat," he says, and the bedroom door closes behind him.

Jake, February 1985

Since the Christmas holidays, I've been doing extra for Mr Horrocks. I can't work in the shop till I'm fourteen, but on Saturdays he gets me to stock the shelves after closing time so he can go up to Mrs Horrocks and get her tea. They've got a little Yorkie dog called Griffin, and they pay me to walk him after school every day. When he hears me coming in the back entrance of the shop to fetch him, he jumps up and licks between my fingers, wanting his ears scratched. He's got this really smooth, wide little tongue, not like the huge slobbery ones you get on big dogs. When he gets really excited he chews at my wrist with his tiny teeth, but he never hurts me, always knows when to stop. It's a doddle taking him out, and I can hardly believe that I actually get paid for it.

Recently, Mr Horrocks asked if I could spare a whole Sunday to help him with a stock-take, and he'd pay me time and a half. I jumped at the chance – I'm saving for a midi system now. I know it'll take ages and ages, but I want my own record player and albums like George's got on the Isle of Wight. So, I arrive at 7.00 a.m. in my scruffy gear, like he told me, and we get started as soon as we've had a cup of tea and a rich tea biscuit. There are sheets and sheets of paper listing the items, and we have to count up what we've got on the shelves, what we've got in the stock room, and what we've got on order, writing down the numbers in all the right columns. It's pretty easy, but you have to concentrate to get it right, so we don't talk much. The blinds at the front of the shop are kept down so that people don't think we're open, and the sunlight stabs through the edges of the windows, cutting across the lazy dust clouds that we make as we work.

Griffin lies in one of the little puddles of sunshine in the middle of the room, getting up once in a while to sniff my feet and beg for a pat. Then he goes back to his sunny patch, bothering the settled dust as he goes, and curls up there like a little mop-head on a spot-lit stage. It's calm, like an old library or bookshop, and you can smell heavy paper and wood and pencils and the peel of varnish. Every now and then, Mr Horrocks clears his throat or scratches his beard with the end of his pencil, and you can hear every movement: the scrape of shoes on the concrete floor, the clink of pickle jars returning to the shelf, the rustle of crisp packets counted in and out of cartons. At ten, Mr Horrocks says it's time for a break, and we go out back to put the kettle on. He reaches up to one of the stock shelves and brings down a packet of Mr Kipling's Fondant Fancies.

"Remember to make that one less on the stock list," he says. When I've eaten one, he tells me to have another. "You're a hard worker. Better keep you fuelled up."

I bite the chewy bit off the top of the cake, then scoop out the fakey cream with my tongue. We never have these at home. The sponge is all light and airy and the sweet icing sticks to my fillings.

"So how's your mum doing these days, Jake?" he asks, pouring himself another cuppa.

"Yeah, she's OK," I answer, wondering what he knows about her.

"I've heard she's not been well since Christmas," he adds, and I stop eating, as my stomach bunches up.

"Oh, that was nothing," I tell him, concentrating hard on digging deeper into the sponge. "She was just a bit, you know, under the weather. She's getting better."

I can sense Mr Horrocks opposite me, leaning up against the big chest freezer, sipping his tea.

"You know, it's a great help having you around, Jake. I don't know how I'd manage without you."

I smile, and look away, embarrassed.

He goes on, "Mrs Horrocks, well, she's not been well for a long time. She gets confused, you see. One day she'll be just like the young Marcie that I married forty years ago; full of life and energy. Then the next she's like this puzzled old woman I don't even recognise."

He looks tired. I'm uncomfortable, don't want him to go on really. Want to get back to the stock-taking.

"It's hard looking after someone like that. But you do it because you love them, I suppose."

I nod, pushing the rest of the Fondant Fancy into my mouth. A little bell rings out from upstairs, and Mr Horrocks leaps to his feet.

"That'll be Marcie. Better go see to her. On you go, Jake, back to work."

I dust the crumbs off my jumper and pick up my clipboard, pausing as I hear his voice from the top of the stairs.

"Hello, dear," he says, *"shall I sort your cushions out for you? There – look – it's* Sons and Daughters *– your favourite!"*

I carefully push through the beaded curtains into the front of the shop, feeling sneaky for listening in like that. I wonder if Mrs Horrocks is lying in bed or if she's up and about. I think about the cup of tea I'd left on Mum's bedside before I set off this morning, and I wonder if she's drunk it or if it just went cold. I wonder if she's got up yet.

We work on through the day, only stopping for a sandwich and a pee. Just before five, Mr Horrocks says we're done, and he goes off to the till to work out my wages on his notepad. He stuffs it into a little brown envelope and writes the amount on the front. As I'm about to leave, he fetches down another box of Fondant Fancies and hands them to me with my envelope.

"For your mum. Tell her you did a good job today, Jake." He rests his hand on my shoulder like he does when he's giving me instructions. "We'll see you in the morning for the papers, then?"

"Thanks, Mr Horrocks," I say, and he bolts the door behind me as I go.

As I walk away, I glance over my shoulder and see movement in the window above the shop front. There's an old woman leaning against the glass, with the nets pulled to one side. She looks slow and sad. But then she smiles at me, and raises her hand in a little wave.

I smile back, and wave, swallowing down my sudden

tears. I don't know what's wrong with me these days.

When I get home, Sandy's there, scrubbing out the oven.

"Oh," I say, when she looks up.

She looks embarrassed. "Oh, hello, sweetheart!" She's wearing this mad, lacy pinny over the top of her velvet track suit bottoms. She must have brought it with her, because it's not Mum's. She gives me a peck on the cheek, and a little stiff hug.

"Hello, Auntie Sandy," I say. I can't remember when she last visited. It must be years.

"Just popped in to see how your mum was, as I hadn't seen her for a few weeks. Well, she seemed out of sorts, so I thought I'd give the place a bit of a spruce up." She wrings the dishcloth in her hands. "You alright, love?"

I nod, and try to avoid her eyes, because she's doing that concerned thing that really annoys me. She's done a good job of the kitchen, and the taps sparkle for the first time in years.

I drop the Fondant Fancies on to the worktop. "She up yet?" I ask, as I open the fridge door to see what there is.

"No, love. I brought round a few bits and pieces, Jakey. There's some milk and bread, and I thought you and Andy might like a shepherd's pie, so that's it over there under the tinfoil. Shall I put it in the oven now, love?"

I nod, and head off to find Mum. The rest of the house is quiet; Andy must be out and about with one of his mates. I tread up the stairs as softly as I can, like she's a sleeping baby who shouldn't be woken.

The darkness from her room spills out into the hall. As I stand in the doorway, I can see her, where she's been for the last two weeks, lying curled up with her face away from me, her lovely glossy hair now matted and dull on the pillow. Sandy's put a fresh glass of water on the bedside table, along with a *Woman's Weekly* magazine. The room smells stale and biscuity, so I go to the window and open up the top pane. It's starting to get lighter in the evenings now, and the sun's only just gone down behind the buildings opposite. The cool air slips through the open window and over my face.

"'s that you, Jakey?" Mum asks drowsily.

I turn from the window as she stirs in her covers, rubbing her swollen eyes with the heels of her hands. I go to pass her the glass of water and my foot clips an empty bottle, sending it spinning into the corner. She takes a weak sip, and puts the glass back on the side.

"C'm here, darling," she beckons, patting the bed beside her. The smell of old gin reeks off her now that she's moving.

I stay standing. "I've got to go find Andy, Mum. I think he's at Ronny's. D'you want anything?"

"Jakey, come on, sweetie. I need you to come here and sit with me. Please? My boy?" Her whole face looks puffed up, her eyes full of tears, her mouth down-turned in a spoilt sulk. I think I hate her. I'm not sure.

"How about a boiled egg? You always like an egg when you've been under the weather, don't you?"

Mum flops back down on to her pillows, turns her face from me. I go and sit on the edge of the bed like she wants. I can hardly bear to touch the sheets she's been sleeping in. Everything feels dirty and damp. She rolls back over to face me, reaching out to take my hand.

"Good boy, Jakey. I love you, you know? Now, you

know where my purse is?"

I'm so tired. I can hardly hear her words, but I know what she's saying. She's gone into these bed episodes before, but this one's gone on and on with no sign of ending. I drop her hand and go to the doorway, looking back at her stuffed into her covers.

"Mum, there's no money left, and I can't get you anything. The money ran out last week. We've been eating the last of the cereals for supper all this week, Mum, and we're just about out of them now. It's just as well they're giving us those poxy free school dinners or we'd starve to death! And you want me to go out and get you more gin?" She's turned away from me again, wishing me gone.

"Mum! You've got to get up! You've got to get up!" I grab at her feeble wrist, tugging her up from the tangled mess of bed. "Mum! That's enough now! Get up!"

I'm tugging and wrestling with her and she's mumbling, "Bugger off, Jakey, leave me alone, won't you?"

Sandy's up the stairs in a flash, pulling me into the hallway, leading me down the stairs by my hand as I look back over my shoulder towards Mum.

Sandy hugs me to her in the kitchen, rocking me, *poor baby, poor baby.* Her tears bounce off my hair and down my cheek. I can't speak, can't cry, I just press my cheek into the sparkling, hard brooch pinned to her chest, encrusted with a thousand orange diamonds. The sharp pain of it feels good, and bright, and the pieces of light dance at the side of my eye.

Andy's key turns in the front door. And then he's in the kitchen doorway, and I'm looking back at him, and Sandy is standing there with tears on her cheeks, and his terrified face says he thinks it's Mum, really thinks the worst. And for the first time, I see he's not just a little kid, I see that he gets it too.

"She's just asleep, Andy!" I shout in a high screech that doesn't even sound like me, but he bursts into tears anyway. He stands there, pale and thin and crying and alone. And Auntie Sandy hugs him up, and she cries enough tears to make up for me.

I flop into the armchair and wish I could just sleep, doze off into a deep, deep sleep, and wake up again when it's all over, when everything is back to normal.

Mary, August 1970

When I arrive at the ferry port, I see Gypsy waiting by the ticket office. An army surplus rucksack lies on its side at her sandal-clad feet, and ribbons weave through the plaits in her hair. She resembles a little sun nymph, smiling at everyone who passes her on their way to the boat. The bright sunshine catches her bare arms, which are slight and tanned.

She sees me approaching, and she jumps up and down on the spot waving her hands in the air. "Mary! You came!"

We hug, and Gypsy squeals, standing back to inspect me better. Her face curls into a frown. "Where's all your stuff? You're not backing out on me, are you?"

I clutch my shoulder bag, feeling slightly embarrassed. "Of course not! The forecast said it's going to be hot this weekend, so I packed light." All my bag contains is a toothbrush, knickers and a jumper.

She claps her hands together, a happy nymph again.

"Good planning. I might go on somewhere else after this, so I've stuffed my life into that rucksack. Not sure where I'll go yet. Might even travel round India, if the mood takes me. Remember Sass and Jojo at St Martin's? Well they're off to a Buddhist retreat in a couple of weeks, and if it comes off, I'll be with them. Buddhism," she rests a hand on my shoulder, "you know, Mary, Buddhism can change your life. It did for Jojo. She's the most chilled woman I've ever met, since she found Buddhism. So. How did Billy take it?"

We join the large crowd heading towards the pedestrian entrance to the ferry, and the sun's rays beat down on us, hot and dry. Groups of travellers herd this way and that, some excited, others seeming in no hurry to go anywhere. Busloads of hippies gaze out of windows with hot, sweaty faces, waiting for their drivers to board the next boat. Many more are on foot, pressed together beside us. The ferry staff appear stiff and disapproving, and the man controlling the pedestrian gate stands with his hat firmly in place, his head held high as he ignores the jostling of the foot passengers. I've never seen so many men with long hair, so many smiling and bearded faces, so many bare midriffs. The women are all beautiful in their own ways, every one of them open and vital. The smell of pot is strong in the air, reminding me of the decadence of art school and life before now.

"Billy doesn't know yet," I shout over the crowd noise, holding on to the chipped handrail as I climb the metal stairs behind Gypsy.

"Know what?" Gypsy shouts back, looking at me over her shoulder. When we reach the deck she grabs my hand so we won't get separated. "Look, there's some empty seats at the end of the deck."

We run, so as not to miss out on the remaining bolt-down deck seats, a row of painted metal chairs which look like they belong in a bus shelter. The metal feels hot on the backs of my knees. Gypsy rummages around in her bag, pulling out two apples and handing one to me. She takes a loud bite from hers. "Billy doesn't know what?"

"That I've gone. I didn't tell him. I just went when he was at work." I'm shocked myself when I hear the words out loud, and I feel suddenly sick.

Gypsy turns to me with mock surprise, instantly becoming the wicked Gypsy I remember from college. "Well, Mary Murray, you dark horse," she says, using my maiden name. "Won't he go mad? Oh my God! Well, tough if he does, because you're here now!" She slaps her little brown knees in delight, and takes another loud crunch from her apple.

"I've left a letter waiting for him when he gets home from work. And I dropped Matthew at his grandmother's. I'd never have got away otherwise. And it's just a weekend." I can imagine him now, reading the letter, rubbing his stubbly chin, wondering if it's a joke. "His mum's always complaining she doesn't get enough time with the baby. So, she'll be happy at least."

Gypsy giggles into her wrist, and gives me a nudge. "To think of you, an old married woman. With a kid! God, it's wild, man!"

A tall thin man with long grey hair and a plaited beard walks along the deck, taking the hands of each passenger in his. "Bless you, child," he says to each, and kisses them on the forehead before passing on to the next one. He wears a white feather boa wrapped around his waist, strangely absurd against his bedraggled disciple robe. A few people move from their seats with suspicious unease, whilst others seem unsurprised when he approaches. When he takes my hands he says, "Be free," and he plucks a downy white feather from his boa, and presses it into my hand. It sends a chill of exhilaration down my spine. The man passes along to the next passenger.

"He thinks he's Jesus," whispers Gypsy. "He's at all the festivals, blessing everyone, and everything. In fact, I don't think he's even got a proper name. Just Jesus."

"Just Jesus," I repeat, enjoying the sound of it in my mouth.

Gypsy glances along the row of passengers towards the robed man. "Yeah. Just Jesus."

"Hallelujah," I say, and we laugh like schoolgirls.

We relax on the deck, feeling our skin singeing in the sunshine, safe in a crowd of happy people. The party atmosphere grows and sways as the boats and masts of the Isle of Wight become clearer, and the harbour of Portsmouth fades away.

It's late on Saturday night, and we're dancing arm in arm to The Doors. There's been an electrical fault, so the band are playing in near darkness, enhancing the eerie quality of the music. We've been drinking cider since we arrived at midday, and my skin glows hot from too much sun. Gypsy's been braiding my hair, in tight furrows that run from my forehead to the base of my neck. My exposed skin feels alert and sensuous. I've been kissed by men, complete strangers in kaftans and waistcoats, and told by Gypsy to enjoy the moment, to chill. This afternoon, she reached out towards me as we lay dozing on the grass, catching the string of my tunic between her fingers like a butterfly. The cheesecloth cotton fell open between my breasts. When I awkwardly tried to gather it back up she said, "Leave it. It looks good a bit lower. Less uptight. You can't see anything anyway. It's a bit more alluring, that's all." She smirked and undid her own shirt one button more. I lay on my back squinting at the too-bright blue sky, and three swans flew past, high above us. "Swans," I said, and Gypsy just laughed.

Now, Jim Morrison's curls glimmer from the shadows of the stage, and his voice hums through my ribcage. I think I'm in love, and I'm happy that my shirt is undone.

I feel a hand on my shoulder, and a white face appears between mine and Gypsy's. "Babe, who's your friend?" His accent is American, nasal.

"Zigg! You genius! How'd you find us? Mary, this is Zigg – from St Martin's. Genius!"

Zigg stands with his hands on his hips. In the night light his skin is translucent pale as if lit up by the moon. His neck is long and elegant, and his white hair grows away from a high forehead, feathering down to his shoulders. He wears a white bed sheet like a cape.

"You two stand out from the crowd, Gyp. It was easy to find you, babe." He kisses Gypsy but keeps his eyes on me, smiling knowingly. "So, you're Mary, then?"

"Isn't it a bit dark for sunglasses?" I say, sounding prim. "It's nearly midnight."

He fingers the little round glasses, which are perfectly black. "I'm albino," he says, and he passes me a joint.

I take a few drags, and giggle, not because of the joint, but because I'm smoking a joint with an albino at a festival.

"She's cool," he says to Gypsy, and we dance. Zigg weaves in and out of us, rising up like a magician, bright and unsettling in the darkness. I see Just Jesus moving through the crowd, taking hands, blessing everyone. You've done me, I think, hoping he'll pass by. Zigg's face moons up at me, and I laugh at the sky, my head thrown back, my throat open wide and loud. *When the music's over, turn out the lights, turn out the lights, turn out the lights . . .*

We're swept up on a sea of good people, all good, all good. As early morning creeps in, Zigg takes us both by the hand and we run through the masses of people and out on to the open plain of land at the top of the festival grounds. I feel the dewy cold seeping into my skin, each little hair standing on end. The damp breeze clings to my face as we run, run, run. The tents and people grow sparser, and we keep going until we reach the top. Inside a large canvas tepee high up on the hill men and women lie about on Indian cushions and rugs, some sleeping, others smoking and talking in low voices. The music still carries towards us, across the fields and valleys of Afton Down. We dance and laugh, and Zigg produces a little black tin. Inside it is a fold of white paper, and inside that, three tiny purple blots of colour. Gypsy's eyes sparkle wickedly.

"*Magie, madame?*" Zigg asks Gypsy.

"*D'accord, monsieur,*" she replies.

We each place one on our tongue, like the Holy Communion, and fall back into the darkness of the tent. We lie together, side by side, the three of us holding hands in our own silence, waiting, waiting. When Zigg kisses me with his cold, white lips, I walk to the opening of the tent and fly up above the fields and lights of the festival.

I look down at the thousands of tents below me, and the illuminated centre stage casts deep shadows and lights across the August fields. I see Gypsy and Zigg in the door of the tepee, waving and spinning in circles, their hair flowing underwater. Fireflies dart between them like meteors, and Gypsy's tongue lashes out, reptilian, catching a bright fly in her mouth, her face aglow. The warm breeze fingers my hair, and I close my eyes to it, letting the currents guide me. Swooping lower, I see couples swaying to the rhythm, and making love on the grass. Breasts and limbs are bared, writhing in a tangle of movement, and all voices join as one union of pleasure. I tumble, on to a landing of amber-scented cushions, my braids trailing around me like a crown of vipers. Gypsy rests her hands on her knees, her wicked eyes on mine as she blows me billows of kisses, and disappears into the dark corners of the tent. When he comes upon me, that great monstrous bird, I'm willing him on, hitching my skirt high above my thighs, allowing him to tug away at my clothing with his rounded beak. His long neck encircles mine, his softly feathered sinews catching against my earlobes with a shiver. The reedy fragrance of him invades my senses, familiar and ancient. His great feathered bulk pushes at my thighs, his black eyes unblinking and hard, and as I push up against the force of him sliding deep inside me, his wings unfold majestically, beating the air with every powerful thrust of his white body.

At her place, Sandy makes up the guest room, then leaves us in the living room in front of the telly. Neither of us talk about it, we just stare at the TV like nothing's happened. After about half an hour, the door goes and it's Dad. He pops his head in quickly, saying he needs to chat to Sandy and Pete on their own and he'll be back in a minute.

They go into the kitchen and shut the door, and I signal to Andy to stay put while I sneak down the hall and listen in.

"Have you seen her lately, Bill?" asks Sandy.

"Well, not really. I mean, when I have the boys I just pick them up and drop them off. Mary and I haven't got much to say to each other these days, you know?"

"Bill, mate, she's not good from what Sandy tells me." Pete sounds a bit nervous.

Dad says something, but it's muffled and I have to press up closer to the door to hear.

Sandy's voice keeps going in and out of focus, like she's

pacing about the room. "She's in her bed, and Jake says she's been there for weeks. Since New Year. God only knows . . . But it's a bloody state round there . . . Jake's been trying to keep on top of it, but he's just a kid, Bill."

Dad doesn't say anything, but I can hear a deep sigh, and I can imagine him in there with his elbows on the kitchen table, head in his hands. I'm hardly breathing, straining to hear better.

"By all accounts Andy's been round his friend's house most nights for tea. Just as well, cos there's no food in the house either . . . She's not eating, and I don't know where she's getting the booze."

There's a long pause, and I get ready to run back to the living room. I listen hard.

"Oh, Bill, love! Come 'ere!" Sandy cries out, and it seems to go quiet for ages.

"Come on, Bill, mate," says Pete, "we'll help you get it sorted. Yeah? Come on, mate."

And I hear the sound of Pete's hand slapping Dad's back. "It'll be alright, mate. You'll see."

Sandy brings our shepherd's pie in on trays, and we eat on the sofa. Pete carries in two cans of Coke, opening them for us and putting them down on the brown glass coffee table. He flicks off the TV, just as we were about to find out how much this big ugly statue was worth on *The Antiques Roadshow*.

"Right, boys, we've been talking to your dad," says Sandy, patting the seat next to her so Dad can sit down. Pete stands at the fireplace, where Mum had stood on the night of the party. "And we think you should stay here for a bit. Not too long, just so's your mum can get herself back on her feet."

Dad's busy looking at the palms of his hands.

"But who's gonna look after Mum, then?" I ask.

"We will," says Sandy. "I'll go in to her twice a day, take her something to eat and clean up around the house. She just needs a bit of a rest. We'll have her right as rain in no time, boys. Just you watch!"

I don't know what to say. I look around at the clean comfort of Sandy's place, and know it's what Andy needs. But Mum'll be in a right state when she realises we've gone. I just know it. And God knows what she'll do then.

Pete's watching me closely. "Jake, let's try it out for one night, OK? Then we'll see from there. Yeah?"

I nod, too tired to argue. Dad smiles weakly, and I see his eyes are red-rimmed.

"Can I go to bed now, Sandy?" I ask, and I leave my half finished shepherd's pie on the coffee table and head up the stairs to sleep.

Early next morning I go with Sandy to collect our school things from home. They're still in a heap on our bedroom floors from Friday night, and Sandy says she'll give them a quick iron to freshen them up. When I go to take a pee, there's blood in the toilet and I flush it away before I use the loo. I hear Mum coughing in her bedroom, a rattling, phlegmy cough that chills me. Sandy comes upstairs and we check in on Mum. She opens her eyes, straight at me, full of hate.

"You didn't come. I called and called for you last night, and you didn't come." She says the words slowly, carefully.

Sandy sits at the edge of Mum's bed. She's wearing

tight snow-washed jeans that I'm sure are meant to be worn by a teenager. She brushes invisible dust off her snowy legs, and gives me an awkward little smile. "They weren't here, Mary, love. I took them home with me. Thought you needed a bit of peace and quiet? You were out cold, sweetheart, and the boys were hungry." Sandy looks really worried, like she's done the wrong thing.

Mum turns her face away. "*I* was hungry," she mumbles.

"That's great news, love!" says Sandy, over-enthusiastically. "I'll go down and get you something. Bit of toast? And a sweet tea, that'll do you the world of good, Mary."

Sandy trips off down the stairs, and I'm left standing in the doorway.

"So did you sleep well at Sandy's then?" she asks, without looking at me. She's holding her hand to her forehead, smoothing out the lines. "Get a decent meal, did you?" She's like a bloody kid when she's like this.

"You need a bath, Mum. It stinks in here." I grab the school bags and head down the stairs.

Sandy rushes to the bottom of the stairs when she hears me coming, whispering and wringing her hands.

"She OK, Jakey? What did she say, love?" Poor Sandy, she's cacking herself. I can't believe how much this has freaked her out.

"She's alright, a bit grumpy, that's all," I say. "Look, you carry on here and I'll take this stuff back to your place for Andy. We'll be late if we don't get a move on."

"Alright, Jakey. Good idea. What shall I tell her if she asks about you and Andy?"

"Tell her I'll be back tonight. Andy can stay on at

yours for a while, but I'd rather come back home."

Sandy stares blankly at me, nodding, wide-eyed.

"OK, love. Whatever you think is best. We'll keep Andy then. Yep, good idea." She leans in and gives me a peck on the cheek. "Have a good day at school, love."

She gets back to buttering Mum's toast, and I pull the front door shut behind me.

Out in the street, it's started to drizzle. It's that nasty wet mist that gets right into your bones, and soaks you quicker than it should. I sling the bags over my shoulder and run all the way back to Sandy's place, up our street, down the side of the park next to the phone box, past the back garden of the Royal Oak, and up Centurion Close to their boxy house, where everything ticks along the same from one day to the next. My hair is cold and wet, and I feel it steaming as soon as I step inside their well-heated hallway. Pete pops his head out of the kitchen, pink-faced and cheerful as ever, and wearing a chef's apron. He's got a spatula in his hand.

"Ready for a fry-up, Jake boy?"

Andy bobs past him into the hall, rubbing his belly and patting his head, with his eyes crossed and his tongue lolling out to the side. He's staggering about as if he's food drunk. Annoying little git. I pretend to punch him and he laughs, ducking to one side.

"She's having some toast," I tell Andy quietly as I pass, and he gives a little nod.

Pete's full of jolly banter, and it's nice to be around him. "How many eggs, Jakey? Two? Look at that! Perfecto, monsieur, if I say so myself. Now get stuck into that, my good man! That'll put hairs on your chest." He slaps me on the back, and busies himself at the sink.

Andy's hanging about the doorway, biting the corner of his thumb, frowning. He's daydreaming. I tip my knife towards the bags dumped in the hallway.

"Get dressed, mate. We're gonna be late."

"Shit!" he says as he looks at the clock above the cooker, and he grabs his stuff, legging it up the stairs.

He'll be alright, I think. Andy's alright.

After a few days, I kind of settle into a routine with Mum. Usually, I get up, make her a cup of tea, and leave it by her bed with a couple of digestives. I discover that she's leaving the house when I'm out, because when I get back after school stuff's been moved about a bit, and she's managed to get herself more booze. I'd like to pour it down the sink, but I know it wouldn't stop her, so it would be a waste of money anyway. So, when I get home after school, I usually go up to see if she's still here, then get myself a snack and have the house to myself. I've figured it's best to leave her sleeping, because if she's sleeping, she's not drinking, and before you know it, she might be back to her old self again. It's weird and quiet, as if I'm completely alone, so I can do what I want when I want. It's like having a dead body in the house, but no one talks about it. But then we don't really have visitors. Most nights, I pop over to Sandy's for a bit of tea and to check on Andy. He's fine, but he's stopped asking about Mum, and he can't meet my eye when I mention her. Sandy makes me up a lunch box for the next day, and I'm usually back home by eight.

This one day, I get back from school, grab a bowl of cereal, and get in front of the telly just in time for *Thundercats*. I love that programme. Mum comes in, looking like she's just woken up, with a real mean temper across her face. I nearly jump out of my skin; sometimes I just forget she's there. But now she's up, and it's just me and Mum, in the front room. Man, is she drunk. She's reeling.

"Don't they feed you at school then, my Jakey?" she slurs. She's giggling like it's really funny.

I just shrug. I don't want a fight, that's for sure. All I want is to eat my cereal and watch *Thundercats*. Cheetara can run at over a hundred miles per hour, and not even break into a sweat. If she wasn't half cat she'd be the perfect woman.

Mum snatches up the mail that I just put on the little table, and she's ripping open the brown envelopes, peeking inside without taking the letters out. She stuffs them all behind the carriage clock on the mantelpiece, and stands for a moment running a finger through the dust.

"So where's my kiss then?" She puckers her liney old mouth. There are pillow creases up the side of her face, making one eyebrow lift up madly.

"Dunno," I say, staring hard at the telly.

"Selfish little bugger," she mutters, and she slopes off, out of the room, leaving me alone in Dad's leather armchair.

They saved up for that two-piece suite, really hard, for years. It came from Morants, and they were chuffed to bits when it arrived in the big Morants van. Everyone rushed in to sit down on it, but by the time that Dad got in the armchair, and Mum was on the sofa with Matthew and Andy, there wasn't any room for me. I was gutted. More than I should have been. Anyhow, Dad only got to sit in that armchair for a few months, before he went.

So, here I am eating my cereal, in the armchair, when Mum sticks her head back in the room and just goes off. Mad.

"Who do you think it is that goes around putting away the sugar? Mopping up your milk rings? The bloody kitchen fairy? I'm no better than a slave around here. That's what you all think!" Her voice is posh; the angrier she is the posher it always gets.

She's standing in the doorway, holding on to the frame, her lank, mousy hair hanging down either side of her Droopy-dog face, and she's just yelling. I could probably slip out of the room and she wouldn't even notice. But now I'm starting to feel mad myself, just like I didn't want to. My cereal is soggy, what with all the interruptions, and I've missed most of *Thundercats*.

"Mum. Can I just watch this? I'll come and clear up the kitchen in a minute. After *Thundercats*." I'm counting to ten, inside my head. "I'll even help you do the washing up from breakfast if you like?"

But then she stands right over me, blocking the telly, and starts to take the mick, you know, copying what I said, in this whiny voice, not like mine, "Muuum. Can't I just watch *Thunder-caaaattts*? Muuum? Muuuuuuummmmm!"

And I can't hold it in any more.

"Oh just fuck off, Mum! Fuck off! You're nuts, you are. No wonder Dad couldn't take any more of it, you fucking nutter!"

Now she's staggering backwards like I punched her in the stomach, and she's wrapping her skinny arms about herself, pulling her granny-cardigan closer. I can see in her face she's getting ready to cry now.

"Jakey – Jakey? Everything I ever did was for you.

You and the other two. My little darlings." She picks at blobs of loose wool on her cardie for a bit, then looks at me sadly. "How could you?"

I know this tactic. So I'll forgive her like nothing ever happened. But it did happen, does happen, every day. I try to talk calmly again.

"Look, Mum. Sorry I shouted. But it's just, well, you're always on at me. Like I'm bad all the time."

Her face evens out, and I think it's worked, but then she spits out the words, "You're not that bad, I suppose – for a bloody Judas!" and I see a sharp flash of light in her dull eyes.

"What's that mean? What d'you mean Judas?" I know what she means, know who Judas was, and I'm mad now. "Why do you think I'm still here, instead of at Sandy's nice house, enjoying a fry-up every morning? Cos I thought you'd be upset! Well, looks like you're upset anyway, so I might as well have gone! Doesn't matter what I do – it's all bloody wrong!"

"You and that Sandy," she yells back, like she didn't even hear me. Her face is red and saggy. "And Pete – and Bill – and the lot of you. Judases! I could die and no one would notice!"

Now I'm staring at her and I don't know what to do next. I'm thirteen, what do I know? Nothing. I can't even get a proper job. If I could get a job, I'd quit school, earn some money and get out of this dump. But there's only one way out, and that's Dad.

Mum's stood up against our fireplace, rocking on her bare heels, sobbing. I try real hard to feel something. I don't hate her. I just don't feel anything. It's all gone, slipped out of me and up the chimney when I wasn't looking.

"Mum?" I say, trying to get her to look at me. "I'm gonna live with Dad. I mean, I haven't asked him yet, but that's what I wanna do. Live with Dad." I've only just thought of this; didn't even know I was going to say it.

Now she's looking at me, clutching her chest, like there's a heart attack coming, and she kind of morphs through all these different faces. She's like one of those mime artists you get on telly; horror, sadness, anger, and then hate, big hate that's hurtling out of her spittly, cat's-arse mouth, in this real mean whisper.

"You wanna live with your dad, do you? Think he'd have you, do you?"

I can't think of anything to say.

"Well, if you can find your dad, then fine, you go live with him. But I can tell you now, your dad's not that loser that disappeared from here three months ago." She raises her eyebrows, folds her arms over her chest. "Work it out, Jakey."

She shrugs, kind of smiling, and turns from me, hobbling from the room like she's just banged her head or something.

So I'm sat here, in the armchair, and my mum has just told me that my dad's not my dad. I'm sat in my non-dad's armchair. So I can't live with him. Because he wouldn't want me, would he, what with me not being his and all. And then I start thinking about me and the other two and how they've both got his nose and I haven't. And I'm smaller than the rest of them; people can hardly believe it when I tell them I'm older than Andy. And anyway, Dad's gone, so he can't want us, leaving us here with this mad woman, while he sleeps peacefully alone every night in his bed-sit. All we get of him now is a measly two hours each Saturday.

"So who *is* my dad then?" I shout after her, down the hallway. She's gone quiet, so I creep down the hall and stand in the kitchen doorway. Mum's leaning on the sink, crying. In a really low voice, she mutters to herself. I don't think she knows I'm there.

"Jimi Hendrix, for all I know, you poor little bugger. You'll be a long time looking."

She reaches for her Benson & Hedges off the window sill and takes a light from the gas. I tiptoe away, leaving my mum surrounded by dirty pots and pans, smoking and staring at the washing line out the window. The only Jimi Hendrix I've ever heard of is that dead guitar guy – and he's black. I don't think either of us really knew what she was on about. So I let it go.

When I get back from seeing Andy it's quite late. I can see the bathroom light on from the street, and I'm dreading bumping into her again tonight. I'd rather just forget about it.

As I creep through the front door, I hear the bath water emptying out of the plug up in the bathroom, and the creak of the floorboards as Mum goes along the landing. I should check on her, but I don't want to start anything up. I slip straight into the dark kitchen and stare out the window at the moonlit slabs of paving. The metal lid of the dustbin has blown off in the wind, and it rocks around on its handle, first this way, then back again. I should go and pick it up, or it'll clatter about all night. Next door's cat runs across the fence, pausing to look over his shoulder at me. It must be true what they say about cats having a sixth sense, how he knows I'm standing here in the dark. Miss Terry's got a cat, she told us in class. It's called Mr

Mistoffelees. *Mr Mistoffelees.* I bet Mr Mistoffelees has a good life. I bet Miss Terry feeds him fresh salmon and lets him sit on her lap all night, being stroked and petted. It must be nice being Mr Mistoffelees.

Andy was playing Monopoly when I arrived at Sandy and Pete's earlier tonight, and he had this massive stack of paper money, and loads of hotels. I don't know if Pete was letting him win, but either way, Andy was chuffed with himself. Every time he got more money or a good Chance card, he punched the air, saying "Skill!" in his stupid voice. Whenever he plays with me I always tell him to shut up with the skill thing, or I'll stop playing. Or I'll give him a dead-leg. Obviously Pete doesn't do either, which is probably why Andy was enjoying the game so much. When Sandy brought me a can of Coke I told her it was half term coming up, and she and Pete looked at each other across the room.

"How's your mum doing?" she asked, and I said, "So-so," and that was that.

I told them not to worry about half term, that I'd already got plans for me and Andy. That we might go to Aunt Rachel's. Andy's ears pricked up when I said this, so now I've got to get out of that one without sounding like a liar. Sandy and Pete tried to not look pleased, but I bet it'll be a relief when we're out of their hair.

Out in the back yard, an empty Hula Hoop packet whips over the fence and flattens against the window pane for a second, before dropping to the ground to dance about near the bin lid. Hula. I remember a film with Elvis in, and the girls on this island were wearing hula skirts. They all fell in love with him instantly, like they always do. It's a good word. *Hula.* I don't think Mum heard me come in, and I wonder if I can get away with putting the TV on quietly. As I turn to leave the kitchen, the door bell goes, making me jump. The noise cuts through the silence like a siren. It's 9.30 p.m., too late for anyone to be calling at the door. Unless it's an emergency. I instantly feel like I've done something wrong, and I'm not sure if I should answer the door. If I don't answer it, whatever's about to happen can't happen. I can almost sense Mum upstairs in the hallway, holding her breath too. Maybe *she* feels like she's done something wrong. The doorbell goes again.

When I hear the faint whining on the other side of the door, I know it's Griffin.

I find Mr Horrocks on the doorstep, pale and shrunken. Griffin bundles into the house, sniffing at every corner, before bombing up the stairs into the darkness.

"I'm sorry to bother you, lad," Mr Horrocks says with a shaky voice. His eyes look dark and hollow. "It's Mrs Horrocks. Well, you know how it is, son."

I stand with my hand still on the latch. It doesn't even occur to me that I should ask him in. I just stare at him waiting for him to speak.

"Well, the thing is, son—" He can't take his eyes off the dog lead folded up in his hand. He turns it over, rearranges it, refolds it. "Well, she's gone. At lunchtime. I shut up shop, and went up to get her a sandwich, and she looked like she was asleep. But she wasn't, and old Griffin was crying and nudging her with his nose, but I knew she was gone. It'd break your heart to see him pestering her like that, too late to help."

I don't know what to say. This is terrible. No wonder he looks so awful. I should get Mum, but she'd be no help. I'm about to offer him a cup of tea, when he thrusts the lead into my hands.

"Can you take him for a couple of days, lad? Just while I sort out the funeral business? He's partial to you, son, so I know he'd be happier that way."

I still just stand and stare at Mr Horrocks. I'm really pleased about Griffin, it'll be like having my own dog. But I'm sad for Mr Horrocks and about Mrs Horrocks, and I don't know how to say, *yes, great, I'll have him*, without sounding too happy, like I don't care about Mrs Horrocks dying. I nod.

"Good lad," he says, looking me straight in the eye with his hand on my shoulder. "Good lad. Pick up his food and bowls when you come for the papers in the morning, son. He's had his supper."

As he leaves, he pulls his collar up against the cold wind, a shiver visibly running through him. He turns back as if to say something, then looks past me towards the stairs, and disappears into the dark street.

I push the door shut behind him, and stand for a moment with my hand still on the latch, wondering what it's like to find someone dead like that. Dead, for ever. I turn, to go find Griffin, and there's Mum right ahead of me, sitting on the bottom step of the stairs in a clean dressing gown, with a towel piled up on her head like a turban. Griffin is in her lap, rolling and licking and fussing all over her like a long lost friend. The colour is back in her scrubbed clean cheeks and the light has returned to her eyes.

"You are adorable!" she tells Griffin, cradling his scruffy face in her hands, rubbing her nose on his. She looks up at me with a shy little smile, and I know she's back.

Mary, August 1970

It's around nine when I reach home, and the August night sky is growing dim. As I enter the living room, I know I've never seen Billy so wounded. I had hoped for an argument, some way to clear the house of the heavy pressure that weighs down on everything. But Rachel is here, through the doorway, in my kitchen, boiling the kettle, making him a cup of tea. She looks up when she hears me drop my bag and keys and gives me a concerned frown. Billy sits at the little table in the living room. He doesn't react to my entrance, but sits with his face down, turning his hands over, rubbing away at a callus.

"Rachel!" I throw my arms around her, and she hugs me, coolly. "I didn't know you were planning a visit! If I'd known . . ."

Rachel shakes her head. "It wasn't planned, Mary." She lowers her voice, and turns back to the tea making. "I phoned, and when Billy told me you'd gone off I came down on the train to help out with Matthew. I didn't know what else to do."

I lean against the sink, and notice how tidy the kitchen is. She's been cleaning up. The taps are sparkling.

"Aren't you even going to say hello to him?" Rachel's annoyed, nodding towards Billy.

I shrug. Rachel tuts, and starts to make me a tea.

"I don't want one," I say, opening the cupboard over the cooker.

"You haven't even asked about Matthew. He's upstairs sleeping. He missed you, Mary." Rachel is trying to keep her voice down, but I know Billy is listening to everything. She looks into my face, squarely. "Where did you go, for God's sake?"

"I'm bursting for the loo!" I snap the cupboard door shut and skip towards the stairs, tiptoeing along the landing so as not to wake Matthew. I peep in on my way back down, but decide not to kiss him, in case he wakes up.

Rachel still stands in the doorway to the kitchen, and Billy hasn't moved. They're staring at me as if I'm completely mad. I laugh.

"Well?" asks Rachel. "Don't you think you should at least tell us where you've been?"

"The Isle of Wight," I say, leaning on the back of the sofa to face them. "The festival, OK? Don't look at me like that, Rach. If Billy can have a family and his freedom, Rachel, then so can I. Who was the one who told me about feminism, about the equal rights of men and women? Or don't you live in that world now, Rach? Not cosy enough for you these days?"

"Equal rights?" Billy stands up so hard that the chair falls backwards with the force. "Equal rights is not running off in the middle of the night, leaving me with no idea if you're alive or dead! I didn't have a clue where you were, you selfish cow! Not a bloody clue!" Billy is mad with rage. His eyes are hooded and dark, and his face is flushed.

Rachel puts his tea down on the table and picks up his chair. He sits in it, and she stands behind him, with her hand resting on the chair back.

"He's right, Mary. That wasn't on."

I stare at them for a moment, and the image brings to mind a Vermeer. Something in the composition. The room tips slightly as I watch them, and my heart shudders. I'm tired. I know they're ganging up on me, the bastards. But I won't bite.

"OK, OK. I screwed up. I'm sorry. OK? Look, why don't I get us all a drink? Yes?"

Billy shakes his head, like a beaten man. Rachel stares at me like she doesn't recognise me at all.

I laugh at them again, holding my palms upwards. "Oh my God, you two. Chill out, won't you? Look, I went off for two nights, that's all. No one got killed, did they? God, it's like having my parents in the house! So, Rach, what's your poison?"

Rachel gives in and sits in the seat opposite Billy. They both still have those stunned expressions.

"You just don't get it, do you?" says Billy, seeming more exhausted than angry now.

I fetch glasses and a bottle of Scotch from the cupboard over the cooker. "Not really," I say, half filling the three glasses on the table in front of them, spilling a splash of Scotch on the table top. "Ice," I remember, going back into the kitchen to open the freezer compartment of the fridge. "Oh, Billy, there's no ice! Why is it always me that has to fill up the ice tray?"

I pull up a chair to join them at the table, one to either side of me. Billy knocks his Scotch back, and Rachel watches him with concern. She turns her eyes on me, and I see she is tired too. The evening light has disappeared completely now, and darkness fills the room through the open curtains. We are lit up by the bulb from the kitchen, which pours across the table catching the amber liquid in its path.

"How was Matthew?" I ask, topping up the empty glasses.

"He's fine," says Rachel, when Billy doesn't answer. "He's grown, since I last saw him."

I smile at her, glad of a kind word. Billy looks up at me, half broken.

"Look," I say, taking the hand of each in mine. "Can we just forget this ever happened?"

Their eyes check with one another, and they both nod. I refill the glasses, and we drink into the night. Billy gives up his frosty silence, and tells me how Matthew struggles to pronounce Rachel's name properly. Aunt Eyeball, he's been calling her. Rachel is giggling after two drinks and I think I'm forgiven. It's good to be home.

The next morning Rachel packs her bag and Billy drives her to the station. Just like that. Before I've even woken, she's gone.

Part Two

Jake, March 1985

When we get into Classics today, Miss Terry is writing "The Lotus Eaters" across the blackboard.

Someone at the back starts singing, "The first picture of you, the first picture of summer . . ." until a whole bunch of them are joining in, drumming at the desk with their pencils and swaying their floppy fringes in rhythm.

Miss Terry claps her hands in fake applause, until the singing stops. "Contrary to what some of you may think, the Lotus Eaters are not just a New Romantic pop group," she says to the back of the class, and taking a seat behind her desk. "OK, page forty-nine in your text books. Let's see where your pop band got its inspiration from, shall we?" She looks at me in my front row seat, and raises her eyebrows with a smile.

I flinch, and quickly flick through to find the right page, bending my head to hide my burning face.

"So, you'll remember Odysseus decided to leave Troy, to seek out his homeland of Ithaca. He filled twelve ships

155

with his men, and set sail. But Zeus had other plans for him, and didn't want him to reach Ithaca yet. A great storm blew up, tossing the ships across the sea until their sails were in tatters."

The illustration in the book shows a ship being thrown high upon an enormous wave, as the men cling to the boat with fear.

"After many days, the ships landed on a strange island, far, far away from their destination. Odysseus now realised that he could not escape the ever watchful eyes of the mighty Zeus. Still, he decided to make the best of it, and sent off three of his men to explore and look for food. Meanwhile the rest of them stayed with the ships, trying to repair the damage inflicted by the fierce storms.

"A few hours later, Odysseus realised the men had not returned, and it was beginning to get dark. 'This is not like my men,' he thought, 'I must go and look for them, to ensure that they are safe.' He searched through the forests all night long, and just as the sun was rising, he came across the men, lying fast asleep, each holding a golden cup to his chest." Miss Terry looks up at the class and smiles.

The class is completely silent, and I wonder if I'm the only one looking at her. Perhaps the others are all asleep, like the Lotus Eaters.

"Sounds idyllic, doesn't it? In the distance, Odysseus could hear the faint sounds of laughter, as if there were people hiding in the trees above. Odysseus did not know that the Lotus Eaters were the inhabitants of this island; a race of beautiful people who ate nothing but the juice of lotus flowers, which caused men to sleep and forget. When Odysseus finally woke his men and told them they must return to their families in Ithaca, they couldn't remember a thing, and they fought him off, wishing only to stay on the island and drink the magic juice for the rest of their lives."

"Was it like vodka, Miss?" someone calls out across the class.

"Yeah, vodka and Coke," shouts another, "that'd make you forget!"

"Make you heave, more like," says Debbie Sutcliffe, who sits along from me.

Miss Terry rolls her eyes and tells them to simmer down. "Actually, yes, it could be compared to alcohol, in that it has a soporific effect. The lotus flower juice had the power to make the men behave in ways they could never have imagined, taking away any sense of judgement. Imagine – they couldn't even remember they had children and wives waiting for them back in Ithaca! It took all of Odysseus' strength to drag the men, kicking and screaming, back to the boats to set sail again. Even then, the men were so addicted to the magic juice that they tried to throw themselves into the treacherous waters, to swim back to the shore. To them, nothing was more important than the magic juice." As she says this, she looks right at me, with a wide-eyed expression, and I'm struck by the sudden fear that she knows, that she knows that I lied to her about Mum's flu all along. My chest tightens and my ears feel as if they're filled with blood.

"Jake, are you alright?" she asks, bending down to my level. "You've gone awfully pale." She puts her hand against my forehead. Her fingers are cool and dry.

I can't look at her, and I can feel the eyes of the class burning into my back. There's lots of whispering and sniggering. Somehow, I'm absolutely certain that they all know. I nod my head, but at the same time push my chair away from the desk.

"OK," she says, leading me to the door with her arm around my shoulders. "Take yourself off to the nurse, Jake. I think you'd better sit this one out. Debbie, make sure he gets there in one piece."

"Grrreat," Debbie huffs as we get out the door, and she looks me up and down like a stray cat. She walks next to me, at corridor width distance, with her arms folded across her chest. We don't speak a word all the way to the First Aid room. I don't know what I'm going to say when I get there. I could say I feel sick. I do feel sick. My eyes never leave the shiny corridor floor, resting every now and then on dried-in lumps of chewing gum or black shoe marks left by the morning rush. I can tell that Debbie isn't happy that she was the one who had to take me. Well, I'd rather have gone alone, if I'd been given the choice. Maybe I should tell her, moody cow.

"See ya later," Debbie says, when Mrs Truman opens the door. She saunters off down the corridor without looking back, in her short, short skirt and poodle perm.

"Right, what can I do for you, young man?" asks Mrs Truman, showing me in and pointing to an orange plastic chair. She doesn't even know my name.

Mary, May 1971

It's early morning. There's a clock on the opposite wall. I'm lying on the hospital bed, and I can see myself as others might, a spent skin of woman, draped over the plastic sheets.

"Time of birth: six fifty-five a.m.," says one midwife to the other as she weighs the baby and wipes away the blood. I can't tell the two women apart.

One of them says, "Good girl, Mary. You did really well. That's the worst part over!"

The morning light streams through the venetian blinds, and I can see it will be one of those bright, clean May days, where faraway views become clear by midday. When I squint, I can see the streams of dust playing in the sunlight.

Billy holds my hand. "Well done, darling. It looked tough. Harder than Matthew?" He looks breathless, bright-eyed.

I nod, still fixed on the clock. 6.56.

"I should've been there for Matthew too," he says, turning to the midwives. "They said I should wait outside last time," he tells them, and he shakes his head.

"Times change, don't they?" says one. "It's becoming quite the trend for fathers to be at the birth these days."

"OK, the placenta should be along in a minute," the other midwife tells me. "When you're ready I want you to give another big push. I'm sure you're fed up with all the pushing, love, but this should be the last one!" She's so jolly, even though she's been up with me all night. "Here it comes," she says, reaching the palm of her hand under my bottom to catch it.

It slips from me like an organ, a complete piece, voiding my womb. A sob catches in my mouth as my stomach sags back against my ribs. The emptiness is devastating.

One midwife hands me my baby boy.

The other says, "Did you want to keep the placenta?"

I try to focus on her.

"It's quite popular, these days," she smiles, and I realise it's a joke. "For nutrition. But, well, it's not for everyone." She scoops it away.

The baby's beautiful, with smooth, clear skin. He's less wrinkled than Matthew was. And his head is rounder. The midwives and Billy fade like ghosts.

"Right, let's stitch you up then," says the midwife with a clap of her hands. "You might want some gas and air for this bit. Dad, you take baby."

My legs feel like dead weights as she guides them into the stirrups. Such an undignified contraption. The first needle entry is like fire. I drag at the gas, pulling the shriek back into my lungs. Again and again the needle tears through my raw skin, as my eyes roll back and my screams are swallowed.

After five stitches, she stops. "Shirley, have a look will you? I think we're going to need the registrar for this one."

The other midwife bends to look between my legs. She sticks her finger inside and wiggles it about. "Mmm. Best be safe. I'd get the registrar." They both disappear into the corridor to locate a doctor.

Billy sits beside me, gazing at the baby, oblivious of the stitching conversation. My head is turned towards him, and I'm drifting into sleep, but I want my baby. Feebly, I hold my hands out towards him, and Billy places him back in my arms.

"Jake," I say, closing my eyes, feeling my cheek against his warm skin.

"I like it. Manly. Unusual. That's cool. Would he be a Jacob?"

"Just Jake." My legs go into shock, still suspended in the stirrups. 7.29. My ankles tremble in the holsters, causing my calves to buck involuntarily. Silent tears stream down my face, on to the baby's head.

Billy jumps to his feet. "You've been stuck like that for twenty minutes. More. I'll get someone."

He leaves the room, purposefully, and I'm left alone with my baby. I cough, and a rush of hot blood exits me, pooling around my buttocks and seeping into the small of my back.

As I glance towards the fingers of light from the window, I see the little girl. She's about nine, and her hair has the whisper of a curl and the dark conker shine of childhood. She wants to come over, but she's shy. A red ribbon that should be in her hair twirls between her fingers.

161

She's got that blue shift dress on, the one for best.

"Do you want to see the baby?" I ask quietly, so the others in the hallway don't hear.

She nods, and walks round to the other side of the metal bed, where she can climb on Billy's chair for a better look.

"What's his name?" she asks.

"Jake. Do you like it?"

She smiles.

"I think he looks a bit like you, don't you think?"

She doesn't answer, but leans in to stroke Jake's soft forehead. There's still blood around his cheeks, but the girl doesn't seem to mind. She pushes her hair behind her ears, in a way that's familiar to me.

"I'm going to feed him now," I say, and I put Jake to my breast for the first time. He suckles instantly.

The little girl smiles again. "Why am I here?" she asks, a little question mark hovering between her eyebrows.

"Well, it's something you do, I suppose," I answer as I close my eyes. I'm slipping.

"Where's your other little boy?" she asks. "Matthew?"

"Oh, Matthew. Of course. He's at his nanna's."

"Is that your mummy?" she asks, tipping her head to one side, as if talking to a child.

"No. No. It's Billy's mummy. Not mine." I open my eyes, and she's still there, with the sunlight catching her hair. "Not my mummy."

She reaches for my hand and squeezes it. "You're bleeding. Does it hurt?"

"No. It looks worse than it feels." I want to reach out and embrace her, but I can barely lift my arms.

"I'm going to get someone," says the little girl. "You've gone all grey." She hops off the chair and pads into the corridor in her bare feet.

"Come back!" I call after her. "Where are you?"

Billy rushes in, and then the room is full of midwives and doctors, but the sound is muted, and I see them in slices of light and grey. I feel the girl's hand in mine, and she presses gently as the lights go out altogether.

"Come again," I whisper, and she's gone.

On one of our days with Dad, we go to Granddad's grave. It would have been his birthday, and we've got to show our respects. We don't do it every year, just when Dad wants to. Mum used to come with us.

"Do we have to get Gran?" asks Andy, poking me from the back seat of the car.

"No. One of your uncles will probably take her separately."

"Oh," says Andy.

He whispers "Skill!" under his breath and I give him the evil eye over the headrest.

When we get there, it takes Dad a while to find the gravestone. "I'm sure it's over this side somewhere," he mumbles, treading through the overgrown grass and weeds.

"Would they have moved it?" Andy asks.

"Idiot. He's buried. They're not gonna just dig up his grave and move him, are they? Idiot." I scowl at

Andy, who's tutting as he shoves his hands deeper in his pockets.

"Show some respect, boys," says Dad, frowning with concentration.

Eventually we find it. There's moss growing up the edges, creeping towards the etched words. Dad tugs away at the dandelions and grass, and soon it's looking much tidier.

"Don't want it looking a mess when your gran gets here," he says.

Andy runs his finger across the letters of Granddad's name. Arthur John Andrews. "He was quite young then, when he died?"

"Yep. I was only a lad."

"Was he born round here?" I ask.

"Southsea, born and bred," answers Dad, looking proud. "See that building over the road? That was his school. He was one of the first pupils, and then when we were old enough to go to school, we went there too. Of course, it's not a school any more. Some posh house now."

The brick building opposite the graveyard has a low stone wall, so you can see the big garden that spreads out the back. There are huge trees around the edges, and a blossom tree just coming into bud. Daffodils pop up everywhere like wild flowers, and I imagine Dad and Granddad running about in the summer. It's much smaller than my old primary school. I think I'd have liked it there.

"It's sad that he died," says Andy. "I wish we could've met him."

"Me too, son," says Dad. "Apparently, he was a bit of

a live wire, my old man."

As we're closing the gate to the graveyard, I see Stu and Malcolm on the other side of the road. Malc looks up and points us out to his dad.

"Bill! What're you doing here? Not your neck of the woods normally?" Stu bounds across the road with Malcolm in tow.

"Just visiting my dad's grave, mate. What about you?"

"Had to pick up Malc this week. His mum's car's on the blink so I said I'd drive over for him." He looks at his watch, rubbing his gingery stubble. "Oh, look at the time, Bill. I must say, I'm feeling a bit thirsty, mate. What d'you reckon?"

Dad grins, checking his watch too, pulling a snooty face. "Mmm. I make it eleven fifty-eight, by this fine piece of digital engineering. Refreshment of the ale kind would be most agreeable, sir. The Anchor?"

"Might as well, good man. As it's nearby."

At the pub, Dad pats me on the back before he heads into the bar. "Jake, we'll get some chips after we've had a pint. Why don't you lads go off and play round the pond. There used to be a tyre swing when I was a lad."

The three of us hop over the fence at the end of the pub garden, into the meadow where the pond is. A huge weeping willow hangs over one side of it, and a raft of old pallet boards floats about near the far edge. A few ducks and ducklings bob around in the bulrushes and reeds, where the sunlight catches the ripples. Just as Dad said, there's a tyre hanging from one of the low branches, and Andy runs ahead to bagsy it.

Malc and me sit on the bench on the other side of the

pond, plopping little stones into the water.

"That's weird, isn't it? Bumping into you like that," says Malc. "Didn't know you ever came over this way."

"Yeah. My gran lives in Southsea. But we try not to see her too much. She's a bit of an old cow. Shame it was my granddad that died."

"My nan's alright. But she lives miles away, so we don't see her much either. But she's nice. Cooks nice cakes and stuff." Malc throws a bigger stone into the water, and the ripples spread out right over to the other side of the pond.

"You staying with your dad tonight, then?" I ask.

"Yeah. It's a bit boring really. He never does much when I come over. You know, pub, park, TV. That kind of thing."

"What d'you like doing, then?"

"I like cycling a bit. And music. I want a midi system, so I'm dropping hints to Dad. And Mum. One of them'll probably get me one."

"Oh, yeah. I'm really into music. I'm saving for a midi player too. It's my birthday in May, and if I keep doing my paper round, I should get enough saved up for one."

"Have you got a job? Blimey, my mum won't let me do anything like that. She reckons I'll get kidnapped or something."

"Who'd kidnap you?" I laugh. Malcolm laughs too.

"You got any music mags?" he asks. "*Smash Hits*, that kind of thing?"

"Yeah. My cousin gave me a load of old *NME*s when I went over there. He's got a brilliant music collection."

"I could come back to yours and look at your music

mags? You know, when they've had their pint."

Over the other side of the pond Andy's got his legs hooked through the tyre and he's hanging upside down with his head and arms dangling. His hair looks like he's had an electric shock.

"Nah, my mum's not expecting us back till late, and she'd be annoyed cos it's her day off from us."

"We could just go to your room and get your magazines then?"

"Nah. Anyway, I can't remember where I put them now." I squat at the edge of the pond and grab the length of rope attached to the raft. I pull it in close, and press down on the edge to test its strength. "Wanna have a go?"

Malcolm shakes his head. "No way, mate. There's no way that'll float. You're mad if you get on that."

I laugh at him, looping finger circles at my head to show him how mental I am.

Untying the rope from its anchor, I pick up the long stick at the side of the pond, slide my bum into the centre of the raft and push away.

"Nuts," says Malc, still shaking his head.

I float into the middle of the pond, using the stick to push myself along. The bottom of the pond isn't that deep. Andy drops down out of the tree, and starts waving at me.

"Over here, Jake! Bring it over, I'll get on!"

I punt over to him, and he carefully eases himself on to the raft too. We shift about a bit, until the balance is good.

"Yahay! Wanna go, Malcolm?" shouts Andy, making the raft bob too much.

"Calm down, idiot," I say.

We push around the pond, trying to do a full circuit, to bring us back round to Malc again. He just sits slouched on the bench with his arms folded over his chubby belly, looking bored.

"Chicken!" I yell over to him.

He gives me the V sign.

As we reach the bulrushes, there's an almighty crash at the opposite end of the pond, as two huge swans hit the water. Malcolm shrieks like a girl.

The swans look instantly calm, not as if they've just arrived from the sky, and they begin to move through the water in Malcolm's direction. I try to punt towards him too, but it's slow going with two of us on the raft. Malcolm's getting to his feet, and backing off behind the bench.

"What's up?" I shout over.

"Bloody swans. They can break your arm, you know." His face looks panicked.

"Can they?" asks Andy, looking worried now.

"Course they can't," I tell him. "It's one of those things that everyone says. But no one's ever met anyone who had their arm broken by a swan, did they? Idiots." We're getting closer to Malcolm now.

The swans look as if they're about to climb up the bank next to Malc, and he yelps and breaks into a run. He scrabbles up the stone wall and sits astride it.

"You chicken!" I laugh at him as he puffs away at the top of the wall. His chubby cheeks are bright red.

The swans turn now, and swim with purpose towards me and Andy on our raft. My stomach bunches up, and Andy grabs my coat.

"Fuckin' 'ell, Jake, they're gonna break our arms," he whimpers.

I shake him off, and start waving my stick around to scare them off. "Don't be bloody stupid, Andy. They're more scared of us than we are of them."

One of them rises up, flapping its enormous wings and spraying us with pond water. It lets out a horrible squawk and comes at us again.

"Get out of there, quick!" shouts Malcolm, waving his arms about. "They're coming! They're gonna break your arms!" He looks terrified, and he's not even in the water.

Andy's gripping the edge of the raft with white knuckles now, saying oh-my-God, oh-my-God over and over. I give three big punts and the raft floats to the edge of the pond. The swans swim off towards the bulrushes, and I start to laugh with relief as I pull us up to the grassy bank.

Malcolm thumps down off the wall and lollops over, still checking for swans out of the sides of his eyes. He holds his hand out to me and I step on to the grass. Just as my weight shifts off the raft, Andy's shifts the other way, and he slides into the water like a sandbag.

"Help!" he screams, flapping in terror. "The swans!"

I really want to help him, but me and Malc are doubled over, as Andy shrieks and rants in the water. The more he thrashes about, the funnier he looks. It's so funny, he looks like he's actually doing it on purpose to make us laugh. Eventually, he manages to drag himself up the bank, gasping and spluttering. There's pond weed in the hood of his parka.

"Bastards," he says as we head back towards the pub garden.

"Spazza," I say, still laughing.

In my dream, I'm in that old-fashioned school of Granddad's. Everything's brown and white, and the desks are all lined up like a classroom, but on the lawn. It's bright and sunshiny, like the best days of summer. We're all watching Miss Terry, who is wearing one of those Victoriany dresses, but with the skirt bunched up around her waist as she tries to climb the apple tree in front of the class. Her feet are bare, and she wears bright white bloomers that stretch tight across her bottom as she climbs.

Then she's in the tree, sitting on a branch with her legs hanging down, and her toes are wriggling like they're dipped in water. I'm in my usual seat, at the front of the class, with my neck craned up to see her in the tree. My neck aches and my legs feel naked because I'm wearing shorts instead of long trousers. Miss Terry isn't looking at me, and I'm trying to get her attention by waving and smiling. She plucks an apple from the branches above her head, and she takes a big bite. I hear it crunch. Then she licks her lips, and holds the apple out on her open hand, letting it roll to the ends of her fingertips, and fall. It falls, slowly, slowly, until it lands in my waiting hands, but it's no longer firm and hard like an apple should be, but soft and warm, like skin. As I bring it to my mouth, I look up to Miss Terry who is now hanging upside down, with her legs hooked over the branch, and the ribbons of her dress are undone. Her breasts are free from her corset, perfectly round and pink with soft brown nipples. She's looking right at me with her green eyes. "Jake," she whispers. And I nod, pushing the soft, warm apple into my mouth, and bite down on it hard. When I sink my teeth into it, it bursts, like a balloon filled with warm water, filling my lap with heat and moisture. I feel my body shudder, and then the dream disappears into the darkness of the night.

Mary, New Year 1972

Matthew and Jake settle quickly in Sandy's spare room. They're tired out and both drift off after just one story. As I close the bedroom door, Billy pulls me close in the darkness of the upstairs hallway.

"You're still a stunner," he nuzzles into my neck. His hands caress the curve of my back and he presses me up against the wall with his hips. He kisses me with force.

"Not here," I giggle, gently pushing him back.

"You wait till I get you home," he growls, and I run down the stairs ahead of him, laughing as I glance over my shoulder.

He follows, close behind, with wicked eyes. In the kitchen, Pete ladles out glasses of Sandy's home-made New Year punch, and passes one to each of us.

"Do I have to?" asks Billy, with mock fear.

"Of course you do, mate," says Pete, puffing out his chest and beating it with his free fist. "It's tradition!"

We all three knock it back in one, just before Sandy

hurries in to fetch more Twiglets.

"Well? How is it?" she asks, looking at our empty glasses.

"Mmm! Delicious!" says Billy, and we all nod in agreement.

"It's the Sandy Special!" she says with glee, and she lights a cigarette at the corner of her mouth, and rushes back out with a tray full of nibbles.

"Another glass?" asks Pete.

"Not on your nelly!" chokes Billy, and he opens the fridge to fix us a proper drink.

Pete slices a lemon up for my gin and tonic, whilst I salt-edge more cocktail glasses for the guests yet to savour Sandy's famous punch. There's a steady stream in and out of the kitchen, but no one comes back for a second glass of the punch.

"I usually have to pour half of it down the sink," Pete says, so that only I can hear, touching his nose with his forefinger. "But Sandy need never know."

I wink at him, and carry on salting glasses.

Sandy returns. "Come on, Mary, love. Pete can do that. You come and mingle. Have a cheese ball or two." She cough-laughs at this and links arms to pull me into the living room.

An over-decorated fake tree dominates one corner of the room, and there are paper chains linked from one side to the other. Tinsel is draped over every surface, and the gas fire throws out a dry heat. But it's very cosy, and the room is already filled with guests.

"Look. Cheese balls," Sandy says, thrusting the bowl under my nose, giggling.

I light a cigarette, and savour my gin and tonic, letting

it remove the sweet after-taste of Sandy's punch.

"Kids go down alright?" she asks, bending down to change the album on the record player. She's wearing an orange and cream shift dress that's way too short. But then she's got the legs to carry it off. Her red hair is held back by a thick purple headband and her eyeshadow is electric blue. There's something about Sandy that's so fun, so irreverent, that I just love her more every time I see her.

"They went straight to sleep. Are you sure it's OK to leave them here tonight?"

Sandy carefully places the stylus down at the start of the album. James Brown. "Sex Machine".

"It's our pleasure, love. When do you ever get a break, eh? Not off that old bat of a mother-in-law, that's for sure. Have you seen her lately?"

I look round to check that Billy's not within earshot. "No. I think I've been written out altogether. Billy pops round there every once in a while with the kids. But even he finds it a struggle. I don't know why she's so angry with the world. Anyway, I've decided to stop trying to make her like me. It's never going to happen!"

"Her loss," says Sandy, and she grabs my hands and makes me dance.

We dance and laugh, and she turns up the volume and we yell out the words to "Sex Machine", and make all the movements, and before long the whole room's dancing and fizzing with energy. Billy waves at me from the kitchen doorway. He holds up his empty glass and raises his eyebrows. I nod, and carry on dancing with Sandy. When the track ends, we flop into the armchairs and both light another cigarette. The volume of chatter in the room has increased along with the music.

"Should I circulate, d'you think?" asks Sandy, eyeing the room.

"No. Everyone's fine. And Pete's in the kitchen. It's all under control."

Sandy nods. "Jolly good show." She laughs and gives me a little shove. She does that sometimes, to remind me that she thinks I'm posh.

"Lord luv a duck," I say, to remind her that she's not.

"Oi," she says, giving me another playful push.

Billy comes, and puts a fresh gin and tonic on the table beside me. He kisses me firmly, pressing me into the armchair.

"Mmmm," he says, smacking his lips.

Sandy's eyes follow him as he swaggers back across the room towards the kitchen. He knows we're watching. I smile, waiting for Sandy to say something.

"Well. You two seem to be very lovey-dovey. What's happened?"

"What do you mean?" I ask, grinding my cigarette out in the Guinness ashtray between us.

"Well," she says in a low voice, "it's not that long since I had you crying on my shoulder about how useless he was. You said you didn't know if you still loved him. Remember?"

I nod, taking a sip from my glass. "I know. But I'll always love Billy. He was my first real passion. I'll never meet anyone who makes me feel like Billy does. He can drive me barmy at times. But I love him." I poke the lemon down beneath the ice cubes in my glass. "Physical attraction is so important, don't you think? Because, even when you love someone, you can hate them sometimes

– really hate them for those split seconds of rage and disappointment. But then, your attraction to one another can break through it all. And then you remember why you loved each other in the first place. Do you know what I mean, Sandy?" I drain the last of my gin and tonic.

She sits quietly, viewing the room. I look at her for a response.

"I think what you're trying to say," she replies, dragging deeply on her cigarette, "is that you fancy the pants off each other." She turns to me with a serious expression, and then we both shriek with laughter until our eyes stream.

When we regain our composure, we sit without speaking for a few minutes, watching the party unfold. Billy reappears on the other side of the room, and waves to catch our attention. He stands in the doorway of the kitchen, his eyes fixed on mine. Led Zeppelin's "Whole Lotta Love" is playing, and as the chorus opens he starts playing his air guitar, legs set wide, his sweaty hair flopping this way and that as he mouths the words to me.

"I mean, look at him, Sandy," I say. "He's irresistible."

And we laugh till our mascara runs.

Jake, April 1985

Gypsy moved in about four weeks after Griffin. When she arrived on the doorstep, she was carrying a dirty great army surplus duffel bag, and wearing a parka jacket to match. Her hair was a blonde mass of curls, and she stood there smiling her bright smile, with her thumbs hooked into her skin tight black jeans.

"Put the kettle on, Jakey, darling," says Mum, once Gypsy has dragged her bag across the doorway. Mum gives her the grand tour, shows her my room, where she'll be staying; Matt's room. Looks like I'll be bunking up with geek-boy for a while. Griffin runs around behind them, following them to each room, standing in the doorway waiting for the next move. He thinks he's Mum's dog now. Mum's been working like a Trojan to get the house spotless for Gypsy's arrival, and it looks great. She even pulled out furniture and hoovered behind. In Andy's room, the carpet behind the chest of drawers was really damp, and when Mum peeled it back at the corner it was swarming with silverfish. They went straight up the hoover nozzle, and the window's been wedged open to air the room ever since. When Mum and Gypsy get back downstairs, I take them their tea, then switch on the TV and pretend not to listen in.

"Sit down, sit down!" fusses Mum, pulling out the chairs, straightening the tablecloth on the fold-out table. "God, Gypsy, you look great. You haven't aged a bit."

"That's one of the benefits of life-without-men," she says, completely seriously. "No one to sap the lifeblood from you. I'm my own woman nowadays, and God, it feels good, Mary!"

There's a pause, as Mum picks up her tea and sips it. The football results are on TV, with that boring voice, Leeds United, one – Ipswich, two. No matter what time you turn on the telly on Saturday daytimes, I swear it's the bloody football results.

"Jakey, do we have to have that on?" Mum asks me over her shoulder. "Where's Andy?"

"At Ronny's," I say, and I lean over and turn off the TV. I pick up one of Andy's *2000AD* comics to read.

"So, Mary, tell me about Billy. I thought you two would be together for ever. Childhood sweethearts and all that. What happened?"

It's weird hearing someone else talk about Dad; and Mum's the only one who ever calls him Billy. Mum glances at me, and talks low, indicating to Gypsy that I'm in the room.

"We just, kind of drifted, I suppose," she says. "And I've been in a bad place for a while, not looking after myself, letting everything get on top of me. So it must've been quite hard for Billy at times."

"But he would have stayed, surely, if he was prepared to fight for you?" says Gypsy quietly, leaning her elbows on the table, looking at Mum like an agony aunt. What does she know about any of it? "I suppose he's got someone else?"

My stomach flips when I hear her ask this. What a cow, coming in here saying shit stuff like that to Mum. It's the last thing she needs. She's been fine for weeks now.

"Oh, no, no, not as far as I'm aware," Mum smiles at Gypsy, "there wasn't anyone else involved. Just us. He's got a bed-sit a few streets away, so he has the boys every Saturday. Gives me a break. Except today, Billy had to work extra this morning, to get a job finished. But I think it's working itself out, you know?"

Gypsy just smiles at Mum, a knowing look on her face. They sip their tea.

"Have you tried yoga?" she suddenly says. "No! Oh my God, Mary, while I'm here I'll teach you – we can meditate together. It'll change your life; it did mine. Look at my stomach."

I look over the back of the sofa as she stands and lifts her T-shirt up, showing her lean, firm stomach. She's well tanned, and I can see the lace of her knickers peeking over the edge of her tight jeans. I can tell she's not wearing a bra.

"I've got the body of a twenty year old, my yogi says. And he's not trying to get in my underpinning, I can assure you," she grins, raising her eyebrows and winking at me. I look away.

"Well, if you can get me one of those," Mum says, nodding towards Gypsy's stomach, "I'm up for it!"

They giggle into their tea.

"Griffin! Here boy!" I call, and he comes trundling down the stairs like a flump. He runs straight to the lead that hangs on the back of the kitchen door, his tail wagging his body uncontrollably.

As I pull the front door shut behind me, I wonder if it's a good idea leaving Mum on her own with Gypsy. She'll be fine, I think, she'll be fine.

I decide to take Griffin to visit Mr Horrocks. He's filling up the crisp racks when I get to the shop. It's about five, so there's only half an hour before he shuts shop.

"Griffin!" he calls out when we come through the door. Griffin runs to him, squirming about on the dusty floor to have his tummy rubbed. "That's one happy little dog, Jake. You must be doing a good job."

Mr Horrocks seems to have perked up a lot over the past few weeks, since the funeral. He kept the shop closed for a fortnight, out of respect, I guess, but once he opened up again, he started to get back to his normal self. But even when he was closed, he kept the paper round going, so I was able to keep an eye on how he was doing. I started taking Griffin on the round with me, so he could visit Mr Horrocks every morning, and wouldn't get too homesick. A couple of times, he ran straight out the back and up the stairs, and we could hear him whining outside the room where Mrs Horrocks used to sit. Both times, I shouted, "Griffin! Come!" as quickly as I could, because I could see it was upsetting Mr Horrocks. He tried to hide it, but I knew he was upset, because he would busy himself with something, turning his back on me so I couldn't see his face. But nowadays he seems fine. I think he's over the worst.

"Want a hand?" I ask him, picking up the crisp box from the floor, and throwing the crisps into the right rack. Mr Horrocks fetches a few more boxes from out the back and starts refilling the cigarette shelves behind the counter.

"How's your mum these days, Jake?"

"Yeah, she's really good, thanks. She's been spring cleaning this week, cos we've got a visitor."

"Oh?"

"Gypsy. She's an old college friend of Mum's. From art college. I don't think they've seen each other since then. Just arrived this afternoon."

I go out back, and get a box of salt 'n' vinegar, ripping open the cardboard tabs as I go.

"How long's she staying for, lad?"

"Dunno. I don't think Mum knows either. Not too long, I hope."

"Why's that? She no good?"

"No, no. I dunno. Sometimes Mum just gets on better when she's left alone. And anyway, she's nicked my room."

"I see your point, son." Mr Horrocks carries on stacking the cigarettes. "A man needs his own space, or he'll go insane. Well, hopefully it won't be for too long, eh?"

"Yeah. We're going to Aunt Rachel's again over Easter, so I guess she'll be gone by then. Off to practise her yoga, probably." I pull a cross-eyed face at Mr Horrocks, and we both laugh.

"So, you won't want any extra work over Easter, then?" he says.

"Nah. Thanks." I suddenly remember the dog. "Oh,

what about Griffin?"

"Up to you, son. I'll have him back if you like. But, well, you can take dogs on the ferry, you know? If you'd rather have him with you?"

I think about Griffin running about over the open fields and hills around Manningly Farm, and how him and Ellie-dog would become best friends. He'd love it.

"Better ask your mum first, son," says Mr Horrocks in a sensible voice, but he looks really pleased.

As I leave the shop to go home, I pass Mum and Gypsy on the way to the Royal Oak. She must see the look on my face, because she grabs me for a hug, and I stand there stiffly with the dog lead in one hand.

"We're just going for an orange juice," she whispers. "Gypsy's on a detox."

Gypsy smiles her white smile at me, those thumbs still hooked in those tight jeans.

"There's a spud in the oven for you and Andy. It'll take about an hour." Mum kisses my cheek and carries on up the road with Gypsy and her little wiggly bum. "Don't forget to turn the oven off," she shouts over her shoulder, without looking back.

Dad rings us the next Saturday to tell us to come to his place a bit earlier, and to bring our coats. It's taken a few weeks for Dad to get back into the normal Saturday routine since Mum's got better, so we've only had one proper visit lately.

Andy overhears me and Dad talking about Bognor on the phone, and shouts down the stairs, "Shall we bring our trunks?"

Dad says, "Tell the daft sod it's April, not bloody

August. See you in a while, mate."

First off we go to the cinema. Dad calls it "the flea-pit".
His folks used to bring him here when he was little, and it's
a really old and crumbly-looking building. In the foyer,
there's a glass window one side where we queue up to buy
our tickets, and then another glass window the other side
where we queue up and get our sweets and drinks. The
woman behind the refreshments window is ancient with
those weird pink glasses that fan out at the sides. She
looks like she got the job here fifty years ago, and hasn't
budged since. Her old, swollen fingers are really slow
when it comes to counting out our change, and she doesn't
look up or smile once.

"There you go, love. Next please." She says the same
thing to everyone she serves.

After a quick pee in the grotty bogs, we go in to get our
seats. The carpet is sticky underfoot, and seems to tug at
my shoes with each step. Dad wants to sit on the smoking
side, which aren't the best seats, but it means he doesn't
have to miss any of the film if he fancies a fag. The fold-
down seats are made of thick, faded red velvet, and you
have to shuffle about in them for a while until you can get
comfy. Dad says it's because I'm a short-arse; that my bum
will disappear down the back if I'm not careful. I give him
a raised eyebrow, folded arms huff, and he laughs.

"What?" I ask.

"You look like your mum," he replies.

We've eaten nearly all our sweets before the film starts,
and I've got that slightly sicky feeling you get when you
eat the wrong stuff on an empty stomach. Then the lights
go down and the curtains open, to this brilliant loud

fanfare of music. Andy leans across Dad to give me a thumbs up. The last time we went to the cinema was when we saw *Popeye*, but Andy would have been about seven, so I don't suppose he remembers much about it. I seem to remember it being a crappy film, and Mum and Dad said it went right over our heads.

Back to the Future, on the other hand, is brilliant, and really funny, and it's great to be in a dark room full of kids and mums and dads, all roaring with laughter at the same time. I can hear Andy squealing and slapping his lap when Marty, the main character, gets into bother. In the break, Dad gives us a quid and sends us down to fetch ice creams while he has another cigarette. We haven't got enough money for three, so I have to send Andy running back up the aisle to get more off Dad. All the kids behind me are tutting because I'm holding up the queue. It seems to take Andy ages to come back with the money, by which time my face is the same colour as the velvet seats. When the ice cream lady says, "There you go, love. Next please," I realise that it's the same old biddy who served us behind the sweet counter. I wonder if she runs the film projector too.

After the film, we get fish and chips on the seafront and wander along the promenade until we find a decent bench to sit on.

"Now, that's a chip," says Dad, holding up a big, greasy, salty chip, and turning it over in the sunlight. "None of your Wimpy, Burger King crap. Proper chips from a proper chippy." He stuffs it in his mouth, closes his eyes and looks like he's in chip heaven.

"Brilliant film, Dad," I say, chomping on chips and watching the tide roll in and out on the beach. It's a nice day, and there are lots of families milling about along the sand. I can see one man quite far down with a bucket, digging with a garden fork, while his two kids run about screaming, chucking seaweed at each other.

"What's he doing, Dad?" asks Andy.

"Rag worms. For fishing. Best bait there is. For sea fishing anyway."

"Do you know how to fish, then?" I ask. He's never mentioned it before.

"Used to. Specially when I first moved back to Portsmouth. I used to get out fishing whenever I got the chance. I'd often catch our supper back then. Except when your mum was expecting you lot. Went right off any kind of fish. Said it made her stomach turn."

"Will you take us?" asks Andy, his face looking all rosy and hopeful. "Fishing?"

"Haven't got the kit now, son. And anyhow, I wouldn't want to eat anything that came out of the water these days. You know, pollution and all that."

We all sit, eating our fish and chips, and staring out to the sparkling sea. The water looks dazzling from here, not polluted. I look over at Andy and he's in a daydream, popping chips into his mouth mechanically, swinging his legs under the bench. My watch says it's nearly two o'clock now, so we've still got a few hours with Dad.

"What now?" I ask.

"Constitutional walk," Dad replies, and we ball up our chip papers and head down the steps on to the beach.

Andy runs ahead, and starts poking about in piles of seaweed with a stick. Wherever we go, Andy always finds himself a good poking stick.

"Urghh! Rank!" he howls, flipping over a dead crab.

One of the things I love about the beach is that you can yell, and scream, and shout as loud as you like, and no one looks at you funny or tells you not to. And sometimes, you just need to scream.

"So, how's your mum then, Jakey?" Dad asks.

"Yeah, really good," I say, truthfully. "She's been fine now for, well, must be weeks. Well, you know, Andy came back just before half term. So since then."

"That's great, son. So what's she up to today then? Bet she was in bed when you left, wasn't she?"

"No! That's the thing. She's up with us every morning at breakfast. And you know we've stopped having school dinners now, so she even helps us with our lunch boxes every day."

"Why've you stopped the school dinners? They're free, aren't they?"

"Yeah, but it's embarrassing, Dad. There's only two of us in my class who has them. No one wants to be a free-school-dinners kid."

Dad doesn't say anything, just carries on along the beach with his hands in his jacket pocket.

"And you know we've got Gypsy staying with us?"

He wrinkles his eyebrows. "Gypsy?"

"Mum's old college friend. She says she remembers you. You know – skinny, blonde, bit of a hippy I s'pose."

Dad looks a bit confused, running his fingers through the hair at the base of his neck. "You mean she's staying at your place?"

I nod.

"How long for?"

"Dunno."

"Well fancy that," he finally says. "Well, if it's doing your mum some good, I don't suppose we can complain, can we?"

"It's not her that made Mum better, though, is it?" I wouldn't want him to think that, because it's not true. "I mean, she was back to normal before Gypsy got there. Although, she has got Mum to give up the fags. She's always going on about the body being a temple, and Mum seems to be going along with it. The only trouble is, Gypsy cooks crappy food that Mum tries to make us eat. I mean, have you ever heard of chick peas? Or couscous? Bloody hippy food, if you ask me."

Dad laughs, and clips me round the back of the head. Andy's down by the water, bent over looking at something.

"Poor bugger's got my skinny legs," says Dad, shielding his eyes from the sunlight as he looks over at Andy.

"Do I look like you, Dad?" I ask, not looking at him.

He thinks for a minute, before answering. "Not so much, son. I think maybe you're more like your mum's side of the family." He turns to me. "Lucky you, eh? You're a handsome little feller, Jakey."

I run off and grab a big bit of seaweed, chasing Andy down the beach. He's faster than me, and I see him stoop to gather up a huge bundle with a mad wide-eyed look on his face. He holds it high, then drapes it over his shoulders and across his head, and starts walking towards me in a staggering zombie walk.

"Creature – from – the – black – lagoon . . ." he says in a monster voice, still stumbling towards me, with his arms stretched out in front.

I weave about the beach, windmilling my arms, yelling

and screaming like I'm terrified. Dad's laughing, and I run behind him, holding on to his jacket.

"Save me, Dad, it's – it's – hideous!"

Andy can't keep a straight face now, and we all end up laughing as he peels off the seaweed, and he realises that it's left a slimy film all over his hair and coat.

"Bog creature," I shout at him, laughing at the state he's in. Trouble with Andy is he just doesn't know when to stop. He'll never get that stink out of his jacket.

When we get back to Dad's place, we pop in to use the loo, and he says he'll walk us back home.

"Give me a chance to say hello to Gypsy, and have a cuppa," he says.

"Oooh-oooh, Gypsy," says Andy in a girly voice, and he pinches out his T-shirt for titties and wiggles about the room like a little prat. "Hellooo, Jakeeeey. Would you like a mung bean?" He gets up close to me. "Or maybe a little kissy-wissy?"

He closes his eyes and puckers up. Dad's grinning. And then I punch him, Andy, right on the ear, hard, and he's lying on the floor, rocking about and holding on to his red hot ear, and Dad's just staring at me like I'm a lunatic.

"Let's go, you two," he says, and we're out the door, Andy trying to kick at me as we go.

When we get home, we find a note from Mum in the kitchen, saying that they've gone out for the day to deliver a food parcel to one of Gypsy's friends at Greenham Common. They'll be back late.

Dad shakes his head as he reads it. "Bloody 'ell, it must be worse than I thought," he says.

"How will they get there?" I ask. I've seen Greenham

Common on the news, and I figure it must be miles away.

"God only knows, Jakey. They're probably bloody hitching or something."

"But we're supposed to be going to the Isle of Wight tomorrow afternoon. Will she be back by then?" Andy looks really worried.

"No idea," Dad answers, not really looking at Andy, who is close to tears now. Dad's busy opening cupboard doors, checking if there's anything to eat. "Right, Jake, there's eggs and bread on the side, and plenty of cereals. And half a pint of milk. Will you be able to knock up a bit of supper for the two of you?"

Andy's gone into the front room now, and I can see the back of his head from where I'm standing by the sink.

"Sure," I say. "What about that cup of tea, Dad? I'll make it."

But Dad hasn't even taken his coat off. "Better not, son. I've got things to get on with. Give us a call in the morning if your mum's not back."

He gives me a quick hug, and leans over the back of the sofa to kiss Andy on the top of the head.

"Be good," he says, and the door closes, and he's gone.

Mary, November 1973

When the first starlings float towards me they're like little murmurs, whispered memories I can't quite grasp. As I stand at the end of the pier, I see something alarming in them, a reminder of a forgotten anxiety, rumbling under the skin, never making itself fully visible. Initially, there are just a few; little soot motes drifting this way and that on the still air. They bomb towards me before being sucked upwards again by some unseen nozzle. It spits them out on the other side of the pier and they disappear from my view. The children are nearby, still sitting on the little wooden bench outside the Brighton Rock pier kiosk, their two ruddy faces zipped into padded green anoraks. They wait expectantly, hoping for candy floss if they're good. The starlings whoosh overhead, the cloud now growing so that they become a thunder of thoughts and wing beats. Up, across, down, swoop. The November sun is turning red behind the old West Pier. Its Victorian facade crumbles in the orange-red glow, and when I squint I can see a legion of starlings taking flight from its hollow eyes, like a plague of locusts. "Mummy," I hear. My breath pulls in sharply as the palpating throng rushes past me like a wave. Other pier visitors gasp and whoop as the starlings perform their aerial display, first for the spectators on the west side, then across to the audience on the east. I feel the sun bouncing off my eyes, and the cool breeze slipping across my sea-damp face. I cast my hat aside and shake out my long hair. Like Botticelli's Venus. The spray from the sea is working up now, and when I lean over the rails quite far the waves flop and lollop around the posts of the pier as if Poseidon himself is stirring within his watery realm. "Mummy," he whines again. Who is this? Who is this? As I run across the decking I can still see the movement of water through the gaps in the wood, and it makes me giddy and drunk. The starlings are now so dense in number that the black cloud is unyielding in its mass, flexing in and out like a lung, pulsating across the sky. Can I hear its heartbeat, for it surely only has one? There! Da-dum-da-dum-da-dum. My name is legion, for we are many. I stare at the crimson sea, cradling my swollen hard belly, concentrating.

"It's important," I'd told him, as he whispered to me down the telephone. "Your grandsons want to meet you." Daddy sounded choked, quiet. "Your mother can't know," he said. And we agreed: 1.00 p.m. Brighton station. I wrote it in my calendar. I wouldn't have got it wrong. He was meant to take us for lunch in The Lanes, but when he didn't arrive the three of us ate chips on the pebbles instead. The boys liked that, as they chased off the seagulls and ate from sheets of newspaper. When Matthew put his arms round my neck, I told him the sunlight was making my eyes water.

The starling cloud draws in its greatest breath, rising to stellar heights, and in one vast exhalation it dives beneath the pier and vanishes. Now, the twittering drowns out all sound and I drop to my knees to press my eye against the gap in the planks. It's so dark beneath the pier that all I can make out is the occasional blur of movement amidst the incessant chatter, chatter, chatter. Then, bam! They're in the air again, in a balloon of dark fog, coursing towards the West Pier until their vapour trail disappears altogether. The rich sun runs across the vivid horizon, blood-like and fluid. When I turn to look at the children, my heart is beating in my ears and my skin throbs. They're fidgeting on the bench and the rest of the pier is empty.

"Did you see?" I shout to them. "Did you see it?"

But they just rub their eyes and start crying. I look back for the starlings but they're gone. The pier is in darkness now, the last of the sun eclipsed from view. As I walk towards the pier exit, the two boys follow, sniffling into their gloves.

"How long?" the older one asks, his hand finding mine.

Perhaps Daddy got the dates wrong, perhaps he'll be waiting for me at Brighton station next Friday, and I won't be there. His grandchild turns inside my womb, and I steady myself on the metal railing, looking out into the sea. As the waves gather momentum, I imagine the weightlessness of the ocean. I lean out, over the barrier, and see the girl there, waxen and still as she floats in the brine, hair shrouding her face in a death mask. Her blue frock ripples on the water, as the moon reflects in the red ribbon which trails from her frozen fingers. She ebbs and flows in the water below, way, way down, beneath the pier.

"Mummy," a voice tugs at me. "Mummy."

"The train," I tell them. "We'll be late for the train." And we run and stumble towards the Queen's Road, the band of muscles tightening around my pregnant belly with each heavy step.

We stand in the vast Victorian station and I scan the busy platforms, searching for his familiar face. The station clock reads seven o'clock, and I know Daddy's not coming.

Jake, April 1985

At about two o'clock the next afternoon, Mum and Gypsy bundle through the front door, out of breath and laughing. They almost seem surprised to see us there. Their hair is all over the place and they've got a layer of dust over their clothes. They look really pleased with themselves; happy and pink-cheeked, like they've got back from some brilliant adventure. Mum comes to kiss me, but I step back.

"The ferry goes in an hour," I say, nodding over to Andy. He's got his knees pulled up against him to hide his face, which is red from crying. "I've packed mine and Andy's bags, but I don't know if we'll make it by the time you've done yours."

Mum looks over at Gypsy, who's filling the kettle in the kitchen, listening to everything.

"Jakey, sorry, darling. We had trouble getting back, that's all. Don't you worry about the ferry. I'll pack now, and we can get a later one. They go every half an hour, and they said you can transfer your tickets easily when I bought them."

Andy is looking at me hopefully, and Mum is looking at me softly. And Gypsy, she's looking at me like a bloody cuckoo that won't get out of our nest.

"I'll go and do it now. Watch me," Mum says as she hurries to the doorway. "I'm up the stairs," she shouts as she goes. "I'm in the bedroom," her voice getting further away. "I'm opening the travel bag . . ."

"Alright, I get it," I yell back, and I see Andy quietly smiling into his knees.

"Cup of tea, boys?" asks Gypsy, handing us both a mug, flashing her silly white teeth. Her hard nipples push out through her thin white T-shirt. Brazen, I think. It's a good word.

"Have you got any kids of your own, Gypsy?" I ask, politely, coldly.

Her smile drops away like a stone. "No, I haven't, Jakey. I guess I'm just not the mumsy type."

She wiggles back into the kitchen, and leans up against the sink where she can see me, one leg crossed over the other. I can't be sure what it is I see in her eyes as she peers at me over the top of her mug. But I don't think it's friendly, whatever it is.

"I'll be off in the next couple of days," Gypsy tells Mum, throwing her eyes my way as they hug goodbye. "Things to do. The Cause needs as much help as it can get," she says, tapping the CND badge pinned to her T-shirt.

"Well, stay as long as you like, and just post the key back through the letter box when you leave. And keep in touch! Promise me? It's been wonderful seeing you again

– really, Gypsy."

Dad arrives to help load the bags into the boot of his car, and we leave Gypsy waving at us from our front door.

"She looks well," says Dad as we turn out of our street.

Mum nods, staring at the road ahead. "She's been good company. A breath of fresh air."

I turn to Andy and roll my eyes, but he's too busy picking a scab off his knee to take much notice. Griffin looks up at me from the footwell with his big brown eyes, and then scrabbles up and settles on my lap, smelling all doggy and warm.

Just as we pull into the ferry terminal, the first spots of April rain hit the windscreen.

"Typical," Mum says.

At Manningly, everything is just how we left it. Griffin and Ellie-dog sniff each other warily at first, and then they're off, rolling about play fighting and wagging their tails like it's a competition.

George's still not back from his friend's house, so I sit in the kitchen reading a book as Rachel and Mum get the supper sorted.

"I haven't touched a drop for six weeks," Mum tells Rachel when she offers her a glass of wine.

"Six weeks?" Aunt Rachel looks amazed. "Are you on a health kick or something?" She runs Mum a tumbler of water.

"No, no. Well, yes kind of," answers Mum. "I just decided to take better care of myself, I suppose. And, my God! I feel so much better for it. My skin's glowing, my hair's glossy, I've got so much more energy. Rachel, you wouldn't believe the difference. At the moment, I don't think I could ever go back to it. It's like being born again!"

"Well, good for you, Mary. I have to say, I can't do without my medicinal glass of wine in the evening. Just the one, unless we've got company. Somehow, it separates the evening from the rest of the day. Anyway, cheers, and well done you!" Aunt Rachel raises her wine glass and clinks it against Mum's water tumbler.

"It's good to be here," says Mum.

"Good to have you here," says Aunt Rachel.

The supper smells delicious. Beef stew with dumplings and mash. I wander over to the pan and have a good sniff, giving it a stir.

"Got a couple of those in specially for you, Jake, darling," says Aunt Rachel as I ogle the blackcurrant cheesecake defrosting on the side. She comes over and hugs me, as Mum looks on smiling. "I'm so lucky you came and found us again, Mary. You and your lovely boys." She kisses me on the top of my head, then goes back to stirring the stew.

"I wish we could live here, Mum," I say, when Aunt Rachel leaves the room to bang the gong.

"Oh, you don't really mean that, Jakey," she says, smiling at me gently, her hand resting around the glass tumbler on the table in front of her.

I look at my feet, crushing a clod of dried mud with my bare toe. "I do," I say, but too quietly for her to really hear.

A couple of days later, we're eating breakfast when

Mum suddenly remembers we have to phone Dad to let him know we got here safely. "I was meant to phone him Sunday night! Alright if I use the phone quickly, Rachel?"

I follow her down to Uncle Robert's study.

"You can do it if you like, Jakey. Hand him on to me when you've said hello." Mum wanders about the room, looking at the pictures as I dial the number.

Dad's phone rings a few times before it's answered. It's Gypsy's voice, "Hello? Hello?" I'm looking at Mum, and she can't hear Gypsy, but somehow her face shows she knows something's not right. I quickly hang up.

"I must've dialled the wrong number," I say, staring at the phone on the desk.

"Try again," says Mum calmly, but this time she holds on to the receiver as I dial in the numbers.

It seems to take for ever before anyone answers.

"Oh, Bill. I wasn't sure if you were in or not. – Sorry we didn't phone earlier. Just got wrapped up in things. – Yes, fine, fine. Jakey's here, wants a word. OK, well, speak soon – bye." The suspicious look has dropped from her face, and she hands me the receiver, and leaves the room.

Dad's fine. He asks me how Griffin's getting on with the other dog, and tells me to phone whenever I like. I listen hard for background sounds and voices, but it's quiet. I ask him what he's doing tonight.

"Not much, son. Might even stay in and watch the box. It's work tomorrow, and we're starting a big job, so I need to be on best form."

There! A noise – maybe the clatter of cutlery or plates being put down on a hard surface.

"Who's that, Dad? I can hear someone else."

"Oh, it's Stu. We've been watching the sports roundup," he says, casually.

"Can I say hello?" I ask, my heart pounding.

"To Stu?"

"Yeah. Can I?"

Then it's Stu on the phone.

"Oh, Stu," I say when I hear it's really his voice. I haven't got a clue what to say to him. "Um, can you say hi to Malc for me?"

"Yeah, course I can, Jakey boy. Want to speak to your dad again?" and he hands me back before I can answer. I can tell he's grinning.

"Happy?" asks Dad. "You have a good week, Jakey." There are voices in the background.

When we've said goodbye, I stay for a while, leaning up against that huge desk, screwing up my eyes as I try to recall the woman's voice that I heard answer the phone earlier. Maybe it was the same voice I heard at Christmas? The one Dad had said was just the TV. But no, this one was clear and husky, and definitely belonged to Gypsy.

I've got that horrible stomach feeling you get when you've forgotten something, but you can't remember what the thing is. The fried breakfast is sitting heavy on my stomach and I feel slightly sick.

I straighten up the phone, and shut the door to Uncle Robert's study as I leave.

"Everything alright?" asks Mum when I return to the living room. She's got her feet up on one of the big scruffy sofas, and she's reading a country magazine. There's a big glass of water on the coffee table next to her.

"Fine," I reply. "Think I'll go and help Aunt Rachel

in the kitchen."

Mum smiles at me and goes back to her reading.

After ten days, it's time to go home. George's made me three different compilation tapes, which we spent hours recording and logging on the cassette sleeves. And he gave me this brilliant black hooded sweatshirt that he says he doesn't wear any more.

As we all pile into Aunt Rachel's car to go to the ferry, Mum runs back into the house to phone Dad and tell him what time to pick us up at the other end. George and Katy stand in the doorway ready to wave us off.

When Mum returns, the engine's already running. Mum quietly slides into the passenger seat. Aunt Rachel toots the horn, and pulls away, and we wave out the back window until we can't see George and Katy any more. The house looks enormous in the distance.

We trundle along, in silence, for about ten minutes, with Aunt Rachel turning to look at Mum every now and then, and Mum staring at the road ahead. Andy seems oblivious to the mood in the car, as he stares out the window, chewing the bubblegum that Katy gave him as we left.

"What is it?" Rachel whispers.

"Nothing," says Mum, with no expression in her voice.

"Mary? What is it? Did something happen with Billy when you phoned?"

"*Billy* didn't answer the phone. I didn't speak to him." They're both trying to keep their voices down but I can hear everything.

"So, who did answer then? Come on, Mary, it's clear

something's going on."

Aunt Rachel slows the car to a stop, as a pair of riders cross the country path ahead, going from one field to the next. The silence seems to expand the insides of the car, and the doggy smell of Ellie is stronger than ever. Griffin stands up at the window and lets out a little whine when he sees the horses trotting off along the field. The car starts moving again.

"Well?" says Aunt Rachel.

Finally, Mum speaks. "My new best friend, Gypsy. Gypsy answered Billy's phone. In Billy's flat."

The two of them sit in the front, stiff as statues, barely seeming to breathe.

"So, what did you say to her?" Rachel asks, turning to look at Mum again.

The car bumps and jostles along a rocky bit of road, and we all wobble and bounce in time with each other.

"Nothing," says Mum, as the road becomes smooth again. "I hung up. I heard her voice, and I panicked. I just hung up."

Neither of them say another word on the subject, until we reach the port.

Aunt Rachel helps us to unload our bags on to the pavement. "You need to phone me when you get back home, Mary. OK? Let me know how things are. Yes?" She's holding Mum by the shoulders, looking down into her face.

But Mum can't look up from the ground. Her body seems to have shrunk, and her shoulders are sloped and weak looking. Aunt Rachel slips me and Andy two quid each, and kisses us on the tops of our heads. I take as much of the luggage as I can and lug it towards the ferry as Aunt Rachel waves us off.

"What's up with Mum?" asks Andy, looking over his shoulder at her, a little way behind us. Her arms are folded and her face is a worried frown.

"Nothing, mate. She's fine. Just don't bug her on the ferry, alright? She's tired."

Andy nods, and looks back at Mum again, who seems unaware that we're even there. She's looking beyond us, appearing to scan the clear horizon for something we can't quite see. When we reach the passenger entrance, I hand the man our tickets and we board the ferry home.

Just as we're about to turn into our road, Mum tells the taxi driver she wants to stop off at the Royal Oak first.

"What're you doing?" I ask her, alarmed.

We pull up in the car park next to the pub and Mum gets out.

"You can turn round and wait here," she says to the driver, "and you boys, stay put."

As the taxi circles the car park and pulls up alongside the pub, I see Mum disappear through the front entrance. I jump out after her, telling Andy to look after the dog.

Inside the pub it's dark, and the outside sunlight seems to flood across Mum as she stands in the doorway with her hands on her hips. The shadow of her reaches across the dusty floor towards the bar. It's half past two, and most of the Sunday lunch-timers have made their way home. The only people left in the pub are Dad, Gypsy and Stu; and a few old men down the other end of the bar. Dad's leaning on the bar with his back to us, chatting to the landlady, and Stu and Gypsy sit in the lounge seats, with their backs to the bay window. When he notices Mum standing there, Stu smiles awkwardly. Gypsy looks shocked for a moment, then flashes her white teeth.

"Mary!" she cries. "You're back! Come and sit down with us – Billy's getting a last round in. Billy!"

Dad turns round, visibly shaken to see us standing there.

"Shit," he says, "did you ring me to pick you up? Shit. I completely forgot you were back today." He puts two pints and a glass of white wine on the table, and sits down next to Stu.

"No detox?" Mum asks Gypsy. "And no Greenham Common either?" Her body is rigid, and her face is white.

Gypsy smirks. "I had a better offer," she replies, turning to look at Stu like a tiger guarding its cub. Stu.

Mum looks at Dad, who shrugs. "Don't ask me," he says.

"So what was she doing at your flat, then?" I blurt out, unable to bear the tension any more. Everyone looks at me as if they've only just realised I'm here.

"You should ask your older brother about that, Jakey," Gypsy smiles at me. She's pissed. She looks all cocky and droopy-eyed, and her shirt has become unbuttoned one too many. In fact, it looks like a man's shirt.

"Matt?" My stomach clenches. "You mean Matt's been back?"

Mum's fingers feel for mine, and I don't know if it's because she needs support to stand up or that she just needs something to occupy her hands.

Gypsy snorts, her mask of friendliness slipping. "Oh, he's been back alright. Pissed as a fart, and climbing into my bed in the dead of night." She looks Mum right in the eye. "Horny little animal."

Mum lunges for Gypsy and Dad leaps up to grab her.

"Billy?" Mum's voice cracks, as he holds his arm around her and she regains her balance.

Dad looks at Gypsy, angry. "It wasn't like that, Gypsy, and you know it. He came back in the early hours without telling anyone – the night you all got the ferry. He'd had a skinful, and he obviously climbed into bed, his bed, and Gypsy was in it. Don't you go making out he's some kind of pervert, Gypsy; that's way out of line, and you know it."

Gypsy takes a drink from her glass, bats her eyelashes at him. "Sorry, Billy, you're right."

"Anyhow, love, the next day Gypsy came looking for me in here, for somewhere to stay for a night or two."

"Which is when I met laughing boy here," Gypsy croons, leaning her chest into Stu, kissing his ear.

Mum looks disgusted. "Come on, Jake, let's go and find your brother." She turns towards the door.

"Matt?" Dad calls after her. "Matt's gone, Mary. He took off almost as soon as he came, love." He looks tired and sad. "I didn't even see him, love. He just took off."

Mum's eyes fill with tears and she leaves the pub before they spill. I look back at Dad, but he's got his head down, running his finger across the wet table. Gypsy and Stu flirt and play fight with each other, giggling and laughing, unaware of Dad's pain as he sits there making patterns out of spilt beer.

Back home, Gypsy's keys are lying on the doormat where she posted them back through. Mum rushes up the stairs and I go straight into the kitchen to see what's what.

Matt's left all sorts of tracks that show he's been here, but they're cold. Like a fox's paw prints in the snow. He's left a dirty cereal bowl on the side in the kitchen, and a coffee mug. The dregs in it have dried solid, so you can tell it's been there for days. There's a used towel draped over the edge of the bath and dried vomit splashes in the basin, and the toothbrush mug lies smashed on the lino floor. He's taken most of the remaining clean clothes from his wardrobe, and dumped off a bin liner full of old ones in his room. There's no note, no sign that he's planning to come back.

I shut the bedroom door and start to unpack my bags, with Griffin following me about the room. When I pull down my Secret Literature money box to stash away Aunt Rachel's two quid, I find it empty. Fifty-two pounds and sixty-five pence. All gone.

Mary, May 1977

I've been trying to guess where we've been heading for the past hour and a half. Billy woke me this morning with a cup of tea, and told me we were going for a picnic once he'd dropped the kids at his mother's.

"You deserve a treat," he had said, throwing open the curtains, "so I've taken the day off. Happy?" I'd flinched against the bright May morning, feeling last night's wine throbbing behind my eyeballs.

Now, as we turn into the car park at Devil's Dyke, Billy puts his hand on my knee. "Happy birthday, darlin'." He kisses me briskly on the lips and gets out of the car.

Billy opens the boot of the car, and unloads the picnic stuff. I fumble in the glove compartment for my sunglasses, and get out to help him with the blanket and flasks that won't fit in the hamper.

"We had a basket just like that when I was little," I say, as Billy struggles with it on the walk up the hill. He's bought it especially for today.

"We didn't really do picnics much when I was little," Billy replies.

"I didn't know that about you, Billy. That's quite sad, really," I say.

"Well, you know Mum. She's never really been one for the great outdoors."

We walk on in silence as the view opens up before us, a calm warm breeze dusting around our clothing.

"It's perfect picnic weather, Billy." The clean air rushes into my lungs, exhilarating, fresh.

Billy spreads the blanket out, weighting the corners with the hamper and flasks. We lie, side by side, watching the birds and clouds float by overhead.

"See that jet stream?" Billy points to a wisp of hazy white cloud left in the wake of a faraway aeroplane. "Reminds me of smoking. Cigarettes. Mmmm." He turns and grins at me.

I tut, annoyed at the reminder. We both gave up in the New Year, after Matthew had kept on at us over Christmas. Sometimes, the craving's almost unbearable.

"I'd kill for one right now," I say, twisting a tassel of the blanket under my fingers. "Just one would do it."

Billy reaches into his hamper, and produces an unopened packet of Benson & Hedges.

"Billy!" I smile at him despite myself, rising on to my elbows.

He widens his big brown eyes. "We could just have one? It is your birthday, after all?" He leans over and kisses me, pulling a daft begging face.

I flop back against the woollen rug, defeated. I try not to respond, but find myself saying, "I suppose one wouldn't hurt. And, as you say, it is my birthday. Just one, OK? And then you'll throw the pack away?"

Billy nods, with a serious expression, then, magician-like, he produces a bottle of wine, two glasses and a corkscrew. We're all alone up on this hill, no one else to be seen. It's just Billy and me, here in the May breeze. Billy's hair flutters around his ears and I think how handsome he still looks. He passes me a glass of wine, and lights my cigarette for me. He raises his glass to my health, and we breathe deeply of our cigarettes, feeling the welcome toxin fill our lungs.

"Heaven!" I exhale, steadying my glass in the grass beside me. I lie back and enjoy the head rush through closed eyes.

"So, this is where your folks used to bring you, then?" Billy's hand brushes my leg as he lies back down beside me.

"Yes. About once a year we'd come up here for a picnic. My mother loved it. And Daddy too." I open my eyes, and see a bird of prey hovering in my eye-line, perhaps a kite, so still against the currents. It dips from view. "You know, it's been over ten years. Since I saw them. Since you met them that one time."

Billy's fingers find mine. "You never talk about them. Does it bother you? I mean, do you miss them?"

"Sometimes. Mostly not at all. But sometimes it feels like it matters. If your mum had been more welcoming it might have been better."

Billy lies quietly beside me. He rolls over to face my profile. "I know, darlin'. But we've got each other, and the kids." He watches me, and I close my eyes. He kisses my knuckles. "Haven't you ever been tempted to call them, or write?"

I sit up and take a deep drink of my wine. "I have. I've written to him every birthday and Christmas, and sometimes in between. For the past ten years." I carefully balance my glass in the imprint it's made in the grass.

Billy sits up too. "Your dad? You never told me." His voice sounds hurt.

"That's because he's never replied to any of my letters. Not even one."

Billy kisses my lips. "You've got me, Mary."

I smile and think about my last letter, posted yesterday, on the eve of my thirtieth birthday. As I stood at the post box, I'd wondered if they were remembering my birthday too, if I might find a card from them in the post this morning. But there was nothing.

"Why'd you just write to your dad?" Billy asks, topping up our wine. "And not your mum?"

"Because she'll never forgive me. Ever. But he would. Might. I don't know. Anyway. Let's forget about them. What've we got to eat?"

Billy lays the food out across the picnic blanket. He's bought all my favourite things. Smoked salmon sandwiches. Grapes and tomatoes. Little pots of chocolate mousse. Madeira cake.

"I got a bit of overtime last week," he explains, passing me another sandwich. He feels about in his jacket pocket, and pulls out a little package, wrapped in red tissue paper. "I hope it's OK."

Under the wrapping is a little black box, and inside the box is a silver pendant on a fine chain. The pendant is a trio of birds in flight, joined together by the tips of their wings. It's pretty and delicate.

"It's because of the boys. You know, to represent the

three boys. See, that one's Matthew, the middle one's Jake, and that's Andy at the end."

My eyes brim with tears, and I can't speak. Billy pulls me closer and fixes it round my neck.

"It's beautiful, Billy," I sniff, and he smiles so gratefully that I want to gather him up and hold him for ever.

But a dog walker passes beside us now, nodding good afternoon, so I squeeze Billy's thumb instead. Between us, we drain the last of the wine and pack up the hamper, before walking along the fields to look at the views of towns and villages nestling below. My fingers twirl at the pendant now resting against my collar bone.

"I wonder what happened with Rachel," I say, to myself as much as Billy.

Billy holds my hand. The sun bathes the grass in a milky light which ripples like the tide. The light is cast this way and that, making my eyes squint against the glare.

"You know what you need," says Billy, dropping the hamper at his feet. He starts to growl, low and teasing, then grabs me round the waist. "You know, don't you?"

"Billy! No!" I scream, and he drops me to the ground and tickles me rampantly, until my legs buckle and I'm merciless beneath his grip. I can't breathe now, and I lash out at him violently, until he falls away from me laughing like Sid James.

"Bastard!" I laugh, pushing him away with my toe.

"Whoa!" he yells, grabbing me to him in a bear hug, and we roll down the hill together as one being, bumping and crunching over thistles and snails, seeing the hill spiral by in a blur of sunshine. When we slow to a stop, we don't pull away. We remain in each other's arms, our eyes just inches apart, our hearts beating downwards towards calm.

"You'll see her again one day," says Billy, and he kisses my forehead and closes his eyes.

Jake, May 1985

Dad's making chicken curry, and the whole house smells of heat and spice.

"You go up and have a good soak in the bath, love, and I'll get on with the rice." He kisses Mum on the forehead, and pats her bum lightly as she walks away.

"Billy!" she whispers to him, trying not to smile, nodding her head in our direction.

Andy smirks behind his hand, and I pretend to be watching *Kung Fu* on TV.

"Ah, Glasshopper!" says Andy, slicing the air with martial arts hands.

"Ah, Master Po!" I say back to him, doing a karate kick in his direction.

He dodges, sniggering. "Velly good, Glasshopper. Velly good!"

"You doing poppadoms, Dad?" I call into the kitchen when Mum's gone.

"*D'accord*," he says, in a crap French accent. He's

been listening to these French learning tapes lately, so he's constantly showing off by dropping words into conversation. We haven't got a clue what he's on about most of the time.

"I'll take that as a yes, then," I call back to him.

He gives me the thumbs up through the steam in the kitchen. He's whistling away, wiping his hands on his apron, tasting the curry every now and then, before adding a pinch of this, a shake of that. The kitchen looks like a bombsite, with pots and pans piled up on all the surfaces. I turn back to the TV and see that Andy's watching Dad in the kitchen too.

"Dad?" Andy calls over. Dad looks up. "Dad, are you and Mum back together then?" Andy's grinning, because he knows it's a dodgy question.

Dad pauses over the pan, his wooden spoon in mid-air. He turns to Andy. "We'll see, son. We'll see."

Andy does a tiny air punch, where Dad can't see it. "Skill," he says. By rights, I should punch him, but I keep it to myself and concentrate hard on the telly, trying not to smile out loud.

Aphrodite was the most beautiful goddess of all, and when she wore her golden, jewelled girdle, no one could resist her beauty. Her son was Eros, and together they would fire their arrows of passion at everyone, melting their hearts with love.

Miss Terry is wearing a gold tank-top today, in keeping with the story. She paces about the classroom using a wooden ruler as an imaginary bow and arrow.

"In Greek mythology, the arrow is too often the messenger of death. But not here – how beautiful!

Imagine an arrow, with the power to intoxicate and captivate its victims. With love!" Miss Terry brings her fist to her chest, and raises the back of her other hand to her perfect forehead. With a sigh, she opens her eyes, claps her hands together and says, "Thank you class! See you next week!"

There's a little cheer, and everyone bundles for the door.

"Good work, Jake," Miss Terry says to me, touching my shoulder as I leave the classroom. "I still haven't decided which Greek character you are, so I think we'll call you Pan for now: son of Hermes." She smiles her mysterious smile, and turns back to tidying up her desk. "But I think I'm going to have to change it as I get to know you better. I'm not certain that Pan's quite right for you."

Pan. Pan: son of Hermes. It's got a ring to it. But I'm not sure it's right for me either.

When I finish my paper round one Saturday, Mr Horrocks asks me to stay behind. He's stacking headache tablets on the top shelf behind the counter.

"So, you'll be fourteen next week, Jake?"

"Yep. Fourteen. Four-teen."

Mr Horrocks beckons me to pass up more of the aspirin packets.

"So, I guess you'll be looking for a proper Saturday job, then?" He carries on stacking, not looking at me.

"Well, yeah, I s'pose so," I say. "I'm saving up for a midi system."

"And what's a midi system when it's at home?"

"You know. Like a stacking record player, with

cassette deck and amp and stuff. I did have over fifty quid, but—" I trail off.

"So, how'd you like to work here on Saturdays? It won't be dull, Jake. Something different every day. Some of the time, you'll be serving in the shop, but I've got other jobs I'd like you to do when it's quiet. Like the stockroom needs a damn good clear out, and the back wall could do with a lick of paint. You any good with a paintbrush, son?"

I shrug at him, imagining how it would be to have a regular job.

"And the pay's not bad. More than the paper round. You'd be able to give that up if you wanted, and still be better off."

"It'd be brilliant, Mr Horrocks," I say.

He climbs down from his stepladder and offers me his hand. "Best we shake on it, son. Good lad."

He goes to the till and pulls out my paper round money, and slips it into my hand along with a bar of Fruit 'n' Nut.

"Now then," he says as we walk towards the shop door, his hand on my shoulder. "Tell me about this Andy of yours. Think he'd be any good on the paper round? Looks like I've got a vacancy to fill."

"Seen anything of Stu lately?" Mum asks Dad one night when he's over again. He seems to be round most nights nowadays.

"Nah, not since that Gypsy came on the scene," he replies, as he peels a potato over the pedal bin. "And even when I do see him, he's all gooey-eyed, so there's no getting any sense out of him."

"Huh," huffs Mum. She's got her back to him as she washes up at the sink. Her new haircut skims the back of her neck, all shiny and healthy looking, and it sways heavily when she talks. Mum calls it a "Mary Quant" cut. "She's a slippery one, that Gypsy. I really thought we were friends, until she said that about Matthew. That – that was low."

Dad nods, carrying on with his peeling. "She always was a bit of a spoilt one, though, even when you were at college."

"But not like that, Bill."

"She's just a user, I guess. She's not really into Stu, you can tell – it's just a place for her to stay. I bet she's spent bloody years bed-hopping around the place, looking for new ways to live rent-free. Pretty smart if you ask me."

"Don't be such a chauvinist, Bill. If it was a man you wouldn't think anything of it, but when it's a woman, well, somehow it's different."

Dad looks up at Mum and shakes his head.

"She's a slapper, Mary. And she's no friend of yours, that's for sure. You haven't got a clue, have you?"

"What's that supposed to mean?" Mum says, pulling her rubber gloves off and dropping them on the side, looking annoyed.

Dad lowers his voice, leans in towards Mum. "She came on to me as soon as you were in the Isle of Wight. I knocked her back; and she moved straight on to Stu. She didn't even pause for breath. And she never gets her money out when he's around. He pays for everything."

Mum leans against the sink watching Dad finish the spuds. Her face is blank.

"You know what, Bill? I want my head examining.

Why can't I see these things coming, for God's sake? 'Soul mates', she called us. She said we were like sisters. And then she goes and tries it on with you the minute I'm out of sight. She fancied you like mad the first time she saw you, at college."

Dad laughs like he's quite pleased. "Did she?" He puts the last of the potatoes into the saucepan. "Well, you're best rid of her, aren't you, love? Anyway, she's not my type," he adds. "Bloody hippy!"

Mum laughs and flicks him with the tea towel, till he grabs her and steals a kiss on the lips. They wrestle like the teenagers you get mooning about down the park after school.

"What's for supper, Mum?" I shout over the back of my armchair, pretending I haven't been spying.

"Fish fingers and mash. It'll be half an hour yet, Jake. Have an apple if you're hungry." She folds up the tea towel and hangs it off the front of the oven. "You know, Billy, Gypsy's not even her real name. It's Jennifer. She thought Gypsy was more bohemian or something. At college, she hated it if anyone used her real name."

"Like I said," laughs Dad, "well rid."

Mary, June 1977

The street party runs in an L shape, all the way from the Royal Oak to the top of our road. The sun is up early, and it seems everyone is out, carrying tables and chairs and bowls of food from the different corners of the neighbourhood. The church has donated all the plastic furniture from the Village Hall, and the pub has dragged out the heavy wooden tables and stools. Mothers and friends rush in and out of houses to fetch extra tablecloths and more sandwiches. The children run wild, excited and boisterous. Apart from Andy, who's close at my heels, I haven't seen the boys for over an hour.

"Don't worry, love. I expect they're with my two," says Sandy, as I look for them. "You look nice, love," she says, between drags on her cigarette.

I smooth my hands over the front of my new white flares, pleased she noticed.

The roads are blocked off so no cars can drive up and down, which creates a kind of reckless abandon in even the smallest children. Andy spots another three year old rolling in the dust, and he throws himself down too. He's wearing his best trousers and shirt.

At midday, Eric the Landlord brings out his heavy bell, the one he uses to call time. He stands at the corner of the street, at the angle of the L, and rings it enthusiastically. All the children know that this is the sign to sit down to eat, and they come roaring down the streets and alleyways, whooping into their chairs, jostling for the best seats. Andy grabs my leg at the noise, and then squeals happily. I manage to find Jake at the other end of the table, with Sandy's older kids.

"Can I pop Andy in next to you, Jakey? Mummy's got to do the orange squash for everyone."

Jake nods and smiles. Both of his top teeth have fallen out over the past few weeks, and he looks like a rascal. I ruffle his hair and he helps Andy to pull his chair up to the table. Andy picks up a smiley face biscuit and presses it against Jake's forehead. Jake laughs and squeezes Andy's chubby cheeks between the palms of his hands.

"Boo-boo," he says, and then turns back to his plate.

I pick up a jug of squash and start at one end of the table, pouring half a cupful into the little white cups dotted along in neat rows. Way down at the other end of the table, Eric's thrown open the windows and doors of the pub, and the tinny sound of music drifts in the air. It sounds like Abba. A line of happy children stretches from me to the corner of the street. So many happy faces. When the drink runs out, I pick up another jug further down the table. A few minutes after all the other children have sat down, Matthew appears with a friend, looking flushed and sniggering. I don't even want to ask him what he's been up to. He looks more like Billy with every passing day. Billy's in the pub with Pete, having a pint, rewarding themselves for lugging the furniture about. He said he'll come and help after a bit of a sit down. We'll see. Matthew and his pal are roaming around the table picking off the best cakes and biscuits. Sit down, I signal to him with a flick of my hand. He smiles through a mouthful of chocolate roll, then shoves in a bit more before sliding into the seat opposite Jake and Andy.

Sandy calls to me from across the table. She's been doing the drinks from the other end. "We need refills, love. Can you get them from your house as it's closest?"

I gather the bottles of squash and empty jugs and jog along to the house. This end of the street is deserted. The quiet is unsettling. As I push open the front door, it catches on the afternoon post piled on the doormat. I put the jugs and bottles down in the kitchen, then pick up the letters. Two of them are for Billy, and the third is a small handwritten parcel, the size of a paperback. The postcode is Brighton, and Mother's handwriting in unmistakable. I feel the blood drain from my face. My hands are trembling as I pull the contents from the packet.

Ten years of unopened birthday cards and letters spill across the kitchen worktop. There's no covering note, no explanation. The shock washes over me like ice. Mechanically, I fill the squash jugs, my heart slowing to a buzz. I lean against the sink, groaning with loss; she has closed all the doors. I know now that this isn't just another of her episodes, one that she'll simply snap out of. The four jugs sit side by side in my dreary kitchen, facing me like sentries.

Still shaking, I cross the living room and dial Rachel's

number from memory, for the first time in seven years. She answers on the third ring.

"Rachel?" My voice is close to crying.

There's a moment of silence, before she says, "Sorry, you've got the wrong number," and hangs up.

I rush to the sink and vomit, my stomach heaving and hollow.

"Why did you leave me, Rachel?" I cry, as I slip to the kitchen floor. "Why did you leave me?" My sobs come now in lurching great waves, wracking and painful. There's no one to hear, and I wail and pound the grubby lino with grief.

When Sandy comes, I've drunk several tumblers of whisky, to calm my nerves. I'm half asleep when she bangs on the door, and I open it without looking up.

"Mary, love, what happened? It's an hour since you went off for drinks. Them kids are parched out there!"

I walk carefully into the kitchen so she won't see I'm wobbly, and turn on the tap to rinse away the sick.

"Ten years," I say, thrusting the bundle of letters at her chest. I push shut the drinks cabinet above the cooker. Click-clack.

"You're slurring, love," Sandy says, her eyes pausing over the empty whisky bottle. She turns the letters over in her hands, frowning as she tries to make sense of them.

"One mistake. And I'm out of their lives for ever. One mistake!"

Sandy shakes her head and embraces me. She rocks me like a child, "Shh, shh, shh, shh," kissing the top of my head, brushing the hair from my face.

I breathe in her cheap perfume and lean on her heavily.

I'm so tired. If I could just sleep, it would all be better.

"You've got to make your own family now, Mary, love. And you've got your friends. Like me. And Pete. We're your family."

I sob against her shoulder. "But it's not the same, Sandy. It's not the same."

It's not the same.

Jake, May 1985

On my birthday I wake up just after six. The birds at the back of the house are making a racket, and I open up my curtains just enough to get a look without scaring them off. They look like house martins to me. This one bird lands on the wire of the nearby telegraph pole. It turns its head, chirps a bit, then flies quick as a flash back towards the house to disappear near my window. They must be nesting in the roof. The sun's starting to shine up through the distant silhouettes of houses and buildings, far beyond the yard and alleyway that runs along the back of our place. It looks like it's going to be a nice day. I crawl back under my warm covers and drift off again, until Andy comes bounding in at seven.

"Happy birthday to you – Happy birthday to you – Happy birthday dear Ja-ake – Happy birthday to you!" He's dancing in the doorway, wiggling his hips from side to side with each word and pointing his fingers in the air like guns. He looks like some demented Milky Bar Kid.

He runs back out and returns with a boxy-shaped parcel in his hands, wrapped in brown paper, with little dogs hand-drawn all over.

"I made the wrapping paper myself – that's meant to be Griffin." He sits on the end of my bed with one knee up, one leg dangling down, waiting for me to unwrap it. "I bought it myself," he says. "Go on, then!"

It's a packet of five C90 Memorex blank cassette tapes.

"For when you get your midi system," says Andy, looking hopeful.

"That's brilliant," I say. I'm quite impressed by his excellent choice. "I'll need loads of these when I get my midi system, won't I? This'll get me started though. Might even make you a tape if you're lucky."

I can hear kitchen noises downstairs; Mum's making tea. Andy can see I'm in a good mood, and lies back on the bed with his hands behind his head. I'm propped up on my elbows deciding whether to let him get away with it just this once, when Mum comes in with my tea. She leans over and gives me a kiss, as she puts the mug on my bedside table, along with two envelopes that must've come through the post yesterday.

I rip open the first one, which is A4 sized and interesting looking. It's from George, and it's a birthday card and a brand new *Melody Maker* magazine. Inside the card, he's written 'Peace, man' and 'Power to the MUSIC!' I feel really bad that I didn't even send him a card; I mean, his birthday's on the same day as mine. How hard is that to remember?

The second card is from the Midland bank, who I've got a young saver's account with. It's got a yellow griffin on the front, and the message inside is printed, not handwritten.

There's nothing from Matthew.

"Right then, Birthday Boy," says Mum, after she's watched me open my cards. "We've got to get ourselves up, dressed and ready. We've got lots to do today."

I frown at her. "Like what? It's my birthday. I thought we were just hanging around here today?"

She smiles, collecting up my dirty clothes as she talks. "Your dad will be here in an hour. We're going out for the day." She's standing in the doorway, looking at me and Andy with our bed hair and matching stripy pyjamas, sprawled out on the tangle of covers.

"Together?" asks Andy.

"Yes," says Mum, picking up one last sock that's got wedged behind the door. "Together. And if you pull your fingers out, we might even get there today."

"Skill!" says Andy, doing the air punch.

I can't let him get away with that, even if it is my birthday, so I give him a dead-leg and he limps from the room shaking his fist at me.

"Why, I oughta . . ." he drawls in a crappy John Wayne accent.

I pretend to go for him again and he runs off down the hall and slams his bedroom door behind him. I grab my jeans and my black George sweatshirt and start to get dressed.

The train to Brighton takes over an hour, but it goes all the way without us having to change. At each stop, Andy presses his face against the window, trying to spot the sign that tells us where we are.

"Is that a real castle?" asks Andy, with his hands flat to the glass.

A castle rises up in the distance, surrounded by a valley of mist. Cows graze in the fields nearby, and it seems we've suddenly gone back in time.

"Arundel," says Dad. "Goes back to William the Conquerer if I remember my history. Went there on a school trip about thirty years ago." He grins at me sitting opposite.

"So, would there have been real battles then?" Andy goes on.

"Of course. It's been rebuilt a few times over the years. That would've been a bugger of a job, lugging all that stone into place without any machinery. And they wouldn't have had a spirit level then, either. Bet it was cheap labour, though. Just a bunch of peasants and slaves, probably."

The castle disappears from view, and the train stops to pick up a single passenger on Arundel station. She's about a hundred and she walks at a snail's pace, getting into one of the carriages further down. She's just the kind of person you'd expect to live in a place like Arundel, with her little knitted hat and knobbly walking stick. I wonder where a little old lady like that would be going on her own. Maybe she's going to Brighton too.

As we get further away from home, the place names get softer sounding, more seasidey. Goring-by-Sea; West Worthing; Worthing; Shoreham-by-Sea; Portslade-by-Sea; Hove. Somehow, the light of the sky looks different too; wider, brighter, and more of it.

"OK, put your coats on," says Mum at Hove. "We'll be in Brighton in a couple of minutes." She's already got her jacket buttoned up, bag held on her lap, perched to jump off the train as soon as we stop.

Dad's just wearing a T-shirt, with a sweatshirt in his hand. He's smiling at Mum, who's sitting next to me, looking out the window. We slow down to a final stop in Brighton, pulling into this huge, domed Victorian station, with pigeons flying about in the rafters and hundreds of people milling about on the many platforms.

"OK, got your tickets? Andy? Jake?" Mum's eyebrows are knitted in a frown.

We wave them at her.

"Stick together until we get out of the station," she says. "It's busy, we don't want to get separated."

Dad winks at me with a smile, and Mum takes Andy's hand and leads the way, marching ahead briskly. Andy looks over his shoulder at us, and I pull a disgusted face at the hand-holding, and he drops Mum's hand like a hot rock. She pinches a piece of his jacket and holds on to that instead. Before we get out of the station, Dad insists that we all get our photos taken in the little booth near the exit. He says we have to do two serious faces, and then two daft ones if we want. I ask him what he wants them for, and he says, "Never you mind." We emerge from the station, into startling light, and the air is filled with the sounds of buses and seagulls. I'm used to seagulls down our way, but this is something else. This is deafening, and constant. It even smells like you'd expect Brighton to smell. Like sea foam and vinegar.

We walk down the Queen's Road, heading straight for the sea. As you get further down the sloping road, the buildings seem to open out, revealing the horizon ahead. The smell of fish and chips is mouth-watering, and the gulls get louder and louder, the closer we get to the beach.

"I can't believe we've never been here before," I say, eyeing up the amusement arcades that flash and chime as we pass.

"You have," replies Mum. "When you were tiny."

"And me?" asks Andy.

"No, I was expecting you at the time."

"What did we do when we came here before?" I ask, looking at Dad.

"Dunno, son," he answers. "I wasn't with you. So! Brighton seafront! Whaddya wanna do first?"

Andy's already climbing on the railings along the front, spinning himself over and back again. There are two piers, one to the left that's alive and buzzing with people and lights, and one to the right which sits quietly on the water, crumbling and deserted.

"That's the West Pier," says Mum. "You can't go on it now, but we used to when we were kids. Before it disintegrated – became a danger, I suppose. It's a shame; such a beautiful thing, left to decay like that."

It's still a beautiful thing, from here, proudly rising out of the calm water. It seems to be the opposite of the other pier, the Palace Pier, with its flashing lights and crowds of holidaymakers.

But still, I can't wait to get on to the Palace Pier and poke about. Near the pier entrance, Dad stops to buy four portions of fish and chips, and we drown them in salt and vinegar, before heading down to the beach to eat them in the sunshine.

"We'll go on to the pier to get pudding," he says, mopping up some salt with a chubby chip.

"Mmmm, pudding!" says Andy, in one of his stupid voices.

"Oh, I know what pudding your dad's talking about," laughs Mum, as she sits beside him on the mound of rolled pebbles, facing the sea. "I guess I can forget my figure for a day."

"There's nothing wrong with your figure, you minx," says Dad, making a grab for her waist.

Mum squeals, catching her chips, stopping them from tumbling from her lap. She gives him one of her looks.

"Urghh," I say, looking at Dad, "not when I'm eating. You'll put me off."

Dad laughs and carries on with his chips.

"Look at that!" says Andy, holding up one of his chips. "That has to be the biggest chip I've ever seen. Look! Jake! It's massive!" It looks like a saveloy, it's that big.

He rolls his head back, and dangles it over his mouth, folding it in slowly, until it's all gone. His cheeks bulge as he chews it with difficulty, smirking all the time.

"'licious," he says halfway through, his cheeks red with the effort.

We all laugh, as he struggles to swallow the monster chip. A scruffy-looking man and his dog are walking along the water's edge. We're all sitting here, watching the dog bounce in and out of the water, and Andy's still chewing away with his fat cheeks, when the dog bounds up the stones, sticks his nose straight into Andy's chip paper, and grabs what's left of the fish before making a run for it. He runs way off down the beach, before his owner even sees what's happened, then stoops down to enjoy his unexpected feast.

Andy's mouth is hanging open like a cartoon. He looks

down at his chips, back up towards the dog down by the water, then over to us. Our eyes meet and suddenly we're all laughing – me, Andy, Mum, Dad, rolling about on the stones with tears running down our faces.

"*Le chien, il a faim*," says Dad, as we all calm down again.

"*Zut alors!*" I blurt out. I just learnt it at school.

Mum and Dad turn and look at me, and we're all laughing again, what's left of our chips lying abandoned beside us, the paper fluttering in the breeze.

After we dump our chip wrappers in the bin, we go back up the beach and climb the stone steps towards the pier. There are people everywhere, of every nationality, wandering about with ice creams and sun hats. You can tell the people who live here, because they carry on walking, uninterested in the flashing lights of the pier entrance, dressed in everyday clothes with no backpacks. I guess we must seem to be somewhere in between.

Dad heads straight for the hot doughnut stand, where he hands over one pound for ten doughnuts. The doughnut man cooks them right there in front of us, plopping the dough mix straight into the fat, already in the shape of a ring. They fry quickly in turn, fizzle sizzle, and he whips them out, tossing them in sugar and into a paper bag. The smell is unique, of battered sugar and heat. We reach the end of the pier, eating our hot doughnuts and leaning on the rail gazing out to sea. No one talks as we enjoy the sweet doughiness of our pudding. There are a few small boats out on the water, and the sunlight bobs over the ripples.

Dad hands me an envelope.

"It's from both of us," he says. "From your mum and me."

I rip it open. The card isn't one of those "son" cards or the ones with your age on, but a tasteful one, with a picture of a boy running across the countryside with his dog. If Dad had chosen it, it would've been a football picture or a racing car. Inside there are two tenners, and the writing says, "Towards your record player."

"I hope you don't mind that it's money, Jakey," says Mum, leaning out over the railings to see past Dad. "I didn't want to choose the wrong thing, and I know you're saving. You must have nearly enough by now?"

I nod, thinking about the day I found my money box cleaned out. I smile back at Mum, and squeeze her hand as she reaches it across.

"It's brilliant, just what I wanted. I want a really good midi system, so I'll save a bit longer. But this really helps."

For a while, there's no need to talk, and we look across the water as the seagulls screech about overhead. Dad turns round, leaning his back against the railings. Mum looks up at him and he nods, taking her hand in his.

"So, boys," he says in a cautious voice.

We turn to face him. Andy looks terrified.

"How'd you like me to move back home?" The pair of them stand there waiting for us to answer.

Andy bursts into tears and buries his head in Mum's chest to hide his face. She rocks him, kissing the top of his head. I feel slightly queasy from all the doughnuts.

"Jake?" says Dad.

"That's brilliant, Dad," I say, trying not to show just how pleased I am. "Brilliant." I can't help it, and a big

232

smile breaks through.

Dad grabs me in a bear hug, taking my breath away, engulfing me in his strong arms. I can smell the clean sweat of his chest mixed with chips and doughnuts and sea spray, and my heart thumps in my own chest as Mum smiles over Andy's head.

"Happy birthday, Jakey," she says, and I swallow hard to dislodge the lump that's risen in my throat. I'm fourteen for God's sake. I swipe away the wet of my eyes, and break away from Dad.

"OK," says Dad, fumbling about in his pocket. "We've got a pound each." He counts out the coins into our open palms. "Whoever wins the most off the slot machines gets to buy the ice creams on the way home!"

Andy runs off towards the blinking lights and thumping sounds of the arcade. Mum and Dad wander along hand in hand, looking into each other's faces from time to time. Mum looks quiet and happy; Dad looks tall and proud. I run after Andy to hear one of the arcade men at the entrance telling him he can't go in there on his own.

"It's alright," I say, pulling myself up to my tallest height, putting my arm round Andy's shoulders. "I'm fourteen."

The arcade man steps aside, nodding for us to go in.

When I pick up Griffin after our day out, Mr Horrocks asks me to come up to his flat for a minute. I've never been up there before, and I'm intrigued to see what it's like.

At the top of the stairs I can see how tiny it is; there seems to be a little kitchen, bathroom and bedroom all off the landing, with a sitting room at the front. Mr Horrocks leads me straight into the front room. It's just how you'd expect, with two of those upright armchairs in a flowery print, and a dark brown display cabinet and coffee table. There's a fake fireplace, and the TV sits on a shelf built into the wall. Griffin runs circles around my feet, begging to be picked up.

"Sit down, son," Mr Horrocks says, reaching for a big book that's lying on the coffee table. "Now, I know it's your birthday, and you're into all sorts of modern stuff that fourteen-year-old boys want, but I thought you might quite like this."

The book is large and old, with a dark green cover and faded gold edging. The bold lettering of the title is intertwined with curling vine leaves and dark grapes. *Greek Mythology for Boys.*

"I thought I might have a son one day, but it never happened. Mrs Horrocks and I weren't blessed that way. And I always loved the Greek stories. I've heard you talk about your Classics lessons, son, so I thought you'd like it."

He hands the book over to me, and I hold it on my lap for a moment, feeling the weight of it. As I turn the pages, beautiful full page illustrations leap out at me, with scripted descriptions beneath them: *Odysseus meets the Cyclops*; *The Wooden Horse of Troy*; *Atalanta and the Golden Apples*. It's the best book I've ever seen.

"To borrow?" I ask.

"To keep, Jake. As a birthday present."

I close the cover, stroking my finger along the gold lettering, imagining it on my bookshelf at home.

"Mr Horrocks, I . . ."

He puts his hand on my shoulder and squeezes it. "Mrs Horrocks kept telling me I should let you have it.

And your birthday seems as good a time as any, son. So it's from both of us really." He stands from his armchair. "Right then, let's find Griffin's lead, shall we? You'd better take some dog food while you're at it. Your mum'll wonder where you've got to."

At the shop door, I try to thank Mr Horrocks for the book again, but he shakes his head and pats me on the back.

"Happy birthday, son. So, we'll see you next Saturday for your first day in the shop?"

I nod and wave him goodbye as he locks up the shop behind me. It's dark now, and as I walk through the quiet streets with Griffin by my side and Mr Horrocks' book under my arm, I think about home. The home where me and my mum and my dad and my brother all live. Together.

Mary, September 1978

9.10 a.m. The house is so still. This morning, as I walked away from the school gates, little Andy looked over his shoulder at me and waved. So confident; so unlike the other two on their first day. His legs looked tiny, still hanging on to a ghost of toddler chub, rounding at the calves, pinched in by short grey socks. There was still a hint of summer in the morning sky, and the sun caught his darkening hair like a halo. Matthew and Jake didn't even look back today; they just marched into their classrooms in line, already slaves to the routine.

The breakfast pots pile beside the sink, and now I have all this spare time to be more efficient around the house. I could clean, uninterrupted for hours, and still have time for a cup of tea and a magazine. If I wanted. But to reach for the taps, to fill the sink, to wash up seems impossible, and I stare into the spaces, battling with the options. I'd feel better if I just got on with it. If I just do it now, I can relax later. The boys would love a home-cooked meal

after school. But I know I'll give them cheese on toast.
Or burgers in a bun. If Jake wasn't so fussy . . . but they
all want something different. At least I know they'll all eat
cheese on toast. I try to imagine what Rachel's kids might
eat when they get home from school. Casseroles and roasts
and vegetables and fruit pies and pavlovas. Sandwiches
and scones at high tea. The pain of her absence doubles
me over and I blink at the peeling corner of kitchen lino
as I clutch my chest, feeling the heart inside pumping too
fast. I sob for my Rachel, who took me into her bed when
I dreamed of the creature inside the light bulb, Rachel
who discreetly took me to the nurse for dry knickers on
my first day of school, Rachel who understood the world,
and left before I understood it too. Eight years. The lino
is maddening. That corner pokes up at the edges of my
vision, and I try to ignore it, but it's always there. I tug at
it, and it lifts easily, like a heavy label from a plastic bottle.
A colony of silverfish swarm and scatter, blown this way
and that by the brightness of light. I have to back out of
the room now, just to keep pulling, hearing the edges pop
out from under the kitchen units. But the last corner just
won't come. I'm sweating now, yanking and cursing at it,
but the heavy weight of the fridge holds it captive. As I let
go, it coils away, slapping back against the concrete floor
like a dropped snake.

In the boys' room, I smell Andy's earthy softness as I
curl up on his bed. His cuggy-bear pokes an ear out of the
unmade bedclothes. I rub the ear between my forefinger
and thumb, in the way that Andy does when he's dropping
off, and I recognise the rhythmic pleasure of the action.
The silky edges run into the balding rough centre of the
ear, rough then smooth, rough then smooth. It's soothing

and unsettling, all at once. Jake's bed is opposite, the bedclothes pulled straight, smoothed down at the edges, the pillow plumped. Who showed him that? Perhaps it was me. But he's only seven. His soft toys have all been put to bed, each little head visible above the neatly folded sheet top. Monkey, Big Ted, Donkey, Alberto, Blanky. Matthew teases Jake that Blanky is just an old rag, but Jake calls it "he" and "him" as if it has a life of its own.

The ring of the phone shocks me, and I'm caught, lying here, not doing the things that a mother at home should do. I leap off the bed and dash down the stairs to catch the phone on the fifth ring.

"Mary, sweetheart, it's me." I can hear Sandy exhaling her cigarette smoke as she speaks.

"Sandy!" My heart's thumping in my shirt.

"Hello, love. So? How's your first day of freedom? Feels good, doesn't it?"

"It's weird, to be honest. Quiet. What are you up to?" The telephone needs a good clean, there's dirt and dust caught up in each of the number holes.

"Not much. I take it Billy's at work? I was thinking, how about you and me go out for lunch and a drink. Just a little celebration, now all the boys are at school. What d'you think? I could call for you at twelve, and we'll go down the Oak for scampi 'n' chips. And a G and T? How about it, love?"

I pause, running my hands through my hair, trying to see my reflection in the glass of the living room window. "I'm not sure, Sandy. I mean, I'll have to pick them up just after three o'clock. And the house is a state."

"Live a little!" she shouts, coughing up her cigarette. "Come on, love, an hour can't kill you, can it?"

I pause, still uncertain. It doesn't seem right.

"Mary? I'm not taking no for an answer. I'll call for you at twelve. See you then, sweetheart."

I hang up, and straighten the curtains beside the telephone, pushing the notepad and pen pot to the edges of the window sill so that they're at straight angles.

Lovely Sandy. The first time we met she said, "God, you're posh, aren't you? Well, I don't mind that. You're alright, you are." And that was that.

The clock says ten, and I get to work with the Hoover. I press it into every corner, even moving furniture to get underneath. When I enter the kitchen, the sight of the rolled-back lino startles me, and I scrabble around on my hands and knees, trying to ease it back into the corners. But of course it won't go back. There are blisters and dips where I tugged and twisted it. I run the bubbles high in the sink, and speed through the breakfast dishes, and wash down the surfaces. I think about a cup of tea, but I don't really have time. The twin tub ran a wash last night. I spin it and put it into the laundry basket, opening the back door to check the sky. It's still clear and bright, with a gentle breeze. The washing line runs diagonally across the small courtyard, to make the most drying space. I select the items of laundry carefully, hanging them from small to large; smallest close to the house, largest at the furthest end of the line. That usually means it goes Andy's, Jake's, Matthew's, mine, then Billy's things. Today, the clothes fit exactly from one end to the other, with not a space remaining, not an item left over. I stand back, admiring my handiwork. With luck, they'll be dry by teatime.

By the time I've bleached the loo and straightened the beds, I've got half an hour before Sandy arrives. I open my wardrobe, and search through the contents. I pull out an old minidress, hold it up, put it back. It's just lunch. My white slacks should do, with my favourite silk ruffle shirt, sunset orange. I stand in front of the wardrobe mirror and brush my long dark hair. "Hair of a goddess", Billy once described it when we first met. "My goddess," he'd said proudly. If I brush it one hundred times, it still shines heavy and sleek, all the way down my back. "It needs a bloody good cut," he said last week when I asked if I should wear it up or down. He laughed, like it was a good joke.

I pick out some chunky bangles and poppet beads and study my reflection from different angles, trying to catch how others might see me. The doorbell rings. "You'll do," I say to the woman in the mirror, and I run down the stairs to let Sandy in.

Jake, June 1985

For the summer term parents' evening, the teachers encourage both parents to come along with their child, so it can be a 'two-way dialogue'. We've never managed both parents yet, but still, it's usually an embarrassing few hours, listening to the teachers talk about you like you're not there.

"Do I look alright?" asks Mum, as we're all getting ready to leave. She's wearing a skirt and a white blouse.

"You look like a secretary," I say.

"He's right," says Dad, barely looking up, his foot up on the armchair as he ties his laces.

"Well, I don't know what I'm meant to wear! I want us to make a good impression. It's important, Jake, now that we're all back together. We've got to take this seriously." She runs up the stairs in her bare feet, and we hear her rummaging about in her bedroom.

Dad looks over at me. "She missed the last one, didn't she? She's just a bit nervous."

I'm still in my school uniform, so all I need to do is wash my hands and face, and check there's nothing spilt down the front of my shirt. All fine.

Andy's school has theirs on a different day, so after tea he goes off to Ronny's and we set off for the school. Mum settled for trousers with the white shirt, which is more her, and Dad has gone the whole hog and put his grey suit on. He's only got one suit, and it does him for funerals, weddings, christenings, and now, parents' evenings.

"You look nice, love," says Dad, as he pulls the door shut behind us. Mum doesn't seem to hear.

"So, Jakey, anything we need to know about before we get there?" she asks.

"Like what?" I say, thinking it's some kind of trick question.

"You know, things that are going well, things that are not so good. Any trouble you've had. I just want to be prepared."

I think hard. School's just a place I go to each day, in between home and holidays. I've never really given it much thought.

"No, it's all fine," I reply. "I can't think of anything special."

"That's good," she says, looking into the distance.

The walk to school takes about ten minutes, and when we get to the gates, Mum pulls out her appointment slip to double check the time. We're twenty minutes early, and we follow the arrows that point to the gym, where the teachers are set up behind single tables, piled with report cards and pencils and pads. Each table has a sign along the front showing the teacher's name and subject. You can still hear the squeak of plimsolls on the gym floor, and smell the sweat of decades of school kids. The ropes are secured against the monkey bars along the wall, and all the benches and equipment have been cleared away. The gym is a hive of noise, as parents and kids wander about, looking for their next teacher and checking their watches. They all carry different expressions: worried, amused, annoyed, beaming with pride, bored. One girl I see is crying into her hanky. I don't know why; it's Sally Jones and she usually gets A's for everything. Maybe she just found out she got a B.

You have to start off with your form tutor, then carry on round the gym, through all your subject teachers in the order given on the appointment slip.

"We've got time to kill," says Dad. "Let's go round and work out where all your teachers are now. Save time later."

"There's no rush, Bill," says Mum. "We've got plenty of time."

"Still, won't hurt," he says. He marches ahead of us, scribbling on the card as he finds the teachers on the list. Mr Thomas: row 3, 2 down. Miss Terry: row 5, top.

Mum's starting to look distracted, and she keeps checking her watch to make sure we're not late for the first appointment.

"I think we should make our way over to Mr Thomas, now," she says. "It's five minutes to five."

Dad nods, consults his list, and leads the way. Looks like his system works.

When we get to Mr Thomas, there are three families ahead of us in the line. The woman in front must be Edward Hampton's mum, because he's standing next to her looking really grumpy. He nods at me, and I nod back.

"What's the delay?" Dad asks her.

"Oh, they always keep you waiting at these things," Mrs Hampton replies. "We'll be lucky to get out of here before midnight!" She smiles at Dad in a twinkling way, then sees Mum nodding, and turns away, flustered.

Edward's got his hands deep in his pockets, his shoulders slumped forwards. He's usually in trouble, so I guess he's not looking forward to this.

"I need the loo," says Mum, suddenly. Her face is a bit shiny, and she looks really agitated. "Where do I go, Jake?"

I look around the gym, and see that they've put up handwritten "Ladies" and "Gents" signs, pointing into the changing rooms.

"Over there, Mum. It's the girls' changing rooms. Want me to come over and wait for you?"

She shakes her head, and disappears through the crowd, clutching her handbag.

By the time we get to Mr Thomas, we've been in the queue for fifteen minutes. Dad's frowning and Mum is daydreaming when he calls us up.

"So," he says, gesturing for us to take a seat. "So, Jake." He sifts through his papers, then looks up over his half moon glasses, eyeing first me, then Mum, then Dad. "Nice lad. Quiet. Never gives us a moment's trouble. Seems to get on with all the other pupils, doesn't appear to be in with any particular group. Which isn't a bad thing. But his work, in general, is unremarkable."

Mum and Dad look at each other, slightly confused. "Go on," says Dad.

"Well," says Mr Thomas, taking his glasses off altogether. His eyes look really old and crêpey. "I can tell he's a bright lad. And he's very articulate if you get into one to one conversation. But he's a dreamer, off in his own world a lot of the time. And I'm afraid it shows in his marks. Mostly C's, a smattering of D's."

My throat's gone dry, as I realise how this evening's going to go.

"However, he does perform well in two areas: Classics and Art. Miss Terry has written a glowing report on Jake's performance in her Classics classes, where it would seem he's her star pupil." He smiles at me, and I blush hotly. "And Art. Well, yes, very good."

"What about music?" asks Dad. "He's very keen on music."

"D," says Mr Thomas.

"Woodwork?"

"C."

We finish with Mr Thomas and rise to leave.

"Nice lad, though," he says, and he shakes my dad by the hand.

We walk away, and I'm waiting for someone else to speak first. In the end it's me who breaks the silence.

"Can we get a drink? The PTA's selling drinks down at the front of the gym. And biscuits."

Dad nods, and we go over and get coffee for them, squash and a shortbread biscuit for me.

"So, Maths next," says Dad, after we've finished our drinks in a bubble of quiet, and we head off to the top end of the gym for my next humiliation.

About an hour in, we arrive at Miss Terry's table. Classics and English, her label says, although I only have her for Classics. She leaps up and invites us to sit down. She looks pink-cheeked, like she does when she's talking about something really exciting in class, like the slaying of the Minotaur or the fearsome Gorgons.

"Mr and Mrs Andrews, lovely to meet you at last. Hello, Jake." She seems much more grown up than usual, and her fingers fiddle with the pencil on the table in front of her. "What can I tell you about Jake? Well, he's my top pupil, straight A's all the way through the year. He seems to love the subject, and his essays have been so mature, so insightful, that at times it's a wonder he's only thirteen."

"Fourteen," I correct her. I can barely meet her eyes, and I concentrate on the sign that hangs off the front of the table, flicking at the corner of it with my fingernail.

"Oh. Of course, fourteen. Anyway, I've brought some of his coursework along to show you. Look at these beautiful illustrations. He just always goes the extra mile." She smiles at me proudly, and her green eyes blink heavily, once, in slow motion.

"But he's all C's and D's in everything else," says Dad.

"Well, I find it hard to believe. Jake's got a lot of potential as far as I can see. And he's a lovely boy. You should be very proud." She doesn't look at me, but keeps her eyes fixed on Mum and Dad.

"We are," says Mum, her eyes welling up.

I grab her sleeve to leave, before she embarrasses me. Dad gives Miss Terry a broad, white smile and shakes her hand, which seems to get her a bit flustered. I'm sure she's blushing. She smiles back at Dad, then at Mum.

"I can see why you do so well in that lesson, Jakey boy," he says, conspiratorially, nudging me as we go.

I warn him off with a stare, and fight the redness creeping up my face. "Dirty old git," I mutter back.

He pokes me in the ribs and makes me yell, so that Mum has to glare at us both as we head for the exit. When we get outside we laugh like kids who've been thrown out of class. I've almost forgotten about all of the crap stuff we've just heard about my school work.

"So, how d'you think that went then, Jakey?" asks Dad, as we walk back towards home.

"Dunno," I answer, head down, kicking at a stone along the path.

Mum puts her arm round my shoulder. "You're doing fine, darling," she says. "Every one of those teachers said you were a nice boy, and that's worth more than a hundred straight A's in my book. And it looks like you take after me, with Art."

"Were you good at Art?" I ask. I've never seen her draw or paint at home.

"Used to be," she smiles, wistfully. "Once upon a time."

"But you could do better, in your academic subjects, Jake," says Dad. "Art's not going to get you a job, after all."

Mum ignores him, and squeezes my shoulder.

"Do what you like, Jake. Follow your heart. And don't let anyone sway you off course. You're a fine boy. A fine, fine boy."

Dad looks away, and we walk the rest of the way home in silence.

I've got this Saturday off work, and I'm going into town with Mum and Dad to buy my midi system. Andy's got another Scout day, so it's just me and them. He's trying to earn his 'Citizenship' badge, whatever that is. As they finish up their breakfast downstairs, I'm getting dressed, pulling on George's black top, as it's the only piece of cool clothing I own. I kneel at the bed and open up my Secret Literature money box, carefully counting out the notes and coins inside, before transferring them into my wallet. I've easily got enough for a decent system, plus a couple of albums. Might even have enough for a new T-shirt if I'm lucky. I push the empty money box back into its new hiding place behind the chest of drawers.

"Come on, Jake, darling. Let's get going!" Mum calls me from the bottom of the stairs, and I hurry down to join them as they go out the front door into the bright June sunshine.

On the walk into town Dad tells me about some of the bands he used to listen to when he was my age.

"Of course, music didn't really come to life until the late fifties – but that was my time. Can you imagine it, a young man on the brink of independence – and rock 'n' roll explodes out of nowhere! Kids used to listen to what their parents listened to before then. And it was all up from there – Buddy Holly and the Crickets, the Stones. Used to head up to London as much as we could, me and a couple of mates, trying to get into the music clubs around town. The buzz! It was another world back then. Of course, that's where I met your mum, London."

He puts his hand on the small of her back, and she smiles at me.

"Who was it you used to listen to all the time, love?"

"Joni Mitchell?"

"Joni Mitchell, that's it. Real hippy stuff. But still, not bad." Dad stuffs his hands into his pockets, with a distant look on his face.

"George reckons Dixons might be a good place to find a midi system," I say.

"Yep, well let's shop around a bit before we decide? You want to get the best value."

Town's only a twenty-minute walk from home, and when we get there Mum says she could do with a cup of tea before we start shopping. I'm itching to get going, but she says I can choose a cake if I'm patient.

We go into the Baker's Dozen, and find a seat near the window. Dad gives Mum a fiver, and she queues up for our drinks. I look out of the window to Currys across the road, hoping we'll have enough time to find my midi system. At that moment, Malcolm and Stu come round the corner, straight through the door of the Baker's Dozen.

"Malc!" I call out, to catch their attention before they walk past our table without noticing us.

"Alright, Bill, mate," says Stu, looking really pleased to see us. "What're you up to?"

Dad stands up and he and Stu shake hands.

"Shopping for this young man," says Dad, giving me a nudge.

Malcom sits down in a plastic seat next to me.

"I'm buying a midi system," I tell him.

"What sort?" says Malc. "I've got one and it's crap. Don't get a Matsui whatever you do."

"How much was yours, then?" I ask.

"Dunno. Mum and Phil bought it for me. They should've let me choose my own."

"That's what I thought, so I've been saving for ages. But I reckon I've got enough for a good one now."

Dad and Stu are talking about the football game on TV last night, and I notice how craggy Stu looks. Too many late nights with *her*, no doubt.

"So, you meeting up with Gypsy, then?" I ask Malc.

He pulls a face, and talks in a whisper. "No fuckin' chance. Not that cow."

"Why?"

"Tried to turn him against me." He nods his head towards Stu. "Wanted him to herself all the time, so come Saturdays, he couldn't always have me over. My mum went ballistic. Anyway, she buggered off – no goodbye, just packed her stuff and went. Good riddance, I say." Malcolm's looking shiftily at his dad to make sure he hasn't heard any of this. He lowers his voice again. "She hated me. Mind you, the feeling's mutual."

"So, just the two of you is it?" says Stu, looking like he's about to sit down.

"No, Mum's here too," I say, nodding towards Mum who's paid for the drinks at the far end, and has paused to pick up spoons and sugar on her way back over.

"Oh. Yes," says Stu, and he seems confused. "Haven't seen you for a while, Bill."

Dad looks towards Mum and pushes his hands into his pockets. "No. We ought to have a drink soon, mate."

"Is that your mum?" whispers Malc.

I remember the incident outside the pub before Christmas, but I'm pretty sure he can't recognise her from then; she looks so different now with her shorter hair.

"Yeah, why?"

"Did she and my dad – you know?" He looks completely serious.

I frown back at him hard. "No way! Don't be an idiot. She hardly knows your dad. She's back with Dad now. He just moved back in."

"Weird," he says, shaking his head. "She looks just like this woman I saw once – just like her. Maybe she's got a double." He chews at the corner of a fingernail, watching Mum closely as she gets nearer.

My heart's pounding, and I don't even know why.

"We'd better get off, Malc," says Stu. "Things to do."

When Mum reaches our table, there's an awkward silence, before we all say goodbye and Malcolm and Stu go and sit at the back of the café.

"You'd really like Stu if you got to know him, Mary," says Dad, tearing open a sugar sachet and pouring it into his coffee. "He's a good bloke, isn't he, Jake?"

I nod, hiding my face behind the huge chocolate éclair that Mum brought back for me.

"I don't rate his taste in women much, though," Dad laughs. He sweeps spilt sugar off the table into his palm, then brushes it from his hands on to the floor. I've seen him do this movement countless times, and I don't know why he doesn't just sweep the stuff straight on to the floor.

Mum stirs her tea for longer than it needs, never looking up from the table.

"But, anyway, it sounds like Gypsy's disappeared, so that's her out of the picture," says Dad. "Poor old Stu, I think he misses family life." He reaches across the table for Mum's hand. "Sometimes I have to remind myself how lucky I am."

We get a brilliant deal when we buy my midi system. It's got a record player, built-in amp, radio, and a double cassette deck, so I can record tape to tape. We traipse around all the electrical shops until we find the right one, and Dad bargains hard at the end to get some money knocked off and a couple of free albums thrown in to boot. I choose *Misplaced Childhood* by Marillion and The Beatles' *White Album*, because Dad says it's a classic that belongs in every serious music collection.

Afterwards, I ask Mum if we can go into Millets as I've got some money left to spend.

"If you want clothes, we should go to M and S or British Home Stores, Jakey. Millets is a camping shop – they won't have much there." Mum obviously hasn't been in Millets for years.

"It's not really clothes, in particular," I say. "They do shoes too – converse, DMs. And monkey boots, you know, like George's got? They're really cool, but I could also wear them for school because they're black lace-ups. Means you wouldn't have to buy me an extra pair for school. And my school shoes are getting a bit tight now."

"Well, let's have a look," says Mum and we head up towards Millets at the other end of the high street.

In Millets, Mum and Dad agree that the monkey boots are a good idea. I also manage to find myself a new army green canvas satchel for school, just like the one George had hanging on the back of his bedroom door. All it needs are some badges and a bit of graffiti, and it'll look just right.

We head home with a handful of bags, a big box, and a tenner still unspent in my wallet. I think about all the new albums I'll buy with my shop wages, and about what I'll write in my letter to George this week. We've already decided that we're going to send each other tapes of any new albums we've bought, so we'll end up with double the amount of music.

Mum pops into the Spar to pick up some mince and carrots to make a shepherd's pie for supper.

"I think we've got onions and plenty of potatoes at home," she says as she comes back out of the shop. "And look, I got one of these too." She holds up a Swiss roll, to have with custard for pudding.

"This day just keeps getting better," I smirk at her and Dad. "My favourite ever supper, and a new midi system! Did I mention that I've got a midi system? Did I? Did I?"

Mum laughs, and bops the back of my legs with her shopping bag.

Dad pats me on the back. "Well, you earned it, son. You've worked hard for that money. You've got a bloody good work ethic, and that's as much as you need to survive in life, Jakey. Well done."

I nod up at him, feeling my chest puffing up with pride. I can't wait to tell Mr Horrocks that I managed to get the midi system I'd been saving for. He's got Griffin today, so I can pop in and tell him about it later, when I pick the dog up.

As we get closer to home, Dad says he fancies a pint in the Royal Oak.

"But I thought you were going to help me set up my system, Dad?"

"Oh, come on, Jakey, I've helped you choose it, haven't I? And I got you a good deal. I'm just going in for a pint or two – you get started and I'll be back to give you a hand in a while." He disappears through the front door of the pub without looking back. Mum stares after him, looking tired.

"Come on, darling," she says, "I'll give you a hand, once I've had a cup of tea and unpacked the shopping. I'm sure there are clear instructions in the user manual."

"I know," I say. "But I just thought that Dad would want to help me set it up."

Mum gives me that understanding look that I've seen a million times, and we carry on up the street towards home.

"He will, Jakey. Just let him have his pint, and he'll be back to help you out. In the meantime, see how much you can get done without him. That'll show him! So. Happy with your ape boots, then?"

"Monkey boots, Mum! They're monkey boots!"

"I know," she says, laughing at me, "I'm pulling your leg, you great hairy chimp!"

I nudge her shoulder with my head, careful not to dislodge the box in my arms, and give her one of my cross-eyed loony faces. She puts down the shopping to pull out the door key and let us in.

"You get started upstairs, and I'll be up to give you a hand in a minute, Jakey. Cup of tea?"

I nod, and disappear up the stairs with my new gear.

Mary, November 1980

I'm woken by the creak of small feet on the staircase. The nine o'clock news is drawing to an end, and the fire is down to its last embers. A child appears in the doorway of the living room, and in the dim light I think it's a little girl. It's Jake, in his dressing gown, rubbing his face.

"What's the time?" he asks, turning to look at the television.

"Must be about half nine," I reply, holding my arms wide to beckon him closer.

In his half sleep, he forgets that he's nine, and pads over to climb into my embrace.

"I'm cold. And hungry," he says, as he stretches over the arm of the chair to reach for the plate of cheese and crackers I'd been eating before I dropped off. His pyjama sleeve catches on my glass, sending red wine splashing up the wall.

"Oh, Jake!" I curse, brushing him off my lap and flicking on the light in one movement. "Why are you always so clumsy? You're always knocking stuff over. Well, get a cloth then!"

He hurries off to the kitchen, and returns with a white tea towel.

I tut. "Not that one. It's red wine, for God's sake. Oh – I'll do it myself."

When I finish clearing the mess I look up to where Jake is sitting on the sofa with his knees under his chin, remorse across his face. I feel horrible, but I can't say anything that might take it back. I uncork the wine bottle and pour the small remains into my empty glass.

"No harm done." I sit down in my armchair again, and pat my knee for him to come back on to my lap, but he pretends not to notice. After a few minutes' silence, I finish the last of my drink and clap my hands together. "Right! It's way past bedtime, darling. Time for bed."

Jake doesn't move.

"Come on, Jakey," I say.

"Where's Dad?" he asks.

"Out."

"Out where?"

"The Royal Oak," I answer, poking at the dying embers with the toasting fork.

"But he was out way before we went to bed," Jake says with his bottom lip hanging out.

"I know. He's met a friend, probably."

I clear away my glass and push the bottle to the bottom of the kitchen bin. My head feels woozy, where I've been dozing.

"He should be back by now," Jake grumbles, climbing back up the stairs towards bed.

"Night," I call after him.

"Night," he calls back.

I sit and gaze at the fire as the flames catch the new log I've placed in the ashes. I switch off the main light and go to the kitchen cupboard for a drink. Click-clack it pings as I gently pull it open over the oven. There's vodka, so I pour myself a glass, topped up with lime cordial and ice.

As I sit in the glowing darkness of the living room, the ice cubes clink about in the liquid like little lights. I'd rather be drinking red wine or whisky, a drink that warms the insides on a cold November night. But the drink is still soothing, and by the time Jake comes back down, I must have had two or three more.

"Is Dad still out?" he asks, lit up in silhouette.

"Uh-huh," I answer, turning back to the orange flames.

"What time is it now?"

"Nearly eleven," I say, looking in his direction.

"Maybe something's wrong?" he says. He looks like he might cry.

"Of course it's not," I say, trying to keep the irritation from my voice. "He's just got caught up with someone."

Jake's quiet for a minute. "I think we should find him. Just in case." He walks to the coat rack by the front door, and pulls down my coat. "Come on, Mum. It's just round the corner."

I look at the clock on the mantelpiece. It's 10.50. Billy had gone out for a couple of pints at six, saying he'd be back for supper. My stomach growls, and suddenly the sight of skinny little Jake, holding out my coat, fills me with hot rage. I imagine Billy in his favourite spot at the bar, supping his fifth or sixth pint and laughing away, without a care in the world. And there's Jakey, worried about his father, who hasn't a thought for anyone. I snatch my coat from Jake's hand, and I wrap him in his, and I march him outside, steadying myself on the doorframe as we go.

"Shh," I whisper as I ease the front door closed behind us. We creep away from the house.

Our breath is white in the black night air, and we trot down the road in small fierce steps, until we're standing outside the Royal Oak, looking in. The windows are steamed up on the inside, and we can hear the bubbling chatter and laughter pressing against the walls and doors.

"You stay here," I tell Jakey.

"No chance!" he says, his eyes enormous. "It's pitch black out 'ere."

"Out *here*," I correct him and we enter through the public bar door. I spot Billy immediately. He's sitting at the far corner, leaning on the bar, talking to Cindy. Cindy is Eric the Landlord's new girlfriend. She moved in a few weeks ago, after his wife moved out. The New Model, Billy and Pete call her. Eric's down this end of the bar, pulling pints and mopping up spills.

"Cindy!" he shouts. "A hand this end, love!" and Cindy totters along the bar to serve the waiting drinkers.

I walk through the bar, with Jake close at my heels, avoiding the stares of the locals. Billy's eyes meet mine as I draw near. Panic crosses them.

"Mary! What're you doing here, darlin'?"

I'm icy.

He notices Jake, smiling shyly as he comes out from behind me. "Jakey!"

Billy's face suddenly turns from pleasure to concern, and he straightens up. "What's wrong? Are the boys alright?"

I get up close to him and whisper through gritted teeth, "They're fine. But Jake was worried. He thought something might have happened to you. As it's been five hours since you went out."

Billy checks his watch, and looks straight past me to Jake. "Oh, Jakey boy! Bless you, son – I'm fine. Just got chatting a bit long, that's all."

Jake smiles at his dad, adoring and gullible.

"Want some crisps?" Billy asks. "Cindy! Come and meet my boy! What flavour, Jakey?"

Cindy gets Jake a packet of smoky bacon crisps and a bottle of Coke.

Billy turns to me. "Mary, darling? What'll it be?"

I want to say, no, I've got to get back to the boys, but Cindy stands there waiting for my answer, all fresh and fleshy in her tight salmon T-shirt, and I know I have to stay for Billy's sake. "Red wine, please," I say, suddenly ashamed of my faded leggings and unbrushed hair.

Jake's face is glowing with happiness, his eyes sparkling and excited.

"He's a lovely boy, Billy," Cindy says as she puts my glass down on the bar in front of me. She wipes the bar down and slowly moves along the surface away from us, taking care to mop up all the spills.

"She seems nice," I say to Billy, as I watch her polish the brass of the drip tray.

Billy speaks low so that Jake can't hear. "Poor old Eric. She's a bit of a slapper, but he hasn't sussed it out yet. See Tony over there? She was with him last Wednesday. On her 'night off'."

I look over to where Tony's sitting, at the other end of the bar. He's a man in his late thirties, with a sad, hungry look about him, and his eyes follow Cindy wherever she goes. Cindy now wipes the bar in front of him, slowly leaning in to make a good job of it. Eric rushes about behind the bar, doing twice as much work as Cindy.

Billy gives me a wink. "Poor old fool," he says.

I laugh, forgetting my bad mood, and wonder whether he means Eric or Tony.

As Eric rings time behind the bar, we finish our drinks and walk out into the empty street. Jake pushes himself between us and holds our hands.

"Can we do this again, some day? Maybe in the 'olidays?" He looks from me to Billy. "Just us three?"

"I don't think so, Jakey. And it's *holidays*. We're not supposed to leave the others on their own, you know?"

Billy ruffles Jake's hair. "Of course we can, son. We'll work something out."

I tut, and scowl at Billy over Jake's head. Jake squeezes my hand and does a little skip-hop between us, blowing his cold breath out in a cloud of white steam.

Jake, June 1985

Dad gets back about half eleven. Mum went to bed hours ago, but I stayed up in my room, playing about with my music. Griffin's asleep on the floor beside my bed, and his ears prick up when he hears the front door go. I flick off the power switch, and jump into bed, pretending to be asleep in case Dad comes up to ask me about my midi system.

But I hear him downstairs, clattering about in the kitchen, searching out the shepherd's pie that Mum has plated up and left in the oven for him. The TV goes on, and I know he's not coming up. I fall asleep to the sound of his fork scraping across the plate, as he polishes off the supper we all started four hours ago.

After Sunday lunch, we settle down in front of a film that Mum wants us all to watch, *The Yearling*. It's about this boy and his poor family. They adopt an orphaned fawn, who becomes the boy's best friend.

"It's a beautiful film," says Mum, as it's just starting.

"Not forgetting it's got Gregory Peck in it," Dad says, easing himself into his armchair. "Apparently he's a 'bit of a dish'. Your mum's words, not mine."

Mum snuggles into the sofa, putting her arm round Andy. "Rather a dish, and a great actor. Now shush, and let's watch the film."

When the film's about halfway through, the phone rings. Mum pulls a face at Dad as he gets out of his armchair.

"Leave it," she says, "they can always phone back later if it's important."

But Dad never leaves a phone unanswered, thinks it's dishonest to pretend you're not in. He sprints over to the window sill, pulls back the curtain and grabs the receiver.

"Bill Andrews speaking." He always answers it like this, as if he's working in an office or something. "Stu, mate, how's it going?" He sounds pleased to hear from him.

Mum turns to look at him over the back of the sofa. He keeps his back to us, one finger over his free ear, his shape silhouetted in the crack of daylight from the half-opened curtains.

"Course I can, mate. What time d'you need me? – OK, let me get a pencil, I'd better jot the address down – I'll only forget otherwise. Yup, yup – OK. See you in about ten minutes, Stu." And he hangs up.

For a moment he pauses in the window light, then he quietly pulls the curtain back across the window, and comes over. He squats down behind the sofa, leaning his arms on the back.

"You don't mind if I pop out for an hour, love?" says

Dad, talking to the side of Mum's face. She's staring ahead at the film with a blank expression.

"Why's that?" she asks.

"It's Stu. He's just moved into a new flat on the other side of town, and he's struggling to get the bed up the stairs. He's got a friend down there with him, but they need another pair of hands. I said I'd take my tools down in case it needs taking apart. He's a mate. You don't mind, do you?"

Mum shakes her head, doesn't say anything more. Dad gathers together some of his screwdrivers in a tool belt and heads out the door. After a couple of seconds I hear his key in the lock, and he pops back in, reaches for his wallet on the side, and pops back out again, giving me a wave as he goes.

I move into his armchair, and me, Andy and Mum watch the rest of the film in silence. The deer has grown up now, but it keeps eating the crops of the family, who are so poor that they are almost starving. When the boy takes the gun into the woods, Mum is already mopping the tears up from her face, and Andy's eyes are watery. Even I'm trying to swallow back the lump in my throat. I pat my lap, and Griffin jumps up for a cuddle. He turns himself over so I can rub his round little belly. He's got these really soft little pink bits under his front legs, where the hair grows thinner, and he wriggles like mad when I tickle him there. I imagine what it would be like if I had to take Griffin out into the woods with a gun, for the good of the family. I couldn't do it. I'd have to just run away with him, I think. I'd have to pack a bag, and run away, maybe to Mr Horrocks. He'd have us.

"What a lovely film," says Mum as the credits roll up

at the end. She blows her nose into a tissue and goes over to draw back the curtains. "So sad."

Andy's staring vacantly at the TV screen.

"Oi, poofter," I say to him, rubbing my eyes with my fists and pulling a boo-hoo face.

Andy snaps out of his trance, makes a rifle with his hands, and pretends to shoot Griffin. I lunge at him, knocking Griffin off my lap, but Andy's too quick.

"You can run, but you can't hide," I shout up the stairs after him.

Griffin's standing by the door expectantly, obviously thinking that all this activity means he's getting a walk. He hasn't been out today, apart from the back yard, so I pick up his lead to take him for a good walk around the park. After all that slushy stuff I need some fresh air.

When I come in at five, Dad's still not back. He's been gone three hours, not the hour he said he'd be.

Mum's up in the loft, and she calls for me when she hears the front door go.

"Jake – can you take these boxes when I pass them down? Andy was meant to help, but Ronny called for him. Some of them are a bit heavy, so be careful."

She lowers down three large cardboard boxes, covered in dust. The first is a Peek Freans biscuit box. I remember having Peek Freans Petit Beurre biscuits at a friend's house, years ago, and thinking they must be rich. The other two boxes are plain cardboard, and sealed with packing tape.

Mum climbs back down the ladder and fixes the hatch back in place. She dusts herself off, and we carry the boxes down from the landing.

Mum starts opening up the boxes. "My old collection."

The boxes are crammed full of records. There must be fifty or sixty albums here, and in the Peek Freans box, hundreds of singles. It would cost you a fortune to buy this lot from scratch. I begin flicking through them rapidly, taking in the band names and the record sleeves, not knowing where to start.

"They won't all be to your taste," says Mum, carefully pulling out a bunch of LPs, "but there are some classics in these boxes. Here – oh, I loved this, *Breakfast in America* – and, look, Bob Dylan. Saw him live at the Isle of Wight festival. Incredible."

I can't believe that this treasure trove of music has been up in our loft all these years. Even more I can't believe that it belongs to my mum.

"When was that?" I ask.

"What – the festival? 1970. It was an amazing line-up – I ended up collecting the albums of most the bands I saw there. Look – I've bunched them all together here – Jimi Hendrix, Joni Mitchell, the Moody Blues . . ."

Mum's eyes are sparkling, and she looks younger as she picks through the album covers, turning them over in her hands.

"Oh God! Look at this one – you must have heard of The Doors – I had the biggest crush on Jim Morrison when I was at art college. I was going to marry him. Then your dad came along," she says with a little laugh. "The 1970 festival is the most famous of the lot. It was Jimi Hendrix's last gig, before he died." She shakes her head, as if remembering someone she actually knew. "What a waste."

"You'd have had Matthew by then. Was he there?" I feel a twinge of jealousy that he might have been part of the adventure, even before I was born.

"No, no.   He was with your dad, back here in Portsmouth."

"Who'd you go with then?"

"Gypsy," she answers, her eyes still scanning the back of The Doors album. She lays it down carefully. "Anyway, they're yours if you want them, Jake. Now you've got a record player of your own."

Mum goes into the kitchen and puts the kettle on. My eyes run over the boxes of music. I wonder why she never gave them to Matthew. I start to pack the records back into the boxes, ready to carry them up to my room.

"Can I phone George, Mum?   Tell him about the music?"

"If you're quick," she calls from the sink. "Don't stay on too long though – it's expensive, Jake. You can always write him a letter, to tell him more about it."

I decide to skip the phone call, and go up to my room to start working my way through the albums.

Mum's still up when I go to bed, waiting for Dad. I'm just drifting off, when the click-clack of the kitchen cupboard disturbs me. There's a pause, and I know she's found the cupboard empty. I checked it earlier, like I do every morning. She closes it again, click-clack. I stare at the crack of light under the door, until my eyes can't stay open any more.

Mary, July 1982

I'm somewhere between sleep and waking when I hear the phone ringing downstairs. It rings and rings and rings. Bright sunlight pushes at the closed curtains, stabbing white lines across the wood-chipped wall opposite. The red numbers of the digital clock read 9.46 a.m. The ringing stops. I reach for the glass of water on my bedside cabinet. It tastes stale in my mouth, but my thirst makes me swallow it to the bottom. As I flop back against my clammy pillow, the phone starts to ring again. I feel suddenly nauseous as the water hits my stomach, so I curl up on my side, cupping my ears with my hands, willing the ringing phone to stop. After a few minutes it does stop, and I slowly ease my legs out of bed, feeling for slippers with my numb toes. I'm halfway along the landing when the phone starts again, jolting me to a stop. I listen. It's so persistent. Perhaps it's Billy. More likely it's some salesman. Or a wrong number. Maybe it's one of the boys. I stumble down the stairs, righting my balance, and pick up the receiver clumsily.

"Yes?"

"Mrs Andrews?"

"Yes?"

"It's Mr Hall here. From the high school. Can we talk?"

I don't like the tone of his voice. Arrogant.

"Of course. What is it?"

"It's Matthew, Mrs Andrews. He hasn't registered this morning. Did he leave for school alright?"

I pause, trying to remember if I saw the boys before they left the house. I don't remember.

"Yes. Yes, he went off as normal."

Mr Hall clears his throat. "Well I'm not entirely sure what normal is for Matthew. In the past four weeks, he's been absent nine times in total. That level of absenteeism doesn't strike me as entirely normal."

There's an awkward silence as Mr Hall waits for my response. I can't give him one.

"Mrs Andrews, may I ask – is everything alright at home with Matthew? He's clearly a very bright boy, but if he doesn't buckle down soon, he'll be leaving school with no qualifications and not much hope for a career."

My mind is whirring through the past few weeks, trying to remember if Matthew has been acting differently or not.

"How many times did you say he's been off school? Because you know, he did have that terrible chest infection just after Christmas." I pull back the nets and watch Mrs Horrocks from the corner shop walk past with her little white dog. It's a beautiful day. No wonder Matthew doesn't want to be in school.

"Mrs Andrews, he's been off nine times in the past month! You do understand, don't you?"

"Yes."

"Obviously, there's Matthew's welfare to think about. He's a fourteen-year-old boy. So, once you locate him today, I'd like you to ring back and let me know he's safe and well. And then I'd like you to arrange to come in and meet me, with Mr Andrews too if possible, so that we can discuss ways forward. Mrs Andrews?"

My heart's pounding. He wants to see us. "I'll call you as soon as I find him, Mr Hall. Thank you."

I replace the receiver and stand rooted to the dreary patterned carpet.

Billy knows where Matthew's gone straight away. "He'll be at his gran's house," he says.

"You can go and get him, then," I tell him, twisting the phone cord round my thumb.

Billy sighs, then talks to me patiently, like I'm an imbecile. "I'm working, Mary. Just give her a call and go and get him. It won't kill you. Just be polite."

By the time I get to Jean's house, it's nearly lunchtime. I missed the first bus and had to wait half an hour for the next one. As I approach the terraced house the curtains twitch and the front door opens before I can knock.

"Mary," Jean says coldly, standing flat against the wall to let me pass.

"Hello, Jean. How are you?" I manage a smile.

"Well, I'd be a whole lot better if I knew what was going on with you and your son," she says, her arms crossed tightly over her chest. "He's not a very happy boy."

I frown at her, and walk ahead into the front room. Matthew's in there with his shoes off, watching TV and eating biscuits. He's got a split lip and a dirty face. He glances at me briefly, then returns his gaze to the screen.

"Mr Hall's been on the phone, Matthew. He says this isn't the first time you've skipped school. Well, I knew that, but I had no idea just how many days you'd actually missed. Matthew! Are you listening to me?"

Jean tuts from the doorway. "Answer your mother, boy."

Matthew looks at Jean and rolls his eyes. "She's not my mother, Gran." He's slurring his words. "She's an old cow. A pissed old cow."

I see victory in Jean's eyes. She shrugs at me as if to say, over to you, Mary, if you're so clever. She scuttles into the kitchen, where she'll still be within earshot.

As I sit next to Matthew on the sofa I fight the tears stinging behind my eyes. I place my hand lightly on his leg. He brushes it off, still staring angrily at the TV.

"Matthew. Why would you say something like that in front of your gran?"

"It's true, isn't it?" His eyes are on me now, hard and black.

"Of course it's not true! All grown-ups have a drink or two. It doesn't make me a drunk, for God's sake!" I'm shaking inside. "So, is your dad a drunk then?"

"No. Dad gets up at six every day and goes to work. Dad doesn't embarrass me in front of my mates. Dad doesn't hide his empty bottles at the bottom of the bin."

I stand, blocking Matthew's view of the TV. "How would you know if I'd embarrass you? I'm not even sure you've got any friends. You never bring your mates back home!"

"That's because you're a pisshead! How could I bring them back home, when you're like that? Remember when I brought Tony Sadler home that one time, and you'd been drinking whisky? You left the bottle on the table next to the ketchup and he kept pointing at it and laughing. Next day, he went round the school telling everyone my mum's name was Scotch Mary. Get it? Scotch Mary, for fuck's sake!"

Jean's back in the doorway, shaking her head.

"Matthew's got it all wrong, Jean. He's the one who's been drinking. I can smell it on his breath!"

Jean shakes her head again.

"Look at me! Do I look pissed to you, Jean?" I stand up with my arms outstretched, smiling with incredulity. "Do I? Jean? Do I look like a pisshead to you?"

Jean walks from the doorway across the green swirl carpet, until we're a foot apart. With a sharp, bird-like movement she sniffs the air between us. "No. But you smell like one," she says, and she starts to lay out the little table for her lunch.

Matthew hangs his head over his lap, now appearing so young and alone.

"Matthew. We're going. Put your shoes on. Now!"

Matthew jumps to attention, and in half a minute we're on the street, marching along the pavement, back towards the bus stop. As we round the corner, I stop him and hold his shoulders in my hands, pressing him up against the red brick wall of the builders' merchants. I pin his eyes with mine.

"Matthew. We need some rules, darling. And the most important one is about loyalty. We're a family, and we do not, ever, go around telling lies about each other. To anyone. What you said to Gran back there – it was a lie. You know it, and so do I. But what must Gran think now? She'll think, that explains why he's skipping school, if his mother's a drunk. But it's not true. So, I want you to promise me that you'll never say anything like this again. OK? OK, Matthew?"

Matthew's been trying to look away all the time I've been speaking, and I realise that I've been shaking him, punctuating my words with each judder. His eyes are now filled with tears and his face is a picture of terror. I release my grip.

"I'm sorry, Mum," he sobs, slumping against me and scrunching his hands into my T-shirt. "I'm so sorry."

Part Three

Jake, July 1985

My last lesson of term is Classics with Miss Terry. After class I hang back to show her my Greek mythology book.

"My friend Mr Horrocks gave it to me for my birthday," I tell her.

Miss Terry takes it from me and places it on her desk like it's a precious antique.

"What a beautiful book, Jake," she says, carefully turning the pages to look at the colour illustrations. "This is a very special gift. And quite old. Mr Horrocks must think a lot of you."

Some of my own drawings slip from the back of the book. The one on top is of Aphrodite handing arrows to Eros.

"Are these yours, Jake?" she says, studying my sketches closely. "You're very good, you know."

My stupid cheeks flush red again. "Look, I'll show you Pan," I say, flicking ahead to the page. I know which page number it's on, because I checked this morning.

There's a picture of Pan standing on a dry mountainside, with his flute raised to his lips. All over the rockface, there are goats and sheep grazing on tufts of grass and flowers.

"You're not Pan, Jake," Miss Terry says. "I knew I'd have to change it. Some kids are so easy to place, but you've been the trickiest this year." She smiles and rubs my shoulder, before turning the book to the index and searching through the pages. "Ah, there we go," she finally says, "Perseus! I was thinking about it last night. You're Perseus the Gorgon slayer. Perseus the rescuer of Andromeda. And when you were slain in brave battle, Zeus set you amongst the stars as one of his particular favourites. So, how about that? Much more fitting than Pan!"

And then she does the most amazing thing. She picks up the book, hugs it to her chest, and kisses me on the cheek.

"You've been a pleasure to teach, Jake. My star pupil. Just stick with it. OK?" She looks at me seriously, and hands me the book. "Have a good summer, Perseus," are her last words, then she turns to wipe the blackboard and never looks back.

It's over a week since we broke up for the summer holidays, and it's a scorcher. After a couple of days off, I started work with Mr Horrocks, and at times I'm glad to be in the cool of his dark shop. Mr Horrocks usually works with me in the shop and stockroom each morning, then takes a couple of hours upstairs after I've had my lunch break. On Saturdays he gives me a pound at around ten o'clock, to go to the bakery and buy two Chelsea buns for our tea break. They're usually slightly warm, and the bready texture gets more and more doughy as you unravel the bun towards its curranty centre. It takes me the best part of my fifteen minute break to unroll it and eat it chunk by chunk, chewing on the dough, crunching on the rock sugar.

When it's quiet, we usually take different areas to work on. Mr Horrocks will stack in the stockroom, while I fill a shelf at the front of the shop, or he'll bring out a new line of biscuits, while I make a space on the shelf. Every now and then we'll stop and chat about this and that. It's good and calm. Today's a Friday, when we usually get the shop stocked up for the busy Saturday.

"It's going to be a hot one," Mr Horrocks says as he tears the tape from a carton of Tunnock's caramel wafers. "They say it could be the hottest in years. Could even lead to a hosepipe ban."

"We haven't got a garden as such, so it wouldn't bother us really," I say.

"Us neither," he says, pausing to put his hands on his hips. "Except Marcie's window boxes. She'd be mad if she thought I'd neglected her window boxes."

I think about the day that I saw her up in her window. The window boxes were old and wintry and dead then. I guess Mr Horrocks must've planted them up since she died.

"Mind you," he says, "they never get it right, do they? The weather. We'll see."

I pull the cloth out of my apron pocket and dust down the shelf before Mr Horrocks stacks the chocolate biscuits in neat rows.

"The book's good," I tell him. "The mythology book.

I'm just reading the bit with Achilles and the golden arrow. I never realised that's where it came from – Achilles' heel. Makes sense, doesn't it."

"Achilles' heel." Mr Horrocks looks thoughtful, like he's just saying it out loud to see what it sounds like.

Griffin plods in from the stockroom, panting with his tongue hanging out. He looks like he's just woken up, hot and tired. He wanders across the shop, and out through the front door to the bowl of water we leave there for passing dogs. He plonks himself down in the middle of the doorway, facing outwards, watching the sunny street. After a few minutes, he gives up and moves into a shady corner beneath the toilet rolls. Mr Horrocks tells me he's off for his afternoon break, and he disappears upstairs with a newspaper. The sunlight pours through the front door, making the inside of the shop seem darker than usual. Every time a car drives by, the motes of dust dance crazily in the sunshine stream, disturbed by the sudden breeze.

After an hour of shelf cleaning, I stand in the doorway, letting the sun fall on my face. The road's quiet today, and I guess most people are either at work or on the beach. Or away on holiday. I wonder what George's up to on the Isle of Wight; maybe there'll be a letter waiting for me when I get home.

A couple of kids pedal by on their bikes, disturbing a wrapper in the road. It lifts and drifts over, landing by my foot. The wrapper's been torn in half, so it reads "angles" instead of "Spangles". I bend over and put it in the bin outside the shop. The sun is beating down, and I feel a thin film of sweat surfacing across my forehead and upper lip. I check my watch. Half past three. Two hours to go. Andy turns the corner at the far end of the street.

He sees me and breaks into a run. He's wearing shorts and a T-shirt, and his knees are wider than his thighs. He's growing too quickly for his body to keep up. He's officially taller than me now.

"You shouldn't wear those shorts," I tell him as he reaches me.

"Why?" he asks, looking down at himself.

"Cos your knees are bloody knobbly," I laugh. "You look like Olive Oyl."

"Fuck off, I don't!" Andy's trying out swearing at the moment, and it makes him sound like even more of a dork than usual.

"What d'you want, anyway?"

Andy looks over my shoulder to the ice cream chest, just inside the door, and raises his eyebrows expectantly.

"Piss off. I mean what did you come here for?"

He frowns, then light crosses his face. "Oh, yeah. Message from Mum. Go straight to the Royal Oak for your tea. We're all gonna be there, in the pub garden if it's still sunny. Dad says we can have scampi and chips or something."

"What's the occasion?" I ask, suspicious.

"Dunno, but they seemed really chipper about it, so something good, I guess. Mum told me to meet her there at five thirty. After she's done the shopping."

"OK," I nod, then I look over my shoulder, grab a Rocket from the freezer chest, and shove it into Andy's sweaty hand. "Go on," I nudge him, "bugger off before I get caught."

Andy grins with his stupid goggle-eyed face, and runs back up the road, the way he came.

When Mr Horrocks comes back down to the shop it's

just after four, and we start our shelf filling, him down one side, me down the other. Customers start drifting in on their way home from work, to buy cigarettes and newspapers, and sweets for their kids. Before I know it, it's 5.30, and Griffin and I are standing in the doorway ready to go.

"See you in the morning, Mr Horrocks."

"See you in the morning, Jake," he replies. He picks up a small dog chew, and hands it to me as he pulls down the door blind. "Look after that dog."

I put my hand up, and wander up the street with Griffin sniffing along by my side. The sun's still hot, and the streets have come to life, as kids return home from playing out, and cars make their way back for the start of the weekend. As I near the Royal Oak, I can sense the party atmosphere spilling over the garden fence; that end of term feeling when there's nothing to think about except the holidays ahead.

"Run after your mum and tell her what you want to eat," says my dad as I come through the gate to the pub garden. "She's at the bar ordering the food now."

Dad and Andy are sitting at one of the bench tables dotted about the balding grassy patch in the back garden. There are quite a few other people sitting in the afternoon sunshine. Most of the men look like they've just finished a day's labouring, in their dusty T-shirts and work boots, joking and buying rounds for each other. Over in the corner there's a smart young couple, teachers or office workers I'd guess, and they seem to be watching the rest of the drinkers with interest. Dad stretches his arms out in front of him, as if his muscles are aching, then he reaches for his cigarettes and lights one behind a cupped hand. He's squinting against the bright light of the sun. Andy's got his head on his folded arms, like he's taking a nap. He doesn't even lift his head to look at me.

Inside the pub, it takes a few minutes for my eyes to adjust to the dark, smoky atmosphere. Mum's leaning on the bar, running her finger down the menu card, telling the landlady what she wants.

"Oh, good – here's Jakey. Jake, what do you want? Andy's having scampi, and Dad's having the steak and kidney pie. What do you fancy?"

I choose a cheese ploughman's and a Coke, and Mum asks me to take the tray of drinks out while she pays. The glasses clink against each other, even though I'm walking super-slow, trying to avoid spilling any of Dad's pint. Dad and Andy point and laugh at me as I approach.

"Don't all rush and help at once," I say.

"Hurry up, son, I'm dying of thirst over here," says Dad. "You look like a little old man, shuffling about in his slippers!"

Andy laughs again, banging the table with the flat of his hand. "Yeah, come on, Granddad!"

I put the tray down on the table, move the glasses off the tray and then give it a good shake on to the grass, emptying the spilt liquids. My hand's wet with a mix of beer and Coke, and I casually walk behind Andy and drag my sticky fingers along his skinny neck. "Spanner," he mutters as he tries to wriggle out of my reach. I lean the tray against the leg of the table and sit down opposite Dad.

"Good day?" Dad asks, lifting his pint to his lips.

"Not bad," I answer, taking a slurp of my Coke.

Mum comes through the back doors and drops two bags of nuts on the table. She slides in next to me on the bench.

"Cheers," she says, raising her sparkling water. The lemon slice bobs in the glass, making the bubbles sparkle in the sunlight.

"Cheers," we all echo.

The landlady appears through the back door, and bustles over to our table.

"Here – you forgot these," she says, and she places our table number in the middle of the table, along with a small half empty bottle of Schweppes tonic water.

"What's that for?" I ask.

"So they know which table we are, when the food comes," answers Mum.

"Not that – the tonic water," I say.

There's a pause, as Mum and Dad exchange a glance.

"It's just the one, Jake," Mum says, sounding annoyed. "I haven't touched a drop in months now, have I?"

"No," I say.

"And anyway, we've got something to celebrate," she adds, with a sweep of her hands.

Dad reaches into his back pocket and drops four little black books on the table. "Know what these are?" he asks.

I flip one over. It's a passport. I look up at Dad with raised eyebrows. He raises his back at me.

"Yup. We're off on holiday. Last three weeks in August. The Dordogne. France." Dad looks chuffed to bits with himself.

My face wants to smile like mad; I've never been

abroad before. But my eyes keep flicking over to Mum's glass like an itchy rash, and I've got that feeling where I can't make up my mind which feeling to feel, good or bad, because both is difficult to feel at once. Andy is doing his skill punch, and the colour has risen to Mum's chest. On the next table a young mother runs back and forth to the climbing frame, to make sure her little ones don't come a cropper from the top bars. Her boyfriend sits at his bench, drinking his pint, not noticing the children all that much.

"But what about Mr Horrocks," I ask Mum, frowning again, "and Griffin?"

"Nothing to worry about, Jake," says Mum, smoothing the hair out of my eyes. I wish she wouldn't. "I've spoken to him, and he knows all about it."

I look at my passport, flicking through the blank pages, until I find the details at the back. And there I am, staring back at myself, pale and serious, in the photo we took in the booth on Brighton station, just before Dad told us he was coming back home. My throat feels tight and bulgy, and my heart is bobbling about in my chest.

"So, what do you think, Jakey?" asks Mum, rattling her ice cubes nervously in the glass.

Andy points at my photo and laughs, and I swipe at him across the table.

"It's great," I say, avoiding Mum's eyes. "It'll be great."

On the Saturday before our holiday, Dad says we've got to visit Gran.

"Ohhh – do we have to?" Andy's whining. "It's miles away. And she'll only have a go at us."

"No she won't. And it's only ten minutes away, you

pansy. Just be on your best behaviour, and she'll be fine."
Dad's checking his pockets for his car keys.

"It doesn't matter how you behave, she still thinks you're up to something," I add. "And why does she hate Mum so much, anyway?"

"She doesn't hate Mum. Now get your coats on and get in the car. We'll be back in time for a sandwich at the Oak. I'll give you some money for a few sweets if you're good."

Andy and me fight over the front seat, until Dad loses his temper and Andy gets in the back. Dad starts the car, pulling his seatbelt across him after we've got on to the main road. He lights up a cigarette, which hangs loosely from the side of his mouth as his tries to wind down the window and drive at the same time. I thought he'd given them up. But then he's always stopping and starting with the fags. I don't bother saying anything about it now, because he just gets pissed off with me.

"What happened to our granddad? Did he die before we were born?" I'm looking at the side of Dad's face, which is set with a deep line between his eyebrows as he squints against the smoke.

"Well, he died when I was little. Don't really remember him all that much. That's why Gran's a bit, you know, grumpy sometimes. She's had a hard life, bringing up four kids on her own." He looks at me and I nod. "I'll see if Gran's got any old pictures of him if you're that interested."

It feels hot and sweaty inside Dad's car, and I fiddle with the air knobs until Dad slaps my hand away. After a while, we turn into Gran's road, which is lined with endless terraced houses, all exactly the same, from one end of the narrow street to the other. It's the house Dad was born in.

When we pull up at the kerb, Gran is already standing on the doorstep, with her pale blue cardigan wrapped around her. Her face is set in stone, and she doesn't smile as she sees us arrive.

"She looks happy," mumbles Andy, and I snigger.

Dad growls at us and we all get out of the car, smiling hard.

"Hello, Mum," says Dad, as he kisses her stiffly on the cheek.

"William," she nods at him. "Boys."

We stand in front of her as she blocks the door to her house.

"Give your gran a kiss, boys!" says Dad, nudging me forward with his elbow.

We both kiss her on the cheek, and she never once unfolds her arms from across her chest.

"Well, you'd better come in then," she says, pushing up at her hair with the flat of her hand. Her hair sits in a stiff shape all round her head, like a piece of moulded plasticine. It looks like it's in a hairnet, even though it's not.

Gran makes a pot of tea and lays it out in the front room. We all sit on dining chairs at the small round table in the front window. There's a crocheted tablecloth, and I remember a time when I spilt my tea on it when I was younger. Gran went mad, telling me that her grandmother had made it by hand for her wedding, and that I should have more respect for other people's things.

She's got net curtains that only go halfway up the window, like in a café. I'd never have nets like that in my house, they're really naff. Outside it's sunny, and the grime on the windows shows up against the bright light of the street. A man passes the house, walking a large black dog, and Gran lifts her bottom an inch, just enough to peek over the top of the nets to see him go by. "Hmph," she says, returning her bottom to the chair.

Andy meets my eye across the table, and I have to look away from him before I laugh.

"I've given up baking cakes," Gran says, slicing up a shop-bought fruit cake. "Not much point when it's just me here."

She hands plates to me and Andy. I know Andy hates fruit cake, and he stares at it like it's a spider. When Gran takes a bite of hers, Andy starts to stuff his piece in his face, chewing and swallowing it down as fast as he can. Poor bugger, I can see it's getting stuck in his throat as he tries to force it down with gulps of tea.

"Greedy guts," says Gran, without a smile, as Andy takes his last mouthful. "I suppose you're after another bit."

Andy's eyes look terrified. "No!" he almost shouts. "No, thanks, Gran. That was lovely. Thanks."

Dad gives him a dry smile, and it's hard to tell if he's annoyed or not.

"So," Gran says, pouring a second cup of tea. "How's that Mary?" She reaches for Dad's cup and saucer, and pours the tea slowly, her eyebrows arched and wrinkled.

"She's fine, isn't she, lads?" Dad replies, patting me on the back, sounding too cheery.

"Still into her clever books and all that?" Gran asks, with a sniff.

"I'm not sure. Jake, is Mum reading anything at the

moment?" Dad looks at me, expectantly. I don't ever remember seeing Mum reading any particular book.

"She reads magazines," I say. "*Woman's Weekly*. That sort of thing. Sometimes Sandy gives her her old copies. What do you mean 'clever books', anyway?"

Gran stares at me like I've got poo on my forehead.

"What?" I ask.

Gran gives Dad a disappointed look, and shakes her head.

Andy looks at me and mouths, "What?"

I shrug and take my last mouthful of fruit cake. It's quite nice actually. I'm glad Gran doesn't bake any more. She'd probably try to poison us if she did.

"So, Mum," says Dad. "Jake here's quite interested in seeing a photo of Dad if you've got any."

Gran wraps her cardigan around her again. "Mmm, not sure about that. Can't be sure where they are. What d'you want to know about that for anyway? You never even met him."

"I'm just interested, really," I mumble.

"Speak up, boy!"

"I said I'm just interested," I say, louder.

"I'm certainly not deaf, if that's what you think!"

Andy covers his mouth with his hand, and stares at the teapot. I can see his shoulders shaking. I mustn't look at him. Dad's fingers start drumming against the underside of the table.

"Well, you can take a look in the cupboard under the stairs, I suppose. There might be an old box of photos in there." Gran starts clearing the table, shaking her head as she goes. "Although I don't know why you're so interested myself."

After a few minutes of rummaging about in the under-stairs cupboard, Dad pulls out a small dusty leather suitcase with rusty hinges. "This is it," he says, sounding really pleased, "I remember it."

As he starts unloading pictures on to the living room table, Gran sits in her high-backed armchair in the corner of the room, and folds her cardigan around her again. Every now and then she clears her throat and pulls her chin in to her chest with an irritated expression. We carry on looking anyway.

"Look at this one, Andy – it's me when I was your age. Blimey, mate, you're the spit of me, son!"

Andy looks at the picture and laughs. "Look at your shorts, Dad. Did you have to wear them in the summer?"

"Had to wear them all year round, son. They were my only pair."

"Don't be ridiculous," says Gran. "You make us sound like paupers."

"Well, we weren't exactly princes, Mum." Dad smiles at her.

"Hmph," snorts Gran, as she turns her eyes to the wall.

Andy passes me the photo, and I can see how like Dad he is. I think about that day when Mum said what she said about Dad not being my dad. I stare at the photo, at this boy's dark hair and dark eyes, his long skinny arms and legs, his wide, white smile. It's just like Andy now, gangly and grinning.

"How would you describe my hair colour?" I ask Dad.

"Mousy," says Gran.

"Well, you were bright white blond as a baby," Dad replies. "And it still goes blond in the summer, doesn't it?"

"Matt looked like you too, didn't he?" I ask, waving the photo.

"How is my Matthew?" asks Gran, her face soft for the first time.

"Fine, Mum," frowns Dad. He carries on rummaging through the box. "It's weird isn't it? Sometimes things skip a generation, don't they?" He searches deeper in the suitcase, then pulls out a brown envelope with the words "Andrews family" written on in biro. "Here we go."

The photos from this envelope are older. Dad hands me a picture of a young man wearing a trilby hat and a suit, one leg up on a pub bench, his hand resting on his thigh. He's got a cheeky smirk on his face. He looks like the Artful Dodger in *Oliver Twist*.

"That's him. That's your granddad. When was that taken, Mum?"

Gran leans forward in her chair. "Not long after we got married. That's the Spotted Cow, off Ship Street."

Dad carries on through the photos, and eventually pulls out a group shot and lays it down on the table in front of me.

"Right. That's a picture of him outside his local school. See if you can spot him."

The picture is browny coloured and faded. There are about twelve or thirteen kids in the photo with two serious-looking school teachers standing at the back row in old-fashioned dresses and rolled up hair. I recognise the garden, from when Dad pointed out the school before. The blossom tree's still there.

"They'd just opened the school," says Gran. "That's why they took the photo. Didn't normally have school photos in them days."

I scan the rows of faces staring out of the misty picture, and suddenly there he is, there I am, staring back at myself from this ghost of a photo. My finger comes down on him with a little thud.

"There! That's got to be him!" I cry out, and I can't believe it because he's so like me it can't be real.

"Get your grubby fingers off that!" shouts Gran. "You'll ruin it! Don't you teach them how to treat things properly, Bill?"

"Alright, Mum," Dad says patiently. "Let's have a look, Jake." He lifts the photograph towards his face and concentrates. "Yep, that's him alright. Bloody hell, he's just like you, isn't he? Mum, have you seen this? Jake's the spit of Dad. The spit!"

I can't stop grinning, and my knee's bouncing away under the table. I want to run about the room, and throw my arms round Dad, and blow raspberries at Gran, and wrestle with Andy, but I don't, I just sit there grinning like an idiot.

"Was he short, like me?" I ask Gran.

She looks like she's thinking twice about answering me. "When he was a nipper, so his mum used to say. But when I met him, he was sixteen and sprouting like a bean shoot. His mum used to say he slept in manure, to grow that fast."

Dad's smiling at me. Andy's staring at the photo, with his gormless mouth hanging open.

"That's weird, Jake," he's saying. "That's weird."

When we go to leave, Gran lets me borrow the photo,

and she wraps it in a used envelope and tells me to look after it carefully. "Don't you make me regret it," she says.

"Can I borrow that one of Dad?" asks Andy.

"No you can't!" snaps Gran. "Is that what you all came here for? To clean me out of photos and eat my cake?"

Andy looks wounded. Dad scowls at Gran, and puts his hand on Andy's shoulder.

"Don't worry, Andy," he says, "I'll ask one of your uncles if they've got one we can borrow. Don't want to ruin Gran's pictures that she looks at all the time." He snaps shut the leather suitcase and runs his finger through the dust on the lid.

Andy's face changes. "Thanks, Dad," he says, smiling at Gran and folding his arms high across his chest. Then he says, "Can we go now, Dad? It's just Ronny's gran said I could call round for tea. Nanny, Ronny calls her. She bakes the best cakes ever. Her grandchildren are round her house all the time. And she said to me that I could be her extra grandson if I wanted. You know, she's knitting me a hat for next winter." He keeps smiling at me and Dad, avoiding Gran.

"Alright, boys, it's time to go." Dad is shoving Andy towards the door.

"She's got photos up all over her living room, of all her grandchildren." Andy looks around the bare wallpapered walls of Gran's room.

Gran doesn't speak. She just keeps clearing her throat and wrapping her cardie tighter.

"See you soon, Mum," Dad says as he kisses Gran goodbye.

Me and Andy clamber into the car before Dad gets a chance to make us kiss her again. Gran doesn't look at us.

"Bitch," whispers Andy, before Dad gets in.

"Shut up, you idiot," I hiss at him. As Dad slams the car door shut, Gran turns her eyes on us again. They're full of water and regret.

"Why can't she be nice to us, Dad?" I ask after a few minutes' driving.

"She just doesn't know how to, son," he says, and he frowns the rest of the way home.

Mary, October 1984

I sit in Billy's armchair in the dark of the night. The boys
are sleeping. The plates from our sandwich supper are still
scattered across the coffee table, surrounded by crumbs
and tea rings. I have Rachel's letter in my hand, its folds
scored deep where I've carried it round with me all week.
I pour another gin, and close my eyes. I think of lying
in my childhood bed, with Rachel just a foot away. Her
gentle breathing, the air that we shared. The secrets we
swore to keep. The belly laughter of our friendship. Then
I weep for the fourteen years we've been apart, and the
memories we can never have.

The bottle's empty. The cupboard above the cooker
is empty. Nothing there. I close it, then open it again to
double check. Click-clack. The washing up is stacked
high, and it's starting to smell bad. I'll do it in the
morning. Tomorrow, I'll get up and have a shower, and
get this place straight again. I don't want Billy coming
round here, sneering at me, as if I can't keep a hold on

things. He'll miss us when he sees how well we're all coping without him.

In the lounge, I plump up the cushions and arrange them neatly across the sofa. The letter feels clammy in my hand, but I can't put it down. I pull a chair up next to the telephone stand and read the letter again, in the light cast from the kitchen doorway. "Robert passed away in July, and it made me think, Mary. That life's too short. I miss you."

I dial Rachel's new number. It rings five times, and she answers, sounding fuzzy from sleep.

"Rachel, it's me," I whisper, my hand cupped over the receiver. "It's Mary."

The silence echoes down the wire. "Mary!" she says eventually. "But – it's nearly two in the morning!"

There's another pause, as I wonder if it was a mistake, calling at this time.

"But it's so good to hear your voice, Mary. It's so good . . ." Her voice cracks. "I'm sorry."

"I love you, Rachel," I say, my voice trembling.

"I love you too, Mary. I'm so sorry I stayed away. It's all my fault. I should have kept in touch."

"I could have made more of an effort too," I answer weakly.

I hear footsteps in the street outside, and put my hand over the mouthpiece, half expecting to hear Billy's keys in the door. The footsteps pass.

"I was so sad to hear about Robert, Rach. I had no idea. He was so young. What happened?"

"It was his heart. The stupid thing is, that's why we moved over here in the first place. To give him a healthier lifestyle. He had one before, you know. A heart attack.

Anyway, the doctor says it was probably just a ticking bomb, waiting to go off."

Neither of us speaks for a moment.

Then she says, "So, how are you and Billy doing these days?"

I laugh, more harshly than I like. "He's gone. He walked out four weeks ago, just before the boys went back to school. He said he still loves me, but he couldn't live with me any more. Or some similar cliché."

"Oh," says Rachel. "How do you feel about it? Are you OK?"

"We're OK."

Rachel clears her throat, and I hear her shifting in her bed. I try to imagine the room she's sleeping in. Just across the water in the Isle of Wight.

"So, you had another baby after Matthew?" she asks.

"Two. I've got Jake, who's thirteen, and Andy who's ten. And Matthew's seventeen now."

"Good Lord. I've got two. George's thirteen, and then there's Katy. She's nearly ten."

"I'm an auntie," we say together, and we laugh.

"So we've both got a thirteen year old. Fancy that. All this time, and we never knew. When was George born?"

"May," Rachel replies.

"No! Jake's May the seventeenth!"

"Now you're pulling my leg," she says, sounding like the old Rachel. "George is May the seventeenth too!"

We chatter away, like old times, excited by one another's news. To think, we were pregnant at the same time, giving birth at the same time. And we never knew.

"I can't wait to tell Jake," I laugh. "They'll have to meet. They're practically brothers!"

Rachel sighs, and I can feel her smiling. "Send me a letter, Mary. Tell me everything that's happened to you in the last fourteen years. Will you do that?"

"I'll do it. I'll start tomorrow. But only if you promise to write back and do the same."

"We can close the gap, Mary. If we really want to. It could be like before."

I'm crying now, hot tears that pour down my face, and I want so much to hold her close, to feel her warm embrace.

"I love you," I say, and I hang up the receiver.

In the morning, I get up at eleven. I watch the digital number rise, digit by digit, from 10.29 onwards, until 11.00 won't allow me to stay in my warm, safe sheets any longer. It's Saturday, and the boys are all up in front of the TV. Matthew gets out of his chair as soon as I enter the room. He takes his leather jacket from the coat rack and slams the front door behind him.

"Want a cup of tea, Mum?" Jake asks, putting his empty cereal bowl down on the coffee table.

"Not dressed yet, you lazy boys?" I smile from the doorway.

Andy gives me his how-dare-you look and smiles back. The TV is blaring out and my eyeballs feel sore in my cottony head. Must be all that crying. They're watching *Roger Ramjet*, and the screechy American accents grate through my eardrums.

"Turn it down, Jakey," I say as he hands me a mug of tea. "And do you have to sit so close? Push the sofa back where it belongs."

Jake picks up one corner of the sofa and starts to heave

it backwards. "Is Dad coming round today?" he asks as I settle against the cushions.

"Don't know," I answer. And I don't. He won't answer my calls to him at work, and he hasn't given me the phone number for his new flat. "Maybe he'll call you later to arrange something," I add, watching Andy's disappointed face.

"Yeah. I expect 'e'll do that," says Jake.

"*He'll*, Jake. *He'll* do that."

"Yeah. He'll do that." He blinks at me with his strange green eyes. "I only do it to wind you up."

"I wish that was true. At least then you could stop it!" I rub the bridge of my nose between my fingers.

"What's up, Mum? You got a headache again?" Jake asks.

"Just a little one."

He disappears into the kitchen and returns with a tub of aspirins.

"There you go. Take a couple of those and I'll make you some toast. You shouldn't have them on an empty stomach."

I watch him from the sofa, his little body silhouetted against the kitchen window, as he carefully butters the toast and hums the theme tune from *Roger Ramjet*. His ankles are bony, and his pyjamas are an inch too short. My heart could burst.

Jake, August 1985

When we arrive in Caen, it's around teatime and the sun is still beating down, hot and dry. We sit in the queue of cars snailing off the ferry, with our windows wound down as far as they'll go. Inside the car we're crammed in next to all our luggage, with our knees pushed up by the pillows and bags in the footwell. Andy and me sit on top of the four sleeping bags, which have been laid out one on top of each other across the back seat. The nylon fabric sticks to the back of my bare legs, creating little wet patches that I have to shift and move about on. I wish I'd worn trousers instead of shorts. In between us is a picnic bag containing the leftovers of today's lunch. Dad got Mum to make up sandwiches for the ferry trip so that we didn't waste our money on the expensive canteen food, which is a rip-off. Andy pokes about in the bag, trying to see what's left.

"How long till we stop?" I ask, once we get through Customs and out on to the main road.

"Dunno," says Dad. "We'll see. When we spot a good

campsite, we'll stop."

One of the straps on the roof rack has come loose, and it begins to flap over the side of the car, whipping in next to my face every now and then. Dad pulls over in a lay-by, opens my door and steps up on the edge of the car to fix the strap. His face is sweaty, and he's frowning with concentration.

"That should do it," he says, and he shuts my door and gets back in the driver's seat.

"I think we should stop before too long," says Mum, as we pull away again. "So that we can settle in before it gets dark."

"We've got ages before then," says Dad. "It's a long way down to the Dordogne, so we might as well get a good start today. Right, boys! Look out for signs along the way: *Camping à la ferme*. If we see a good one, we can camp up there."

But we seem to be driving through town after town, little grey places with bent-over pensioners and the odd stray dog. No sign of any farms or campsites around here.

"Will Aunt Rachel be at the house when we get to the Dordogne?" I ask.

"Yes, they'll have been there a week when we arrive. Rachel said they'll stay on for a few days after we get there, then we'll have another week by ourselves." Mum smiles back at me from the passenger seat.

"Will I get to share a room with George?"

"Well, Rachel says the inside of the place is tiny – it's only half converted. But there's loads of space outside, so I don't see why you shouldn't camp out together if you want."

"Brilliant," I say, feeling the hot breeze battering my cheeks. "Brilliant!"

"Can I?" asks Andy.

"No way!" I growl at him. He's not butting in on me and George.

"We'll see," says Mum.

Andy gives me one of his smug little smiles and I shake my fist at him to let him know there's no chance. "Git," I whisper at him through gritted teeth.

"Wanker," he mouths at me so Mum can't hear.

"Later," I whisper back at him, quietly bringing my fist down into the palm of my other hand. "Later, geek-boy."

Andy tuts and turns to look out of his window. "Yeah, yeah," he says. "Knob."

Eventually, as the sun begins to set, we find a *Camping à la ferme* site, and decide to stop there, whatever it's like. Turns out it's really shit, with lumpy, hard ground, pre-war style loos, and a weird old witch of a farmer's wife who can't keep her gnarled hands off Andy's white cheeks. But we get the tent up before it's dark, and cook baked beans over the Calor gas. Mum and Dad open a bottle of wine they picked up in one of the little villages we drove through, and we eat baked beans and baguette and nectarines by the light of a gas lamp. The damp cold comes down quickly, and soon we're stuffed into our sleeping bags with the tent zipped up.

"Love you," I hear Dad tell Mum.

The further south we drive, the brighter the sunflowers, and the wider the fields. The plastic smell of the vinyl car seats hangs heavy in the air, and even the breeze blasting through the four open windows seems unable to shift the suffocating heat. We've been on the road for the best part of two days now, and when we start to pick up the local directions that Rachel wrote out for us, we can hardly believe we're nearly there. The car winds uphill alongside a steep drop that looks down on to jagged rocks below, and I can tell that Mum's nervous by the way she grips at the steering wheel, leaning further forward as if to urge the car on. From time to time we pass little bunches of flowers, laid down carefully on the dry grassy bank.

"So," says Dad, who's navigating, "it says, 'Take the turning on the left marked Ferme Fourniers, and follow the road all the way down, even when it starts to look like it's no longer a road.' There should be some deserted barns on the right along here. There! There they are. OK, we're on the right track. Now, Rachel's place is called La Font de Paul."

The road is rough and bumpy, hardly a road at all, and thick hay-like grass grows across it in heavy clumps. As we pass the deserted buildings, the road disappears altogether, and the grass grows long. It just looks like a dried up old field.

"What now?" asks Mum, pulling a disbelieving face.

"Like it says, carry on anyway."

Mum drives on a few yards then brakes to a halt. "We can't just drive up there. We could get stuck in a rut or something. We don't even know it's the right way."

Dad huffs, and gets out of the car, clutching the directions in a rolled up bundle. He's wearing his faded denim shorts that he's had for years, and a tight stripy T-shirt. I wonder if the shorts are too short as he stretches his arms and legs at the side of the car.

"Won't be a tick," he says, and he marches off through the long grass, and disappears through a haze of heat into the opening of a heavily wooded area. Mum turns off the engine, and the three of us sit in the car listening to the chorus of insects around us. After a few minutes, we all get out, hoping it'll be cooler on the outside of the car, but it's not. The heat is stronger than any I ever remember before, and the sweat pours from my head freely. I run my fingers through my hair, feeling the dampness spread across my scalp.

"Jake! Jake!" shouts Andy, as he scrabbles about in the dusty grass. "Look at the size of it."

He's got a grasshopper in his cupped hand, and he takes it over to the car and releases it. "Skill!"

The grasshopper is light and bright, and it hops about on the hot white bonnet with noisy little taps, until eventually it manages to leap off into the grass and escape.

"Get me a drink, Jakey," says Mum. She's leaning over one of the open doors, fanning herself with the map of France.

I grab the bottle of water from the picnic bag. It's half full, and warm to the touch. Mum throws her head back and gulps it down, chucking the empty bottle on to the front seat when she's done with it.

"Run up and see if you can spot your dad, Jake," she says, "but don't go any further than the opening to the trees up there."

I break into a run, and as I get halfway to the trees, Dad appears, waving his arms in the air, beckoning us to follow him. Andy and Mum get back into the car and drive slowly through the long grass until they reach the

spot where I'm now standing with Dad. We both take our
seats back in the car, and Mum carries on at about a mile an
hour through the trees and across the uneven track.

"It's definitely up here," says Dad, looking excited.
"All the signs match up with Rachel's directions."

The path through the wood is so narrow that the
bushes and branches on either side drag along the doors
of the old Austin, making a screechy, scrapy noise, like
they're trying to hold us back.

"It's a good job it's not an Aston Martin," says Dad.
"I'll have to get the car polish out when we get back
home."

On and on we drive, slowly, slowly, with the mounting
pressure of anticipation growing inside the car. Andy and
me are both up on our knees, craning forward to see if
we can spot La Font in the distance. Gradually, the track
opens up and we're driving through the cool, dim woods
towards the bright sunlight beyond the trees. We emerge
on the other side of the wood, and the car slows to a halt.
There it is: La Font de Paul, a crumbling old barn made
of ancient stone, surrounded by wide, singed grasslands,
nestled against a backdrop of magnificent fields and
valleys. In all its solitude, La Font could be the last place
on earth, and we could be the last people.

"They're here!" screams Katy. Barefoot, she runs from
the barn in a little blue swimsuit, her pigtails flying behind
her, free.

"*Bienvenue!*" Aunt Rachel shouts over, as she beckons
us to drive closer to the barn and park in the shade. She's
wearing faded black shorts and a bikini top, with her hair
piled up under a scruffy straw hat. Her skin is deep nut

brown, and she's so skinny; not in a weak way, but in a lean, busy sort of way. She reminds me of Jane Fonda in those old Vietnam photos of her.

"Wow," says Mum as she gets out of the car. "You said it was in the middle of nowhere. But this – this is beautiful!"

Rachel hugs Mum, then me and Andy. She pecks Dad on the cheek. "How are you, Billy? Good to see you."

Dad smiles, then busies himself immediately, unloading the boot of the car and laying it all out across the dry grass with a concentrated look on his face.

"So, you'll want the grand tour then?" Aunt Rachel puts her arm round my shoulder and gives me a squeeze as we walk towards the earthy ledge that leads down to the fields and valleys surrounding the barn.

We stand in the heavy, dry heat, looking across the landscape of scrub and plain.

Aunt Rachel cups her hands around her mouth. "Cuckoo!" she calls out in a sing-song voice, her eyes surveying the land. "Cuckoo!" We all pause, watching her face, as her eyes scan the valley. "Cuckoo!" Her voice bounces across the land, echoing perfectly as it drifts through the sunlight.

Then, in the distance, we see a little dot plop out of a tree, creating a dust billow as it lands. "Cuckoo!" it calls back, and it starts to run towards us, leaping over dried up streams, and sprinting through fields, in and out of view until it becomes clearly visible as George. "Cuckoo!" he calls out again, closer still.

Before he's got as close as a field away, I'm running down through the gorsy earth to meet him. I approach the wire fence that separates us and he's smiling widely, waving both his arms in the air, looking like a marooned sailor giving an SOS signal.

"Jake, mate! Don't . . ."

I grab the wire to leap over it, and bang, I'm on my backside in the dust, feeling like someone's just whacked both my hands with a rounders bat.

George has caught up with me on the other side, and now he's hunched on his heels laughing between gasping sobs as he catches his breath from the run. "It's electric," he eventually manages to say. "The fence, you idiot. It's electric."

I stare at him; I can't believe he's laughing so much. I've just been electrocuted. When I don't say anything, he looks suddenly worried.

"Jake, mate? Are you alright? Jake?"

He looks so terrified that I snap out of my shock and start to chuckle nervously. He frowns at me, like I've got brain damage. I laugh even more, get up, brush myself down, still shaking. "George, mate! Your face!"

"Bastard," he says, and he puts his ear up close to the fence, concentrates for a moment, then grabs the wire and jumps over it in one swift movement.

"How'd you do that?" I ask. "You didn't get a shock."

"Special knack. You've gotta know how to listen for the wave to pass. I'll show you later if you want."

George holds out his hand and we shake, and slap each other's backs like men.

"You're gonna love it here," he says.

Inside the converted part of the barn there are two rooms, the kitchen and the bedroom, with the bedroom split in two by a sunflower yellow curtain. Aunt Rachel sleeps on one side of the curtain, with George and Katy in the two narrow beds on the other side. Until the others leave in a few days, our family will be sleeping outside in the tents. Dad has already started putting the larger tent up, sorting out the poles and pegs, quietly laying them out in order. His T-shirt is in a crumpled bundle by the peg bag, and he looks strong and serious as he paces around the grass, in his faded shorts and bare feet. He runs a hand through his hair, and it sticks up at the front where the sweat slicks through it. Normally, he'd be shouting for Mum to come and help out by now. George and I start to pitch the smaller two-man tent a few yards from Dad's spot. We strip off our T-shirts too, and our brown bodies seem smooth and unnatural in the washed out landscape. As I bend over for the peg bag, I have to grab at my shorts as they slip down at the back.

"Oh my God!" screams George. He chucks his T-shirt past me where it lands on a prickle bush. "Your white arse! I – I – I think I've gone blind! The light! It's – so – white!"

"Bet yours is no better," I laugh, and I lunge at him, to flick his nipple and poke him in the ribs.

"You gay-boy!" he shouts. "Nipple twitcher!"

"If I did fancy you it'd only be cos I thought you were a girl!" I shout after him, swiping at him as he comes back at me.

We're too hot to carry on larking about, so we get on with the tent. After half an hour, it's up, and Dad is cursing his poles as he unscrews them again and wipes the sweat from his brow.

"Bloody poles. They should label them or something.

Bloody things."

Me and George offer to help Dad with the poles. He looks a bit pissed off, but I can tell he's glad of the help. Even though it's late afternoon now, the sun's still beating down on our backs, and the moisture seeps up through my scalp and down my neck as I bend and twist the metal tubes into place. I've done this a couple of times now, and soon the frame is up, ready for the canvas to be dragged over and pegged down. Aunt Rachel brings out a tray of drinks: clear lemonade and a bottled beer.

"It's not fridge cold, but you'll get used to it," she says, handing the beer to Dad.

"Nice spot you've got here, Rach," he says, nodding to the barns and the land beyond.

Aunt Rachel stands balancing the empty tray on her hip, taking in a deep breath as she smiles at her countryside with a face of quiet happiness. The gaps between her toes are bright white against the conker brown of her feet. "It's Robert's place really."

Dad looks at the ground, silent for a moment.

"I know I only met him the once, but I could see he was a good man." He turns his eyes up to Aunt Rachel now, who continues to survey the valley. "And I'm sorry we lost contact, Rach. I know it broke Mary's heart. I can't tell you how happy she is to be here."

Aunt Rachel shakes the drips off the drinks tray, reaches out and squeezes Dad's shoulder gently, then ambles back to the barn as we grapple with the canvas to finish the tent. We've done a good job, with the tent doors opening on to the best view. We're close enough to the barn, but far enough from the stinking chemical loo that sits in the stone woodshed a few yards from the kitchen door.

"Piss in the bushes, unless you can face the Chamber of Horrors," George says, pointing over to the toilet shed. "But keep an eye out. You wouldn't believe the wildlife here. A viper slithered right across my feet yesterday. No lie! Right across my feet. I was mid-piss, so there was nothing I could do but carry on. Mum said that's probably what saved me – if I'd panicked it might have reared up and bitten me. Urghh."

Over at the opening to the woods, George shows me the standpipe, sticking up out of a cement box built into the earth.

"This is where we get water from. Not for drinking though – you'll get the squits. For washing and cooking with only. We keep a trough filled up by the shit-pit, so you can use that to wash your hands and face in."

"What about having a bath?"

"You can either stand under the tap here, or we fill up a tin bath and leave it out in the sun to heat up through the day."

"What, you think I'm gonna get my kit off and stand under a tap in the middle of a wood? No chance!"

George laughs. "There's no one here! This is it – just us. It's miles to the nearest town, mate. The only living creatures likely to get a flash of your skinny knob are the snakes in the wood. And I know which one I'd be most scared of."

He turns the stiff faucet between his two hands, and a gush of cold water spurts out. We duck our heads under it, feeling the shock of the cool stream pouring down our hot, sweaty backs. Refreshed, we sprint back towards the house to add the finishing touches to our tent. As we pass the toilet shed, a tiny green lizard darts up the pale stonework.

"*Lézard vert*," says George. "They're impossible to catch. Believe me, I've tried."

My head feels weightless, and my eyes drift to the heat haze shimmering between us and the two women who stand beside the door to the kitchen. It's like a mirage in the desert. As my heart slows to a steady thump-thump, I see Mum raise her hand to us as she smiles and blinks against the glare of the sun. My hearing is swallowed up inside a vacuum of fuzz and I'm aware of my knees crashing to the dusty ground, as my body follows.

Mary, New Year 1985

The smell is all wrong. Before I even realise I'm in someone else's bed, the smell is wrong. My breath grows shallow as I rise up from the darkness of sleep, and I feel the unwelcome warmth of a strange body next to mine. Stu rolls over and flops his arms above his head, releasing a musky tone into the room.

"Morning, tiger," he says, with a self-satisfied expression. Like the cat that got the cream, my mother would have said. "Sleep well? I did," he chuckles, noisily rubbing his chin with his knuckles.

I pull the sheets up under my chin and stare at the ceiling. My heart's trembling, as I grasp at piecing together the events of last night. I remember stumbling through Stu's front door, laughing, his hand on the small of my back, urging me up the stairs. "How long have you known Billy?" I ask, searching for common ground.

"Years, on and off," he says. "But we've only really been mates since I moved down the road a few months back." Stu shifts in the bed, wafting his stale scent over me again.

"Oh," I say, trying not to touch his naked body under the sheets.

"He'd be alright about this though, wouldn't he? I mean it's not as if you're together any more, are you?"

"No. I suppose not."

Stu scratches his armpit and yawns. "Anyway. Don't suppose he needs to know about it at all, does he?"

I turn back to the ceiling, noticing the greying damp patches in the two corners near the window. "So, where did you live before?"

He swings his legs out of bed, and sits on the edge trying to step into his boxer shorts. "Southsea. But me and the missus split up and she got to keep the house – and the kid. So I get to live in this shithole. Not for long though. I'm looking for something else. Something a bit classier, if you know what I mean. Tell you what – give me ten years, and I'll have made my first million!" He laughs raucously, and leaves the room without looking back. I hear him peeing loudly in the bathroom down the hall. He clears his throat and flushes the loo.

"Ah, my fuckin' 'ead," I hear him say. "Wanna coffee?"

"OK," I call back. I'm horrified that I'm here, with this stranger who means nothing to me, and cares nothing for me. I gasp at the thought of Billy knowing, of the boys finding out, of this horrible secret. I ease myself out of bed and start to dress. From the hallway, Stu breaks wind and applauds himself, and the bile rises in the back of my throat.

In the kitchen, Stu and I stand at an awkward distance.

There's a picture of a tubby boy stuck to the fridge. He's got Stu's small chin.

The coffee is too strong and it clings to my unbrushed teeth. "Is that your son?" I ask.

Stu nods proudly. "Yup, that's my Malc. Chip off the old block. Or he will be if his mother and her idiot feller don't end up spoiling him rotten. He comes here once a fortnight. Your Jake's met him once or twice."

Jake.

"What time is it?" I ask, looking round the kitchen for a clock.

"Ten thirty," he says, pulling back his sleeve to reveal a huge digital watch. "Shit! You'd better go. Malcolm's due here any minute, and I don't want him to see you here. He wouldn't get it."

I think Stu must think I'm disappointed, because now he leans in and kisses me on the cheek and pats me on the back. "It was a laugh, Mary. Thanks for spending New Year with me. Honest, I mean it." He belches under his breath. "Christ, I can still taste that bloody awful punch of Sandy's. Repeats something rotten. So we're agreed that Bill doesn't need to know?"

I nod, then he's steering me towards the door with my coat and bag, and I'm outside. I stand rigid on the icy doorstep, looking up and down the deserted street. A drink can rattles at the far end of the road, blown along by a cold wind. I shiver. When I look back up the other end of the street, a blue Cortina is driving this way, eventually coming to halt a couple of doors down. A boy jumps out of the car, clutching a rucksack. He's plump, with black hair cut in an odd bowly style. The car pulls away, and as the boy gets closer I realise it's Stu's son, Malcolm.

I pull my coat in tight, and hurry off with my head down. I run and run, along the sleepy streets towards home. At the Royal Oak, I perch on the pub bench and try to slow my thoughts. The boys must still be with Sandy, and Billy will be asleep in his bed-sit. And my house will be empty. Nobody home. I wonder where in the world my Matthew has gone. My first baby, out in the wilderness. How can I protect him, when I don't even know where he is?

A car passes, beeping its horn. "Happy New Year!" the passenger shouts from the window, and the car slows briefly as they throw out a ball of party streamers. It lands in a sad pile at my feet. I watch as its acid colours grow darker, sucking up the damp of the pavement. The sudden clatter of the pub doors makes me jump, and I turn to see Eric the Landlord, up and about as if today's any old day.

He puts his hand up, as he starts to sweep up the fallen leaves that litter the forecourt. "You just off home, Mary?" he jokes.

I smile, standing and brushing the frost from the seat of my coat. "No. I'm off to fetch a pint of milk," I lie, and I scurry off towards my street.

"Happy New Year, love," Eric calls after me.

Outside my house, I stand and stare for a moment, looking along the row of doors, all closed up against the New Year. Ours is the only one without a Christmas wreath. As I open the door to my cold, empty home, I see Andy's tatty slippers, still where he kicked them off last night, before we left for the party. The little Christmas tree stands limply in the corner, its lights off and most of its needles lying on the carpet. The house is silent and grey, and shame falls over me like mist.

There's a massive rope hammock hanging in the corner of the cool, dark kitchen, and after she's given me a glass of water, Aunt Rachel helps me into it and tells me to rest there for a little while. Outside the front door, I hear Rachel telling George to show everyone around the fields and woods, to give me a bit of space. Mum strokes my head and goes off to join the others.

I sway gently, gazing at the beamed ceiling above me. I feel fine, but it's nice being here, alone with Aunt Rachel as she potters about the room, placing plates and pots on the table in preparation for supper. The table is huge, and it looks like a great slice of a tree, because it has the wobbly bark edge still attached. It looks bruised and scarred from years and years of use.

"I know it sounds mad, but I think I'll light a fire ready for tonight. We haven't had one yet, but it gets so cold in the evenings. I hope you'll all be warm enough in the tents." Aunt Rachel starts to roll up newspaper for firelighters. She doesn't do big, quick, bunchy ones like Mum does. She settles herself at the table and lays a sheet of paper in front of her. Then she begins rolling the paper tightly, as thin as a cigarette, until she gets to the end and has a long thin stick to curl up and place in the grate. She repeats this action again and again, as I swing slowly in my hammock, hypnotised.

"I think the heat got to you," she says, still rolling.

"Yeah, I think so," I reply.

"How's it been having your dad back?" Rachel looks up from her sheet of newspaper and pauses.

"It's good, really good," I say.

"What about Mum? How's she been recently?"

I frown at Aunt Rachel. "How d'you mean?"

"I'm her sister, Jake. I know the signs."

I turn my face back to the ceiling, not answering.

"She used to get, well, I suppose you'd call it low, when we were youngsters. Her moods – she'd get high, then low. Do you know what I mean, Jake?"

I nod, without looking down from the ceiling.

"I saw that in her at Christmas. And at Easter when you came over. I recognise the signs, even after all this time. It can't always be easy for you boys. And it's hard work being a mum too. I know that."

I look at her now, and she's watching me, her hands folded in front of her with a pile of finely rolled firelighters littering the tabletop. I nod again. Aunt Rachel looks at me for a long time, and I don't turn away.

"I think you all need a break," she says. "You'll rest here, because there's nothing to do except walk and eat and rest. It'll do you all a lot of good." She bends into the large fireplace, arranging the firelighters underneath twigs and sticks and small branches. "If you ever need to get away from it all, when you're back home, just let me know, Jake. You're welcome at Manningly any time."

She lights the paper, and we watch as the smoke spirals up the blackened fireplace. Spiders and beetles start dropping out of the chimney, smoked out for the first time in months. Some of them fall straight into the rising flames, but others bounce and fall short of the fire, scrabbling and scuttling for shelter in the corners of the room. Rachel lets out a little shriek, and looks back at me wide-eyed. We both laugh, then she darts over to where I'm hanging, tells me to budge up and climbs up next to me in the hammock.

"That's better," she says, staring at the ceiling with her arms crossed over her chest.

"But they can still drop down on you, from up there," I say, pointing to a big black spider hidden behind one of the beams.

"Ahhhh!" she shrieks again, and we lie there swinging and laughing, as Aunt Rachel hides her face behind her hands. "Some country girl I turned out to be," she says.

"I won't let it get you," I say, grinning at the spider, giving the wall a little push to make the hammock swing more.

"I know you wouldn't, Jake," she says, in a serious tone. "You're one of the good ones."

"Your hair's nearly as long as George's now," says Mum, standing behind me and gathering it into a small bunch at the back.

"Get off!" I moan at her, shrugging my bare shoulders to shake her off. My hair is released and flops back around my ears.

George sits next to me at the table, and Aunt Rachel tells everyone else to come and sit down for the meal she's been making.

"Don't you boys want a shirt or something?"

"Nah," we say at the same time.

"You two look like you're straight out of *Lord of the Flies*," she says. "Gone feral."

Rachel plonks a couple of bottles of wine on the table, along with a big bowl of salad, a couple of French sticks, and a casserole dish of *boeuf bourguignon*. We all serve ourselves as Rachel pours the wine.

Dad's been down at the standpipe for a wash, and he's the last to sit down at the table, opposite me and George. He reaches for his wine, brings it to his lips, then looks up at us over the top of his glass. He pauses. His eyes look directly at George, then at me, then back to George. He puts his glass back on the table. Then looks at us again.

"There you go, Bill. Help yourself to the casserole," says Aunt Rachel, pushing the pot towards him.

He looks up at her, and nods. Rachel frowns, as if she's puzzled. Dad's face looks quite pale against the brown of his arms. He looks back at me, then at George again.

"You alright, Dad?" I ask.

He helps himself to the casserole and passes it along to Mum. "I'm fine, son."

"Maybe the heat got to him too," suggests Andy.

"Maybe it did," says Dad, and everyone laughs.

Supper goes on for ages, and everyone talks and laughs throughout. Dad's really enjoying himself and Mum and Rachel seem a bit tipsy as they go on to the second bottle of wine.

"*Salut!*" says Dad, raising his glass again.

"Bottoms up!" say Mum and Rachel together. We all cheer.

For pudding, Aunt Rachel has bought a *tarte au citron* from the *pâtisserie* in the nearest town. She gets out a pudding wine to go with it, and me and George are allowed a bit. It's disgusting, but I drink it anyway.

"You always did know how to do everything just right, Rachel," says Mum. Her words are slurring.

Dad turns his face to the tabletop. Aunt Rachel gives a small smile, like a polite one that she doesn't really mean.

"D'you remember? Mother always used to get you to make the dessert for Sunday lunches? You were always so good at that sort of thing. A much better wife than me!" She splutters the last few words, like it's the funniest thing ever.

"I'm not sure about that, Mary," says Rachel, "I'm not sure Robert would say I was the best wife in the world, if he were here. Actually, sometimes I was a rubbish wife."

Dad's eyes flicker up at Aunt Rachel, then back to the table.

"Well. You're still better than me. Anyway." Mum stands from the bench, steadying herself as she swings her legs out from under the table. "I need a wee. Oh God! Can I pee in the bushes, Rach? I can't bear to use that portaloo thing at night time. It stinks!"

"Go on," says Aunt Rachel, "go round the side of the house."

Mum goes out through the back door, and I can see she's trying to walk steadily and upright. Andy and Katy take their cards into the bedroom, along with one of the gas lamps. They've played Pairs over and over again since we arrived, because Andy's determined not to lose out to Katy. She keeps winning, so he has to keep playing.

"More wine?" Dad asks Aunt Rachel, emptying the rest of the bottle into her glass.

Aunt Rachel rubs her eyes with the heels of her hands. When she looks up at Dad, it's like a warning.

"The last time we saw you was way back, before Jake was born," Dad says. "How did it get to be so long?"

Rachel starts to clear the table. "It wasn't through choice, Bill," she says, her voice controlled and clipped.

Dad starts fiddling with the candle wax that's dripped on to the table.

Aunt Rachel picks up her wine glass, one hand on her hip, and something in her eyes is really mad. I've never seen it before and it reminds me of Mum. "Boys – go and check on Mary. It's pitch black out there – she might stumble if she's not careful. Here – take the lantern."

We leave them in the light of the fire, and walk round to the side of the house where Mum's meant to be. Even before we get there, I know she'll be gone.

"Where could she go from here?" I ask George, feeling impatient.

George leads the way, holding the lantern in front of us. "She hasn't got a torch or anything, so she won't have gone far."

We track round the whole building, but there's no sign of her.

"Try the portaloo," I suggest. "She might have changed her mind, and gone there instead of the bushes."

We knock on the wooden door of the toilet shed, but she's not there. My forehead is getting cold and sweaty again, like it did when I passed out earlier. I start to run about, calling her name into the darkness. George catches me by the sleeve and tells me to slow down.

"She can't have gone far, mate. She's fine." He puts his hand on my shoulder.

I nod. "Yeah, you're right, George. Thanks, mate." I'm glad of the darkness, to hide my panicked eyes.

We carry on round the house, and into the main barn, where George holds the lamp above his head, throwing light up into the beams. The barn is huge, so high and wide. I feel tiny under the lamplight.

"Jakey!" we hear Mum whisper from above. All I can see are the rafters and ladders around the old barn. "Jakey! There's an owl – a barn owl," she gasps.

George walks to the centre of the barn, the lamp still held high, and in a wide, clean swoop, the owl glides across the barn, casting its enormous shadow over the beams in the ceiling. I spot Mum. Up in the rafters, at the top of a long, thin ladder, she perches, with her knees pulled up to her chin. Her face is lit up like a child's at Christmas.

"Jakey! Did you see it? Did you see it!"

George turns to me, looking terrified. "Shit. Get your dad, mate. She could kill herself up there. That wood's rotten all the way through. Get him now!"

I run back to the house, stumbling in the darkness, and grazing my knee on a rock as I fall. As I pass the window, I see Dad and Rachel, now both standing up in front of the fireplace. Rachel has her arms folded across her chest and Dad has his hands on his hips. Across the garden I can hear Andy and Katy, now outside, pointing out the stars and talking. At the back door, I pause.

"You've just got to look at them, Rachel!" says Dad.

He's angry. "They're practically identical!"

"Well, you're wrong, Bill. You've got it all wrong."

"Why else would you have stayed away from Mary for all these years?" He's nearly shouting now. "Maybe she knows. Maybe that's what's got into her?"

"Mary doesn't know!" Aunt Rachel cries, her voice cracking now. "She can't know!"

"What?" I yell, as I stand in the doorway. "Mary doesn't know what?" My heart's thumping again, and I know Mum's up on that rotten ladder, but I know that's not as important as this thing.

Dad and Rachel stop and stare at me. They look as if they've seen a ghost. I know they're not going to tell me. Just like everything else.

I hate them both right now. I flop down on the edge of the fireplace, exhausted, and I tell them. "Mum's stuck up a ladder in the barn. George says the wood's rotten. She could fall and die." It doesn't even sound like my voice.

They both rush out of the door and I'm left alone in the firelight. Out of the corner of my eye, I see a little mouse run in through the open door and straight up the table leg on to the top. It grabs a little hunk of bread that's crumbled on to the table, and runs back out again. When it's gone, I wonder if I dreamt it.

In the morning, I'm the first up. As I emerge from our tent, I find everything covered in a thick layer of dew, and a heavy mist hangs over the valley. I stick my head into Mum and Dad's tent and see she's still lying on her side, in the same position they put her in after they'd got her down from the barn. Dad's snoring, facing the opposite way. I roam around the buildings, looking for signs of life, but it's as if the whole of the world is asleep, except me. It's too early for the lizards, too late for the barn owl. Even the cicadas have fallen silent. As I jump down the rocky ledge and sprint across the field below, I could be going at a hundred miles an hour. My hair is streaming behind me and I feel the damp mist clinging to my skin, soaking through my white T-shirt. Further into the valley I run, leaping over streams, and dashing past brambles that tug at my clothes. But I keep going, enjoying the cool air of the morning and the feeling that the world is mine. On the far side of the valley, I see the sun breaking through the mist. I settle on a dusty mound with my back against an old olive tree. I can see La Font de Paul perfectly from here: the old barn that faces me, hiding the converted house at the back; the two tents – one large and one small; the little white Austin and the big dusty Volvo. Over the back of La Font, I can just about make out a handful of cows, milling about on the land above. They're so slow though, I can't be sure if they're really moving at all. I sit and sit and sit. I know that the rising heat will force the others out eventually, as the slow sunshine turns the tents into saunas. A large yellow butterfly drifts past me and across the fields. There's not a breeze in the air, and I see the steam coming off my damp T-shirt as the heat of the day takes hold. Sure enough, George appears from the small tent. He stretches and stands for a moment looking in my direction, before taking a leak next to a nearby tree. He wanders off, towards the house. Food. It's the first thing he thinks of when he wakes up. Soon after, Andy and Katy come out from the house, probably woken by George's clattering about. They pick up the tennis rackets and take them down to the dry field in front of the barn. I can see them batting the yellow tennis ball back and forth between them, but they never keep it in the air for more than a few hits, because Andy keeps whacking it so hard. Katy's doing all the work, running to fetch the ball all the time, and Andy looks like his body's saying, oh come on, Katy, try a bit harder. George runs down into the field, and they all stop and talk, before he leaves them and heads off towards the woods at the side of the house. I guess he's looking for me. Aunt Rachel is up now, and she's got her hands in the tin bath that balances on the large rocks at the entrance to the barn, scrubbing at the clothes she left soaking last night. One by one, she lifts each piece from the tub, dunks it into another bucket of water then squeezes it, flicks it out and takes it over to the washing line that runs the length of the garden. They'll be dry by lunchtime. I watch her doing this for ages, trying to work out what each piece of washing is. I wonder if Mum will do ours later. I'm starting to run out of underpants and socks already. Dad appears from his tent. Like George, he stretches and stands for a moment looking this way. Rachel stops hanging out the washing and they exchange a few words before Dad goes into the house. He comes out a moment later with a bottle of water, then rolls back the door of his tent and stoops to go back inside. I squint to see if I can get a view of what's going on inside the tent, but it's impossible. I just sit and wait, drawing pictures in the dust with a stick. When Mum and Dad finally come out, I can see from here that Mum's not good. She's up, but she's all curled in and her head hangs forward, like it does when she's in a rough patch. She stands outside her tent, with her arms wrapped around herself, as if she's cold. Like an old woman. Rachel and Dad go off to the house, and come back with a folding table and chairs. "Katy!" Rachel shouts and Katy and Andy drop their rackets and run back towards the house. They start laying out food and drinks on the table, and it looks like they're going to have breakfast in the sunshine. Dad settles Mum on to one of the folding chairs and fetches her a blanket from the tent. She doesn't look at him. George appears again, running across the grass, and he stops at the table to talk to them all. He turns towards the valley and moves his arms in a wide sweep, pointing to the woods, then towards the back garden. In the dusty earth, I've drawn a Gorgon, with wild snake hair and menacing eyes. I run the palm of my hand over it to make it disappear. There one minute, gone the next. George sits down on the picnic blanket to eat his breakfast. They're all there now. Mum, Dad, Andy, Aunt Rachel, George and Katy. Everyone's eating except Mum. The others are all eating and talking, as if she's not there.

Suddenly, as if something terrible's happened, Mum leaps from her seat, dropping the blanket at her feet. She grabs George's hand and drags him to the stony ledge. She's talking to him, and he's shaking his head, shrugging.

She lets go of his arm, and George turns in my direction. "Jake! Cuckoo! Cuckoo!"

He doesn't know I'm here, hidden in the shade of this old tree. He's just guessing, because Mum's making him. I stay quiet.

Mum turns back to Dad, who's getting up slowly, brushing the crumbs from his lap. He walks over to her, puts his arm round her shoulder. She shakes it off, waving her arms wildly.

"Jake!" shouts Dad across the valley, "Jake!"

Soon they're all at it. Jake! Jake! And the sound of

my name is echoing and bouncing over fields and dried up streams. I can see them all running around the house, in and out of the barn, down into the field, up the path to the woods. Only Mum stays still, hunched in her folding chair with her head in her hands. I sit in my shady place, feeling the world tip slightly, as I imagine Miss Terry walking through the hazy valley, bringing me water. My heart slows, like it did yesterday, and I close my eyes where everything is dark and cool. The earth is moving, but I'm not sliding with it, I'm still planted to the dry earth under this gnarly old tree. When the valley falls silent again, I come out from the shade. I come out into the sunshine and slowly make my way back.

"Cuckoo!" I call, to George.

"Cuckoo!" he calls back.

They all appear in a line along the rocky edge to the garden, shielding their eyes from the sun, scanning the land for me. George suddenly points and breaks into a run, followed by Andy and Katy. We meet at the electric fence.

"Where were you, mate?" asks George, frowning. "Your mum was going mental. Proper mental."

"Man, you're in trouble!" grins Andy, and Katy giggles.

"No, you're not," says George. He holds his ear close to the wire, listening for the current to pass, then nods for me to hop over. "We were all just worried. In case you were lost or something. Come and get some breakfast, mate."

As planned, Aunt Rachel, George and Katy pack up to go home the next morning. Their car isn't half as crammed as ours was, so before long, everything's in its place and we're all standing in the morning sunshine, preparing to say our goodbyes. Mum's still quiet but she's there with us, hugging Aunt Rachel and pulling her cardigan around herself. I'm so hot, I can't believe she can wear a woolly in this heat. Andy and Katy are leaning on the bonnet of the car, playing rock-paper-scissors and slapping each other's hands when they get it wrong. Katy's giggling like mad, trying to pull her hand away in time.

"I've left instructions on the table," says Rachel, more to Dad than to Mum. "Directions to Beauville – you'll need to get some groceries I expect, and there's a list of things you need to do before you lock up next week. Disconnect the gas canister, do the shutters – that sort of thing. Apart from that, it's all yours!"

I suddenly remember a book I've promised to lend to George and I run to grab my rucksack out of the tent.

"Hold this," I tell him, when I return to the group, and George holds on to the straps of my rucksack as I riffle through and pull out a bunch of books.

As I balance one book on top of another, searching for the right one, my jotter falls open and the photo of Granddad flutters out and lands on the grass by Mum's bare feet. I'd forgotten it was even in there; I only put it there to keep it flat. Mum stoops to pick it up.

"What's this?" she asks, frowning at the old black and white image.

"It's Granddad," I reply, leaning in to point him out. "There. Dad's dad. He looks exactly like me, doesn't he?" I'm laughing, seeing again just how similar we are.

Mum stares at the photo, then slowly lifts her eyes to look straight at George. George doesn't notice, he's too busy reading the back of the book I've just given him. Mum turns to face Dad, who stuffs his hands deep into his shorts pockets and rocks on his heels, avoiding her eyes.

"Better get you on your way, then," Dad says to Aunt Rachel, sounding jolly and slapping George on the back.

Aunt Rachel doesn't reply, but leans in and takes the photograph from Mum's hands and looks at it hard. Her eyes scan the picture from one side to the other. She brings her hand to her mouth and shakes her head, just a little.

"It's amazing, isn't it?" I say. I can see she can't believe how like my granddad I really am.

Aunt Rachel looks at me over her cupped mouth and nods. Mum turns and runs to the house and everyone stands and watches her go.

After an awkward silence, Dad says, "She's not herself, Rachel. Don't worry about a thing. I'll make sure everything's alright."

Aunt Rachel kisses me and Andy on the forehead, and gets into the driver's seat. She fastens her seatbelt, and looks up at Dad through the open window. "I think we need to talk, Bill. We need to sort this thing out."

Dad nods, not smiling, and the blue Volvo rocks along the dusty grass, and disappears into the cool, dark trees.

Something shifts in our little corner of France. The heat presses down like a wet blanket, and the drill of the cicadas buzzes inside my ears. Around the back of the barn, I spot Mum, sitting on a rock, staring out across the valley. Her skinny brown legs hang over the edge, and she looks like a little girl from this distance. I stay in the shadows and lean against the cool stone wall. Andy is hunched on his heels a little way from Mum, scratching at the dusty grass with a little stick. Every now and then he looks over at her, pausing as if he's trying to work out what to say. Then he goes back to his scratching, flicking up little puffs of dust as the hole grows bigger. He's guarding her.

"Where's Dad?" I ask him, casting shade over his hole.

He shrugs, and carries on digging without looking up.

I nudge him with my foot. "I said, where's Dad?"

Andy looks up at me now. "Fuck off, Jake," he says. "I wish you'd never been born." His eyes are hard. There's a buzzard overhead, and its shadow distracts me briefly.

I push him over sideways, and stand over him. "Cockroach," I whisper, turning to walk away.

Mum looks up, and silently slides off her rock. She passes us without a word or a look and goes through the back door into the house. Out of the corner of my eye I see a dot moving in one of the fields across the valley. Dad. He's left us to it. Mum reappears, now wearing her bikini, sunhat and glasses, and dragging a deckchair behind her. She sets it up beside her rock, then goes back inside the house. She comes back out carrying a bottle of wine and a large glass. The bottle's more than half full. Just before she settles in her chair, she turns and rests her eyes on me. It's not an angry look, or a sad look. It's a puzzled expression, like when you're trying to make out something tiny in the distance. She sits, pours a glass of wine, and stays there with her back to us, gazing out over the valley. Dad has now disappeared from view, leaving nothing but a heat haze in his place.

"Careful you don't burn, Mum," I call over to her.

But she doesn't answer or move. Over the back of the deckchair, all that I can see of her is her hand, dangling over the armrest, limply cradling the full glass of red wine. It disappears for a few seconds, before returning to position. I wonder how long she'll be gone for this time.

When Dad gets back, we lay a picnic out on a rug beside Mum.

"We'll have to get to the market in the next couple of days." Dad's talking all jolly, pretending everything's normal. He looks up to see if Mum is listening. "Well, it's Sunday today, so we'll have to make do for now," he adds, breaking up a dried up old baguette. "Don't know what it is with this French bread, but it goes stale before you've had a chance to eat it."

He puts a few bits of bread and cheese on a plate for Mum, but when he offers it to her she waves it away, and drains the last of the wine into her glass.

"Go and get that other bottle, will you?" she mutters to no one in particular. It's the first thing she's said since Aunt Rachel left.

Andy meets my eyes, then looks down quickly. He unpeels a cheese triangle and squishes it on to a piece of bread with his thumb. "*La vache qui rit,*" he whispers.

I flop down on my side and watch the *lézards verts* dart up and down the wall of the barn. One. Two. Three. The first one disappears inside a hole so tiny that I didn't even know it was there. I can hear a grasshopper somewhere nearby. I know it's a grasshopper because its chirp is different to the cicadas'. I wish I could see a cicada; they're like these secret insects that make this enormous noise, but never let you see them. They sound more like birds. The sun is beating down on the side of my face, and I can feel my nose beginning to sweat. I close my eyes and smell the dry grass and earth.

"Jake, sit up and eat your food," says Dad, nudging me with his sandal.

The three of us sit cross-legged on the blanket, finishing off the last of the bread and cheese in silence.

"What've we got tonight?" asks Andy, unfolding his legs in front of him.

"There's a couple of tins of cassoulet on the shelf, and we've got some spuds. That should do us."

"What's cassoulet?" me and Andy ask at the same time, and he breaks into a smile even though he's meant to be mad at me.

"Beans and sausages. But with a posh French name."

"I said, can you get me that other bottle, Bill?" Mum says coldly, wiggling her empty glass over the armrest. She's just an arm and a hand with a voice.

"There is no other bottle," Dad replies.

"Yes there is," she snaps back, "there's another red on the side. Oh, for God's sake, I'll get it myself." She lunges out of the deckchair, making it rock on its wooden legs. She steadies herself, and shuffles towards the back door in her flipflops. I'd never noticed how bony her knees were before now. Her bikini bottoms sag around her bum.

"We drank it last night, Mary," Dad calls after her. "You just finished the last bottle!"

We hear her banging about in the kitchen, moving jars and pans out of the way. Andy fiddles with a loose piece of blanket, pulling it until it unravels. Dad's rubbing his eyebrows with both hands, blowing air through his lips. Mum appears in the doorway, leaning on the frame, with a mean face.

"Well, thanks for leaving me a little drop, or else I'd

have had nothing at all, would I? The amount you and my sister must have put away last night. I suppose you sat up after I'd gone to bed, chatting and putting the world to rights? I'll bet you had no end to talk about. After all these years."

Dad just stares at her.

"Well?" she screams, and she hurls the empty glass across the grass, where it bounces without breaking.

"Mary, there's nothing to say," Dad says, calmly clearing the plates from the ground. "When you went to bed, so did we. We all went off at the same time, but I guess you don't remember much about it after your second bottle of red." He leans his weight on to one leg, and looks at her kindly. "I don't know why you're getting yourself so worked up."

"Bastard," she whispers through gritted teeth, and she takes herself inside again.

The next thing we hear is the slam of the car door, and we're all up and running to the front of the house where Mum's at the steering wheel, still in her bikini, starting the engine.

"What're you doing, for Christ's sake, Mary?" Dad leans in through the window and grabs the keys. "You're not even dressed!"

"We need food!" she screams at him, jumping out of the car to wrestle the keys back. Her hat falls to the ground and rolls away like a Frisbee. As she thrashes about, I think she looks like a little wild animal.

"Take a walk, boys," Dad says.

I frown at him.

"Jakey, just take a walk. I need to sort this out."

"You bastard! You bastard!" Mum shrieks, slapping at

his hands and chest.

Dad holds her away with one hand, flinching out of her reach.

I nod at Andy and we head off along the track into the woods. When I look over my shoulder, Mum seems to be calming down and she's flopped on the grass, pulling a sulky face. The darkness of the woods is cool, with the occasional flash of warmth as the sun breaks through a crack in the canopy. Andy carries a long stick, which he swishes across the path in a sweeping motion, to scare off snakes. He's terrified of being bitten by a viper. The only sounds in the woods are from the birds high above us. They fly from tree to tree, keeping pace with us, and it's almost as if they're following us, spying down from their treetop look-outs. We don't talk until we come out at the other side into the heavy sunlight.

"Why does she do it?" Andy asks, kicking at the high grass.

"I dunno, mate," I answer. "She just does. It's what she does."

"But none of my friends have got mums like that." His face is hurt, tired.

"I know, mate," I say, and I pat him on the back. "Let's just forget about it. Dad'll calm her down. She's just pissed."

We carry on through the overgrown field, until we come out at the winding road. We decide to follow the road down, the way we'd driven in on the first day, with the steep drop just beyond the thin grass verge. There's a squashed snake in the middle of the road, flat and grey, and huge, and Andy starts poking it with his stick, trying to unpeel it from the grit. I tell him to leave it alone, in case a car comes along and squashes him. He sniffs and leaps back on to the grassy verge. There are berries growing on bushes along the roadside, and we can't decide whether they're for eating or not.

"I think they're sloes," I say, picking one and inspecting it. "But I wouldn't risk it. We'll check with Dad when we get back."

Andy picks a berry, balances it on the palm of his hand, then flicks it over the edge of the roadside. He kneels on the dry verge, carefully craning his neck forward to see down below.

"Oh my God, Jake. Have you seen how far down it goes?" He pushes a little rock off the edge. "I can't believe we drove up here before. I'd have pooed my pants if I'd realised how dangerous it was."

I lean over to look, and step back quickly as my stomach lurches. "Come on. Let's carry on a bit." I hold out my hand to help Andy up. He gives me a nervous frown, as if he expects me to push him over. "Don't be an idiot," I say.

The heat is intense, and I wish for the cool cover of the woods again. My T-shirt sticks to my back, and I feel the bridge of my nose burning. It's about one-ish, I guess. The worst time to be out in the open sun, Aunt Rachel told me yesterday. Andy starts moaning because the back of his neck is getting sore. We take off our shirts and wrap them round our necks like scarves.

"Alright, we'll head back," I say. "We've probably been gone an hour anyway. They should've sorted it out by now.

Andy runs a bit further down the road to look at the bunches of flowers left on the roadside. "Did people die here?" he asks, looking horrified.

I nod, making an up and over motion with my hand, whistling a sound effect. I'm standing a little way from Andy now, and I spot a large bird floating on the horizon behind him. It's amazing, and I point at it to show him, but Andy raises his arm too, and points beyond me, his face suddenly pale. As I turn and look up the road, back the way we came, the world tips again. I feel it; like the axis has slipped. At first, everything is blurry, but I'm not surprised when it appears. Our old Austin comes into view, with Mum at the wheel, hurtling towards us down the dusty grey road. Time seems to slow, as I see her eyes staring blankly through the windscreen at some unseen distraction in the distance, and I think she'll drive straight into us, and that will be that. But she doesn't; in the time it would take for me to blink, she turns her head, just slightly, and I look into her eyes and I see her, completely clear and awake and knowing, and even though her face isn't smiling, her eyes are. I take a step to one side, and the car screeches briefly and sails off and over the cliff edge between us like a great metal bird. Whoosh. One minute she's there, the next, she's gone. We stand motionless, Andy and me, staring at the empty space where the car had just been. Dropping to our bellies, we lean our faces over the edge of the burnt grass precipice to view the wreckage below. Way, way down, a tiny fire burns brightly amongst the craggy rocks and dried up streams.

Mary, August 1985

As the horizon rears up before me, shimmering and bright, I feel her beside me.

"Are you OK?" she asks, touching my wrist lightly.

I nod, with my eyes on the road ahead. "Do you see it? The bird?" I ask.

A bird of prey hovers in the distance, and seems to pull the sluggish car forward, drawn along by invisible force. A line between me and it. Umbilical. The bird bobs in the heat stream, like a totem. I'm so tired, I could sleep now, and let the bird do all the work.

"What kind is it?" the little girl asks.

"It looks like a kestrel to me. I don't know." The road descends steeply, and the speed picks up. This old banger's never gone so fast. If Billy could see me! He'd die! I laugh aloud, and the little girl laughs with me.

"Eeeeek! You're like Stirling Moss!" she giggles, clapping her hands. "Look at Jake and Andy."

There, framed against the steep backdrop of rock and

sky, I see them, my two boys, bare-chested and brown as berries. The kestrel hovers between them, a wing tip on either shoulder. My foot is pressed hard against the floor of the car, and the speed is exhilarating. I forge towards them, a great pike, coursing through this ocean of blue sky. Jake sees me, cocking his head to one side, trying to work it out with his strange eyes.

"Does he see you too?" I ask the girl, turning to look into her deep face. "Does he see you?"

She shrugs, unconcerned, and as I tumble towards them, spitting grit and dust off the narrow mountain path, I smile at Jake, sending my heart out to him, longing for him to understand. The kestrel drops from view and the two boys part, making way for me to pass. Jake nods, a slight tip of his head, and when the car tyres leave the road, I'm really flying.

Jake, August 1985

By the time we reach the old barn, we're drenched in sweat. The air is thick with heat, and the dust from the wooded pathway clings to our bare legs. Nestling into the side of its valley, La Font feels more alone than it did before. It's miles from anywhere, and apart from our cousins, we haven't seen another soul in days.

Inside the cool, dark kitchen Dad sits motionless, his hands resting on the table in front of him. When we stumble through the open doorway, breathless and wild, he turns to us with wet, brown eyes.

"What is it?" he whispers, standing to face us.

Andy and I look at each other, scrabbling for the right words.

"It's Mum," I say, "the car – it just, it just—"

"—wouldn't stop," finishes Andy. "It just wouldn't stop, Dad. We saw it – it went over the edge. On the bend, Dad. The bend with all the flowers. She just went over . . ." His voice trails off into this pained whimper, as the shock of the moment washes over us all. I can still see Mum's calm expression as she raced by, still hear the throbbing beat of blood rushing past my eardrums.

Andy and I stand in the doorway, our shadows stretching deep into the kitchen as Dad blinks against the sunlight. He stares at the stone floor, one hand limp at his side, the other cradling the back of his head like he's holding it all in.

"Stay here," he says, close to a whisper. I go to answer him, but he grips me by the shoulders and locks his eyes with mine. "Stay here and look after Andy," he tells me, and he sprints across the sun-baked grass, in his denim shorts and sandals, and disappears into the woods.

It's more than an hour before Dad returns. He's sweaty and covered in dust, and I guess he must have tried climbing down to the car. When Dad left, Andy sat down in the shade of the doorway, staring after him into the woods. He hasn't moved since. Now, he gazes up at Dad, his face desperate with hope.

"What's happening, Dad?" I ask.

His face looks grey against his dark brown chest, and he avoids my eyes.

"Dad?"

Dad shakes his head, his firm expression breaking loose, and then we know it's all real. Andy starts to cry into his knees, in great juddering sobs. Dad gathers him up and rocks him gently against his body, and he looks so small. My little brother.

My mind scrabbles about for something useful, something practical. "What should we do, Dad? Shouldn't we tell someone?"

Dad looks at me over Andy's head, his face growing calm again. "It's alright, Jakey. It's all sorted. There's nothing else we can do now."

The next morning, I wake to the sound of the cock crowing across the valley. Just like any old morning. I stare at the ceiling of the bedroom. Last night was my first night sleeping in the house, and I'm in the single bed next to Andy's on the furthest side of the room. Dad slept alone in the double bed on the other side of the yellow curtain. The uneven walls seem to ripple in the morning sunlight that floods across the room through our open window. I pick up the extinguished nightlight from the bedside table as I swing my legs out of bed, feeling the cool stone floor beneath my feet. The shallow wax in the bottom of the metal case is full of perfectly preserved tiny moths. There are so many, layered one on top of the other, that it's impossible to count them. They must have singed their wings in the flame. Andy's still sleeping, his mouth open and his arm thrown back over his head. I pull the sheets down at the end of the bed, to cover up his toes. Dad's face is buried in his pillow as I creep past carefully, so as not to wake him. I think he could do with a lie-in, what with yesterday.

Outside, the mist is rising up from the valley. There's dew twinkling across the dry grass, and thousands of fine cobwebs weave across the wide stretch of land at the front of the barn. I shudder as I almost step on a giant slug on my way to the stinking chemical loo. I'm more afraid of them than the snakes, if I'm honest. The day we got here, I saw Andy tread on one and its orange innards shot up the back of his leg, all the way up to his thigh. Andy screamed like a girl, and George and me laughed like mad, but it made my stomach churn. Why would God create such a useless, ugly creature? Not that there is a god. In the rising heat, I hold my breath against the stench of the toilet, and I get it over with as quick as I can. I don't know why Aunt Rachel doesn't just get a proper loo fitted somewhere.

Afterwards, I dunk my hands in the tin trough beside the shed and look out over the waking fields, letting the water slide off my fingers and into the cracked earth. Far beyond the tree line, I can see the mist rising around the old olive tree.

"Mum's dead," I mouth silently. "Dead." The word feels alien in my mouth. Dry as the ground under my bare feet. Dead. Last night Andy cried himself to sleep, but I still haven't shed a tear. I'm not sure I know how to.

Dad comes out and stands beside me, laying his hand on my shoulder. "We're going to have to watch what we use over the next week," he says, his calm gaze on the valley. "I've worked out we're here for another ten days, and we've only got twenty nightlights left. We'll be in darkness by Wednesday if we don't ration them out now."

I turn to him, aghast. Mum's just driven off a cliff, and he's worried about the candles running out?

"Tell you what," he goes on, "if it was my place, I'd get some of the lads over to put electricity in, and running water. It'd be a whole lot easier with lights and a fridge. And I'd cut that path back too, save scratching up the paintwork every time you drive through."

I run my hands through my hair. Maybe I imagined the whole thing. How great that would be, if it was all just a weird, horrible dream. "But, Dad, won't we have to go home early now? You know, because of the accident. Doesn't anyone need to talk to us? About Mum?" Even I know there are things you need to do when someone dies. Official things.

Dad rubs my back, and shakes his head. "Jake, I told you, it's all sorted. The holiday won't last for ever, mate, so let's just make the most of the time we've got left."

I'm frowning at him, and I don't know what to say.

He smiles gently. "Look, we've got to be strong for Andy. OK? I think we can get by on what we've got, so long as we're careful. If we really have to, I can walk to the nearest town. Rachel put something about it in her instructions; Beauville's forty minutes away on foot, so it's not out of the question."

He slaps me hard on the back and picks up the poo shovel that's leaning up against the trough.

"I'm off to dig the hole. I'll need a hand, so you and Andy grab a spade from the shed and come and help me. I'll be up behind those sloe bushes."

Andy comes to the doorway, rubbing his nose. His eyes are all puffed up like slugs. "Help with what?" he says.

I stare at Dad's bare, brown back, the way it muscles as he walks. "Why are you doing the shit hole? Can't it wait?" I shout after him.

"Jobs to be done, Jakey," he replies, his voice normal and even.

"Oh," I mutter, not knowing what to do next. Andy runs after him in his bare feet, and I fetch the spade from the shed.

Dad picks a spot away from the house, under some

old orange trees. They're not in fruit, and I'm not even sure they're still alive. The ground is so hard that Dad has to break up the top layers with a pickaxe he found in the shed. He's hammering it down into the dry grass, levering up great big clods of earth, as his back sweats into the waistband of his shorts. When he decides that the hole is big enough, the three of us go back to the shed to fetch the slurry. It's so disgusting that Dad has to carry it on his own, as we run ahead of him gagging and retching. It's foul, and Andy can't even look at it without sounding like he's really vomiting. At the dug edge, Dad plants his feet wide apart, cautiously tipping the filth into the gaping hole.

"Urghh, look, Andy. Look at the size of that one. That's got to be one of yours," I say, sniggering.

Andy gags and walks away with his hand over his mouth.

Dad stands up straight and rubs the small of his back as he puts the empty barrel to one side. He picks up a spade and starts to fill the hole with the old soil. I just stand and watch, enjoying the sound of the earth covering up the filthy soup.

"Go and rinse the barrel out, Jake," Dad says over his shoulder.

"Why can't Andy do it?" I ask, annoyed that it's always me.

"I'm not doing it," Andy shouts over from his safe distance. "It's rank. You do it, Jake. He asked you, not me."

He pulls a fist at me, and I go for him, pinning him to the ground and punching his puny arm.

"Get off me, you bloody psycho!" he shouts, and he

brings his knee up, right between my knackers.

Andy jumps up, and for a moment I'm floored, but I grab him by the calf and pull him back down and twist the hair behind his ears until he screams.

"Mum!" he shouts. "Get him off me."

We all stop still, our silence made louder by the constant click of the cicadas. Andy's face is ashen, and his lips tremble as his chest rises and falls rapidly. Dad leans on to his spade, with his head hung low, and doesn't move. Andy turns to me, horrified, then back to Dad.

"Dad?" I say, standing beside him at the poo pit. I touch his shoulder blade with the tip of my finger.

A single sob empties out of him, like a moan. He pushes the spade over and strides off down the garden, before breaking into a run over the shimmering fields below. We watch him till he disappears from view. Andy's twisting his thumb this way and that, like he does when he's worried, his gaze still on the valley. When Dad doesn't come back, I pick up the two shovels, and together we finish the job in silence. We flatten the mound of earth with the back of the spades, pounding it as level as we can. Afterwards, Andy doesn't speak; he just wanders off alone, to pick around in the grass for wildlife. I go round to the front of the barn, and scan the valley, but I can't see Dad at all. Maybe he's found the old olive tree, like I did. I carry the poo bucket into the cool woods and rinse it from the standpipe. He'll be back, when he's feeling better.

That night, as I struggle to sleep in the humid darkness, I can hear Dad behind the curtain. He's crying, but so softly it could be mistaken for deep breathing. Andy won't hear; he's asleep, a frown stamped across his tanned forehead. He's curled towards me on his bed, naked in the awful heat, and in the candlelight his body looks too long for his baby face. After a while, the only sound from the other side of the curtain is Dad's gentle snoring. The wax nightlight flickers on my bedside table, and I watch as the moths fly to their deaths, one after another. The night goes on and on, unchanging, until the owl glides in through my open window, lighting up the walls with her shadow. In the silent dark of the night, I blink to prove she's real. On the third blink, I feel the breeze of her wing beat, and she's gone.

After a few days, we get into a sort of rhythm. Every morning, I'm up first and I go down to the standpipe to fetch water for the kitchen. I go round opening up shutters as the water pan comes to the boil on the hob, and I sweep out the insects that have crept under the door in the night. All my clatter usually brings Andy out, and he gets to work making a pot of tea. The milk is UHT, so it tastes a bit weird, but if you put in extra sugar it's passable. Without fail, Andy goes out the front in his bare feet and treads on something on the way to the loo; a slug or a prickle or a mound of rabbit droppings. He'll scream theatrically, and I know he does it on purpose to get Dad up, because it always works.

This morning, Dad seems pretty chipper, and he's full of plans. "Righto, boys," he says with his mug in one hand, running the other across the dusty window sill. "Think we need to clean up a bit today. The place is looking shoddy." He walks us round the rooms, pointing out what needs doing. "Jake, you can run a broom through the house, and dust every surface. Andy, you can clean the gas hob and polish the kitchen windows. I'll clear out the fireplace and fix up the hole in the back door for Rachel. We can't leave it like that till she next comes. She'll have a colony of wildlife in here before she knows it."

We all laugh. Last night, as we sat at the table eating some cheese and crackers, a toad as big as a dinner plate squeezed through the hole in the bottom corner of the back door. We all stared as it lolloped a few paces across the floor, before a second one squeezed its way in too. Andy cried out and jumped up on the table. "They're monsters!" he yelped. Dad opened the door and shooed them out with the gas lamp, then propped a stack of logs up against the hole. "I bet they've been living in here all the time it's been empty," said Dad, and he shuddered, "urghh!"

We get to work on our various jobs. Dad looks content to be doing something useful, and he strides about with a pencil behind his ear. It feels good to get the place in order. I've been keeping the area round my bed in pretty good shape, but the mess of the rest of the house has been niggling me more and more. As I sweep through our shuttered-up bedroom, the dust rises in billows, catching the light from between the slats. Just like you see in the old gangster movies. I push the broom far into the corners under mine and Andy's beds, straightening the bedclothes as I go. I fold all my clothes into a neat pile on the bedside table, and chuck the dirty ones into a heap on the floor. I'll do a wash later. I watched Aunt Rachel doing her washing in the two metal tubs, so I know what to do, more or less. Andy's corner is a dump. I tell him to sort out his dirty laundry once he's done the kitchen. Pushing the shutters back against the outside wall, I stop for a minute to look out across the view. The dull glare of sunshine makes my eyeballs ache briefly. Far off in the distance, I can see the small figure of a man herding his cows from one field into the next. You can see the farmhouse from here, but I've never seen anyone in the valley before. I feel a little stab of disappointment, that we're not really all alone in this corner of the world.

"Boo!" says Dad, his head popping up outside the window in front of me.

"Oh! Bloody hell, Dad!" I gasp, clutching my chest. "You nearly frightened me to death."

He smiles and carries on past the window to do whatever he was doing. I scoop up all the used nightlight cases and take them through to the bin in Mum and Dad's room. I push back the yellow curtain and tie it against the wall. The air in here feels suddenly still. Dad has slept with the window closed tight, and the stifling smell of warm bodies is heavy. All the items that litter the dressing table are in shadow, and I'm almost afraid to open the shutters for fear of what I might find. In this light it looks as though someone's still sleeping in the bed. I bundle over to the window and throw the shutters wide, breathing deeply from the outside air. My heart hammers away as I turn back to the room to find it normal in daylight. I dust the surfaces carefully, setting down Mum's things exactly where she left them after Rachel had gone. I smell her perfume bottle, and run my fingers down the decorated glass edges. It smells of her hair, when she's just washed it and it's clean and shining. I sweep far beneath the double bed, and all sorts of dead insects and dust balls come out with the broom. There's even a tiny dried up frog corpse. I put it to one side to show Andy later, and empty the rest of the sweepings into the bedroom bin. Mum's clothes are draped over the back of a wicker chair in the corner. Her shorts are in the same place that she took them off on that last day, and they lie like two small hoops on the floor. Her bra dangles off the bed knob. It's salmon coloured. I hear Dad whistling round by the back door, as he starts to bang about mending the hole, and I lean out of the window to see him bent close to the ground, sorting through a small tub of nails and screws.

"I'm going to wash our clothes," I call over.

"Good plan," he says, not looking up. His arms look dark and strong as he pushes himself to standing. "Mine are all on the floor in there."

"I know," I say.

Dad carries on measuring and marking up a piece of wood. He looks up at me, where I'm still leaning out of the window. "What?" he says.

I look away, then back at him. "What about Mum's stuff?"

He doesn't answer, and he starts to saw away at the piece of wood, holding it steady across an old stool. "Whatever you think, Jakey," he says when the cut wood drops to the ground. He disappears round the corner to fix the door.

The next afternoon, I'm out fetching the washing off the line when the first drop of rain hits my cheek. At first I think it's bird poo, it's been that long since I felt rain on my face. I look up, and see that one half of the vast skyline is black and threatening, whilst the other half remains in bright sunshine.

"You'd better get that lot in!" Dad shouts over from

the shed roof, pointing out the sudden fork of lightning in the distance. He climbs down the ladder, and puts the tools back in the shed. He's been replacing the broken tiles for Aunt Rachel, ready for the winter.

I run down the long line of washing grabbing it down in big bundles and dumping it into the tin tubs. Most of it is Mum's; I decided it would be best to wash it all in the end. A deafening crack of thunder smashes through the air, and I run clutching the first tub and dropping it on to the stone floor of the kitchen. I sprint back for the second one just as the rain comes down, and in the few seconds it takes to get back to the house, I'm drenched. Andy and Dad stand in the doorway cheering me on.

"You dropped your kecks!" laughs Dad, and I look back to see a trail of smalls that have fallen off the pile as I ran. "Might as well go back for them, as you're already wet," he grins.

I shrug and run back along the length of washing line to the furthest sock, scooting round as I pick it up. The water sits on top of the ground like a big puddle, unable to soak into the baked earth, and as I run back towards the house I lose my footing and land flat on my back with a thud.

Andy whoops hysterically, and Dad is bent double slapping his thighs. When I get to the door, I grab at them both, pressing my wet body up against them to soak their clothes.

"Go and get changed," says Dad, pushing my hair off my face.

In Dad's bedroom, I peel off my wet clothes and they drop to the floor with a slap. I wrap myself in a bath towel, and go back through to the kitchen where Dad and Andy are watching the storm from the window. It's as dark as dusk outside, and the storm must be right above us, because the thunder and lightning are constant. Like the world's splitting open. I stand next to Dad and shiver.

"You alright, son?" he asks, putting his arm round my shoulder. He stoops slightly to see through the window.

Suddenly, I'm so cold I can't even answer him. My shivering grows and travels through me until my legs are shuddering and my teeth chatter.

Andy leans past Dad to look at me with a frown.

"You don't look good, mate," says Dad. "You're freezing." He wraps his arms round me, and rubs my back dry through the towel, like he used to when I was little.

The tubs of washing sit on the floor beside the table, with Mum's clean clothes spilling out all over the place. One of her stripy socks lies in a ball under the bench where it rolled out of the washing tub, still turned inside out from the last time she wore it. My body swells up as I sob into Dad's shoulder, my cries coming loud and harsh. Dad holds me tight, my arms pinned beneath the towel, and the thunder crashes down all around us, drowning me out.

"You're alright, boy," Dad whispers into the top of my head. "I'll make a nice fire, and you'll be alright." He smooths back my hair again, and kisses me on the forehead, and I realise that he's never done that before.

After five days, we're sick of instant mash and tinned frankfurters every night. For lunch today, we had crackers with Marmite, and I'm still starving. I poke about the dark kitchen, looking for something else to eat, while Dad lies on the picnic blanket at the back of the house. All the fresh food ran out days ago, and I'm desperate for some bread, some of that lovely, warm baguette, all crunchy on the outside and soft and doughy in the middle. One of the best things about France is the *boulangeries* that we stopped in en route to La Font. The smell as you walk into one is like nothing I've smelt before, not even in an English bakery back home. It's warm and bready, but with a layer of sweetness, like icing sugar dust that billows up when you put it through a sieve. There are always piles of French sticks and big flat loaves behind the counter, and glass display cabinets filled with strawberry tarts and intricately decorated gâteaux. At the first one, we all crowded into the shop together and Dad asked for "*Deux baguettes, madame*", and the old woman behind the counter smiled at him like he was a film star and she asked, "*Anglais?*" and he smiled back and said, "*Oui, madame.*" She handed him the bread then put two little custard tarts in a paper bag and said, "*Pour les garçons,*" and pointed to us. "You've got the charm of the devil," Mum said, rubbing his shoulder as we walked back to the car. He looked chuffed to bits with himself. I thought about how Dad's been practising his French on us, and I realised that he'd had this trip in mind for months.

On the shelf in the kitchen are several jars of *framboise* jam that Aunt Rachel left for us. Strawberry jam and warm baguette would be heaven. There are stock cubes, salt, sugar and flour, but other than a few more cans of sausages and beans, there's nothing else. The worst thing is that we're on to our last two bottles of mineral water, and Aunt Rachel said that under no circumstances were we to drink from the taps over here. Katy got gastroenteritis one year, and she nearly died, she said. I expect she was exaggerating, but the screaming runs is not something I really want to risk.

Outside, Dad is still lying on his front on the blanket, wearing his denim shorts and sunglasses. His back is a deep red-brown now. The sun's blistering today, and all the rain from the thunderstorm has dried up as if the storm was never really real. He's reading one of the books that Mum had packed, *Cold Comfort Farm*. Dad never reads books. I kneel down on the warm blanket beside him.

"Any good?" I ask.

"Not bad," he replies, pushing his sunglasses up his nose.

"I finished my book the day before yesterday. That's three I've read on holiday, altogether."

Dad nods. "That's good, son."

I take off my T-shirt and lie next to him, in the same position. He carries on reading, swatting a hoverfly away with his hand.

"Watch you don't burn," he says, still looking at his book.

"I'm alright," I say, feeling the scorch on the back of my neck. "Dad?" I ask, and it comes out all whiny.

"Yup?"

"How about we go into town, Dad? There's nothing left, and we're going to have to work out how to get home on Monday. You know. With there being no car and all."

Dad carries on reading and I wait for his reply.

"And we're nearly out of water. We'll get the shits if we drink from the tap. We definitely will, Aunt Rachel told us."

Dad puts his book down. I shift up on to my knees

next to him.

His silence is killing me. "Dad, I think I'll die if I have to eat another tinned sausage. I haven't had any fruit in a week. I could get scurvy. Can we, Dad? Go into town? We've got loads of francs left." Thank God Mum didn't have anything with her when she took the car. I wonder what they thought when they found her down there, with nothing but a pink bikini and a straw hat.

Plucking at the frayed edges of the blanket, Dad is still silent. Andy's been listening from the bedroom window, and he comes out and plonks himself down with pleading eyes. A small green lizard sprints across the grass and up the brickwork of the old barn. The dip of skin behind my knees is filling up with sweat, and Andy's eyes meet mine across Dad's bent head, and I nod at him. For a brief moment everything stands still.

"Dad?" Andy starts, but his voice trails off, and he sounds like he might cry.

I look across the scrubby grass, and wipe the sweat from my lip. I don't think I've got the fight to ask again, and I flop back on to the blanket. Andy makes a 'go on' face at me, and I close my eyes to him.

"Alright!" shouts Dad, startling me on purpose. "We'll do it! Can't let you get scurvy, can we, Jake?" And he's laughing, and poking me in the ribs. "Look at the state of you! You're a bag of bones! And you're not much better," he says to Andy, squeezing his knobbly knee, and making him shriek. "How did a fine figure of a man like me end up with a pair of twigs like you, eh?"

Andy punches the air, before running off, barefoot, to fetch pen and paper. "Skill!" he whoops as he goes. I don't think it would be right to punch him right now, though.

Andy writes the list, as we all say what we want.

"Baguettes. Get four. Cow cheese – you know, *vache qui rit*. Lemonade. Peaches – no, nectarines are better. Some of those little cheesy crackers, like Ritz."

"Water?" says Dad.

"Oh, yeah. How many? Six?"

"That should do it. What about for supper? I could get some chicken pieces and fry them up with a few vegetables. I'm sure I could knock something up." Dad rubs his chin.

"Oh! Milk! And some Petit Beurre biscuits. They were lovely," says Andy.

"Ice cream?"

"Don't be daft, Jake, I'll be on foot."

Andy and me both stop and frown at Dad.

"Well, I'm not taking you two. It's nearly an hour away, and someone should stay here. I'm not leaving either of you on your own, but you'll be fine together."

"How will you carry it all back?" I ask.

"I'll manage. There might even be a bus service or something."

"Well, I don't think we should add anything else to the list, though," I mumble, snatching the paper off Andy.

"Pez!" he says. "Did you see in one of the shops before, they did Pez? They're only small." Andy grabs the list back and writes "Pez" at the bottom.

Dad changes into some fresh clothes and heads off through the woods.

The hours tick by, slow and stifling, as Andy and I loll about in the shade, flicking through cards and quiz books to fill the time. We've found a spot under one of the trees at the back of the barn, on the edge of the grassy bank that leads into the valley. Andy goes in and fetches one of Mum's crosswords.

"Wanna help?" he asks me as I line up a game of patience.

I shake my head, and start turning over the cards.

Andy fills in a few squares, but after a couple of minutes he starts huffing and tutting to himself. "What's this: Bits and pieces, 4-3-4? It's got to be something 'and' something."

"Dunno," I reply, carrying on with my game.

"OK then, what about American for football?"

"Soccer."

"Really? I've heard people call it soccer before. Didn't know it was American."

My card game runs out of steam and I scoop up the cards and roll over on to my back. Every movement is a great effort, and even in the shade it's too hot to do anything. I can feel the dry heat on my tongue when I breathe in through my mouth. Andy chucks the crossword book to one side and lies next to me quietly. The cicadas are going crazy today, click-click click-click. They chorus on different levels, like singers in a choir, so it becomes a harmony of clicking. I squeeze my eyes shut and try to filter out the different voices and layers.

"Will you miss her?" Andy asks.

We lie shoulder to shoulder gazing up at the sunburnt leaves. A rare breeze rustles through the branches, and is gone.

"I'm not sure yet," I answer.

Sometimes the cicadas just stop altogether. They do it now.

"Shh!" I tell Andy, and after two quick beats, they start up again.

"What will we tell people, when we get home?" Andy props himself up on his elbows to look at me. "I mean, people won't believe us, will they?"

I close my eyes again.

"Maybe we should say she had cancer. Or a heart attack? That sounds better, doesn't it?"

"Better than what?"

"Than driving off the edge of a cliff. I mean that just sounds like we made it up. It's embarrassing. People would laugh."

"Why would anyone laugh, you idiot?" I say, looking up at him now.

"She was drunk."

"Well we won't tell people that bit, will we? That bit's not important. We could just say it was a car accident. And that's it."

Andy's face brightens. "Oh, yeah. Brilliant, Jake! It was a car accident. Anyone would believe that."

"That's because it's true, you spanner. It *was* an accident."

Andy lies back, his bare shoulder brushing mine. I shift away, not wanting to be touched. I can't take the heat for much longer.

"Do you think we made her go off the road?" he asks, his voice near a whisper.

"What?"

"If she hadn't seen us, maybe she would've stayed on the road. On that bend."

I don't know how to answer, because I've thought about it too. "No I don't think that. She would've gone

355

over anyway. We couldn't have stopped her."

"Mmm," he says.

I feel a weird sensation across my feet. "Urghh!" I yell, sitting up to see a *lézard vert* sprinting across the dried grass and up the tree trunk. "Oh, that was horrible. They've got little claws. Urgh."

Andy laughs. "I'm gonna try and catch one." He jumps to his feet, only wearing a pair of tatty Y-fronts, and starts to do karate moves in front of me. "Ahhhh! Glasshopper. Only with the patience of the cobra will you master the lizard-beast. When you have achieved inner lightness, you will be ready to tame the green one." He tiptoes in exaggerated steps, all the while making cooing karate motions, and looking over his shoulder to see if he's making me laugh. "Ahhhh! Glasshopper!" He looks at me with raised eyebrows, as if he's discovered something incredible. "Patience of cobra!" He gets right up against the tree and presses his body against the trunk. He looks ridiculous, and so skinny that he actually looks malnourished. His Y-fronts bag around his no-bum.

"Quickly as you can," I say, in my Master Kung Fu voice, "snatch the lizard from the tree. When you can take the lizard from the tree, it will be time for you to leave."

He stands motionless, staring up the tree. He suddenly snatches up into the branches, then screams like a girl and throws something at the ground as if it bit him. "Shit! Shit!"

"What is it?" I crawl across the rug, out of the shade, to look at the thing on the ground.

Andy crouches next to it, and cautiously pokes it with his finger.

"What is it?" I ask again.

"It's its tail. I pulled its bloody tail off."

We stare at it a bit longer with the sun's rays burning down on our backs.

I stand up and press my palms together to do a Japanese bow. "Ahhhh! Glasshopper! Indeed, you have patience of cobra. Your initiation is complete!"

Andy stands and returns the bow, and I suddenly see us as others might, as two skinny boys in baggy pants, standing in the middle of nowhere in the scorching midday sun. I start to laugh, but it's a nervous kind of laugh, one I can't control, and it takes me over till I'm on my knees pounding the dry ground with my fists, screaming and laughing like a madman. Andy's with me, rolling about on his back, clutching at his belly as tears roll down his face. "Glasshopper!" he howls. "Glasshopper!"

The heat sends us crawling back into the shade, as our laughter subsides and we flop back against the rug, exhausted. The sun's so bright beyond the trees that I struggle to keep my eyes open. I hear Andy's breathing as it becomes deep and slow, and together we drift into a warm slumber of grief, surrounded by the soothing clicks of a million cicadas.

When the *gendarmes* arrive at La Font, we're still dozing in the tranquil air. The holiday is over. We trudge beside them through the dappled light of the wood, and towards the opening to the grassy meadow. A black and white police car fills the view, strange in the dazzling sunlight.

Dad leans on the roof of the car, his head resting on his folded arms. As we break out of the shadows, he looks up and nods at me, his stern face full of relief. "It's time to go home, boys," he says.

Andy's fingers feel for mine. "Skill," he whispers, looking up at me with half a smile.

I squeeze his hand, and lead him to the waiting car.

Acknowledgements

There are so many people who have spurred me on in the writing of this book – too many to name them all.

Special thanks to the creative writing staff at the University of Chichester for their inspiration and encouragement; in particular to Dave Swann, who helped me to spot the novel inside my short story; to my MA workshop friends for their generous and insightful readings; to Adrian Weston and Jemima Bamford at Raft PR for their invaluable advice and enthusiasm; to Candida Lacey, Vicky Blunden and Corinne Pearlman at Myriad Editions for their expertise, humour and tender care of *Glasshopper*; and to Paul Walshe, for sharing the magic of La Font de Pepicou with the Ashdown family.

Most importantly, thank you to my family and friends. Particular thanks to my warm and talented mother, for a rich childhood and unconditional love; and to my wonderful husband, Colin, and our two beautiful children, Alice and Samson, for their endless patience and belief.

Glasshopper

BOOK GROUP GUIDE

Questions for discussion

BOOK GROUP GUIDE

- Having read the novel do you find yourself more attached to either Jake or Mary?

- What makes the family in *Glasshopper* dysfunctional?

- Does the novel attempt to attribute blame for their troubles?

- Does the novel tell us anything about the experience of children with alcoholic parents?

- What does *Glasshopper* say, if anything, about good or bad parenting, and motherhood in particular?

- Do you feel sympathetic towards Mary as a character?

- What is gained by having both Jake and Mary narrate their stories, and what limitations does this present?

- Is Bill a good father?

- How does the behaviour and moral code of one generation impact another in the book?

- What kind of character is Gypsy — is she sympathetic? How does her behaviour also reveal Bill, Stu and Mary's characters?

- Does our impression of Rachel change as the novel progresses?

- What does Matt — and his absence — add to the story?

• Are there any turning points in how we see Bill as the story progresses?

• How important are the time shifts within the novel?

• How does the shift in location to the Dordogne change the atmosphere of the end of the novel?

• How does Bill react to the news of the accident, and how is this reflective of his character?

• How does Jake deal with what happens in the Dordogne, and his father's reaction to events?

• Could the family have survived Mary's alcoholism had the novel ended differently?

• Is the novel judgmental or prescriptive in its depiction of alcoholism?

• What is it that unbalances the family — could it be secrecy? Addiction? Betrayal?

For the downloadable Book Group Guide plus Author Q&A, please visit *www.isabelashdown.com*

January 2010

Sarah waits at the kerbside, her winter coat buttoned up tight against the cold night air. The tang of sea spray whips through the lamp-lit High Street, as the distant rumble of clawing waves travels in from the dark shoreline, up and over the hedges and gardens of East Selton. It's an ancient echo, both soothing and unsettling in its familiarity. She checks her watch. She's early.

At the far end of the Parade, an old Citroën turns the corner and rattles along the street, drawing to a stop alongside her. She stoops to peer through the window, and sees John Gilroy smiling broadly, stretching across to open the passenger door, which has lost its outside handle. She slides into the seat, pulling the door shut with a hollow clatter.

"It's good to see you, John," she says, returning his smile, not knowing whether to kiss him or not. She runs her fingers through her hair. "This is a bit weird, isn't it?"

John pinches his bottom lip between his fingers and frowns. "Yeah, *really* weird."

There's a moment's pause as they look at each other.

"I suppose we'd better get it over with, then?" he says, releasing the handbrake and pulling away.

They cruise slowly along the deserted Parade as the wind buffets the faded canvas roof of the car, whistling out across the night. Sarah draws the seatbelt across her body, clunking it into place between the seats.

A disquieting recollection rattles her, a sense of having been here before, with John at her side. She studies his face as he struggles with the gear-change from second to third, a slice of mild irritation still lodged between his black eyebrows. "Sticky gearbox," he mutters as it grinds into gear.

Sarah gazes out at the shop windows as they pass through the High Street. She remembers old Mr Phipps from the tobacconist's. Every Saturday morning Dad would take her there on the way back from the paper shop, and she'd choose something from the jars at the back of the counter. It was a tiny vanilla-smelling store, its walls adorned with framed black and white photographs of the screen greats: Clark Gable; Bette Davis; Victor Mature. She notices the estate agent's, on the corner opposite the war memorial, although the name over the top has changed.

"I couldn't believe it when I got your email," she says. "It's been years."

"Twenty-four years," John replies.

She nods.

"I worked it out. It was just before your sixteenth birthday, wasn't it?"

"You've got a good memory."

He keeps his eyes fixed on the road ahead. "Well, one minute you were there, and the next you'd gone. It sort of sticks in your mind."

Sarah shivers against the cold. "The town gives me the creeps, to be honest. When I checked into the B&B this afternoon, the woman who owns it seemed familiar, but I don't know why. I guess she's just got that Selton look."

"What's a 'Selton look'?"

"Don't know. But it puts me on edge, whatever it is."

John scowls, feigning offence.

"Not you, though!" she says quickly. "You don't count."

She notices he's wearing a knitted waistcoat under his jacket. It's a bit hippyish but she's pleased to see he's no longer in the black prog-rock T-shirts that seemed to be welded to his torso throughout the eighties.

They turn into School Lane.

"So, who are you dreading most tonight?" John asks.

"Oh, God, what a question! It would be easier to say who I'm not dreading."

"OK, then. Who?"

A light mist of freezing fog has started to descend, and the windscreen wipers squeak into action.

"Actually it's the same people. I'm looking forward to seeing certain people but dreading them at the same time. Tina and Kate are the obvious ones."

"Dante?" John asks, briefly turning his eyes on her with a small smile.

She blinks. "He probably ended up in some rock band in LA. That was the trouble with Dante. Too cool for school."

John laughs, rubbing his chin.

They pull up in the new car park at the rear of the girls' building, a few rows back from the large open double doors of the gym. Sarah scans the area, trying to make sense of the layout. "This bit used to be the netball court," she says. "Can you believe they've built a car park on it?"

John shrugs. "Well, I suppose the schools are even bigger now than in our day. I'm surprised they haven't merged the boys' and girls' schools into one. It would make sense, wouldn't it?"

Sarah's fingers fiddle nervously with the charm bracelet beneath the sleeve of her coat. She rolls a small silver conch between her thumb and forefinger. "Do you mind if we just sit here a moment?" she asks.

John shifts in his seat. "We can sit here as long as you like." He reaches inside his jacket and brings out the postcard-sized invitation. "I wonder who designed the cheesy invites? Look at this: '*Wanna know what your old school friends have been Kajagoogooing? Then put on your leg warmers and Walk this Way for a Wham Fantastic night out...*'"

"Stop!" Sarah laughs, clapping her hands over her ears. "I can't believe I let you talk me into coming."

"It'll be fine," he says, slipping the card back in his jacket.

A taxi pulls up outside the entrance to the gym and a small group of men and women disembark. The men are clutching cans of lager, and they stumble on to the pavement, laughing and shouting to each other. Sarah recognises one of the women as a girl from her class, but she can't quite grasp the name. Melanie? Or perhaps it was Mandy.

"Bloody hell," says John, grimacing. "Look at the state of them."

Sarah blows air through pursed lips, watching her white breath slowly drift and disperse inside the car. Her eyes rest on the funny little gearstick, poking out of the dashboard like a tiny umbrella handle. "Is this a Citroën

Dyane?"

John leans into the windscreen to wipe the moisture away with a sponge. It's a stiff synthetic sponge, and all it does is turn the condensation to water, which runs into a pool on the dashboard. "Yep. My trusty old Dyane. It's a bit of a renovation project."

"Thought so," she says. "It's freezing. Just like my dad's old car."

He sticks the sponge under the dashboard. "I know. I really liked his car. Used to see it chugging through the town sometimes, and I thought, one day, when I've got a bit of money, I'd like one of those."

Sarah leans across and kisses him on the cheek. It takes them both by surprise, and she draws her hand to her mouth.

"Sorry," she says from behind her glove. "I'm a bit nervous."

John shifts in his seat so he's facing the windscreen. "Me too."

Two screaming women run down the side of the car towards the school, click-clacking on high heels. Sarah tries to make them out, but they're strangers to her. She draws a smiley face on her misted side window.

"We'd better go in," says John, "before the car steams up completely."

Sarah stares ahead, her fingers curled around the still-buckled belt strap. "Just five more minutes."

MORE FROM MYRIAD EDITIONS

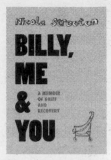

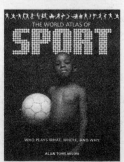